ONE CHANCE IN AN INCONCEIVABLY
LARGE BUT FINITE NUMBER

ONE CHANCE *in an* INCONCEIVABLY LARGE *but* FINITE NUMBER

a novel

CHERITH REYNOLDS-CLARK

PalmCity
Publishing

Published in the United States of America
by Palm City Publishing LLC, 2023

Paperback ISBN: 979-8-9890057-0-3
eBook ISBN:979-8-9890057-1-0

Book design by Danna Steele

For Rob –
my love, my muse.

Two roads diverged in a yellow wood,
And sorry I could not travel both
And be one traveler, long I stood
And looked down one as far as I could
To where it bent in the undergrowth;

Then took the other, as just as fair,
And having perhaps the better claim,
Because it was grassy and wanted wear;
Though as for that the passing there
Had worn them really about the same,

And both that morning equally lay
In leaves no step had trodden black.
Oh, I kept the first for another day!
Yet knowing how way leads on to way,
I doubted if I should ever come back.

- Robert Frost

PROLOGUE

I never believed in the multiverse. As a theoretical construct, it's certainly interesting, but there's no evidence for it. As an engineer who values data and proof, I dismissed it as the machinations of some theoretical physicist wishing to escape their disappointing life. If I had believed in its existence, I would have assumed that anyone fortunate enough to explore it would become consumed by the search for the perfect life and never want to leave.

But I had the perfect life. Not because *I* was perfect in any way, far from it. But it was *my* life, *my* choices, *my* consequences. I never truly appreciated how valuable of a thing that is.

The surprising fact about the multiverse, at least in my experience, is that it's not as abstract as I once imagined. There are no worlds made of goop, no utopian timelines where everyone lives in harmony, singing Kumbaya around a metaphorical fire. The world is always the same – full of shitty politics and imperfect individuals who, for the most part, are trying to do what's right and just get by. I simply want to return to my own universe.

Yet here I am, trapped in this paradox of time and space, forced to watch myself live my life over and over and over. It can be entertaining, exciting or endearing at times, often cringeworthy. But all I want is to go home – to my own life, to my own wife. I just don't know how. I've tried everything.

At first, I attempted jumping in front of moving vehicles, but they passed through me like water through a sieve. Next, I hurled myself off the edge of the Grand Canyon. I hit the ground, but the impact was soft, as if I had merely jumped from my bed into a pile of pillows on the floor. I'm at a loss for what else to do, and suppose I've resigned myself to the fact that I'm trapped here indefinitely.

My parents were church-going folk, so I'm familiar with the notions of heaven and its counterpart. We always envision that other place as a fiery pit where sinners burn for all eternity. But what if it's not? What if it's a place of desperate and profound loneliness, where you can observe the world and the people you love, but never truly be a part of it? You're a ghost. A shadow. I can think of nothing worse.

After much contemplation, I have come to the conclusion that I must be dead, and this is hell.

CHAPTER 1

March 3

S he's in the car with Mike, heading to his parents' house. The sun
set hours ago, and a large cloud has rolled in, concealing the moon,
leaving them to navigate the winding mountain roads in total darkness.
It begins to drizzle, then rain, as Mike speeds around the curves. He
grew up on these roads and could drive them with his eyes closed. She
has one hand on his leg and nervously bites the fingernails of the other,
unsure whether it's their audiobook or the drive that is causing her more
anxiety.

As they round a sharp corner, she spots the deer first. She gasps, and
Mike jerks the wheel, attempting to avoid the eight-point buck standing
directly in their path. They were so engrossed in their book that neither
of them noticed the temperature dropping, the ice forming on the newly wet roads. The car goes into a spin. There's a wide shoulder here but
no guardrail, and they're careening towards the cliff. Mike struggles to
regain control, but the slick road proves too much for him. They slide
across the gravel – she can hear the crunch under their tires – but it does
nothing to slow their trajectory. And then they're airborne.

For a moment, they seem to hang there, and she instinctively
reaches for Mike, clasping his face in her hands. There's so much she

wants to say, needs to say, but there is no more time. "I love you," she cries out.

They're falling.

Sailee awakens with a start, her breathing hard and fast. She lies still, taking deep, deliberate breaths, attempting to calm her pounding heart. "It was just a dream," she reassures herself.

Commanding control of her body, she rolls onto her side and flips the pillow, looking for a cool spot in a bed warm with sleep. She wants to waken enough to shake off the dream but not so much that she won't be able to fall back asleep. Through squinted eyes, she sees him lying next to her – the man from her dream. He has rolled towards her in his sleep, and she observes his thick brown hair curling at his temples ("he could use a haircut," she thinks), and the salt and pepper scruff defining the contour of his jaw. His face peaceful as he slumbers on. She has never been more grateful to find him in bed beside her.

Gently planting a kiss on his cheek, she turns over once again. He stirs and reaches for her, one arm finding hers under the pillow, their fingers interlocking, while his other arm pulls her against him. Sailee's heartbeat slows, her breathing deepens. She is safe; she is loved.

The next time she wakes, the room is bathed in light. Sweating, Sailee throws off the covers and glances at her already-awake husband.

He turns to her, his green eyes sparkling. "Good morning, love! How'd you sleep?"

She rubs her eyes, trying to grasp the remnants of the dream that linger on the fringes of her memory. "Ok, I think. Weird dreams."

"Would you like a cup of tea?" he asks.

"I'd love one," she replies.

Mike gets out of bed and walks over to the wet bar in their bedroom, where the water is already hot. Placing the tea on her nightstand, he gives Sailee a kiss and settles back down beside her with his own cup. This has been their morning ritual ever since she first slept over. She can't imagine a morning without it.

They sip their tea and scroll through their phones, reading the news and checking emails. After an hour, they get up, make the bed, and head for the shower. "Do we have any plans for tonight?" Mike asks as he puts on his shoes.

"Mm-hmm," mumbles Sailee, her mouth full of toothpaste. She spits, then answers, "We're having dinner with Steve and Katie, that couple we met at the bar last week."

"Right, I forgot about that," replies Mike. He pulls Sailee to him, giving her a lingering kiss. "Mmmm, minty fresh," he says with a laugh, wiping toothpaste off his mouth. Then he turns to leave. "I love you."

At his words, she has a momentary flashback to her dream, but quickly dismisses it. "Love you too," she responds.

That evening, after a delicious dinner and a few cocktails, Sailee's laughing so hard that her face hurts. Steve has been sharing hilarious stories of travel mishaps on their catamaran when Katie looks at him affectionately and says, "Spending two years on a boat with a person really tests your relationship. We've been married for almost forty years, and that was the first time I ever truly considered killing him!"

Steve laughs, replying, "And there were definitely times I thought about trading Katie in for a newer model." He winks at his wife, then turns to Mike. "Speaking of newer models, how did you convince Sailee to marry you?"

Mike grins. With a thirteen-year age difference between them, he's accustomed to the question. He looks at Sailee. "Do you want to tell the story, or should I?"

"You start, and I'll jump in with the details," she replies.

"We met at a conference in 2015," Mike begins, recounting how he had been giving a presentation when a gorgeous blonde caught his eye. "It was love at first sight. I hurried out to find her after the session, but she had disappeared. I searched for her all week but never saw her again. On the final night, during the cocktail reception, I thought I heard someone call my name. I turned around just as a server walked by, and her shoulder bumped my arm, spilling my glass of red wine—"

"All down the front of my dress," interjects Sailee. "My *white* dress."

"I didn't recognize her initially, I was so flustered and embarrassed," Mike responds. "I was apologizing profusely and handing her a stack of napkins when I finally looked at her face."

"He was so excited to see me, but I had no idea who he was," explains Sailee.

"She was trying to be good-natured about the whole thing, but I could tell she was irritated," Mike continues. "And I was afraid that once she walked away, I'd never see her again. So, I offered her my sport coat and invited her to sit at my table, promising to track down some club soda to help salvage her dress."

"She fell for that?" scoffs Steve.

"I didn't have time to go back to my hotel and change," clarifies Sailee. "And I needed to be at the dinner because one of my clients was the keynote speaker. Besides, I didn't feel like answering questions about my dress all night."

Mike gives Sailee a warm smile. "We ended up having a blast, although my ego was slightly bruised when she admitted she hadn't paid any attention to me or my lecture. When the dinner was over, I didn't want the conversation to end, so I suggested we change and meet for a drink at the hotel bar, and she agreed."

They had chatted late into the night, and Mike confesses how disappointed he had been to learn that Sailee was engaged. "Although she didn't seem too thrilled about it," he adds, nudging her playfully.

Sailee looks down at her drink, slightly embarrassed. "Things weren't going well," she admits. "I had been contemplating ending the engagement for some time, and talking to this smart, kind, interesting man certainly wasn't helping."

Mike take's Sailee's hand in his lap. "Long story short, we became friends. What started as an update on her dress (which, thankfully, was not ruined) turned into emails about business opportunities, previous jobs, and college experiences. That led to conversations about life, family, and our upbringing. We discussed books we were reading, vacations we were planning, and shared restaurant recommendations for cities we were visiting. On the rare occasion when we were in the same place, we'd meet for a drink and talk until we were hoarse."

"I tried to convince myself that my decision to end the engagement had nothing to do with my blossoming friendship with Mike," says Sailee. "Maybe that's naïve. Regardless, I finally gathered the courage to call it off. Mike, who had been divorced himself, was an immense support and helped me understand that my stages of grief were normal after ending a seven-year relationship."

Mike gently squeezes her hand. "My friends got tired of hearing me talk about Sailee and kept urging me to ask her out, but I always had some excuse. 'We're just friends… She needs time… She's too young for me…' Finally, three years after we first met, I was in DC on business, where Sailee was living at the time, and I invited her to drive down with me to visit my parents in North Carolina."

"Mike was by best friend," says Sailee, "but I fell in love with him that weekend – watching him joke around with his mom while he did the dishes, listening to fifties music and dancing in the kitchen, hearing him play the banjo for his dad… At his parents' house, he wasn't the hotshot entrepreneur or CEO; he was just a boy at home, and I was head over heels."

"We got married a year later," Mike continues. "Sailee moved to San Francisco, and it has been Christmas every day since!" They exchange grins, sharing an inside joke.

"Wow, Mike" says Steve, glancing over at Katie before looking back across the table. "Imagine if you hadn't been such a klutz!"

"I know!" Mike exclaims, brushing off the jab. "If either of us had made a different choice in our lives, we would have never crossed paths. It was a once-in-a-lifetime chance."

Steve looks from Mike to Sailee. "Well," he says with a smirk, "I can understand why you were attracted to Sailee. But Sailee, what the hell did you see in Mike?"

"Wait a minute," she replies, raising a finger. "We have talked on and on about us. I want to know what Katie saw in *you!*"

"That's easy," answers Steve. "My big penis!" Everyone bursts into laughter, and Sailee nearly chokes on her drink.

Katie nods her head and chirps, "Guilty as charged!"

An hour later, they're on their way home. Mike is driving, and Sailee has her hand on the back of his neck. "I've been thinking about something," she says. "Do you really believe that we only had one chance to meet?"

Mike glances at her, then returns his gaze to the road. "Just think about it!" he replies. "We didn't grow up in the same place or even at the same time. We lived in different cities and worked in different industries. I only presented at that conference as a favor for a friend I made through my former brother-in-law. If I hadn't married Caroline, I wouldn't have known him or been asked to speak. And you weren't even supposed to be in that session. I hadn't planned to attend the cocktail hour because I was supposed to meet an investor for drinks, but he fell ill and canceled at the last minute. If I hadn't spilled wine on your dress, I wouldn't have had an excuse to offer you my coat or invite you to sit at my table."

He pauses for a moment, then continues. "If you hadn't been uncertain about your relationship, you probably would've been married already and likely living and working elsewhere. All the choices we made led to that particular moment in time, and if either of us had made any other choice, we wouldn't have met."

Sailee ponders this. "I know there's no evidence of any universe existing apart from our own, but I'm fascinated by the idea that there could be an infinite number of parallel universes branching out from each and every decision we make. Theoretically, couldn't we be together in another universe, having met a different way?"

"I think," says Mike, "in other universes, we made different choices, and those choices led us to do other things, have different jobs, meet other people. I'm sticking with my statement. Even if the multiverse exists, I believe you and I are only together in this one. A one in—"

"A one in infinity chance?" interrupts Sailee.

"No," replies Mike slowly. "Infinity is a mathematical concept used to explain something that has no bounds. It's not a number."

Sailee chuckles. "Alright then, dearest engineer, what is one less than infinity?"

He ponders this for a moment. "I suppose it would be… one chance in an inconceivably large but finite number."

Sailee laughs harder, throwing her head back. "Oh baby, talk nerdy to me!" she says with a playful grin. Then, still not quite satisfied, she asks, "What about soulmates? Do they exist, or do people just happen to stumble upon the perfect person for them?"

Mike contemplates the question. "I'm not sure I believe in soulmates," he answers. "There are so many people in the world, and theoretically, you could end up with anyone. I just feel lucky every day to be married to you."

Sailee smiles at him. "And *I* am lucky to be married to you."

She leans over and shower's Mike's neck with tiny kisses – his favorite – when suddenly, there's a flash of light and a thunderous crash. For an instant, Sailee thinks, "Is there a storm?" Then everything goes black.

CHAPTER 2

He awakens and lies still for a moment, listening. He expects to hear the chorus of birds perched on his balcony railing, or the rustling of trees, or Sailee's heavy breathing (she never wakes up first). Or perhaps less favorable sounds – like the four dogs next door barking at the UPS truck or the hissing of brakes and the loud *THWUMP* of the trash being collected. But he hears nothing. It's completely silent. Mike opens his eyes.

It's dark; the kind of darkness that his eyes don't adjust to. He closes them but can't shake his awareness of the darkness. It wraps around him like a shroud. It feels heavy but not oppressive. Beyond that, he feels nothing. He's neither warm nor cold. He doesn't feel the gentle breeze from the fan overhead or the touch of the Egyptian Cotton sheets against his body. He feels... nothing. He wonders if this is one of those sensory deprivation tanks he's read about. But how did he end up here? He recalls driving home with Sailee. She was kissing his neck, and he was thinking about taking her home and kissing her elsewhere. But now he's here. Now he's... where?

He opens his eyes again, and the darkness is overwhelming. He's annoyed that his eyes aren't adjusting, that he's not getting any clues as to his whereabouts. He lifts an arm, and it moves without resistance. When he lowers it, it doesn't make contact with anything. It just sort of... hovers.

No sight, no smell, no touch. How about speech? "Hello?" he calls. The word leaves his mouth but falls dead in the air, like being in an anechoic chamber.

"This must be a dream," he thinks. Sailee dreams all the time and loves to share her nocturnal adventures with him. He wonders if he'll recount this one to her; if he'll even remember it in the morning. And what would he say? "I dreamt I was trapped in... nothingness. I think it was a nightmare, but I can't explain why."

She'll proceed to tell him about all her dreams, and by the time she finishes, this will fade from his mind forever.

But how to wake up? Usually, with a nightmare, he'd start thrashing or whimpering, and Sailee would gently shake him.

Sailee.

He says her name out loud, and once again, the word fades before it fully leaves his lips. Yet, there's solace in uttering it. "Sailee..."

That's it! He's going to keep repeating it, louder and louder, until he wakes himself up or she rouses him. "Sailee. Sailee. SAILee! SAILEE! **SAILEEEEEEEE!!!!!**"

There! The darkness is lifting. He senses it more than he sees it. The weight begins to dissipate, and there's a faint shimmering at the edges. Then, like a sunrise, it gradually becomes brighter and brighter and brighter.

CHAPTER 3

March 4

Sailee awakens with a start. She thought she heard Mike calling her, but it must have been a dream. Usually, her dreams are so vivid that she remembers every detail, but this morning everything feels hazy. She tries to recall the events of the previous evening. They had dinner with Steve and Katie, right? Why can't she remember anything after that? She turns her head to the left, and a sharp pain shoots through her skull. "How much did I drink?" she wonders.

Attempting to rub her head, she discovers her right arm won't budge. She tries her left arm, and it feels heavy, as if she's lifting a weight. Letting it fall back onto the mattress, she slowly opens her eyes, and the light sends another sharp pain to her forehead. Squinting, she tries to read the clock beside the bed. But there is no clock, no lamp, no nightstand. Where is she? Did they drink so much that they ended up staying at the Mitchells' place?

Sailee closes her eyes again and tries, despite the throbbing in her temples, to focus on the last thing she remembers. They were in the car, driving… home. So, they didn't stay over. They were talking, and she had leaned over to kiss Mike. She vaguely remembers thunder, or perhaps lightning. Was there a storm? She doesn't remember if it was raining. It was a beautiful night when they left the Mitchells' house. She had even commented on the stars. Did the weather change suddenly?

They were almost home, she thinks. But she doesn't remember getting wet running into the house. In fact, she doesn't remember arriving at the house at all. "Think, Sailee, think." There were lights. Red lights. Twinkling lights. And people talking. Were they talking to her or about her? Was she dreaming about a Christmas party? Or was that last night?

She turns her head to the right. Is Mike awake yet? He'll remember. He drove home, so he clearly didn't have as much to drink as she did. Sailee barely opens her eyes and experiences another flash of pain, but there's no sign of Mike – just the edge of the bed. Why is she sleeping in a twin bed? Nothing makes sense. Frustrated, Sailee concedes she's going to have to endure the light so she can figure out what's going on.

"Okay," she says to herself. "On the count of three. One…two…" on three, she takes a deep breath, and the pain that shoots across her body is so agonizing that her eyes fly open.

Her surprise momentarily distracts her from the pain. The unfamiliar room is small with yellowing walls. There's a TV in the upper left corner and a large gray curtain to her right. Something is tugging on her left arm. Sailee turns, trying to focus without lifting her head, and realizes she's hooked up to an IV. Her right arm lies at her side in a cast. Her entire torso is wrapped. Her right leg, from hip to knee, is encased in a cast and hanging in a sling. She resembles a mummy. No wonder she can't move. Nearby, something is beeping, and the realization finally dawns on her. "I'm in a hospital bed!" she thinks.

She looks around for Mike. Why isn't he here? She tries to remain calm but can feel panic rising in her chest. The heart rate monitor, which she identifies as the source of the beeping, is accelerating. Where is Mike?! She moves her eyes around, head spinning, searching for signs of him. Finding none, she begins looking for some kind of call button when the curtain whips open and a nurse rushes in.

"You're awake! That's good!" Her voice is high-pitched, and Sailee flinches, jarred by the sound. The nurse immediately begins checking Sailee's vitals. "How do you feel?" she asks.

Sailee tries to answer, but her tongue is like a dead weight. She licks her lips and tries again. "Like hell," she manages to croak out. "Where am I?" And then, pushing aside her mounting dread, "Where's Mike?"

The nurse's face remains expressionless as she hangs the stethoscope back around her neck. Flashing Sailee a tight smile, she says, "I can give you some more medication for the pain. The doctor will be in shortly to explain everything to you." With that, she rushes back out.

Sailee closes her eyes and lies as still as possible. Agony sears the inside of her eyelids, but at least, if she doesn't move, the scorching pain reduces to a constant but dull ache. She remains in this position until she hears the sound of the curtains being drawn. When she opens her eyes, a doctor is standing by the bed.

"Sailee," she begins, her voice soft and warm, "I'm Doctor Hammet. You're in the Trauma Center at San Francisco General Hospital. Last night, you and your husband were in a car accident. You were T-boned by a drunk driver. You have three broken ribs, a shattered femur, and a fractured right arm. You have a concussion, but thankfully, there are no signs of brain damage or bleeding. However, we'll continue to monitor you closely over the next several days."

Sailee tries to absorb it all – the lights, the people, the crash. It wasn't a dream. When she swallows, her throat feels sore. "Where's Mike?" she asks again, her voice shallow and raspy.

The doctor pauses for just a moment, and Sailee catches the hesitation. "We'll discuss Mike in a minute. First, can you tell me what you remember?"

Sailee is trying her best not to get angry. Why won't anyone answer her question? Pushing her anxious thoughts aside, she recounts everything she was just thinking about – everything she remembers – which isn't much.

"Well," says Dr. Hammet when she finishes, "leaning over to kiss him probably saved your life. You were hit on the passenger side, and the impact pushed the door clear through to the middle of the vehicle. When the emergency crew arrived, they didn't expect to find any passengers alive. But you were tucked in between your husband and the door of the car. Your injuries are severe but not life-threatening, although it will be a slow recovery. We just need to keep an eye on the brain swelling."

Sailee feels like the wind has been knocked out of her. "And Mike?" she breathes out, her voice quavering just above a whisper.

There's a pause before the doctor answers her, a pause that feels like eternity to Sailee. Then, "Physically, he fared much better than you did. Other than some bruising on his face, his body is okay. You shielded him from the brunt of the impact. However, he must have hit his head in the crash." The doctor takes a deep breath. "He's in a coma, Sailee. I'm sorry to be the one to tell you. We have him in the ICU—"

Sailee hears nothing after that. Coma. What a strange word. What does it even mean, really? Her stomach clenches into a knot. She can't dwell on that. She won't think about that word – coma. She'll think of it as... her mind searches for an alternative... a comma. Yes! Just a pause in their normal routine to deal with this abnormality, but then life will resume. Because it has to. Because that's what happens after a comma. The sentence continues, and so will their life.

The doctor is still talking, but Sailee isn't listening. "Where is he now?" she interrupts.

"He's in the intensive care unit," repeats Dr. Hammet, patiently.

"I need to see him. When can I see him?" pleads Sailee.

"We can't move you in your current condition, and we need to be completely sure there's no brain trauma. Right now, Mike isn't in any danger. All his vital signs are stable. You can see him as soon as you're able."

"Which is right *now*," Sailee snaps. She can see the doctor's point, but nothing makes sense at the moment, and despite her love for logic and sense, she wants nothing to do with it. She *has* to see Mike. She's certain that if he hears her voice, he'll wake up. They're connected, attuned to each other.

"I'm sorry, Sailee," the doctor says again. "We just need to keep you here a little longer, and then I promise we'll take you to see Mike. In the meantime, you need to rest. We'll be back later to fill out paperwork, and the police need to speak with you about the accident. We're putting together a care plan for you. Although it appears you've suffered no internal damage, you'll require a significant amount of physical therapy. Your parents are on their way from Vermont. It was smart to have your emergency contacts on your lock screen. That made it easy for us to reach them."

"Do Mike's parents know?" Sailee asks. As an only child, he is their whole world. This will devastate them.

"No," Dr. Hammet replies. "We couldn't find their information. Now that you're awake, we thought you might want to make that call." She smiles kindly down at Sailee. "I know this is difficult, but it's a miracle that you're both even alive." She nods at the nurse, and they exit, closing the curtain behind them.

Sailee's heart is pounding, fear and guilt paralyzing her. It's all her fault. If she hadn't been kissing Mike, distracting him, perhaps one of them would have seen the car approaching, and they could have avoided the crash.

She looks down at her broken, bandaged body, caring little about her own injuries. She only cares about Mike. He's somewhere nearby, alone. If only she could see him, hold his hand, apologize for getting them into this mess. Maybe if she concentrates hard enough, he'll sense her thoughts. Maybe if she speaks to him, he'll hear her somehow.

"Baby," she says out loud, "You're right and..." She pauses. That phrase they always use, the secret to their happy relationship, the words she loves both hearing and saying, now cause immense pain. She clears her throat and tries again. "You're right, and I love you. There's only one chance in infinity, or whatever you said it was, for me and you to meet and share this life together. So you can't leave me in this one." Her voice cracks. "You just can't." She finishes with a whisper, tasting the saltiness of a tear that has escaped and trailed down her cheek unnoticed.

She can feel the medication taking effect, lulling her to sleep, easing the pain. She doesn't want to sleep. She wants to be awake in case there's any news about Mike, but she can't fight it. She sinks down, down, down, as the darkness envelopes her.

CHAPTER 4

The light continues to intensify until Mike can see his surroundings. However, this perplexes him even more than the darkness. He finds himself standing in a coffee shop, and after enduring such a prolonged absence of sensory input, this sudden flood overwhelms him. There's the constant hum of voices intermingled with the occasional burst of laughter rising above the clamor. The sound of the bell rings out, signaling someone's entrance or exit, while the barista calls out, "JOHN? Latte!" Then, the piercing *KSHHHHHHH* of the cappuccino machine slices through the chaos like a roaring train, momentarily eclipsing all other noises.

While the coffee shop is unfamiliar, Mike knows it's a Starbucks because they all have a similar look. Glancing outside, he observes an endless parade of people in winter coats bustling by, hunched over to shield themselves from the gusts of wind whipping between the buildings. It's snowing! Snow is a rarity in the Bay area, and Mike walks toward the window, peering outside. Wait... this looks like New York! How did he end up here? Then, in the window's reflection, he catches sight of Sailee.

She's sitting at a table in the corner, typing furiously on her laptop. The coffee shop is crowded, with only one vacant chair at her small table. She must be waiting for him. Something about her seems different, he notices. Younger, perhaps? It's hard to tell with her hair in a ponytail.

He approaches her. "I'm having the strangest day," he begins. "It started with a bizarre dream, and now, I can't for the life of me remember what we're doing in New York. I must be going senile!" He chuckles, expecting Sailee to respond with a sarcastic comment about his age, but she doesn't laugh, look up, or even acknowledge his presence. She acts as if she can't hear him at all.

"Sailee!" He says louder. "Babe!" Nothing.

He extends his arm to pull out the chair that sits empty across from her, but his hand passes right through it. What is happening? He must still be dreaming. The bell jingles, and instinctively, he glances at the door. To his astonishment, he sees… himself?!… enter the coffee shop. A younger version, seemingly in his late thirties, but it's unmistakably him. "What the hell…?"

The Shadow Mike (as he's starting to think of himself) watches this other Mike as he stands in line, places an order, and pays. While waiting for his drink, he removes his coat and scarf, draping them over his arm. A few minutes later, they call his name. "Mike – Earl Grey!" He picks up the cup, holding it awkwardly as he scans the room. His gaze lands on the vacant chair at Sailee's table, and he approaches her.

"Excuse me," he says, "do you mind if I set my things here for a second? I need to fix my tea, and I don't have any free hands."

"Go for it," she replies, barely looking up.

He adds milk and sugar to his tea, then returns to pick up his belongings from the chair when the man at the adjacent table stands up. "Are you leaving?" Mike asks him. "Can I take your table?"

"Sure thing," the man responds.

Mike slides into the seat, his back to the wall. He stirs his tea, takes a sip, and lets out a long sigh. Sailee stops typing and glances over at him. "Long day, huh?" she asks.

"You could say that," he replies.

"What do you do, if you don't mind my asking? Just so I can make sure I never have that job!"

Mike chuckles and runs a hand through his thick, wavy hair. "Do I look that bad? I'm a broker."

"Ah," she says, nodding in understanding. "I've heard it's a tough time to be a broker."

"I won't lie, the past two years have really kicked my butt." He pauses. "But nothing a cup of tea can't fix!" Smiling, he raises his cup to her. "You seem to be working hard. What do *you* do?"

"I'm a writer for Saturday Night Live." Sailee answers. "With all the politics these days, it's a great time to be in the satire business!"

"A writer, huh? What do you write?"

"A little bit of everything," she replies. "But parodies are my specialty."

"Parodies?"

"Yeah – spoofs of popular songs. Those are my favorite. I've been writing them for fun since I was a kid, and now I get to do it for a living."

"Is that what you're working on now?" he asks.

"Yep!"

"What's it about?"

Sailee leans toward him and lowers her voice. "Can you keep a secret?"

"Sure, I can!" he says, intrigued.

Her face lights up, and Mike notices her eyes for the first time. A brown ring encircles her black pupil, followed by a green ring in the center, and the perimeter is a dark gray, not quite hazel. He hasn't seen eyes like that before.

"Our guest in a few weeks is a golfer. I can't tell you who – it's top secret – and I'm working on a song for the opening!"

"Can you sing a little of it for me?"

She hesitates, debating whether she should give it away, then says, "In the opening monologue, the golfer complains about how much it sucks being famous – how girls are constantly hitting on him, hanging all over him, and what a nuisance it is. Then one day, he's on the course and sees this chick sink a forty-foot putt, and it's love at first sight. The music for 'Baby Got Back' comes on and he starts rapping…" Sailee raises both hands in the air, forming a stereotypical thug gesture with her fingers, and raps,

"I like big putts and I cannot lie
You other golfers can't deny
When a lady walks in with a golf skirt on
And sinks a hole in one
You get sprung
It's out of the rough
And you notice that the putt was tough
Deep in the green she's clearin'
I'm hooked and I can't stop starin'
Oh baby, I wanna get wit'cha
And take yo pict'cha
My partners tried to warn me
But that putt you got makes (me so horny)

Oooo Rumple-smooth-skin
You're as hot as Taylor Dowd Simpson
So excuse me, you amuse me
Hit it hot, watch it seduce me
When under pressure
she acts so put together
She's sweat, wet
Hits her driver like a turbo jet
Should be on the magazines
Has a handicap in the teens
She's no average person with a four-jack
And she loves to talk some smack
So fellas (yeah) fellas (yeah)
Have your girlfriends got the putt (hell yeah)

She's smokin (yeah) outspoken (yeah)
With a stroke into the cup
Baby got smack"

She stops. "You get the idea."

"Oh, no, no, no," Mike says, laughing. "I definitely need to hear more."

Sailee grins. "Well, you'll just have to watch the episode then! I'm imagining one of the male cast members prancing around the stage with a putter, wearing a wig and a golf skirt with butt pads."

Mike shakes his head in disbelief. "That was amazing," he says. "By far the best thing that's ever happened to me in a Starbucks!" Then he stands and begins gathering his belongings. "Unfortunately, it's back to the grind for me. It was nice to meet you…"

"Sailee," she replies.

"Sally?" he repeats.

"No, Sailee. Like a sailor on a boat."

"That's a pretty name," he says. "I'm Mike. Thanks for brightening my day. I'll have to make an effort to catch SNL from now on!"

He extends his hand, and she returns the handshake with an impressively firm grip.

"Great to meet you too, Mike," she says. "Hope things get better for you."

CHAPTER 5

Shadow Mike can't shake this dream. Instead, it seems the only thing he can do is follow Young Mike around. For the next eight months, he trails him to work, to the gym, to drinks with his friends. He grimaces at the women Mike dates, most of whom he meets at bars.

Now they're on the subway, heading to Mike's apartment, when a blonde woman steps onto the train. Shadow Mike's heart skips a beat.

Young Mike apparently recognizes her as well. "Hey!" he says, smiling.

Sailee looks up from her phone, recognition slowly registering on her face. "Hey!" she smiles back. "Mike, right? How are you?"

He looks pleased that she remembers him and says he's doing well, that things are going better. They chat for a bit, and Mike tells her that he hasn't missed a single episode of SNL since they met. He loved the golf sketch and always tries to guess which skits she writes. Sailee laughs, and it's a bright, happy sound.

They come to a halt. "Well," she says, "this is my stop. It was great running into you again." She steps off the train.

Frustrated, Shadow Mike yells at this obviously stupid version of himself, "What are you doing, dumbass? You let her slip away once. Go after her. Go!" It seems his plea gets through because suddenly Mike jumps out of the train.

"Sailee!" he calls. She turns around, surprised. "Would you like to grab dinner sometime?" he asks.

She smiles, and her entire face lights up. "Sure!" she answers. Taking out her wallet, she hands him a business card. *Sailee Roberts. Writer.* "Shoot me a text and we'll arrange something. Saturdays don't work for me!" She winks at Mike. Well, sort of. Both her eyes kind of half close. Then she laughs. "I know – I can't wink. But you get the point. Gotta go!" She races up the stairs to the street, taking two steps at a time.

Mike looks after her until the next train arrives, then continues his way uptown.

A week later, they meet for dinner. Mike had wanted to take Sailee to Nobu 57, but she said that was extravagant for a first date and suggested a place in the West Village instead. Over platters of sushi, Sailee tells Mike about her experiences growing up on her grandfather's dairy farm in Jericho, Vermont. Her parents live next door to her grandparents, and most of her aunts and uncles on her mother's side live within half a mile. She loved growing up on the farm but needed a change, and New York City was about as different as she could get. The thing that surprised her the most, coming from the country, was discovering how lonely a place with so many people can be.

Mike tells Sailee that he grew up in Marion, North Carolina – a small mountain town near Asheville. He was the football captain and high school valedictorian, and he received a full scholarship to play football at Yale, which he did until he tore his rotator cuff. He obtained an engineering degree, then later attended Harvard Business School. He landed a job on Wall Street right after graduation and has been there ever since.

"Let me guess," says Sailee, taking a bite of sashimi. "You live on the Upper East Side?"

"Upper West," Mike replies.

Relationships? Not really. They've both been focused on their careers. He's had a few girlfriends, but nothing serious. Sailee's last boyfriend was in college, and he ended up marrying her roommate. "It's cool," she says. "They're great together, and I was even in the wedding!"

"Wasn't that awkward?" Mike asks.

"Not really. Except when the photographer wanted all the brides-maids to kiss the groom, and everyone looked at me, wondering what I would do."

Mike cringes at the thought. "What *did* you do?"

"Nothing! We all just laughed hysterically and made it so awkward that the photographer finally gave up and moved on to another pose. He couldn't figure out what the big deal was."

"How did you end up at SNL?" Mike asks, grabbing a piece of spicy tuna roll with his chopsticks.

"My first job after graduation was making cold calls for the Vermont Symphony Orchestra," explains Sailee. "Glamorous, I know. It's like that song from the Broadway show *Avenue Q* – 'What Do You Do with a BA in English.' Which is my degree." She laughs and rolls her eyes. "Anyway, one of my co-workers was pregnant at the time and telling us how her husband had taken to calling her Grumpopotamus. I couldn't stop thinking about that song by the Flight of the Conchords, 'Hiphopapotamus vs. Rhymenocerous'. Do you know it?"

"It sounds vaguely familiar," he replies.

"Well," she continues, "I went home and wrote a parody. And then I made a recording. And *that* wasn't enough, so I decided to make a music video." She laughs. "It was terrible. I did the entire thing in two hours. But it still cracks me up, and it ended up being my audi-tion piece for SNL. They loved it, and I got the job."

"What did your co-worker say about the parody?" asks Mike.

"She told me I was weird." Sailee laughs, shrugging her shoulders. "It's a fair assessment."

"I'd love to see that video," says Mike.

"It's on YouTube. Maybe I'll show it to you sometime."

They finish up their meal, and as Mike signs the receipt, he says, "I can't remember the last time I had so much fun. I'd love to do this again."

"It's not that late," says Sailee, looking at her watch. "Unless you have to go, why don't you come over to my place. It's only a few blocks away. It's nothing fancy, as you'll see, but I live alone. I'll show you my YouTube video, and you can play me that song you were telling me about. I have a guitar."

Mike loves the idea, so they walk. He can tell Sailee's hands are cold by the way she's rubbing them together, so he offers her his arm, and she wraps both her hands around his elbow, keeping them close to his body, which is radiating heat. Her touch is both new and exciting, yet somehow comfortable and familiar. He's grateful for the cool evening, a reason to be close to her. This is the best time of year in the city, in his opinion, when the oppressive humidity and summer stench are replaced with mild sunny days and crisp, cool evenings.

"Do you know what today is?" Sailee asks.

"The perfect day," replies Mike, without thinking.

"Yes, exactly!" she answers, excitedly. "It's October 10, 2010. 10/10/10. The perfect day!"

She squeezes his arm and leads him up the stairs to her apartment.

CHAPTER 6

A year has now passed since Sailee and Mike first met in the coffee shop. "A year," Mike says, "from the day I was stupid enough to not get your number."

They've been on a few dates over the past four months, but their busy schedules haven't allowed them to spend as much time together as they would like. Mike leaves for work early every morning, and Sailee has many late nights. He works weekdays and some weekends, and Fridays and Saturdays are her busiest days. He has had an inordinate number of business trips this year, and she spent a significant amount of time at home with her family during the holidays, leaving the day after the SNL Christmas Special aired. They squeeze in dinners and drinks (and a few quickies) when they can and talk on the phone every day. Since Mike's office is in the Financial District, not too far from Sailee's apartment, he spends most of his time in her neighborhood.

Sailee has been to Mike's apartment once, briefly. He took her to lunch one day at his favorite spot in Columbus Circle, a cash-only hole-in-the-wall with amazing Pho, only to realize he had left his wallet on his kitchen counter. Sailee would have offered to pay, but she never carries cash. So, they made a quick run up to his place, grabbed his wallet, and dashed back to the restaurant. She was half an hour late getting back to work, but it was worth it.

Today is Thursday, and to celebrate the anniversary of their first meeting, Sailee left work early, and Mike took Friday off. Instead of going out, they decide to cook dinner together at Mike's apartment. Sailee prepares a salad while Mike selects a bottle of wine to accompany the steaks he's grilling. Growing up in a family of non-drinkers, Sailee hasn't had much exposure to fine wine, but she's eager to learn. They dance in the kitchen, laughing as Mike grabs Sailee's hand and spins her around while she tries not to spill her Brunello, both of them singing along with the music at full volume.

After dinner is finished and everything's cleaned up, Sailee makes her way to the living room. She settles herself onto the couch, draping a blanket over her lap. She's casually flipping through the book lying on the coffee table, but she's not really paying attention to it. She can't get over the incredible view. Or Mike's apartment, for that matter. Granted, he's a few years older than her (thirteen, to be precise) and has had more time to establish himself. He has also worked his ass off. Still, this beautiful two-bedroom apartment on the twenty-third floor, with its expansive windows overlooking the Hudson River, is a far cry from her tiny studio apartment in the West Village.

Mike enters the room, drying his hands with a dishtowel, and joins her on the couch. "Interesting read?" he asks, nodding toward the book in her hands. It's titled, *Reality Is Not What It Seems.*

"Very," she responds. "But a bit too complex for me. I was never particularly good at science. Do you ever miss it, having studied engineering and all?"

"Yes, sometimes," Mike replies wistfully. "However, one of the reasons my firm hired me was because of my engineering background. I think differently than typical business types."

Sailee nods. "That makes sense." Looking back down at the book, she says, "I love thinking about hypothetical situations and have always been fascinated by the 'what-ifs'. What if there's an alternate universe? Or, what if everything we're experiencing in life is merely a computer simulation designed by some graduate student for his master's thesis? It keeps life interesting and it keeps me creative!"

Mike leans over and kisses her. Sailee lays down on the couch and pulls him on top of her, their legs intertwining. Soon, all thoughts of science are forgotten.

Hours later, they emerge from the bedroom. They have never had so much unscheduled time and have made good use of it. Glancing at the clock, they realize it's much later than they had anticipated. Although Sailee doesn't have to be at work early the next day, she doesn't have the day off either. She's standing in the living room, wondering how frequently the express trains run at this hour, when Mike walks up behind her. Sliding his arms around her waist, he whispers in her ear, "You could just stay, you know."

"I don't have anything with me," she replies. "No toothbrush, no makeup, no clothes. If I go in tomorrow wearing the same thing, I'll never live down the 'walk of shame' comments!"

Mike spins her around to face him, a mischievous grin on his handsome face. "So don't worry about living them down. Own it! Wear it as a badge of honor. 'Hey, I had such an incredible night, I didn't even go home. I bet it beats the hell out of whatever y'all did!'"

Sailee laughs, enjoying it when his southern accent slips out. "What about a toothbrush?" she asks. "There's no way I'm letting you kiss me if I can't brush my teeth!"

Mike considers this. "I'm sure I have an extra one around here somewhere. Every time I go to the dentist, they give me a new one. But I use an electric toothbrush, so I stash them somewhere."

"For moments like this?" she jokes.

"Exactly," he replies with a wink. "But it obviously hasn't worked out so well for me, since I can't remember where I put them."

"Fine," Sailee answers, after a beat. "I'll stay." She stands on her tiptoes, kissing his cheek.

"You can borrow one of my shirts to sleep in if you want," he offers, walking into the bedroom and returning with a dark blue t-shirt.

Sailee takes it from him. The fabric is wonderfully thin and soft. "This is perfect," she says, slipping it over her head. "Thanks."

Mike can't stop staring at Sailee. She looks so cute standing there in his t-shirt, which just barely covers her butt. He has started thinking of it as the Mona Lisa – a work of art.

"What?" she asks self-consciously, tugging the shirt down.

"Nothing," says Mike. "You're perfect." He's definitely falling in love with this woman. "Let me go find that toothbrush for you." He walks into the bathroom while Sailee gathers her clothes, which are scattered across the living room floor.

She shakes them out, folds them, and lays them on the couch. "At least I won't look *too* disheveled tomorrow," she says out loud.

"Found them!" Mike calls from the other room. Sailee follows his voice into the bathroom and finds Mike putting toothpaste on a brush for her. He has double sinks, and she likes the way it feels standing side by side, brushing their teeth together. Mike grins at her in the mirror, and she can tell he's thinking the same thing.

It's February, and the tiled floor feels cold on her feet. Mike has kept her warm for the past few hours, but Sailee can feel the chill creeping into her skin. They walk back into the bedroom. "Is there a particular side you sleep on?" she asks.

Mike thinks for a moment. "Ummm," he says, "the left side, I guess. That's where I keep my phone, anyway."

Sailee's apartment can only accommodate a double bed, so sleeping in a king-sized bed will be a luxury… if she can manage to sleep. She slips under the covers, pulling them up to her chin. She's freezing.

Mike climbs into bed next to her. "I always sleep naked," he says. "I hope that's okay."

Sailee laughs. "You've been naked for hours. Why would it bother me now?"

"Touché," he replies, reaching over to turn out his light. There's a moment of awkward silence. "Um, are you a cuddler?" Mike asks.

Sailee contemplates how to answer. It's not the time to tell him she's never actually done this before. While she's had sex, she has always gone home afterward or made up an excuse for why they needed to leave. "Not really," she finally replies. She doesn't know, of course, but she doesn't want to pressure him into feeling obligated to hold her if that's not his preference.

"Ok, good," he says, clearly relieved. "I'm not either."

"And I'm sorry if I snore." Her roommate in college never complained about it, but it seems prudent to apologize in advance, just in case.

Uncertain about what to do next, she's deciding whether to roll over onto her side or pretend she has already fallen asleep, when Mike leans over to kiss her. "This has been a truly wonderful evening," he says softly. "The best I've ever had. You're really special, Sailee Roberts. Sleep well."

Sailee rolls over to face him, placing her hand on his side. She's wondering how many times she's going to get up in the middle of the night to brush her teeth, paranoid about morning breath, when Mike interrupts her thoughts. "Sailee!" he exclaims loudly. "Your hand is freezing!"

She quickly pulls it away. "I'm sorry!" she says, apologetically. Then, after a pause, "You should feel my feet!" She shifts her legs under the blanket and gingerly rests her left foot on his calf.

"Oh my gosh, it's like an ice cube! I need to warm you up. Put both of your feet on me."

"No way!" she retorts. "They're too cold!"

"Nonsense!" Mike replies. "I'm always hot. It'll cool me down *and* warm you up."

She scoots closer to him, placing both her hands and feet on his body. He wasn't exaggerating. He radiates heat, and it feels wonderful.

They lay in silence like this for a while, not sleeping, just enjoying the closeness. Then Sailee begins to sing softly. Mike recognizes the melody – it's John Mayer's "Your Body Is a Wonderland." He's growing accustomed to her mind – the way it makes connections, how something triggers a song in her head, and she hums it incessantly until another one takes its place. He's feeling quite pleased that his touch evokes that particular song for her.

But then he pays attention to the lyrics she's singing. "Wait – those aren't the words!" he exclaims. "What are you singing?"

She sings louder. The tune is correct, but she's changed the lyrics. "Your body is a furnace, man! If I'm not careful, I'll burn my hand. Your body is a furnace mahaaaaan…" she slides her voice up in a perfect impression of John Mayer.

Mike laughs. "Is that one of your SNL songs?"

"Nope." She replies. "This one is all for you!" She kisses him, rolls over, and they both drift off to sleep.

CHAPTER 7

Over the next seven months, they fall in love. While Sailee still maintains her apartment, she has all but moved in with Mike. They begin prioritizing their relationship over their careers, something neither of them had done in previous relationships. Mike takes fewer business trips, and Sailee makes an effort to come home earlier, bringing her laptop so she can write while they sit together on the couch. Mike has a great sense of humor, inspiring Sailee with some fantastic sketch ideas.

They've established a new Saturday morning ritual. They go out for breakfast, and afterwards, Mike walks Sailee to Rockefeller Center, kissing her goodbye before he heads to the gym or the office for a few hours. And when she returns home late, after the craziness of the live show is over, he's waiting up for her with a glass of wine. They sit and rehash the entire show (because, naturally, he watched it) – what worked, what didn't, what sketches were a hit and which ones fell flat. Which guests were easy to work with, and which ones were a pain in the ass. And then, exhausted, they fall asleep in each other's arms, because it turns out, they *are* both cuddlers.

Although they've been eating more meals at home, tonight they are going out. Mike has discovered a restaurant he's been eager to take Sailee to – a charming Italian eatery on 58th and 2^{nd,} boasting a Michelin

Star and receiving rave reviews. He adores taking Sailee to nice restaurants. She has a genuine appreciation for good food, and Mike loves the way her face lights up when she takes her first bite of something extraordinary.

They decide to dress up for the occasion. While Mike normally opts for jeans and a sport coat, tonight he dons a suit. Sailee emerges from the bedroom in a sexy yet tasteful red off-the-shoulder dress that complements her blonde hair.

"Ready?" she asks.

Sailee is always punctual; another quality Mike adores about her. He helps her with her coat. "You look absolutely stunning," he says, offering his arm.

"And you're quite dapper yourself," she replies.

During dinner, Mike is restless, the ring burning a hole in his pocket. But he won't propose at the restaurant – he knows Sailee wouldn't appreciate that. He'll wait until afterward, when they're walking through Central Park on their way home.

Observing everything, Shadow Mike can see that Young Mike knows this Sailee as intimately as he knows his own. Although they're the same person, they are also different – shaped by their distinct choices that have made them unique individuals. In some ways, it's challenging for Shadow Mike to not feel envious of these two. They are younger and will have more years together. They don't have the baggage and battle scars from broken engagements and divorce. They were fortunate to start their romance right away. Shadow Mike also respects the fact that Young Mike's initial attraction to Sailee was not solely based on her appearance but rather her creative mind; and it remains his favorite thing about her.

However, he reminds himself that he and his own Sailee spent three years building a friendship in a way these two never will. They will never experience the anticipation of waiting for an email or the warm, somewhat awkward hug when they first see each other after she called off her engagement – when they weren't sure where things were going, but they knew they were going somewhere. He wouldn't trade those moments for anything.

Watching Mike and Sailee walk arm in arm up Broadway, a diamond now glittering on Sailee's left hand, Shadow Mike somehow knows that these two will have a magnificent future together. They'll marry in Central Park, exactly two years from their first date. They'll form a band and make a name for themselves in the city, working tirelessly during the day and playing gigs into the late hours of the night. It will be hectic and fun, and they'll be exhausted in the best way. After a few years, Sailee will get pregnant, and they'll swap late night gigs for late night feedings, and they'll be exhausted in an even better way. They'll have a little boy, and soon after, a little girl, and their apartment, as spacious as it seemed initially, will begin to feel small. So, they'll move out of the city, and raise their children somewhere with grass and ample space, reminiscent of their own childhoods – where the kids can run freely, build forts, and sled in their backyard. Mike will teach them to fish and hunt, and Sailee will give them piano lessons. They will love being parents together, and although there will be moments of impatience and anger, they will always be quick to say, "You're right, and I love you." And Shadow Mike is thrilled that they, too, will discover and embrace this phrase.

Back at the restaurant, Sailee is telling Mike that she can't believe they met and found each other, that she never thought she'd find "her person." "What are the odds," she asks, "considering our different ages and backgrounds, that we would end up together?"

Mike ponders this for a moment. "One in an inconceiv..." he pauses. "... basically, one in infinity."

"Two in infinity," says Shadow Mike, as the blackness envelopes him.

CHAPTER 8

March 6

It has been two days since Sailee woke up in the hospital, and despite her pleas, they still haven't allowed her to see Mike. She's going out of her mind with worry, and being confined to the bed with nothing to occupy her has only intensified her anxiety.

Well, it's not that she has had *nothing* to do. Yesterday, she spent a considerable amount of time with the police. She had wondered what they would say. Was she responsible? Were they planning to arrest her? However, they assured her that the accident was not her fault and that nothing could have been done to prevent it. This somewhat eased Sailee's guilt.

She then wondered if they would ask her to press charges, but it turns out she and Mike were the lucky ones. The man who hit them died on the way to the hospital. She's sorry for that. He had a wife and three children. She's sorrier for them.

Thankfully, her parents arrived from Vermont and have been keeping her company. She's grateful for their presence and tries her best to show it, but she's constantly distracted, worried about Mike. They have been allowed to see him and informed Sailee that he looks good, which should make her feel better, but it doesn't. She should have been the first to see him.

The worst part was the call to Mike's parents. She had been dreading it, knowing it needed to be done sooner rather than later, but she had to be in a state where she could get the words out without completely breaking down.

They took the news like she expected – hard. Mike's parents are older with some health issues, making it impossible for them to travel to California. That was the most heart-wrenching part, knowing they would have to cope with the news from afar, without being able to see or speak to Mike. Sailee promised to call them every day with an update, even if there was no update, promised to stay by his side and take care of him.

Meanwhile, the doctor has concluded that Sailee has no brain damage, and she has been moved out of the Trauma Center. They informed her that tomorrow she'll be able to visit Mike. At that point, they will most likely discharge her, but she doesn't want to go home. She doesn't want to be that far away from him.

CHAPTER 9

Shadow Mike doesn't know what to do with himself in the void, as he has come to think of the blackness, this empty space. He may be here for seconds, years, or maybe even millennia, and he still has no idea where "here" actually is. Nevertheless, he finds ways to pass the time.

He flips through his memories like a photo album: the Christmas he got his first bike, the first time he asked a girl out and she said yes, the day he was named captain of his high school football team, standing beside his college dorm freshman year, watching his parents drive away. And, of course, memories of Sailee: the day they met, their first kiss, their first dance, their first night together, their wedding day, and the way she looked walking toward him through the vineyard. Then there are the everyday memories: morning tea in bed, lunches together on their patio, dancing in the kitchen while they cook, and Sailee's constant humming to herself. He calls her the human jukebox because she remembers every song she has ever heard. Sometimes a particular song gets stuck in her head, and she sings it incessantly until he grows tired of hearing it and "reprograms" her by singing something else. And she'll transition to that song for a while until he repeats the process.

He's humming an old Keb Mo song when he suddenly feels a pulling sensation, and is whisked from the darkness. Before, the light gradually appeared around him, but this time it's quick, catching him off guard. The light is too bright, too sudden, and he struggles to find his footing. Stumbling, he regains his balance and stands upright, scanning his surroundings.

It appears he is in an airport, with people swarming around him. Some are leisurely strolling, surveying the variety of restaurants and shops, while others are walking briskly. Others are running, weaving in and out of the throng in hopes of making their connecting flights. He has spent a lot of time in airports over the years and never truly minded the travel. In fact, he loved it. It was a major contributing factor to the downfall of his first marriage.

Caroline was an immunologist, and always needed to be in her lab. Apart from attending a few conferences each year, she couldn't travel. On the other hand, he was an entrepreneur and couldn't stay at home, so they ultimately decided to call it quits. The split was amicable. They had met in college, married young, and grew apart over time. They both had fulfilling careers and different social circles. They still maintain contact through Facebook and run into each other occasionally. Caroline is now happily remarried and sent him a nice card upon hearing of his nuptials to Sailee.

Shadow Mike wanders over to the arrival and departure screens. It's 2:55 p.m. on August 1, 2029, and he's in Atlanta. "Wait, 2029?" he exclaims, double-checking the board to confirm. "This is the dream that never ends," he says to himself. Unsure of what to do, he roams around for a while before remembering an art exhibit that he enjoyed between Terminals T and A. He wonders if it's still there. Turning towards the escalators, he nearly walks into (or through) himself.

He's older this time, which makes sense if it's 2029. He'd be 57. He's trim, handsome (if he does say so himself), and wearing a pilot's uniform. Shadow Mike can't see this Mike's hair due to the hat, but it appears he still has some. That's a relief! He has been worried about losing his hair. He notices how women turn their heads to watch Mike as he walks past. With broad shoulders and slender hips, the uniform suits him well. "Atta boy," thinks Shadow Mike. "Fifty-seven and still got it!" He turns and follows him.

They arrive at gate E7, and Pilot Mike makes his way to the front desk. It appears they're flying to Athens, Greece. "Hopefully there's an empty seat," thinks Shadow Mike. "That's a long time to amble around an airplane." He wonders how his ethereal form will handle turbulence without a seat belt. Although he can't be seen, heard, felt, or manipulate the environment in any way, he still seems bound by the laws of gravity.

As he ponders this, Sailee appears at the gate, accompanied by another woman. Her light brown hair is tied back, and he notices a few silver strands at her roots. His Sailee always complained that she was going gray prematurely, and he assumes this version is no different. Wearing a flight attendant's uniform, she looks lovely in the purple dress, which accentuates her small waist and curvaceous hips.

Mike is conversing with the gate agent as the two women approach. He greets them briefly, then resumes his conversation before doing a double take and turning back to Sailee. "Hi," he says, extending a hand. "I'm Mike Black. I don't believe we've met."

She shakes his hand. "I'm Sailee Anderson. It's nice to meet you, Mike."

The other flight attendant interjects. "Number four's out sick this week, so Sailee was called off reserve. This is her first international flight."

"I've never been out of the country before," says Sailee gleefully. "Usually I get the flights to cities like Milwaukee and Sioux Falls, so I'm *really* excited about this!"

Mike can't help but noticed that this beautiful woman isn't wearing a wedding ring. She's probably too young for him, but he's drawn to her. He can't get over how pretty her eyes are. "Anita, I assume you'll be showing her the ropes?" he asks.

"Sure thing, Captain!" Anita smiles at Mike, and it's clear she's attracted to him.

The gate agent opens the door to the jet bridge, and Mike proceeds to the plane, while Sailee and Anita wait for the flight paperwork and greet the other six flight attendants. As they make their way down the bridge, Anita leans over and whispers to Sailee, "The captain's a catch, eh?"

Sailee smiles politely. "Yes," she replies. "He has a nice smile."

"*And* a nice ass," giggles Anita.

To Shadow Mike's disappointment, the flight is completely full, and he sits on the floor in the back for takeoff, trying to stay put as best he can. Throughout the flight, he wanders up and down the aisles, grabbing a seat for a few minutes whenever someone gets up to use the facilities. Dinner apparently didn't agree with the woman in 28C, much to the annoyance of the other passengers waiting in line for the bathroom, and Shadow Mike occupies her seat for nearly forty-five minutes.

Most of the time, he keeps his eye on Sailee. He loves observing her interactions with people. She has a warm smile and a way of making them comfortable. She walks up and down the aisles, checking on the passengers, distributing headphones and collecting trash. When she walks by his seat, he reaches out to her, longing to pull her into his lap, but she simply passes through his arms and moves on to the next row.

Eleven hours and five minutes later, they touch down in Athens. It's 11:35 a.m. local time, and the crew is exhausted. They have twenty-nine hours on the ground before their return trip, and Sailee is ready to collapse. She has flown plenty of domestic flights, but that overnight leg nearly did her in. Her body keeps reminding her that it's 4:35 a.m. in Atlanta, and she should have been in bed hours ago. When she gets to her room, she barely undresses before falling into bed.

She wakes up abruptly, and for a moment, can't remember where she is. Shaking her head to clear the haze, she looks at the clock on the nightstand. It's 3:38 p.m. "Oh no!" she panics, suddenly alert. She was supposed to be at the airport at noon! Grabbing her phone, she checks the date, relieved to find that it's still August 2nd. She only slept four hours. "Stupid jet lag," she murmurs. Her stomach rumbles, and Sailee pulls on some clothes before heading downstairs to the lobby, hoping to find a nearby restaurant or café.

The elevator stops at the fifth floor and when the doors open, the captain is standing there. He smiles at her as he steps onto the elevator. "Up already?" he asks.

"I couldn't sleep anymore," she explains. "My brain thinks it's 9 a.m. and won't let me forget that I haven't had breakfast." As if in agreement, her stomach growls loudly.

Mike laughs. "Ah, yes. I remember my first international flights. I could never sleep for more than a few hours either."

"Why are you awake now?" Sailee inquires.

"I can't sleep right after a flight," he answers. "Too much adrenaline. A habit from my old navy days, I suppose. I find that I do better if I stay awake all day, then go to bed late so I can get a full night's sleep and wake up at a decent hour Eastern time. Plus, I enjoy exploring the cities during the day. Have you been to Athens before?" he asks, obviously forgetting she had said this was her first time outside the United States.

"I haven't," Sailee replies, as they walk out the front doors of the hotel and into the sunshine.

"Well then," he remarks, "if you have no other plans, let me take you to a wonderful lunch place around the corner, then show you some of the city!"

Sailee smiles. "I'd like that!"

"Excellent," replies Mike. "It's Sally, right?"

"Sailee. Like a sailor on a boat," she explains. She's accustomed to people getting her name wrong. Sally, Siri, Sarah, Selah… she answers to anything remotely close.

"That's an unusual name," he says. Then, putting his hand lightly on Sailee's arm, he turns her toward a charming little restaurant. When he opens the door, the smell of garlic, dill, and gyro impale Sailee's senses, and her stomach growls once again.

"Sounds like I made a good choice!" Mike remarks. He winks at Sailee, causing her heart to skip a beat. He really is very handsome, she thinks.

She orders a traditional Greek salad, a gyro pita, a chicken kabob, and lemon potatoes. "I'm so hungry," she says, slightly embarrassed. "And I love Greek food."

"Then you've come to the right place!" Mike responds cheerfully. He appreciates a woman who's not afraid to eat. And Sailee, it appears, is not.

Over lunch, Sailee asks Mike how he got into flying. "I was a navy pilot," he reveals. "I was ROTC in college, then flew for the navy for fifteen years. I retired in my late thirties but missed flying, so I decided to go commercial. I've been with Delta for the past twenty years. It's a good company to work for. I don't mind the hours, and I like seeing the world. How about you?"

Sailee pauses, chewing, then swallows and responds, "My husband died five years ago in a motorcycle accident. I was fortunate to be working from home at the time, which allowed me the flexibility to be there for my kids and run them around to all their concerts and games. But they're nineteen and seventeen now – my oldest is at Emory, and my youngest is a high school senior – and I need something that gets me out of the house. I love to fly and have always wanted to see the world. I actually worked as a flight attendant after college for a few years but quit when I got pregnant the first time. Now that my kids are more independent, it seemed like a natural choice to pursue it again. It'll be years before I have enough seniority to be scheduled on the international flights with any regularity, so I was thrilled to be called off reserve this week. I suppose I moved up in the ranks when everyone took that early retirement buy-out last year."

Mike smiles at her. "And where does your younger…"

"Son," Sailee fills in the blank.

"…where does he want to go to college?"

"He's hoping to get into the engineering program at Georgia Tech," Sailee replies.

"I went to Georgia Tech!" exclaims Mike. "They have an outstanding engineering program."

"I think he's leaning toward aerospace," she says. "Seth inherited his love of flying from me, but his aptitude for math from his father. My older son, Braden, takes more after me. He's studying pre-law and is an exceptional cellist."

"Do you enjoy music?" Mike asks.

"Absolutely!" Sailee gushes. "I have a degree in music." She pauses to take a bite. "I almost enlisted in the military myself, you know. A week before my freshman orientation, I accompanied my best friend to the Air Force recruiting office, and they nearly convinced me to join the Air Force band. My dad was in China for work at the time and freaked out. He called me every day, begging me not to do anything rash." She chuckles at the memory. "Anyway, do you like music?"

Mike is leaning in toward her now, and Sailee can read the interest in his face. It sends a shiver of excitement through her. It has been a while since someone paid this much attention to her.

"I love it," Mike declares. "When I was ten, my dad gave me a banjo, and I learned how to play bluegrass. I taught myself guitar in college, mostly to impress girls, but it ended up being a lifeline for me. Music helped me get through my deployments and some other tough times in my life."

"It certainly has that ability," Sailee agrees. Music was what sustained her during the first few months after her husband's passing. Whenever she felt overwhelmed, she would retreat to her old upright piano and play and play and play until she found solace.

Mike watches in amazement as Sailee cleans her plate. "If you weren't here, I'd probably lick the bowl," she admits sheepishly, using a piece of pita bread to mop up the last remnants of tzatziki.

Mike laughs. "You practically did!" Then, pushing back his chair, he says, "So, Sailee, are you ready to explore Athens?"

"Absolutely," she replies, standing up. "Lead the way, Captain!"

CHAPTER 10

He takes her to the Acropolis first. "A wonder not to be missed," he declares.

Sailee is awestruck. "Look at the detailing!" she cries, pointing to the top of the pillars at the Parthenon. "Imagine accomplishing that without our modern machinery. It's astounding!"

As darkness falls, Mike realizes they don't have much time left. "You mentioned you enjoy reading?" he asks.

"I love it," Sailee replies.

"In that case, there's one more thing you need to see."

They leave the Acropolis and walk downhill until they reach some ruins, where only four pillars remain standing. Sailee gives Mike a questioning look. After the magnificence of the Acropolis, he knows she's wondering why he brought her here.

"This," Mike says, gesturing dramatically, "is Hadrian's Library. It was built in 132 AD to house papyrus scrolls!"

"Oh! An ancient library!" Sailee exclaims, clapping her hands in delight. "Imagine what it must have been like in its heyday – scrolls stacked from floor to ceiling! I bet it was beautiful." Mike can't help but smile at her enthusiasm.

On their way back to the hotel, they detour through Anafiotika, strolling along its narrow streets and perusing the shops. They stop at a small café for a glass of Assyrtiko. "Normally, I prefer reds," says Mike, "but this white wine is exceptional."

They clink their glasses. "This has been so fun, Mike!" Sailee exclaims. "I appreciate you forgoing your normal routine to show me around."

"It was my pleasure," he replies sincerely, feeling a twinge of sadness that his time with her is coming to an end.

As they sip their wine, Sailee asks, "Do you have any children?"

"I do!" Mike says proudly. "My daughter, Emily, is thirty-two, and she and her husband live just outside Washington, DC. She works for the National Institutes of Health. My son is twenty-nine, and he's a computer programmer. Currently, he resides in the guest cottage at my house."

"That must be nice," she says. "I hope my kids decide to stay somewhat close by, but you never know these days. My family is all still in Vermont. I'm the only one that moved away."

"I know you're based in Atlanta, but is that where you live?" he asks.

"Yes," she replies, "In Westview. And you?"

"I live in Jupiter, Florida," says Mike. "On the east coast, just north of West Palm Beach. I love fishing, and Atlanta doesn't offer much in terms of ocean access!"

"That's true," she laughs. Sailee acts as if she's going to say something, then pauses. Finally, she asks, "Are you married?"

"No," he answers. "I'm divorced."

"Oh," she says, sheepishly. "I'm sorry. That was rude of me to ask."

"It's fine," he replies. "Military life isn't for the faint of heart. My wife was a good woman who did a wonderful job raising our kids. I was on active duty and away a lot of the time, and she got lonely. During my last deployment, she found someone to keep her company. I came home a week early, intending to surprise her, and found them in bed together. And that was the end of it."

Sailee opens her mouth to say something, but he continues, "I couldn't really blame her. We had an okay marriage in the sense that we got along fine, probably because I was away so much, and we parented well together. But there was never a lot of passion. We didn't have much in common besides the kids. The split was tough at first, but I got over it, and I've maintained a good relationship with my children. I've dated some over the years, but the constant travel makes it difficult, and I've never found anyone I really connected with."

"I understand that," Sailee says. "It's one of the reasons I *wanted* to get back into this profession. I'm tired of people asking me when I'm going to start dating again. 'It's been five years,' they say. 'You're still so young, with so much life left, so much to offer.' Blah, blah, blah." She rolls her eyes. "Having a travel job with crazy hours is a good excuse not to date. Like you, my marriage was fine. Paul was a good man, a good father, and a good husband, for the most part. On the surface, we were the picture-perfect family. But I felt stifled. Paul expected me to be the traditional wife and stay-at-home mom who cleaned, cooked, and played bridge, but that wasn't me. I wanted to work, but he always made me feel guilty whenever I brought it up, saying I should be home for the kids. A year before he died, I found a part-time job writing commercial jingles. Although it took some convincing, Paul reluctantly agreed to it since I could do it from home."

She takes a deep breath. "Life after he died was hard at first, especially getting the finances squared away. I was better with money, but Paul believed that was the man's job, even though he didn't manage it well – which I discovered after he died. Fortunately, he had a decent life insurance policy through work, and my jingle-writing brought in a small income. My priority over the last five years has been my boys, but now they're grown, and I'm ready to dedicate some time to myself. I don't need another man in my life telling me what to do."

Sailee drains her glass, then looks up at Mike. "I'm sorry," she says. "That was far too much information. I don't usually overshare like that. It must be the combination of the jet lag and wine. Thanks for letting me prattle on like the crazy old lady I'm becoming."

Mike laughs. "You're not old," he replies. "Or crazy. I actually find you eloquent and very impressive, and I appreciate you sharing all that with me."

He empties his own glass and signals for the waiter to bring their check. It's nearly 10 p.m., and he can feel the jet lag hitting him. On the walk back to the hotel, Mike entertains Sailee with stories from his days at Georgia Tech and boot camp, and Sailee laughs so hard that tears stream down her face. She wipes them away as they step onto the elevator. It stops at the fifth floor, and Mike steps off.

"Thank you for such a lovely day," she says.

"No," he replies, "Thank *you*. Goodnight, Sailee."

"Goodnight, Mike." They stand there looking at each other until the doors close between them.

The next day, Sailee arrives at their departure gate, and the crew is waiting for their plane, which has just landed. She's exhausted but happy, unable to remember the last time she had as much fun as she did yesterday. She spots Mike and walks up behind him, holding her Starbucks cup. "I do not handle jet lag well," she says with a laugh, rolling her eyes.

He turns and smiles at her. "Coffee?" he asks, nodding toward her cup.

"No, tea. I'm not a coffee drinker," she replies.

"Neither am I," he says. "I prefer Earl Grey with a little milk and sugar."

"Like Captain Picard!" Sailee exclaims. "Tea, Earl Grey, Hot," she says in a low voice, doing her best impression of Patrick Stewart.

Mike laughs. "Don't tell me you're a Trekkie."

"Oh, yes," she replies. "I'm a Next Generation girl all the way. I was thrilled when they came back with that new series in the early 2020s!"

Anita watches them suspiciously. She opens her mouth to join in the conversation when a tall man with graying hair and a beer belly walks up to them. "Mike? Mike Black?"

Mike spins around. "Doug!" he cries, throwing his arms around the man. "You've got to be kidding! What are you doing in Athens?"

"I was in Singapore for work last week," Doug explains, "and thought it'd be nice to visit Greece on my way home. Donna flew over and met me in Santorini for a few days. You remember my wife, right?" He turns to the tall, slender brunette beside him.

"Of course, I do," says Mike. "How are you, Donna?" He gives her a hug. Sailee is surprised when she feels a twinge of jealousy. She would like to feel those arms around her.

"I'm great!" Donna replies cheerfully. "It's good to see you, Mike. You look fantastic."

"Thanks," Mike responds, beaming. Not wanting to be impolite, he introduces everyone. "This is Sailee, Anita, Patrick, and Amelia. Some of our crew. And this," he turns back to the couple, "is Doug and Donna Winters. Doug and I were roommates in college, until he met Donna and ditched me." He winks at Donna. "Not that I blame him!" They all shake hands.

"So seriously, man," says Doug, turning back to Mike, "you look good. Did you lose weight or something?"

"Yeah," Mike replies. "I stopped eating gluten a few years ago due to joint pain and lost thirty pounds!"

"You're kidding," exclaims Donna. "That's amazing!"

"It's tough with the travel," Mike continues, "but I've been trying to keep up with regular workouts and have lost another five in the last few months."

"Geez," quips Sailee, "if you lose any more weight, you'll be in *my* pants!"

Everyone turns to stare at her. There's a moment of awkward silence before Mike bursts out laughing, everyone else soon joining in. Sailee can't figure out what's so funny until she realizes what she said, and her face turns a deep crimson. "Oh my gosh," she says, hiding her red face in her hands. "You'll *fit* in my pants. If you lose any more weight, you'll *fit* in my pants."

Mike wipes his eyes. "Wow, Sailee," he remarks, "you sure have a way with words." And they all break out in another round of laughter.

As the crew is making their way down the jet bridge, Anita sidles up to Sailee. "That was hilarious," she remarks. "And a clever way to hit on the captain."

"I wasn't hitting on him!" insists Sailee, blushing again.

"Right…" says Anita, unconvinced. "Well, you two sure seem to have hit it off."

"He's nice," Sailee replies, trying not to sound defensive. "We ran into each other in the elevator yesterday afternoon, and he showed me around Athens. That's all."

Anita purses her lips. "Oh really. That sounds like fun."

Sailee detects jealousy in her tone and wants no part of it. She likes Anita, but she's not going to let her spoil her memories of a nice day.

"Too bad we aren't flying to Paris next," Anita continues. "The most romantic city in the world. I'm *sure* Mike could show you a good time there."

Sailee can't take it. "Is something wrong, Anita?" she asks bluntly.

Anita is taken aback, and her eyes widen. "What do you mean?" she asks, innocently.

"You seem to be reading more into this than there is, and I don't appreciate what you're insinuating."

Anita scowls at her. "Sorry," she mumbles and stalks off onto the plane, muttering under her breath, just loud enough for Sailee to hear, about how some people can't take a joke.

Sailee feels bad for being short with Anita and tries to catch her eye the entire flight home, wanting to apologize, but Anita ignores her. "Oh brother," thinks Sailee. She had told herself she was going to keep her mouth shut and stay on people's good side. So much for that. One trip with this new crew and she's already blown it.

They land in Atlanta, and when the crew disembarks, Mike is standing in the door of the cockpit, thanking them. He smiles at Sailee when she walks by, but she merely nods, barely looking at him, and hurries up the jet bridge. The rest of the week she's polite, but does her best to avoid him. She doesn't want to start any rumors.

CHAPTER 11

Captain Mike can't stop thinking about Sailee. He thought they'd hit it off that day in Athens, but the rest of that week she had avoided him. Every time he approached her, she would come up with something she had to do, and leave. And he never saw her during their layovers. He has been wracking his brain, trying to figure out what he could have said to upset her. He should just let it go. It's unlikely he'll see her again anyway, but he can't get her out of his mind.

Several months later, he's covering a few domestic flights for a friend and finds Sailee's name on his roster, causing his heart to beat a little faster. He looks around and spots her in the bookstore across the terminal. Unsure if she's still avoiding him or simply hasn't noticed him yet, he walks over to her. "Hi, Sailee!" he says cheerfully.

She looks up, surprised. "Oh, hi, Mike!" Sailee gives him a friendly smile, but it quickly fades from her face. "I didn't see you walk up," she says, her tone suddenly cordial. She takes a step back from him. "How are you?"

"I'm good," Mike replies. "I just flew in from DC. I spent a few days with my daughter—" He stops abruptly. Sailee is looking around distractedly. "Is something wrong?" he asks her.

She turns back to face him, flushing slightly. "No… sorry. I was just looking to see if Anita is working this flight."

"Anita?" Mike repeats, glancing at the paper in his hand. "She's not on the roster."

Sailee visibly relaxes. "Oh," she says, trying to sound nonchalant. "Anyway, you were saying that you spent time in DC with Emily?"

Mike can't figure her out. "Sailee, what's going on?" he asks bluntly.

"Nothing!" she replies quickly. "Everything's fine."

"No," he says slowly, "everything isn't fine. You've been avoiding me since Athens. Did I do or say something to offend you?"

"Oh goodness, no! Not at all." Sailee shakes her head vigorously. "It's just that Anita made some comments when we were leaving Athens, and I didn't want people to get the wrong impression about us—" she stops abruptly, her face turning crimson.

Ah. Anita. He should have guessed. Mike nods, understanding the situation. "Enough said," he replies. "But let's clear the air on this. I've been working with Anita for over five years now, and for the first three, she repeatedly asked me out. I turned her down every time. She's a nice person, but I'm not interested in her. To avoid leading her on, I've always maintained a professional but not overly friendly approach, and I would never offer to spend time with her on a layover.

"I imagine she was green with envy to know that you and I explored Athens together and was doing everything she could to make you uncomfortable. It's not the first time she has interfered in my friendships with other colleagues. I'm sorry she did that to you. Most of the crew are familiar with her antics, and I assure you they don't think anything of us spending time together. It's common for the crew to socialize during layovers. I simply avoid it when Anita is part of the crew due to our history." He pauses. "So, are we good?"

Sailee smiles brightly, obviously relieved. "We're good. Thank you for clearing that up. And I apologize for acting so... childish. I really wanted to maintain a good relationship with everyone. Making friends with women has always been challenging for me, and this industry is dominated by them." She shrugs.

"Well," says Mike, "you're a beautiful woman who's also interesting and competent, so it's not surprising that women are intimidated by you. But don't let that change who you are, Sailee Anderson. You're special." With that, he tips his hat to her and returns to the gate. Sailee blushes, smiles, and makes her way to the checkout counter with her book.

The flight goes according to plan, and they arrive in Seattle at 10:37 a.m. Since her time in Athens, Sailee has made it a point to use every layover as an opportunity to explore a new city and has discovered some hidden gems. Although being a flight attendant isn't the most glamorous job, her days spent handing out snacks, collecting trash, and dealing with unpleasant restroom incidents, she is experiencing things she never imagined, and she's determined not to waste a minute of it. When the crew arrives at their hotel, Sailee takes her belongings to her room, then quickly heads back down to explore.

She's not surprised to find Mike in the lobby. "So," he exclaims. "You've come to the dark side."

"I have," she confirms.

Curious, Mike asks, "Where are you headed today?"

"I'm not entirely sure," she responds. "I have a few places on my list: the Space Needle, Pike Place Market, Kerry Park, the Ferris Wheel, a ferry ride to Bainbridge Island, Lake Union, Mount Rainier... There's so much to see here! I probably won't get to all of them today, but I'm going to do as much as I can."

Mike smiles at her. "That's an ambitious list," he agrees. "I recommend starting with the market since it's nearby, then exploring the piers, including the Ferris Wheel, on your way to the Space Needle."

Sailee jots that down on her map. "What's your plan?" she asks.

"I'm going to do what I always do in Seattle," he replies. "Eat sushi! My favorite little spot is just a few blocks away."

She laughs. "Well, if you don't mind company, I've always wanted to try sushi, and I'll need sustenance for my adventures."

"I would love your company," Mike replies, glad they're back to normal. He offers Sailee his arm, and she takes it.

Mike enjoys watching Sailee eat. At lunch, she orders gyoza, seaweed salad, a sashimi platter, three sushi rolls, and two mochi. "Not to be rude, but how do you manage to stay so slim?" he asks her as she finishes her last bite. He's jealous, as he has to work hard to keep the weight off.

Sailee laughs. "I worry. Anxiety is a fabulous diet!"

"Well, don't get too skinny," Mike says, a devilish grin spreading across his face. "Or I won't be able to get in your pants!"

Sailee lets out a squeal, covering her face with her hands. "Oh my gosh," she says, "that was so embarrassing! I can't believe I said that!"

"That was one of the funniest things I've ever heard," responds Mike.

"I'm always putting my foot in my mouth," she continues.

"I'll look forward to it then!" he replies, winking at her.

"My kids yell at me for it. 'Mooooooooom, you can't *say* that.' I embarrass them."

"That's what parents are for!" Mike retorts.

"Which reminds me," says Sailee, "at the airport, you started telling me about your visit with your daughter. How was it?"

Mike picks up the check, and they start walking. They talk all the way through Pike Place Market, making a brief stop for fresh cheese and chocolate-coated Bing cherries, a ride on the Ferris Wheel, the Space Needle, and the walk up to the overlook at Kerry Park. "My husband didn't enjoy traveling," she tells Mike as they gaze at Mount Rainier posing majestically behind the city skyline. "Aside from visiting our families, we never went anywhere. Now I want to see everything."

And Mike wants to show it to her.

On the Uber ride back to the hotel, Mike inquires about Sailee's music. She explains that while most of her work required writing short, catchy tunes, her real passion is in composing classical music.

As they enter the deserted hotel lobby, Mike points to the piano in the corner. "Will you play something for me?" he asks.

Sailee shakes her head. "I hate playing in front of people."

"But I'm not just people," he replies. "I'm your friend."

"Alright," she reluctantly agrees. "One song."

"Play me something you wrote," he suggests.

She contemplates for a moment, then says, "This is called 'Stasia's Waltz.'" Positioning her fingers on the keys, she begins to play a haunting melody reminiscent of a Russian dance. Mike is mesmerized, unable to fathom how this music came out of her brain. "Bravo!" he exclaims when she finishes. "That was beautiful." He sits down beside her on the piano bench. "You're amazing, Sailee," he says, gazing into her eyes. "Would you mind if I kissed you?"

She smiles. "I would not."

He leans in and gently kisses her lips. They are plump, and lush, and soft, and firm all at the same time. They're warm and perfectly moist. He wants to melt in them. Deepening the kiss, Sailee places her hand on the back of his neck, holding his mouth to hers.

When they finally part, they're both breathless. "I would very much like to ask you to come to my room, Sailee," Mike says. "But you deserve better than a tired pilot on a layover. We have an early morning, and I don't want to be rushed. I'd like to take my time with you. Would you be willing to spend a night with me on our next week off? I'll take you wherever you want to go."

Sailee looks into his eyes. "I would like that very much," she replies.

CHAPTER 12

They had one more day after their Seattle adventure, which consti-
tuted a brief layover in Rochester, NY, but they didn't have time
to do any sightseeing. Instead, they hung out with the rest of the crew,
doing their best to hide their feelings for each other. The following week,
Mike resumed his international schedule, and the week after that their
days off didn't align, further delaying their much-anticipated date.

Finally, the long-awaited day arrives, and Mike is waiting at their
gate in the Atlanta airport, having just flown in from West Palm Beach.
He had considered inviting Sailee to his home but thought that might
be too presumptuous for a first date. Instead, he let her choose the destination, and was delighted when she selected New York City. He wants
this weekend to be perfect and has meticulously planned two full days,
including a room at the Westin Grand Central, a Broadway show, a carriage ride in Central Park, and dinner at one of his favorite restaurants.

His eyes twinkle when he sees Sailee approaching. She's wearing
jeans, heels, and an off-the-shoulder top that accentuates her long neck.
She looks different, and Mike realizes it's unusual to see her in an airport
without her uniform. Sailee typically wears her hair up when she's working, but today it's down, swishing at her shoulder blades as she walks.

When she arrives at the gate, Mike gives her an awkward hug and a
quick kiss. Sailee has never done anything like this before, and she

feels giddy – like a teenager going on her first date. She was a virgin when she got married and hasn't been with anyone since her husband passed away. Her last first date was twenty-four years ago. "I don't remember how to do this," she thinks.

She's been nervous for days and spent hours last night trying on outfits, searching for something classy yet sexy. She had her hair highlighted and packed too many pairs of shoes. She took a long bath and shaved *everything*. Afterward, she had stood in front of the mirror naked, assessing herself. She noted her prematurely graying hair and the deep wrinkles on her forehead. Her once taut body has gone soft, and despite her efforts to stay in shape, she has long accepted that she will never look like she did before having children.

Turning around, she grimaced at the stretch marks snaking their way up her buttocks and the cellulite forming on her upper thighs. With a sigh, she put on an oversized t-shirt and crawled into bed, wondering why she had agreed to this trip in the first place.

But now that she's with Mike, all her nerves have been replaced with excitement. She can't remember the last time she flew for fun, and it feels strange to be a passenger rather than the person handing out disinfectant wipes and helping passengers fit their luggage into the overhead bins. She was anxious about the looks she would receive when she showed up with Mike and the gossip that would inevitably circulate by the time they returned to work. But fortunately, it's a New York-based crew, and she doesn't know any of them.

As if reading her mind, Mike takes her hand. "Don't worry," he whispers. "We aren't doing anything wrong. We're allowed to date."

She smiles at him, feeling assured.

Their time in New York is magical. They laugh and take selfies on the carriage ride through Central Park, then rent a boat and leisurely paddle around the lake for an hour. That evening, they attend *The Music Man*, which was one of Sailee's childhood favorites. Mike pays little attention to the show because he can't take his eyes off Sailee, who leans forward in her seat, mouthing the words to every song, completely captivated by the performance.

And then they stroll to dinner, her small hand nestled in his large one. Mike helps Sailee with her coat and notices how all the men in the restaurant pause to admire her. She is lovely, to be sure, but more than that, her zest for life is infectious, and his face hurts from smiling.

They order a bottle of wine, two appetizers, a salad, two entrees, and two desserts, happily sharing everything. Mike playfully remarks on the unfairness of Sailee being nearly half his size but eating exactly half of everything. She cleans her plate, casually tosses her napkin on the table, and jokingly sings, "I'm so full I think I might explode all over the wall..." Mike laughs, appreciating her wit.

Stuffed, they leave the restaurant, and Sailee suggests walking back to the hotel instead of taking a cab. She loves the city at night, with its vibrant lights and bustling sounds. Mike agrees, relishing the extra time he has to hold her hand. When she gets chilly, he puts his arm around her, and she snuggles against him. She fits perfectly in the crook of his arm.

Upon reaching their hotel room, Mike helps Sailee remove her jacket, and she quickly ducks into the bathroom. He can hear her brushing her teeth and smiles at the innocence of it. Then she opens the door and is in his arms. He kisses her softly at first, then with growing intensity. Her hands are on his waist, his chest, in his hair. His hands caress her face, then work their way downward, exploring her body. He kisses her mouth, her neck, and she tilts her head back in pleasure. Sailee raises her arms, and Mike lifts her dress over her head. Stepping back to admire her body, he lets out a low, soft whistle. "You are so beautiful," he whispers.

Feeling self-conscious, Sailee's instinct is to argue – to point out all her flaws, all the things she doesn't like about herself. But then she looks into Mike's eyes, and his sincerity and admiration transform her, giving her confidence. She undoes his belt, his buttons, and he scoops her up, laying her down on the bed, kissing her long and deep.

As promised, Mike takes his time, getting to know her body as well as he knows her mind. He asks her what she likes, what she doesn't like – something she isn't accustomed to. And when she tells him, he listens. Over the next few hours, they explore each other. And when she finally reaches her climax, she yells out in pleasure, releasing his own, and they collapse, exhausted, on the bed together. Sailee looks over at Mike, grinning, and gives him a high-five, eliciting a laugh from him.

What she doesn't tell Mike is that she has never been cared for in such a way, never had an experience where her pleasure was the sole focus. She used to feel guilty for taking a long time and would often feign her orgasm, attending to herself later. But Mike's patience with her, and the way he communicated with her and loved on her, put her more at ease than she has ever been in bed. "Now I know why they call it making love," she thinks. And she wants more.

When their time in New York comes to an end, neither of them is ready to say goodbye, so Mike invites Sailee to his home in Florida. She makes some calls, confirming that Seth can stay with a friend, then agrees. "Will your son be okay with it?" she asks.

"My son will be fine," he replies. "I've arranged for him to stay in a hotel for a few days so we can have some privacy." Sailee giggles.

She falls in love with Mike at his home. They sleep in every morning, and Mike wakes Sailee with a cup of tea in bed. They skinny dip in the pool. He takes her out on the boat and teaches her how to fish. They cook together. They sing together. She teaches him how to play tennis. They talk nonstop and laugh often. It's a relationship unlike anything they have experienced before.

And then the time comes for Sailee to return home, but already they're making plans for her to move to Florida as soon as her son goes to college. And while they wait, they renovate the house together – knocking down walls, painting, creating their forever home. And when she finally moves in, they christen it "The Oasis," because their life and love thrive there, transforming what was once a desert. Their children join them for a small wedding ceremony beneath their tiki hut, overlooking the grove of newly planted citrus trees in their backyard. It's perfect.

Their home becomes a haven for their children and grandchildren. They create a pirate's walk down the pier, hanging skeletons and skulls, and the grandkids love climbing up the rope ladder to the platform that Mike builds, overlooking the mangroves and the river. He climbs up after them, wearing an eye patch and brandishing a plastic sword, shouting, "I am the dreaded pirate, Michael Black! Surrender or die!!"

In the evenings, they listen in rapt attention as Mike captivates them with tales of the great pirate Edward Teach, who was actually Edward Black, and reveals that he, Papaw Mike, is a direct descendant of Blackbeard, and that the pirates' blood that runs through his veins also runs through their veins. And they squeal with delight that they themselves might just be pirates.

Secretly saving his money, Mike surprises Sailee with a grand piano, fulfilling her lifelong dream of owning one. Braden brings his cello, Mike plays the guitar, Seth rocks out on the bass, and their granddaughter showcases her budding clarinet skills as they all jam out together in the living room.

Sailee gazes at Mike over the piano, her hair silver now, and silently mouths, "I can't believe this is our life." And he tells her that he would make every choice he ever made, both the good and the bad, all over again if it meant he could live this life with her. Because there was only one chance in an inconceivably large but finite number that they would find each other. But they did, and it's beautiful.

Shadow Mike smiles, and his world goes black once more.

CHAPTER 13

March 9

They move Sailee into a wheelchair, and she's thrilled to finally be out of her hospital bed. She's been eagerly awaiting this moment! She'd like to go see Mike alone but can't maneuver the wheelchair with only one functional arm. So instead, her dad pushes her into the ICU and locks her in beside Mike's bed. Understanding her need for privacy, he slips away, telling Sailee to call him if she needs anything.

Sailee's hardly listening. She looks at Mike's face, and it's as if someone has taken a giant vacuum and sucked all the air from the room. They had been watching an old TV show together – The Expanse – and she imagines this is how it feels when they open the airlock.

"He looks dead," she thinks, then quickly pushes the thought away. Glancing at the monitors on the wall, she observes his heart rate – slow but steady. Confirmation that he's alive.

This is the longest stretch of nights she has spent without him since they got married. She wants to crawl into the bed next to him, rest her head on his chest and feel his heartbeat, be enveloped by his arms. But she can't. So instead, she reaches forward with her good arm and takes his hand in hers, gently playing with the ring on his finger – the ring they designed together. It matches hers. Four ropes intertwined, like their lives, their hearts. Four ropes signifying friend-ship, affection, harmony, and love. It's their story.

Part of her wants to cry, to release the emotions that are choking her. But the tears won't come. Finally, she clears her throat. "Mike, my love, it's me. I'm sorry it took me so long to get here."

CHAPTER 14

There's a shimmering on the edges of the darkness, and Mike anticipates the light that will soon illuminate his world. The question is, which world will he find himself in? His own? Or some distorted version of it? He still clings to a sliver of hope that this has been some horribly long, drawn-out dream, and he'll wake up in his own bed, his own Sailee snuggled up beside him.

Instead, he finds himself in an atrium, surrounded by a couple hundred people. Some mingle, others are engrossed in their phones. The brightness of the space, with sunlight streaming through a forty-foot wall of windows, forces him to squint as his eyes adjust from the pitch-blackness he emerged from. Towering banners hang from the ceiling, displaying the words "Aviation Global" in large red letters. This must be his current location. There's a small stage in one corner, and a middle-aged man with thinning hair steps up to the microphone.

"Good afternoon," he begins. "If I could have your attention directed to the stage for a moment, we're going to have a few remarks." The attendees make their way slowly toward the platform, a few pausing first at the food table. "My name is Scott Tempers," the speaker continues. "As Chairman of the Board, it's my pleasure to welcome you today. This is an exciting day for Aviation Global. Over the past ten years, we've built a lean, fast-moving, and innovative company, revolutionizing aviation technology. We consistently rank as one of the best companies to work for in Vermont, and establishing our headquarters in Burlington has helped transform the city. With a mere twenty-five employees during our startup phase, we have grown to over five hundred employees today. Since going public, our stock has outperformed all our predictions. And today, I'm pleased to announce our acquisition of Take-Off Tech. By incorporating Take Off's technology, we will gain access to new markets and unlock further opportunities for research and innovation. With a new valuation of $2.5 billion, Aviation Global is poised to revolutionize the way we fly." The audience responds with polite applause.

"Furthermore, this acquisition will bring us an additional forty-five employees and 440,000 square feet of space, allowing us to dream bigger, develop prototypes, test new ideas, and showcase Aviation Global as a world leader in technology and innovation!" There is more applause, louder this time. "None of this would have happened without the leadership of one man. Please join me in welcoming to the stage the visionary whose unwavering dedication made this achievement possible, Vice President for Research, Dr. Michael Black!"

There is enthusiastic applause, and Shadow Mike sees himself (he doesn't think he'll ever get used to this) jump up on the stage. This version is quite different from the last one. He's older than Young Mike but younger than Pilot Mike. He suspects he's closer to his own age, maybe a little older – late forties, early fifties. He's heavier and sports a thick mustache.

Taking the microphone out of the stand, this new Mike, obviously full of energy, paces while he talks. "Thanks, Scott, for that wonderful introduction, although I can't take sole credit for this achievement. This wouldn't have happened without my team. They're the ones who have worked tirelessly to bring this vision to life. So please, give them a round of applause." As people applaud, Mike nods and silently mouths 'thank you' to different members of the audience.

"I joined AG after its initial public offering and immediately recognized its tremendous potential," Mike continues. "For a small company in the aerospace industry, we possessed extraordinary talent. Our employees are intelligent and driven, and our technology is innovative. However, we weren't getting the attention on Wall Street that we deserved. Over the past six years, we have more than doubled our annual revenue and expanded our workforce. We take pride in being one of the leading technology companies in the state, particularly for our commitment to diversity. As Martha in active noise control used to say, 'If you're a woman at AG looking for a boyfriend, the odds are good, but the goods are odd.'" Everyone laughs, and many women in the audience nod in agreement. "That's not so true anymore, although the goods are still a little peculiar… myself included!" Everyone chuckles.

"However," Mike goes on, " what I'm most proud of is the sense of family we've fostered. AG is a close-knit community that supports and uplifts one another." Another round of applause ensues. "We're exploring new areas of research and discovering that the best solutions often lie in interdisciplinary approaches and have recruited some of the country's top talent to tackle these challenges."

He pauses, scanning the room. "This marks AG's first acquisition, and I am immensely proud of everyone who contributed to its success – the legal team, the finance team, and the research team, who produced numbers and answered emails from me at all hours of the day and night. Thank you. I'm excited to see where our journey takes us in the years to come!"

Cheers erupt throughout the room. "Lastly," says Mike, "none of this would have been possible without our fearless leader and CEO, who grasped the vision, understood its significance for AG, and entrusted us with the reigns to make it a reality. I'd like to invite her onstage to give a few words…"

Shadow Mike tunes him out. He knows how these events typically unfold. The CEO will speak, then someone from Take-Off Tech, and then people will start getting restless. Eventually, everyone will disperse and return to work. Grateful, for once, for his invisibility, he roams around the room, examining the display of AG's various technologies and patents. There's some interesting work showcased here.

He thinks back to his days as a student at Georgia Tech and his early career as an engineer. He vividly recalls the moment when he had to decide between staying at an established company or starting his own venture. He loved the security his position afforded, and his ability to make changes on a broad scale, but the allure of having the flexibility and freedom to explore new avenues tempted him.

When he conceived the idea for his first company, it was daunting to let go of his stable nine-to-five job at Goodrich, where he was rapidly advancing, and make a leap into the unknown. Fortunately, he had a couple of exceptional business partners – a friend from grad school and his former Ph.D. advisor – and the company was a success. When it sold, he started another, and then another. He has truly enjoyed his career, collaborating with brilliant and interesting individuals across various industries. His work has granted him opportunities to serve on several boards and deliver keynote speeches on entrepreneurship worldwide. Observing this version of Mike on stage, he contemplates what his own life might have been like had he chosen to stay at Goodrich.

And then it dawns on him. He isn't dreaming! He's in the multiverse, traversing different timelines and witnessing the outcomes of alternate choices he could have made in his life. He knows it as sure as he knows the three laws of thermodynamics:

First law: the best you can do is break even.

Second law: you can only break even at absolute zero.

Third law: you can never reach absolute zero.

He can't believe he didn't figure this out sooner. Of course, he still has no clue how he got here and even less of an idea how to escape. He wishes he could share this revelation with Sailee. She would find it remarkable.

He glances out into the main lobby and notices that the event has concluded. Most people have departed, although a few still linger. And that's when he sees Sailee. She's within a small group of people engaged in conversation with the CEO. Then she smiles, and the already bright room gets brighter still. Shadow Mike knows he's partial, but he senses that others share the same sentiment. She looks so much like his own Sailee it makes his heart ache. Appearing to be in her mid-thirties, her black and white striped dress cinches at her waist and hugs her hips – those perfect hips. She hates them, but he adores them.

Dr. Black (as Shadow Mike is now calling him) approaches the group, apologizing for the interruption, and shakes hands with Jolene, the CEO, thanking her for her kind words and support. "I see you've met several members of our research staff," he says proudly. "These are some of our brightest minds." His gaze sweeps across the group and lands on Sailee. He hesitates, not recognizing her. "Are you new to our department?" he inquires.

Sailee shakes her head. "No," she replies. "I work in talent management. I'm a recruiter. I joined AG last month." She extends her hand. "Sailee Harris. It's a pleasure to meet you, Dr. Black. Everyone speaks very highly of you."

He smiles and shakes her hand. "Sailee? Did I pronounce that correctly?" She confirms that he did. "That's a good, firm handshake. So, you're going to recruit top graduates from the world's best engineering schools to join our team, right?"

"That's my goal," Sailee replies.

"Excellent. Best of luck." He acknowledges the rest of the group. "Outstanding work, all of you." With that, he walks away.

So much for love at first sight, thinks Shadow Mike. Then he notices the wedding band on Mike's finger, and his heart sinks. Ah, perhaps in this universe Mike is happily married, and he and Sailee don't end up together. The probability of that happening three times, including his own life, already surpassed what he believed to be possible.

Mike and Sailee run into each other around the office occasionally, and although Sailee frequently talks about Mike, touting his successes and the growth of the research division, she doesn't think about him beyond that. In their limited interactions, Mike notices that Sailee is professional, has a good eye for talent, and works hard, but he doesn't give her much thought either.

Eight months into her employment, Sailee is in Chicago with her boss, Hannah. She took the 5:00 a.m. flight and spent all day recruiting at Northwestern's Career Fair. Exhausted, she's looking forward to back getting to her room. She has another full day tomorrow, including an event at the University of Illinois with Dr. Black. This will be her first time working with him directly, and she's nervous. Hannah, who is friends with Mike, has warned her about Dr. Black's high expectations and zero tolerance for staff who waste his time. She's under tremendous pressure and wants to make a good impression.

While driving back to the hotel after their dinner meeting, Hannah receives a text. "It's from Mike," she says, handing Sailee her phone. "He just arrived at the hotel and wants to grab a drink. I've already made plans to meet up with a friend who lives here in Chicago. But you should go."

"I don't know," Sailee replies. "I doubt he wants to have a drink with me. And I wouldn't know what to say."

Hannah chuckles. "First of all, you could talk to a wall, so you'll be fine. Besides, he's super laid back. And it would be good for you to have some face time with him. Just send him a text back and say, 'Hi Mike, this is Sailee. Hannah's driving. She has plans to meet a friend for a drink at the bar across from the hotel, but we can meet you there, and you and I can always chat once her friend arrives. It would be good for me to learn more about your new initiatives. It will help with recruiting.'"

Sailee types it out, then hesitates. She's worried he'll respond and say, "No worries, I'm just going to head to my room then. Will see you all tomorrow," and she'll feel foolish.

"Don't be ridiculous. Just send it!" Hannah insists. Heart pounding, Sailee hits the 'Send' button. She can see Mike typing a reply. Then the text pops up. *Sounds good. See you there.*

She breathes a sigh of relief. "See?" says Hannah, laughing at her. "That wasn't so bad."

At the bar, they order drinks and make small talk, the four of them chatting together until Hannah gives a nod to Mike and says, "Blake and I are going to grab a table over here and catch up."

"No problem," Mike replies. He turns to Sailee. "Do you want to grab this table? It'll be less crowded." She agrees.

Trying to avoid any awkward silences, Sailee bombards Mike with every question she can think of. What are his plans now that the acquisition is complete? Will AG be bringing in all of Take-Off's employees, or will there be layoffs and restructuring? How did he end up in his current role? Where was he before AG?

Then Mike starts asking her questions. How did she get into recruiting? Where did she go to college? What did she study? What does she do for fun?

Sailee tells him she has a degree in business, and her main hobbies are running, music, and sports. Mike's face lights up. "You're an athlete?" he asks.

She shrugs. "I dabble. I played field hockey in college, and soccer and softball throughout high school. I'm not great, but I can throw a baseball better than a lot of men."

Mike laughs. "Are you doing anything with sports now?"

"I'm currently training for a half-marathon," she replies. "I played in a community soccer league for a while, but I was too busy to make most of the games."

"I'm an athlete too," Mike explains.

"Oh, really?" Sailee responds. "That's cool! What sports do you play?"

"I lettered in football, basketball, and baseball in high school. In fact, I recently joined a softball team here in Burlington," he says.

"You did?!" She leans in to hear him better. The bar is getting loud.

"Yeah," he yells back. "One of our engineers in the vibrations department is the captain. He asked me to join. My first game with them is in a few weeks."

"I'd love to watch you guys play sometime!" Sailee exclaims.

Smiling, she thinks that Hannah was right. Mike is surprisingly laid back, and it's nice to know him better as a person. He's much less intimidating now. Downing the last of her cocktail, she explains that she's been up since 3:00 a.m. and needs some sleep. She pulls out her card to settle the tab, but Mike insists on taking care of it. "Are you sure?" she asks.

"Of course," he replies with a grin. "I can expense it!"

Several months later, Mike and Hannah are having lunch at a café down the street from AG, and Hannah asks how the softball team is going. "Great!" Mike replies. "I'm loving it. Unfortunately, Rachel just informed us that she's leaving. She's moving to Minneapolis for graduate school. So we're short a player."

Hannah ponders this for a minute, chewing. Then she suggests, "I hear Sailee has a mean arm, but quite the temper. Didn't you recently lose your pitcher as well?"

"Yeah," says Mike, chuckling. "Matt threw a bat at him and that pretty much ended his involvement." He recalls that practice. Patrick had been nagging Matt all evening, and he finally reached his breaking point. Mike had never seen him so mad. "That's a good idea about Sailee," he says. "I forgot she played softball. I'll discuss it with the team."

After that evening's practice, Mike sends Sailee an email.

Hey Sailee,
Would you have any interest in joining my softball team,
Satisfaction Guaranteed? One of our outfielders just left,
and we're looking for someone to fill her spot. Hannah
suggested you. If you're interested, we'd like to have you
come out and meet the team, and maybe play for an in-
ning. Let me know what you think.
Thanks,
Mike Black

The email takes Sailee by surprise. She hasn't played softball in a while and isn't sure she needs to add another commitment to her already busy schedule . But she's ambitious and recognizes the potential networking opportunity of playing on a softball team with the VP of Research at AG, a lead engineer, and other business professionals in town. She decides to give it a shot and confirms that she'll be there.

Shadow Mike can't figure out why he's still trapped in this universe. It's torture. Mike and Sailee cross paths occasionally, but there's no connection between them. Not even a spark. They're friendly, but professional.

On the surface, they both appear to be happy, contented people. But Shadow Mike senses that things may not be quite what they seem. He detects Mike's reluctance to leave work at the end of the day and the mounting tension the closer he gets to home. He can also feel the relief that washes over Mike when he leaves for work again the next morning, always early, long before anyone else is awake. Every version of himself that Shadow Mike has observed has been a hard worker, but for this Mike, work borders on obsession. And then one day it's clear.

It's the night of the game, a chilly October evening, and the stands are packed with friends, family, and colleagues. Sailee arrives with her husband, David, and scans the crowd for Hannah, spotting her on a bleacher near the dugout, where she's sitting with her wife and a tall, heavy-set redhead. Hannah is buying rounds, and Sailee orders a water for herself and a beer for David. Meanwhile, Hannah's wife introduces them to the redhead, who's apparently already had several drinks. Her name is Tiffany, and she's Mike's wife.

Sailee, adept at small talk, immediately joins the conversation. Her husband, in contrast, sits quietly beside her, watching the game. Tiffany, having downed another beer, looks at David sympathetically and remarks, "It appears you enjoy this shit as much as I do. Let me buy you another drink." She gets off her stool, wobbling a bit as she makes her way to the concession stand.

When the game is over, Mike introduces Sailee to the rest of the team. Her husband left after the fifth inning, right after Sailee played. They appeared to have an argument about it. David had wanted Sailee to go home with him, but she insisted on staying until the end to help pack up and get to know the team. Irritated, David told her not to do anything stupid and had taken an Uber home.

Mike goes in search of Tiffany, finding her laying on the bleachers with an empty beer can in her hand. He whispers something in her ear, then lifts her off the bench, saying, "Well, gang, that's it for me. I need to get Tiffany home. See y'all at practice next week."

The rest of the team is going to the new pitcher's house for a drink, and Mike is clearly disappointed to be missing out. They invite Sailee, but she politely declines, explaining that she'd love to join them, but David would be furious. As she walks away, Shadow Mike hears her mutter something about not wanting to be called a twat again.

Mike carries Tiffany to the truck, and she immediately starts giving him hell. "Why do you even do this? You were a decent athlete once, but you don't have a shred of talent left anymore. Only a moron would play in public when they're as terrible as you. I guess you're just a moron. And you know how much I hate being left alone, yet you always abandon me at these things. You're such an asshole." Mike sighs, apparently accustomed to this treatment. He drives her home, saying nothing.

"You should have come home earlier," Tiffany continues berating him as he carries her into the house and up the stairs to the bedroom. "All you care about is work and your precious little softball team. Maybe you should prioritize your *wife* a bit more." Mike pulls the covers over Tiffany, then undresses and gets into bed, turning out the light. "You're not even going to kiss me?" she screeches at him.

He sighs again, leaning over to give her a brief peck on the lips. "Goodnight, Tiffany," he says. Then he rolls over onto his side, facing away from her. The next morning, he rises at 4:30 a.m., showers, and is out the door in fifteen minutes, long before Tiffany wakes up. Shadow Mike understands why.

CHAPTER 15

Nearly a year has passed since Sailee's try-out, and she's now a full-fledged member of the team. Outside of work, Sailee sheds her professional demeanor, and Mike sees a different side of her. Hannah hadn't exaggerated when she said Sailee had a temper. Her level of competitiveness is second only to his own, and Mike finds her outbursts amusing. Off the field, she and Matt, the short-stop, are constantly provoking each other, pushing the limits of appropriateness, and although Mike wants to join in the fun, he's careful to always keep his interactions with Sailee professional. They're slowly becoming friends, but as she's employed at AG, he knows he must establish suitable boundaries.

Then one day, out of the blue, Sailee calls Mike for advice. One of the companies she has been recruiting from has offered her a sales job, and while she thinks it's a good opportunity, she wants his opinion. After listening to the details, Mike helps Sailee negotiate a counteroffer, and in the end, she accepts the position.

Several months later, they're hanging out in Matt's kitchen after practice, as has become their custom, and Mike asks her how the new job's going. Sailee's expression falls. She hates it, she replies. Absolutely despises it.

"Why?" he asks.

"One, the CEO has no idea how to run a company. Two, they treat their employees like crap. If I were still a talent manager, I couldn't, in good conscience, recruit anyone to work there because it's dreadful. Three, the product they hired me to sell doesn't even exist. It's merely an idea, and they haven't allocated any resources to develop it – which they conveniently neglected to mention during my interview. So, I'm just spinning my wheels. I've always been passionate about my work, but I have no passion for this."

She pauses momentarily. "I'm sorry," she finally continues. "I shouldn't complain. It's valuable experience and I *did* want to see what it was like on the sales side of the fence. And thanks to your great advice, at least I make decent money. But I feel like I'm losing my mind. I actually enjoyed working at Burger King in high school more than this job.

Matt comes over and hands Sailee another glass of wine – his fix for everything – and she offers him a slight smile. "Thanks," she says, taking a sip.

Mike can't help but feel sorry for Sailee. For as long as he has known her, she has always been enthusiastic about her work. While he recognizes that this is a good experience for her, he wishes there was something he could do to help.

The last week of April, six months after Sailee's departure from AG, Mike is driving back to his office after an out-of-town meeting when he remembers it's Administrative Professionals Day and decides to stop and buy chocolates for his two assistants. Getting off the nearest exit, he realizes he's just around the corner from Sailee's new office and thinks it would be a nice gesture to drop some off to her as well. It seems both her work and home life have been challenging lately, and he hopes this will brighten her day.

He calls her, asking if she can meet him in the parking lot, and Sailee appears a few minutes later, looking happy to see him but slightly confused since he has never visited her office before. "Hi!" she says, waving to him.

"Hey!" Mike replies, motioning towards the passenger door. "Hop in for a second." She complies. "I was around the corner picking up some gifts for my admins and thought you might appreciate some chocolate as well."

Sailee's face lights up. "Oh my word, that was so thoughtful. Thank you!" she exclaims. "You know how much I love chocolate!"

He shows her the three varieties he has picked out – dark chocolate with peppermint, milk chocolate with peanut butter, and dark chocolate with caramel and sea salt. She chooses the latter. "These are my favorite," she says, opening the box and popping one into her mouth. "Do you have time for lunch?"

"I don't, unfortunately," Mike replies. "I have meetings this afternoon. I only had a moment to swing by."

Sailee gives him an awkward hug, the best she can do in the confined space of the car, then returns to her office. Mike continues on to work, feeling good about having done something to make her day a little better.

Things are going well for Mike at Aviation Global. After the restructuring, he was promoted to Chief Technology Officer. While he's excited about the position, the new job requires longer hours and frequent travel, and Mike soon realizes the need for someone to manage this aspect of his work. As he's drafting the job description for a new Chief of Staff, he finds himself thinking that Sailee would be perfect for the role. She has excellent interpersonal skills and already knows many of the people from her time at AG. Besides, she hates her current job and is itching to jump into something that's a better fit. This could be the opportunity she's looking for.

Mike weighs the idea carefully. They would be working closely, even traveling together on occasion. Is he comfortable with that? They've become better friends since she left AG, which might be an advantage. He could be himself around Sailee. She knows him and wouldn't be intimidated by his Type-A personality and no bullshit manner. The job will be challenging, but nothing she can't handle. The question remains: would she even be interested?

During practice that evening, Mike cryptically remarks that he has something to discuss with Sailee and asks if she'd meet him for lunch. Intrigued, she agrees, and the following week, Mike tells her about the new position he's creating, asking if she would be interested. To his delight, Sailee loves the idea! It aligns perfectly with her skill set, she says, and she'd be thrilled to work for him. A month later, after a formal interview process, she officially accepts the job.

While work has been going well, Mike's personal life has deteriorated rapidly, and a few weeks before Sailee's start date, he announces at practice that he and Tiffany are getting a divorce. Things have been bad for years, he explains, and his final attempt to salvage their marriage had ended in a disastrous, alcohol-fueled meltdown.

"You guys are my closest friends," he says. "I haven't told anyone besides you and my parents, and I appreciate you keeping this confidential for a while." He pauses, then offers a faint smile. "And I might need to crash on one of your couches for the next couple of months while we sort things out."

Sailee is shocked by Mike's announcement. Although he never seemed in a hurry to go home after practice, she had no idea things were so strained between him and Tiffany. They always put on a good front, and Mike never spoke negatively about her. There were a few instances when Sailee sensed tension between them, but she never asked Mike about it, and he never brought it up. She empathizes with him. Her own marriage is broken beyond repair, and her therapist recently told her that she needs to make some tough decisions sooner rather than later.

Over the following months, Mike is grateful to have Sailee on his staff. In the throes of divorce proceedings, he appreciates that he doesn't have to hide his emotions from her and can be open about the struggles he's facing at home.

Then one day, Sailee arrives at work clearly distraught. Mike can tell that she has been crying and calls her into his office to check on her. He asks if everything is okay, and she tells him that she and David separated over the weekend. "I'm so sorry to hear that," he says, understanding her pain all too well.

"Thanks," Sailee replies quietly, looking down at her lap. "I know it's the right decision. It's been a long time coming, and honestly, even though we really did try to make it work, I gave up on my marriage years ago. But it's such an emotional rollercoaster. Yesterday was the absolute worst day of my life. And although I woke up this morning feeling relieved, another part of me still feels sick about it. It's just so hard!" She wipes at a tear before it escapes down her cheek.

Mike listens sympathetically, unsure of what to do. As Sailee's friend, he wants to hug her, but he hesitates, wondering if that might be awkward given the dynamics of their working relationship. Instead, he walks around the table, placing a gentle hand on her shoulder. "I know what you're going through," he says. "If you ever need someone to talk to, I'm here. I'm your friend first and foremost."

She nods, drying her eyes. "That means a lot – thank you."

Pausing at the door, Sailee attempts to compose herself, and Mike's heart breaks at the pain in her face. "Screw it!" he thinks, stepping forward to embrace her. He can feel her relax in his arms.

"I don't want to make a big deal about this in the office," she says finally, pulling away. "And at some point, I'd appreciate your insight on lawyers and such. I don't even know where to begin, and I know you're going through it yourself."

Mike assures her he's willing to help in any way he can. "You're a wonderful person, Sailee, and I wish things had worked out differently for you. But I know you'll find someone who makes you truly happy, if that's what you want." And until then, he thinks, she'll probably break a lot of hearts.

CHAPTER 16

Over the next several months, Mike and Sailee try to stay focused on their productivity and not the frustrations of their divorce processes. Both are moving along, Sailee's faster and more amicably than Mike's. They've developed a strong work partnership and a better friendship. Sailee can anticipate Mike's needs before he even asks, and being together is easy.

Since she's so good with people, Mike has started making Sailee point person for most of their partnership visits, and traveling with her is a lot of fun. This week, they're on the road, visiting the Air Force Research Labs in Albuquerque, New Mexico, and then driving to Santa Fe to meet with several clients. Knowing Sailee's love of classical music, Mike plans to surprise her with tickets to the outdoor opera on their last night in Santa Fe. They've been working sixty-hour weeks, and he hopes this will provide a much-needed break for them both.

Upon their arrival at AFRL, they're greeted by Mike's good friend, Valerie, who leads one of science divisions. While giving them a tour of the lab, Valerie shares some of the research areas they're currently focused on, and Mike talks about the new technologies being developed at AG and potential partnership opportunities that could be mutually beneficial. Dinner follows, and Mike has just ordered another bottle of wine when Sailee pushes her chair back.

"I'd love to stay and hang out," she remarks, "but the jet lag's killing me, so I'm going to bed." She turns to Valerie. "It was great to finally meet you. Mike always speaks highly of you, and I'm glad to know he's not exaggerating!"

Valerie chuckles. "Great to meet you too. I'm sure I'll see you again. Sleep well!" They watch Sailee leave, then Valerie turns to Mike. "So…?" she says, looking at him expectantly.

"So, what?" Mike asks, clearly confused.

"You and Sailee," Valerie continues.

"What about us?"

"You two have a lot of chemistry. Have you ever considered asking her out?"

Mike laughs. "No, actually, I haven't. We're just friends. We play softball together. Besides, she works for me! And she's significantly younger than I am. Sailee's great… I mean, really great, and we get along well… but I just don't see how…" His voice trails off.

Valerie looks at him and smiles. She has known Mike for a long time and is aware of what he went through in his marriage. She places her hand on his arm. "For what it's worth, I think you should consider it." And then she changes the subject. "So, how are the kids?" And that is that.

But Mike can't stop thinking about the seed that Valerie planted. Is she right? Is there chemistry? Could they be compatible? He acknowledges that he's attracted to Sailee. But he has always pushed those thoughts out of his mind. She's just one of the guys, one of his friends, one of his teammates, and one of his employees.

And what would Sailee say? Would she be interested? Would she think he's too old? Normally, he would never consider asking someone out who's that much younger than him – thirteen years, to be precise. But Sailee is different. He never feels the age difference. She has lived a lot of life in her forty years and has a maturity that belies her age. In fact, they are so similar that being with Sailee is as effortless as being alone.

Mike keeps his thoughts to himself, and the next few days pass normally, at least on the surface. Internally, however, he scrutinizes all their interactions – the way Sailee smiles at him and jokes around, the way she embraces him when he gives her the opera tickets. He also evaluates his own feelings for her. Has he been deceiving himself all this time, convincing himself that he only sees her as a friend? No – that part he knows is true. It was Valerie's comment that made him wonder if there could be something more. Personality-wise, he's certain they would make a great match. But is there chemistry? He's beginning to drive himself crazy. "I need to stop overthinking this," he mutters to himself.

On their final day in New Mexico, they stop for lunch before heading to the airport. They are debriefing about the trip and discussing the opportunities at AFRL when Sailee exclaims, "Valerie is great! I'm glad I finally got to meet her! I just wish I hadn't been so tired that night. I really wanted to stay up and hang out with you guys. Did you have fun?"

"We did!" Mike replies without thinking. "We talked about our families and how things are going with my divorce. She asked about you…" He trails off, unsure of how to relay the conversation.

"About me?" Sailee asks, puzzled.

"Yeah," says Mike, trying to sound nonchalant despite his suddenly racing heart. "It was funny! She mentioned that we have a lot of chemistry and asked if I had ever considered asking you out." He laughs nervously.

Sailee laughs too, but with genuine amusement, leaving Mike unsure how to interpret her reaction. "That *is* funny!" she replies. "What did you tell her?"

"I told her we're just friends – that you've always been one of the guys."

"And what did she say to that?" Sailee inquires, clearly finding this conversation entertaining.

"She said that we seem a lot alike and it's obvious we have fun together, that you have a great personality and I clearly trust you…"

"And…?" Sailee presses.

"…And she thinks I should consider it." Mike attempts to make this last statement sound as if he finds the idea ridiculous, but it comes across more thoughtful than he hoped.

"And are you?" she asks, now watching him intently.

"Am I what?" Mike asks dumbly. Her gaze becomes too intense, and he looks away.

"Are you considering asking me out?" Sailee's tone shifts, and this time she turns away, her face flushing slightly. He can see she had meant it to be a lighthearted question, but the conversation is taking a serious turn.

"Well, I really hadn't," Mike responds, all jesting gone from his voice. "But the more I think about it, the more I wonder if she's right. We get along great – that's hard to deny. But you work for me, so it's not as simple as me just asking you out… if you were even interested," he adds quickly.

Sailee's quiet, which is rare. She's an outward processor, and Mike is used to hearing her work out a problem. When she's not bouncing ideas off him directly, he often catches her talking to herself. It's cute. Now he's trying to read her and can almost see the gears in her head turning as she's taking in all this information.

She looks at him, then away, then at him again. "Yes," she says finally.

"Yes what?" Mike asks. A little clarity would be helpful.

"Yes, I'd be interested."

Mike's heart gives a little leap, but before he can say anything, Sailee continues. "It can't be that difficult to figure out if it would work or not. We know we get along; we know we communicate well. We share common interests and values, even though you're better at living by them than I am." She makes a funny expression – scrunching her face and half blinking both eyes – and Mike realizes she's trying to wink. He's never seen her do that before and didn't realize she can't. It's adorable!

"Plus," she goes on, "I know that if it didn't work out, we could go back to being friends. I would never want to jeopardize that. I like you too much as a person."

She's right, thinks Mike. They could go back to being friends. There's just that one little problem… "Dating me could impact your job," he states. "Are you willing to do that?"

"What do you mean?" Sailee asks, sounding concerned. "Would I get fired?"

"Oh, no, no," Mike says quickly, "but if we decide to date, you can't report to me. It might change the nature of how we can work together." Sailee is quiet again, thinking. Mike knows how much she loves her new job.

"Here's the deal," she says finally, and he appreciates that she's always so direct. "You email your boss and tell him what you're thinking, and make sure it's even okay. And while you're doing that, I'll talk to someone in Legal or HR, if that's okay with you, and see how this might affect me. And then we can decide whether or not it makes sense."

"Deal," he says. And they shake on it.

CHAPTER 17

The evening of their first date, Mike picks Sailee up at her new apartment. The past month has been strange, to say the least. They had talked about wanting to have dinner, but then had to wait while they jumped through all the appropriate hoops at work. The tension between them has been palpable. Like waiting for a sneeze, thinks Mike. You know when it comes that it's going to be satisfying, but the wait is excruciating. They've been trying to maintain their professionalism in the office, but it's impossible not to flirt. It's a delicate line to walk.

The CEO and the head of Human Resources both gave their approval, and Sailee is no longer reporting to Mike, although they're still able to work together to some extent. As there is no point in unnecessarily waking the monster that is the court of public opinion, they decide to keep their relationship quiet, giving themselves time to determine if this is going to become something serious or not. They're enjoying this secret, this delightful spark in their lives, and want to keep it to themselves for as long as they can.

Deciding beforehand that there would be no shop talk on their date, Mike had wondered if they would have anything to say or if it would be awkward, given that they spend so much time together already. But he needn't have worried. It's as easy as always, and he thinks that with Sailee, they'll probably always have something to talk about. The girl's a chatterbox! But he doesn't mind. After twenty-eight years with Tiffany, alternating between forced conversation and the silent treatment, it's refreshing.

Halfway through their meal, Sailee pulls out her phone. "I wrote something for you," she says.

"For me?" Mike asks, surprised.

"Yes," she replies, hardly able to contain her excitement. "I wrote you a rap!"

"You wrote a rap about me?" Mike probes, trying to understand.

"Yes!" Sailee answers, then clarifies. "Well, no. I mean, I wrote it and it's about you, but it's for you to rap, not me!"

Mike laughs. "Do I seem like the rapper type to you?"

"Mmm, not so much," she answers honestly. "But I think you'll like this. A lot of people at work are intimidated by you, because they don't know you, and I thought this would help. It could also be a fun way to break the ice with new employees!" She goes to push play, then pauses. "Don't judge me," she says sheepishly. "I wrote it at work, then found a background track on YouTube. I recorded it in my office and didn't want anyone to know what I was doing, so I'm basically whisper-rapping!" She laughs and shrugs. "Anyway, here it is."

She presses play and Mike holds the speaker up to his ear. A guitar riff leads into a country-style rap beat. Then Sailee's voice comes in on top, barely more than a whisper. Mike has to strain to make out the words.

> *You probably know me as Doctor Black*
> *But what you prob'ly didn't know is that I love to rap –*
> *'Cause who I am at work is not the whole me*
> *And I wanna share with you and see if you agree*
> *That I can be way more than maybe meets the eye,*
> *I work hard but I play hard and can be a real wise guy*
>
> *I'm a country boy, a Carolina hick,*
> *And here are some things that really make me tick:*

I was Senior Vice President of Research
You mostly see me in a tie, but I prefer my t-shirts.
The best days are the ones where I can ditch my suits,
And trade them in for a slick pair of cowboy boots.
I'll admit that country music is mostly my jam,
And the nerdy part of me loves the block diagram.
I've been playing the banjo since I was ten,
And blues guitar really helps me find my zen.

I'm domesticated too, you know I smoke a mean brisket,
And if anything breaks, you damn well bet I can fix it.
I got three kids, and they are all really smart,
And all four of us are trained in the martial arts —
So you better watch out, 'cause I could break your neck,
But I'd much rather be chillin' with you out on my deck.

In high school I played basketball, baseball, and football
But got injured so in college I was captain of the bar crawl.
These days I prefer red Italian wine
Got my Brunellos and Barolos while I wine and dine.
Love my lunches at Panera, 'cause they got variety
But I cannot eat the bread because I'm gluten free.
Have meetings all day and events I must attend,
But have a house on Lake Champlain where I spend my
weekends.
I can really bust a move on a slalom ski,
And it's when I'm on my boat that I feel the most free.

So now you know just a little more about me,
And I feel lucky to be such a part of this society
So when you pass me in the office, now you'll know what
I'm like —
That I'm not just the CTO, I'm Cowboy Mike.

Laughing, Mike hands the phone back to Sailee, who looks at him expectantly. "Well?" she asks. "Do you like it?"

"I love it!" he replies. "I can't believe how well you captured me. And you're right – if I did this at one of our holiday parties, people would go crazy!" He chuckles again, shaking his head. "I just can't get over the fact that you wrote me a rap!"

Sailee smiles, obviously pleased. "You have to promise me that if you ever do this, you'll make sure I'm there. I need to see it live!"

He laughs, picturing it. "You got it!"

It's late when Mike finally looks at his watch. The restaurant cleared out, and they hadn't even noticed. "I suppose we should go," he says reluctantly.

He walks Sailee to the car and opens her door. When he gets in on his own side, they sit facing each other, still talking, not wanting the night to end. Finally, he can't resist any longer. Her lips have been calling his name all night, and she's looking at his, which he interprets as mutual desire. Mike hesitates briefly, reminding himself that once they cross this line, things will change. They'll no longer be just friends. Then he leans over and kisses her softly.

Sailee returns his kiss, their lips coming together as if they were made to be that way. There's no awkwardness. Instead, it feels like they've been kissing their entire lives. Something inside Mike melts. He has never, in all his life, been kissed like this. "Wow," is all he can muster when they finally pull away.

"Wow," Sailee echoes. "I would definitely like to do that again."

Mike laughs, placing his hand gently on the back of Sailee's head and pulling her toward him. He's looking forward to kissing her properly, when he can truly hold her. But for now, this is enough. When they come apart, Mike chuckles, saying, "You know people are going to give us hell for jumping into this so quickly after getting divorced."

"You're probably right," Sailee agrees. "But honestly, I don't care."

Shadow Mike, delighted to see them finally come together, feels something inside him tighten at Sailee's words. He doesn't know why, but he senses a storm is coming.

CHAPTER 18

Although Mike has been to Lausanne many times, he still can't get over the backdrop of the Swiss Alps behind Lake Geneva. This evening, he's meandering along the Rue de St-Laurent. Typically, he walks fast – a man on a mission. But tonight, he's sauntering slowly, lost in thoughts of Sailee. He can't remember the last time he was this happy. Apart from the softball team, they still haven't made their relationship public and have been happily flying under the radar.

This week, a speaking engagement brought him to Switzerland. He invited Sailee to join him, but she declined, choosing to spend some time alone at home decompressing after her divorce finalized. Mike misses her, but he understands why she needed some time to herself. As he passes by a café, he stops to savor the scent of freshly baked bread, wishing he could indulge, when his phone rings. It's AG's general counsel.

Annoyed, Mike answers the phone. He's used to the never-ending drama at the company; it comes with the job. But just once, he'd like to have an evening free of crises. As he listens to what Bob is saying, his face turns pale. Then his legs buckle, and he frantically searches for a place to sit. Bob is speaking rapidly, and Mike struggles to fully grasp the details. "Lawsuit… Sailee… attorney…" He's normally adept at controlling his emotions, but tonight Mike can feel the anger building inside him.

Working hard to control his tone, he says, "I need to go back to the hotel and get on my computer. And I need to call Sailee. She should hear this from me. Then I'll join the conference call." He hangs up and sits there for a moment, staring at his phone as if unsure of what just transpired. Then, slowly, he dials Sailee's number.

She picks up on the first ring. "Hey babe!" she greets him cheerfully. "How was your dinner?" Mike hesitates a moment too long, and she notices. "Mike?" she asks, sounding concerned, "Are you alright? Is everything okay?" He doesn't answer. He opens his mouth to speak, but no words emerge. "Mike!" she says, her tone firm now. "What's going on?"

"Sailee…" he's uncertain how to begin. "There's a crisis at AG."

Sailee laughs, letting out a sigh of relief. "What else is new?" But when Mike remains silent, she stops abruptly. "What is it, Mike? Is it bad?"

"Yeah," he replies. "It is."

"Do you want to talk about it?" she asks, her voice trembling.

He realizes he has upset her, which wasn't his intent. He just doesn't know how to break the news. "There's a group of former employees," he finally starts, "who are upset about something that allegedly happened in one of the labs years ago, before I even came to AG. Long story short, they're suing the company."

"Wow," says Sailee. "That's going to be a real pain in the ass to manage, isn't it?"

"That's not all," Mike continues. "They need someone to target, so they're launching a massive smear campaign against the executives. They accused the CEO of insider trading, the COO of lying about his credentials to advance his career…" He takes a deep breath. "… and they accused me of having an affair with you, claiming I hired you because we were sleeping together."

"What?!" Sailee cries in disbelief. "Are you kidding? But that's a lie! We did everything we were supposed to! We asked permission. We even changed my job and who I report to! How can they say that?"

"I know, babe," Mike says, trying to keep his voice steady. He sounds calmer than he feels. "But they did. And…" He pauses, running a hand anxiously through his hair. "…they leaked their lawsuit to the press. It's going to be published in the Burlington Gazette tomorrow morning." He stops, letting that sink in.

Now it's Sailee's turn to be silent. "But," she finally says in a weak voice, "my parents read that paper. And we haven't told them, or anyone, about us. So everyone will assume it's true!" Mike hears her breath catch as she tries to stifle the mounting panic in her chest. "What can we do?"

"Right now? Unfortunately, nothing," answers Mike.

"So they're allowed to tell lies about us, and we can't do anything to defend ourselves?"

"General Counsel told me that you can say whatever you want in a lawsuit, true or not, and it's protected by law. So right now, our hands are tied."

Neither of them say anything for a long time. When Sailee finally speaks, her tone is hardened, bitter. "Well, this blows, doesn't it?" When Mike doesn't respond, she softens her voice. "Mike, are *you* okay?" He nods but doesn't say anything. "Mike?" she asks again.

"Oh, right." He replies, realizing his mistake. "Yeah, I'm okay. I'm worried about the company, of course. This won't sit well with our shareholders, and it'll take time to disprove their accusations. This could drag on for years. But mostly, I'm worried about you. We're going to be okay, though. You know that, right? We didn't do anything wrong, and everything will be fine. But it's going to get pretty ugly, I think."

Mike pauses, trying to figure out their next steps. "Listen," he says, "just try to forget about this and enjoy your weekend. I'm sorry I had to tell you, but I didn't want you to hear it from someone else. And please don't let this get to you, Sailee. We can discuss it when I get home." He stops again, thinking. "However, you should probably call your parents… and David, and give them a heads up. It's better that they hear about this from you than read it in the paper."

Sailee lets out an anxious sigh. "Before you go, I just want you to know that you're the best person I have ever met," she says. "I'm sorry you have to go through this. I miss you, and I wish we were together right now. That would make this a lot easier."

"So do I. I miss you too. Gotta go deal with this now." He hangs up.

A few days later, Mike meets Sailee at her apartment. They've spoken by phone a few times since Mike dropped the bomb, but mostly he's been in endless calls and meetings. He's worried about Sailee, who has continuously assured him over the phone that she's fine. But when she answers the door, he can see that she's not.

Her hair is disheveled, there are dark circles under her eyes, and she looks like she has lost a considerable amount of weight. "Hey babe," she says with a wan smile. "Come on in." Mike enters the apartment and wraps his arms around her. He can feel how tense her body is. Then he steps back and looks at her again. He hasn't been able to sit still since the call, his nerves and frustration fueling his energy. It appears the anxiety has had the opposite effect on Sailee. He pulls her into another hug and kisses her on the head. "How are you?" he asks tenderly.

"I'm…" she pauses, and Mike knows she's trying to decide if she's going to be honest. "…trying to be fine," she eventually replies. It's closer to the truth.

"Talk to me," he encourages. Then, thinking it could be beneficial to get her out of the house, he suggests, "Let's go grab lunch and we can talk there."

Sailee shakes her head. "I'm not hungry."

"When was the last time you ate something?" Mike asks, concerned.

"I've been eating a little," she promises. "The thought of food makes me sick, but I've been nibbling on crackers and protein bars because I know I need to."

"Oh, Sailee," Mike says, his heart breaking. He has never known her to have no appetite. "I am so sorry about all this. I can't *believe…*"

He slams his fist down on the counter, startling her. "…those assholes dragged you into this."

Sailee shrugs. "This impacts you more than me. But I hate those people. I really do. I know I shouldn't, and I'm trying not to, but how can people who don't even know us be so cruel?"

She can no longer contain her feelings, and the dam breaks, the words rushing out of her. "They twisted everything, Mike. Did you see that? They even twisted the chocolates you gave me. You were just being nice! They didn't mean anything. And how did they even know about them? Is my old boss part of this too? I don't trust anyone anymore."

She takes a deep breath and continues. "Do you know how awkward it was calling David and telling him this would be in the paper, and trying to assure him it isn't true? Or having to coach my parents on what to say when their friends inevitably ask about it? My phone has been buzzing incessantly. A few friends have said, 'I'm sorry you're going through this, it's so screwed up.' But most people are like, 'Are you really banging Mike?!' And I've had to explain, 'We're dating, but no, we didn't have an affair, and yes, we asked permission, and no, I'm not working for him anymore, and yes, we chose not to publicize it…' But I shouldn't have to justify my personal life to anyone, regardless of the circumstances. It's nobody's business. And no matter what I say, people are going to believe what they want to believe anyway. Facts don't matter anymore. That's just the way the world is."

She's getting hysterical. "And you know what else? Because they used my title, my LinkedIn views have gone up 1600% in the last three days! I'm contemplating shutting down my profile, but I shouldn't have to do that. I'm a professional and have worked damn hard to get where I am. But they've portrayed me as some gold-digging whore who slept my way to the top. And I can't do anything about it, which makes me so *fucking angry!*" She's yelling now, her fists clenched.

Mike puts his hand on her arm, and Sailee takes a deep breath to calm herself. "I feel selfish even saying all this to you because I know, as much as this hurts me, it harms you more. You're the actual target, I'm just collateral damage. And I absolutely *hate* that they are using me to hurt you." Spent, she slumps into a chair.

Mike kneels on the floor in front of Sailee, taking her hands in his. "I can't pretend to know what the outcome of all this is going to be, but I do believe we'll be okay." He pauses, not wanting to say the next part because he's terrified of her response. But he has to. He has to give her the choice. "But I also know that it's going to get worse before it gets better. So if you want out, I totally understand."

Sailee looks at him, surprised. Then she shakes her head adamantly. "No. No way. That's not at all what I want. You're my best friend, and we were friends first. Besides, what would that accomplish? It wouldn't change what they did. I love you, and I'm with you all the way, no matter what happens."

In spite of their circumstances, Mike smiles. "You love me?" he asks. She's never said that to him before.

She looks into his eyes and nods. "I do."

"Well, that's great news, because I love you too."

Sailee smiles, then leans over and kisses him. Mike lays his head in her lap, and for a moment, all their troubles are forgotten.

The lawsuit against Mike is eventually dropped, but the damage is already done, and Shadow Mike can see the toll it has taken on both of them. While Mike's reputation and career lie in ruins, the entire executive suite having lost their jobs due to pressure from the shareholders, his primary concern is how it has affected Sailee. The experience has fundamentally changed her perspective on life, turning her from an optimist into a cynic, from a trusting person into a cautious one. Fortunately, her basic good nature remains intact, and their commitment to each other remains strong. By facing adversity together, they grow closer. They learn to rely on each other during the most challenging times. Mike is Sailee's rock, and she is his joy. They learn that it's not the things that happen to you in life that matter most, but how you respond to them. Shadow Mike realizes that the friendship they cultivated over all those years became the foundation they built their entire relationship on, and they will maintain that friendship for the rest of their lives.

Mike and Sailee are in bed together now. Years have passed, and while the course of their lives has been forever altered, the wounds of that time have faded to dull scars. Mike is lying across Sailee's chest while she reads aloud to him, her free hand gently running through his hair. They are happier than they ever imagined they could be. Shadow Mike smiles as the world darkens around him.

CHAPTER 19

March 25

S ailee's parents returned to Vermont yesterday, leaving her home
alone. While their constant presence was overwhelming at first, she
couldn't have managed without them, and is grateful they were able to
stay so long. Her dad, who had already been considering giving his notice, retired the day he received the call from the hospital. At the time,
they had no idea how dire the situation was, or what Sailee's recovery
would entail, and he wanted to be available to help in any way possible.
Her mom used all her available time off, including most of her Family
Medical Leave, and eventually had to return to work. With their departure, the house is now as quiet as a church on a Monday morning.

Sailee is still confined to a wheelchair, and it's challenging to navigate on her own. Since their house isn't handicap accessible, her parents set up a bedroom for her in the living room on the first floor.
Sailee hates being helpless. She has always been incredibly independent, but now struggles with everyday tasks such as cooking, cleaning,
getting into bed, and using the bathroom. It's difficult, and with her
parents gone, it's also lonely.

She's still on medical leave. Until now, she couldn't even get off the
toilet unaided. Going back to the office is out of the question. More
importantly, there's no way she could focus on work. Mike remains

unresponsive, although his vitals are strong; and the doctors maintain hope that he'll emerge from the coma.

While her leg still requires a brace, Sailee has finally discarded her arm sling. She hopes to progress to crutches by the end of the week, which should make getting around a bit easier. Her doctor has advised her to spend more time in bed since rest is crucial for healing ribs, but there's no way she's staying home.

Instead, she spends each day at Mike's side. Sitting in the wheelchair beside his bed proves difficult because she can't fully see his face. Nevertheless, she holds his hand and talks to him. She avoids discussing the accident or her own injuries. It's been said that coma patients can often hear people speaking, and if Mike can hear her, she doesn't want him to worry. Instead, she tells him stories.

She doesn't want to bore him with things he has already heard, but coming up with new content is challenging because they talked about everything. So she delves deep into her memory to recall things he won't know. Stories from her childhood. Her first boyfriend, the crush that sparked her first parody, the time in sixth grade when her friends suddenly abandoned her, and how it was her first encounter with bone-crushing sadness. She reminisces about the time she cut her hair and looked like a boy, and the time she wanted a bikini but her mom disapproved, so she cut her one-piece in half. When that failed, she had blamed it on her little brother, and her mom punished him by withholding his allowance until he bought Sailee a new swimsuit. Unable to bear the guilt of his undeserved sentence, Sailee eventually confessed. In the end, she had to repay her brother the same amount he would have given her, for retribution, *and* buy herself a new swimsuit, all on an allowance of two dollars a week. She was broke for a long time after that.

She tells Mike all the things she had wanted to be when she grew up – a dancer, a writer, a marine biologist on the moon (her mom had to explain the impracticality of that one), an astronaut, a pilot, a flight attendant, a comedian, a concert pianist, an inventor (until she realized she didn't enjoy science), and a conversational therapist. "Yes, that's right," she says with a chuckle. "At one point, I actually believed someone might pay me to keep them company." Her life could have gone any number of directions, but she wouldn't change a thing because it ultimately led her to Mike.

Days pass, and if Mike can hear her, he now knows every detail of her life, down to the Sunday School songs she still remembers and the telephone numbers of her best friends growing up. Sailee just keeps talking, hoping he'll get sick of listening to her and wake up.

It reminds her of a particular incident during one of their trips to New York. They were on the plane, and Sailee woke up from her nap in a foul mood. She began venting to Mike about everything she was upset about – politics, work, disinformation, and the perils of social media. She ranted throughout the rest of the flight, all the while they were deplaning, and the entire bus ride to the airport. Mike simply nodded, not saying much. When they reached the terminal, he interrupted her diatribe to inform her that he needed to use the bathroom. He returned a few minutes later, laughing, and Sailee asked him what was so funny.

"I was standing at the urinal," Mike explained, "when the guy who sat behind us on the flight approached me and said, 'You're a good man. That's a *lot* of listenin'.'"

Sailee burst into laughter, realizing she had been talking incessantly. She stood on her tiptoes and kissed Mike's cheek. "You *are* a good man. The best. Thanks for being so patient. I'm sorry about that – it's all out of my system now."

Mike had put his arm around her. "I don't mind. I love to listen to you." They still laugh about that.

CHAPTER 20

Shadow Mike hears the next universe before he sees it. Even before the darkness dissipates, he's jolted into focus by a cacophony of sound. It's loud and chaotic. There's a barely perceptible coordination to the rhythm, but not the notes. It reminds him of something he's heard before. As an ear-piercing squawk rises about the noise, he puts his finger on it: an elementary school band.

The room brightens, and he finds himself standing in an empty hallway. Peeking through the window of the nearest door, he's not at all surprised to discover the source of the racket, which he had correctly identified. "That's painful," Shadow Mike thinks, plugging his ears. He was never in band. The only instrument he played growing up was the banjo, at his father's insistence. He was mostly into sports, and now, listening to this clamor, he's glad he never subjected his parents to such torment.

He strolls down the hall, glancing into classrooms. Some students are sitting in rapt attention, while others are hunched over their desks or dozing off. A few are turned around in their seats talking to the person behind them, and Shadow Mike recalls Sailee once telling him how her high school English teacher had claimed to know her ponytail better than her face. He smiles at this.

Wandering the halls, he searches for a version of himself. It's unlikely he's one of the students because if he's in elementary school,

Sailee hasn't been born yet. A teacher, perhaps? If that's the case, he desperately hopes Sailee isn't one of his students. Stepping outside, Shadow Mike gazes up at the building. The words "Marion Elementary School" are prominently displayed over the door in large black letters. It's his alma mater, but it looks different somehow. Smaller.

He continues his exploration until he reaches the main office. Peering inside, he finds himself seated in a chair. This Mike is wearing jeans, a faded t-shirt, and a baseball cap. He's absorbed in his phone and doesn't seem to notice when two children enter the room. The boy, appearing to be about nine years old, is sporting a green backpack and a black eye. Accompanying him is a girl of similar age, perhaps slightly older. She's taller than the boy, though that's not uncommon at this stage. She has large green-brown eyes, and a blonde braid falls down her back. Shadow Mike does a double take. This girl is a miniature version of Sailee. He looks at Mike again, confused, as their ages don't seem to match up.

"Hey, Papaw," the boy says softly.

Mike lifts his head, and Shadow Mike is shocked to hear the boy refer to him as "papaw." This Mike doesn't appear much older than forty.

"Hey, kiddo," he replies in a thick southern drawl. "I heard you got into a bit of a scuffle. Wanna tell me about it?"

The boy hangs his head. "Not really."

The girl interjects. "I can tell you what happened!" she says loudly. "Tommy was making fun of him because he plays the flute. Hunter tried to ignore him and walk away, but then Tommy pulled the flute case out of his hand. So Hunter yanked it back and pushed him away. Tommy fell into the lockers, which made him mad, so he punched Hunter in the face."

Hunter looks at the ground. Even with the black eye, Shadow Mike can see that he's a cute kid. He has short, thick brown hair and rosy cheeks.

Mike (or Papaw Mike, as Shadow Mike has now nicknamed him) looks at Hunter. "Is that how it happened?" he asks gently.

Hunter nods, keeping his eyes fixed on the floor. When he lifts them to meet his grandpa's gaze, Shadow Mike notices that they're the same shade of green as his own. "I didn't mean to push him, Papaw. I tried to do what you said and just ignore him, but he tried to take my flute, and I was gonna be late to band practice. I didn't know what else to do." Papaw nods understandingly, then pulls the boy to him and tousles his hair affectionately.

"Tommy picks on Hunter all the time," the girl says.

Mike turns to her. "And what's your name?" he asks.

Pleased to be the center of attention, a big, crooked-toothed smile brightens her face. "I'm Olivia!" she answers. "I used to sit next to Hunter when I played the flute. But now I play the trumpet." She stops, as if this information is sufficient. Then, realizing she should per-haps give some further explanation as to why she's here with Hunter, she adds, "My mom asked me to walk Hunter to the office. Tommy won't pick on him when he's with me because my mom's a teacher!"

"I see," says Papaw Mike. He stands and is about to tell the girl that she can go on back to her class when a woman rushes in. She's obviously related to Olivia. They have the same eyes, nose, and hair.

"Olivia!" she says sharply. "I asked you to escort Hunter to the office then return immediately to your class."

"But mom," replies Olivia, sounding like an annoyed teenager, "I had to tell this man what happened."

"I'm sure Hunter can tell him everything he needs to know. Now scoot." She smacks Olivia lightly on the behind and watches as she skips down the hall. Then she turns to Hunter, kneeling down so they're on eye level. "Are you okay, Hunter?" she asks kindly. Hunter nods. "Has this happened before?" Hunter doesn't say anything, just stands there frozen, his eyes on the floor.

The woman sighs, then rises to face Mike. "I'm sorry," she says. "I feel responsible. I try to be in the hallway to keep an eye out for things like this, but I got distracted today. Hunter's a terrific kid and a talent-ed musician. He's going to be a great flautist someday if he keeps at it." She looks back down at Hunter, placing her hand on his shoulder. "And I hope you *will* keep at it," she adds. "Don't let the other boys bully you into quitting something you love." Hunter nods slightly, still not saying anything. Mike nods brusquely to the woman, then turns the boy toward the door.

They're both quiet on the way home, the only sound being the country music playing on the radio. They drive about ten minutes out of town when Mike pulls into the driveway of a small gray ranch. He turns off the truck and faces Hunter.

"Okay, kid," he says, "what's going on?"

"It's nothing, Papaw."

"Why do the boys pick on you?"

Hunter stays silent for a long time while Mike patiently waits for him to speak. Finally he explains, "Because I'm weird, because I don't talk much, and because it makes me uncomfortable to look at people when they're talking to me. But mostly because I play the flute. They say it's a girl's instrument and that I must want to be a girl." He pauses. "But I don't want to be a girl, Papaw. I just want to play the flute." He lets out a deep sigh.

Mike places his hand on the boy's shoulder. "There's nothing wrong with that. And there's nothing wrong with being different. It doesn't make you inferior, or stupid, or weird. As you get older, you'll realize that being different isn't such a bad thing." He opens the truck door and steps out. As they walk up the sidewalk, he asks, "Do you have any friends at school?"

"Yeah," Hunter replies. "Jim and Brady are alright. But they're afraid of Tommy and won't hang out with me when he's around because they don't want to get picked on too. Olivia is always nice to me, and she isn't afraid of *anybody*."

"Is she in your class?"

"No, she's in fifth grade, like Tommy."

Mike nods. "Let's go inside, get your homework done, and then we'll order pizza for dinner." At this, Hunter's face brightens. "We were gonna go see Nana and Papa tonight," Mike continues, "but they would freak out if they saw your face, so we'll see them tomorrow instead."

Hunter tosses his backpack onto the kitchen table. "I told mama about Tommy last week when I went to visit, and she said he's just a 'dumb fat fuck,' and that I should kick him in the balls if he messes with me again. She's gonna be mad that I let him punch me."

Mike sighs. "Hunter, watch your mouth," he says sternly.

"But I was just repeating what mama said—"

"You know you can't repeat everything your mom says, and you'd do well to not take most of her advice. But we do need to take care of this Tommy business."

CHAPTER 21

On Saturday morning, Mike's phone rings. When he answers, a little girl's voice chirps, "Hi, is Hunter home?"

Mike looks surprised and hands the phone to Hunter, who is sitting at the kitchen table eating Cheerios and reading a book about rockets. "It's for you," he says.

Hunter's eyes widen in disbelief, but he takes the phone. "Hello?" After listening for a moment, he says, "I'll ask. Hang on." He puts the phone against his chest. "It's Olivia. She wants me to come over and play this afternoon at two o'clock. Is that okay?"

"Do you want to go?" Mike asks. Hunter nods. "That's alright with me then," Mike replies. "But I need the address."

Hunter gabs a piece of paper from the kitchen drawer and says excitedly into the phone, "My papaw says I can come! Where do you live?" He writes down the address and hands it to Mike. "See you later!" he remarks cheerfully before hanging up. He gives Mike a big smile and goes back to his Cheerios.

They pull up to the cinderblock apartment building at precisely 2:00 p.m. Mike has always disliked being late, and he's trying to instill the importance of punctuality in Hunter, who tends to amble along, concerned only with whatever is happening in his brain at the time. They locate the second-floor apartment, and Hunter rings the bell.

The door opens, and Olivia's mom is standing there, her hair up in a messy bun, glasses sliding down her nose, and a dishtowel in her hand. She's wearing baggy sweatpants and a faded sweater with holes in it. Hunter seems a bit taken aback, but not as much as she does. "Oh, hi Hunter!" she says brightly, though sounding somewhat confused. "What are you doing here? Can I help you with something?"

Now it's Hunter's turn to look perplexed. "Um," he stammers, "Olivia called me this morning and asked if I wanted to come over and play." He looks at the ground and shuffles his feet.

"Oh, she did, did she?" the woman replies, shaking her head slightly. Just then, Olivia pokes her head around her mom. "Hi Hunter!" she says. "Oh yeah – Mom, I asked Hunter if he could come over and play today. That's okay, right?"

The woman glances at Mike, who raises an eyebrow, clearly amused. "Yes, that's fine," she says. Then she gives Olivia a scolding look. "But a little heads-up would certainly be appreciated next time. Do you understand?"

"Yes. Sorry mom!" the girl says, grabbing Hunter's hand and pulling him into the apartment, leaving Mike standing awkwardly at the door.

The woman looks back at him, throws the dishtowel over her shoulder, and extends her hand. "Hi," she says warmly. "I'm Sailee. I'm sorry I didn't introduce myself the other day."

"Mike," he replies, shaking her hand. She has a good, firm grip, and it throws him off a little. "Er, sorry about this. I assumed this was all cleared with you. That's my fault. I can always bring him back another day—"

"Oh, no, no." Sailee interrupts. "Please come in. I'm glad to see Olivia taking an interest in having a friend over. And Hunter is such a nice kid. I just wish I wasn't so... unprepared." She looks down at her clothes and gives an awkward laugh, then pushes her glasses back up her nose. "She's such a precocious child, that girl. Sometimes I don't know how I'll make it through her teenage years." She opens the door wider and ushers Mike inside.

"Can I get you something to drink?" Sailee asks, heading into the tiny kitchen. "Unfortunately, all I have to offer you is tea or YooHoo – it's that chocolate milk stuff. I think it's gross, but Olivia loves it. Sorry I don't have any coffee."

"Tea's good," says Mike, sitting on a stool at the bar. "I'm not much of a coffee drinker anyway."

"Me either," responds Sailee. "I love the smell but hate the taste. I grew up drinking tea. It's the Irish blood, I guess." She puts some water in a kettle and sets it in on the stove. "I used to have one of those fancy plug-in water heaters," she explains. "But it got lost in the move, so we're back to doing it the old-fashioned way."

Mike nods. "Yeah, those are nice. I got my mom one for Christmas, but she still uses her old tea kettle."

"Old habits die hard," replies Sailee. There's a bit of an awkward silence until she asks, "Do your parents live around here?"

"Yeah," says Mike. "Just a few doors down from me. I grew up in Marion."

"That's nice! It's a beautiful place to live," she remarks. "Do you work here in town?"

"Yeah, I work at Metal Industries. I'm a mechanic."

"How long have you worked there?" Sailee inquires, trying to make conversation. She can see that the whole situation at the front door has made Mike uncomfortable, like he has barged into their home uninvited.

"Twenty-four years," he answers. "My dad worked there, and I always had a knack for fixing things, so he helped me get a job as soon as I graduated from high school."

Sailee does the math and looks surprised. "You were smart to wait to have kids," she says. "I was nineteen when I had Olivia. Just a kid myself."

Mike chuckles. "Yeah, well... Hunter's actually my grandson." Sailee's eyes widen. She was surprised to find out how old he was. Now she's shocked he's so young. "It's a long story," he explains, seeing that she doesn't know how to respond to his confession.

Sailee glances around the corner at the kids, who are engrossed in a game of Chinese Checkers. "Well, no pressure," she says, "but it seems we have some time."

Mike nods as if he's going to tell her the story but then says, "So, you teach at the school?"

Sailee is caught off guard by the abrupt change of direction. "Yes," she replies. "I'm the music teacher. This is my first year at Marion Elementary." The kettle starts whistling, so she takes it off the burner and pours the steaming water into two white mugs, sliding one over to Mike. "I have green, black, and mint tea," she says. "What would you like?"

"Black, please," he answers.

She drops a tea bag into his cup. "Milk or sugar?"

"A little of both if you have it."

"Sure thing." She grabs the milk from the fridge and sugar from the cabinet and sets them in front of Mike. "I'll let you do it, since you know how much you want. I drink mine black and will probably overdo it."

Mike smiles. "So, where were you before you came here?" he asks. "You don't have an accent, so I assume you're a transplant."

"I was teaching at a school in Vermont, where I grew up," Sailee answers.

"And what made you move to Marion?" he asks, curious. "It's a pretty small town."

"That is also a long story," she replies cryptically. They sip their tea in silence for a moment, watching the kids.

"It's good seeing them play together," says Sailee. "Olivia's outgoing, but she hasn't made many friends here yet. Ten's a tough age. Girls can be so... cliquey. I didn't think about that when we moved here. I went to the same school from kindergarten through senior year, so I never experienced being the new kid. I didn't realize how difficult it would be on her. She and Hunter sat next to each other in band for a while, and he was always very kind to her, which I appreciated. She almost didn't switch to trumpet because she didn't want to move away from him. But she was turning her flute sideways and spitting in it, so I told her she needed to play a brass instrument instead." Mike laughs at this, and Sailee notices that he has a nice smile. He hasn't said much, but there's a warmth about him.

"I'm glad too," he says. "Hunter's a quiet kid. He mostly keeps to himself and hasn't gotten invited to many playdates. Is that what they're called these days? Anyway, he was so happy when Olivia called, which made me happy, which was why I neglected to do my due diligence. Sorry, again, about that."

"It's really okay," Sailee replies, smiling.

They make small talk for the next few hours while the kids play. Mike tells Sailee about growing up in Marion: how his dad would take him hunting and trout fishing in the mountains, how he saved his allowance and bought a small six-pack cooler that he and his best friend would take to the river, filled with beer, and drink it under the guise of fishing. He talks about his days playing sports in high school, where he lettered in baseball, basketball, and football.

Sailee talks about growing up in Vermont on her grandfather's dairy farm. He passed away a few years ago, and they recently sold all his land, which was hard on the family, even though none of them wanted to continue running the farm. She tells Mike that while she played soccer in junior high, she was more of a music nerd, participating in band, choir, and all the drama productions. "I don't have the temperament for sports," she admits. "I'm way too competitive and I get mad. And mean."

Mike laughs, unable to picture that. Glancing at his watch, he realizes it's already 5:30 p.m. The time has flown by, with those first few minutes of awkwardness turning into comfortable and easy conversation. "It's nearly dinnertime," he says, rising. "I better get this kid some supper and leave you ladies to enjoy the rest of your evening. Thanks for the tea." He checks on Hunter and Olivia, who are now working on a large puzzle together. He hates interrupting them. He hasn't seen Hunter so at ease in a long time.

As if reading his mind, Sailee says, "Would you like to stay for dinner? It's nothing fancy – Hamburger Helper. I'm not much of a cook."

Mike hesitates for a moment, then agrees on the condition that she let him help.

"You can cook up the burger, if you want," Sailee suggests.

"I can do that," he replies.

While they cook, Sailee tells Mike that when she was twelve years old, she had informed her mom that she was old enough to start dating. Her mother, graciously, hadn't laughed at her. Instead, she had thought for a moment and then said, "Okay, Sailee, that's fine. But dating comes with a lot of responsibility, and you need to prove that you're ready for it. So here's the deal. If you can prepare Thanksgiving dinner for the entire family this year, including planning the menu, shopping, cooking, and the clean-up afterward, then I think you'll have shown that you're ready to date. But you have to do it right. Fresh vegetables, not frozen ones. Homemade pies, no instant mashed potatoes, and a real turkey."

Sailee started planning, and realizing how much work it was going to be, promptly decided that she could wait until she was sixteen. "Therefore," she says, "I never learned how to cook."

Mike laughs. "Your mom sounds like a smart lady."

The dinner table is quiet, everyone busy stuffing their faces. After each bite, Olivia closes her eyes, swaying back and forth to some silent rhythm. Hunter watches her curiously for a while and finally inquires, "Why do you do that?"

"Do what?" asks Olivia.

"Dance after every bite."

Olivia blushes slightly. "Um, I have synesthesia," she says.

Hunter furrows his brow. "What's that?"

Olivia looks at her mom, who nods encouragingly. "It means my senses are kind of... tangled up," she explains. "Whenever I eat, I hear music. When I eat my favorite foods, like Hamburger Helper, I hear happy music, and it makes me want to dance. Some foods make me hear scary music, or sad music."

"Are most people like that?" asks Hunter.

"No," interjects Sailee, seeing that Olivia isn't quite sure how to answer. "It's not very common. Olivia's kind is especially rare. More often, a person with synesthesia will see colors associated with particular words or sounds."

Hunter's eyes widen. "Like when I play the flute?"

Sailee looks at him curiously. "What do you mean?" she asks.

"Whenever I hear the flute I see the color green, which is my favorite color. That's why I wanted to play it!"

Sailee laughs. "Well, Hunter, it does seem quite possible that you have synesthesia as well."

Hunter smiles, but then his face falls. "Does that make me even more weird?" he asks.

"No," says Olivia, reaching over and placing her hand tenderly on his arm. "It makes you even more special."

Mike's heart swells, and he glances over at Sailee, who is looking at Olivia with pride, tears shimmering in her eyes.

When Mike and Hunter finally take their leave, they agree to get together again. Mike shakes hands with Sailee, and Olivia fist-bumps Hunter. Though they're quiet on the ride home, there's an energy in the air that can only come from one thing – joy.

CHAPTER 22

Olivia and Hunter have several playdates over the next few months, and Mike and Sailee coordinate so that one of them can drop off their child at the other's house, allowing them some time to run errands, go to the dentist, and take care of other day-to-day tasks that are challenging for a working single caregiver.

Mike has noticed that Hunter's friendship with Olivia has boosted his confidence. He's still reserved, but he's finding it easier to interact with the other kids in school. While he doesn't voluntarily speak up in class, he no longer stares silently at his desk when he's called upon. Mike has done some research on synesthesia and has gained a better understanding of it, but he still has questions. He would like to find a time to get together with Sailee again and pick her brain; see if there's anything more he can be doing to support Hunter.

One evening in February, they're at Mike's parents' house. His dad was diagnosed with Lou Gehrig's disease seven years ago, and although he can still get around with a walker, Mike bought a house just a few doors down from them to make it easier to help out as his dad's condition deteriorates. Hunter adores his great-grandparents and often brings a book to read to his Papa or a puzzle to solve with his Nana. Meanwhile, Mike takes care of various tasks around the house for his mom, such as changing lightbulbs, mowing the grass, and whatever else needs done.

Living so close to his parents turned out to be a blessing in disguise. Mike's shift at the plant starts at 6:00 a.m., so every morning Hunter walks down to his great-grandparents' house, where he catches the school bus. Mike has always been the type to arrive early and stay late at work, building a strong reputation for himself over the years and earning several promotions. But there's only so far he can advance without a college degree. And it has been more challenging with Hunter. Mike has had to leave work early on numerous occasions to pick Hunter up from school due to illness or, most recently, the incident with Tommy. His boss is aware of his situation and tries to be understanding, but it's still frowned upon.

His mom does what she can to help, but her time is increasingly devoted to caring for Mike's dad. She always wanted to be a grandmother and didn't have much opportunity to get to know Mike's own daughter, Jessie, and she cherishes the time spent with Hunter. She's good to him and for him, inventing imaginative games, trying to engage him and break him out of his usual reverie. Every time Mike sees them together, he's reminded of how fortunate he is to have his parents.

Tonight, he's grilling steaks on the carport when his mom joins him outside. "Mike," she says, "your dad and I have been talking, and we've decided to give you that piece of land we purchased thirty years ago."

"Yeah, Mom, of course," he replies. She's referring to the seventy-acre wooded property on one of the mountains that he and his dad used for hunting. "But why are you giving it to me now? Why not keep it? I can still use it, right?" Mike loves that land, as it holds countless cherished memories with his dad.

"Well," she explains, "we're concerned that as your dad's condition worsens, if he needs to go into a care facility, the state might seize the land to cover his medical expenses. We always intended to pass it on to you if you wanted it, but it seems more sensible to give it to you now. Your dad can't go up there anymore anyway, and now that you've fulfilled your child support obligations, the land won't be considered an asset in your payment calculations."

Mike looks down at his mom, sensing her worry. He puts his arm around her in a side hug. "Ok," he says. "If that's what you want to do."

She looks up at him lovingly. "You know," she says, "it's not too late for you to go back to school and pursue that engineering degree. You're still young, and I know it's what you always wanted."

"No, Mom," he replies. "I have to take care of Hunter."

"You could take classes during the day while he's at school. Asheville isn't that far away—"

"It just won't work," Mike interrupts, his tone sharper than he intended. He softens his voice. "It's alright. That ship has sailed. I have a good job at the plant, and it's important that I be available for Hunter. And for you guys."

She sighs but nods in understanding. "Alright then." Giving him another squeeze, she says, "You're a good man, Mike, and I'm proud of you."

He squeezes her shoulder in return. "Thanks, Mom."

That evening, after dinner, Mike is back at home, sitting at the kitchen table with a cup of Earl Grey tea, his favorite, and thinking about the land. He hasn't gotten up there much in recent years. There was too much going on with his daughter that consumed all this free time. Those woods have always been his sanctuary, but he was too stressed even to go hunting last year.

Just then, Hunter walks into the room, and Mike gets an idea. "Hey Hunter," he says, "how would you like to explore the land on Saturday?"

"What land?" Hunter asks.

"Papa's woods, where I hunt. I haven't been up there in ages and want to check it out and see what kind of condition it's in. Wanna go?"

Never one to give a quick answer, Hunter thinks about it. "Sure," he says finally. "Can I bring Olivia? She loves nature."

"Yeah, that's fine. I'll give her mom a call and see if they want to join us. They might both enjoy the change of scenery," says Mike, secretly hoping for some alone time with Sailee to discuss synesthesia and get her perspective on how to handle Tommy. Although he has backed off somewhat since the black-eye incident, due to the amount of trouble he got in, Tommy still seems to have it in for Hunter. Mike's instinct is to tell him to fight back, but he's not sure if that's the right approach. He never had these issues with his daughter; usually, Jessie was the bully, not the other way around.

He calls Sailee. "Hi," he says when she answers, "it's Mike Black. Hunter and I wondered if you and Olivia would like to join us for a hike on Saturday. Being new to the area, we thought you might enjoy exploring the mountains. My parents have some land, and we're gonna walk the ridge line and check things out. It's pretty this time of year. Are you interested?"

"Sure!" Sailee replies enthusiastically. "We've been cooped up for weeks. I've been putting in extra hours preparing for our upcoming concert – you're coming, right?" Mike assures her that he'll be there. "And Olivia had the flu last week, so fresh air would be more than welcome."

Mike tells her to meet at his house at 10:00 a.m., and they can all go together. "Dress warm," he advises.

"Will do," she responds. "See you then."

On Saturday morning, Sailee pulls into the driveway at 10:00 a.m. sharp. Mike is pleased that she's so punctual; he has never had to wait for her, which he appreciates. As usual, Olivia jumps out of the car and rushes up to Hunter. She seems to intuitively understand that he's uncomfortable with a lot of physical touch, so she usually gives him a high-five or a fist bump, occasionally tousling his hair. Today, she gives him a small side hug, and to Mike's surprise, Hunter doesn't shy away but reciprocates it.

Sailee steps out of the car wearing snow pants, a winter jacket layered over a hoodie, a winter hat, gloves, and thick wool socks. Mike laughs. "I know I told you to dress warm," he says, "but it's fifty-five degrees today, and you're dressed for the frozen tundra!"

"Listen," she replies, laughing, "I get cold if it's seventy-five degrees and there's a breeze. So if I'm going to spend the entire day outside, this is how I have to do it."

"Are you serious?" Mike asks. "I thought you were a northern girl."

"Doesn't matter," says Sailee. "I'm cold-blooded."

"Like a snake?" Hunter inquires.

"Precccccisssssssssely," Sailee hisses, playfully "winking" at Hunter.

Oliva rolls her eyes, and Mike shakes his head, laughing. "Alright," he says, "let's roll." They all climb into his truck.

Mike has never really brought anyone to these woods, at least not since high school when he'd bring a different girl every week. At first, the woods were his playground, but they later became his escape. Pulling in, he has a moment of apprehension about the whole plan. He has no idea what kind of shape Sailee is in. He likes to walk at a brisk pace, and what if he has to keep stopping and waiting for her? He isn't the most patient man.

However, his worries prove unfounded as Sailee charges up the hill. At one point, she sprints ahead of him up a steep slope, catching up with the kids and pulling Olivia down with her into a pile of leaves. "Mom," says Olivia, sounding annoyed. "What are you doing?"

"This reminds me so much of my summers as a kid, exploring my granda's woods. I just wanted to prove to myself that I could still run up a hill in my old age."

"Old age?" repeats Mike, snorting. He remembers her briefly mentioning that she had Olivia when she was nineteen. "What are you – twenty-nine?"

"I'll be thirty in June," replies Sailee. "Can you believe it? Thirty!"

"A baby!" says Mike, throwing an armful of leaves at her. Then he laughs and offers Sailee his hand, pulling her out of the pile.

Hunter looks back and forth between them. "What's a granda?" he asks Sailee.

"It's the Irish term for 'grandpa' or 'papaw'," she explains. "That's what I call my papaw since he was born in Ireland."

Satisfied, Hunter nods and runs ahead of them. "Ms. Roberts," he yells, "look at this!"

Sailee follows Hunter, who's picking something up off the ground. It's a deer skull, with the horns still intact. "Wow," she remarks, "that's really cool!"

"Papaw," says Hunter, "can I take this back to the house?"

"Sure," Mike replies. "We can mount it on the wall in your room, and you can hang your coat and hat on it."

"Sweet," Hunter retorts, putting the skull into his backpack.

They reach the top of the ridge around noon, and Mike calls everyone over to him. Pointing in the direction they just came from, he says, "Look over there. In the winter, you can see the entire valley."

"It's beautiful," says Sailee. The sun is high overhead, lighting up the ridges on either side of the valley.

"This is a good place to stop for lunch, I'd say," says Mike. He pulls a large blanket out of his backpack and lays it out on the ground. Then he sits and begins unpacking containers of food – sandwiches, sliced vegetables, and potato chips.

"You've been carrying all this the entire time?" asks Sailee, surprised. "What a great idea! But I feel bad. I could have brought something. Or at least carried something."

"Nah," Mike replies. "This is easy. I hope you guys are okay with ham and cheese."

Hunter and Olivia scarf their food, then head out to explore some fallen trees. "Don't venture too far!" yells Sailee. She turns to Mike. "I'm only letting her do this because she's with Hunter. I know *he* won't misbehave."

Mike smiles. "He's a pretty good kid most of the time." Then he turns serious. "He's had a hard go of it, you know."

Sailee looks thoughtful. "Care to expound?"

Mike takes a deep breath. Being from a small town, everyone knows his story – or at least they think they do. It's strange to have to share it.

"It's crazy how your life can change directions so quickly," he begins. "I was on track to be the valedictorian in high school and had planned to go to Georgia Tech for engineering. I remember watching Star Wars for the first time as a kid and thinking, 'I'm getting the hell outta this town.' Yet here I am, twenty-four years later, still in the same town, working at the same factory, and living a few doors down from my parents. It's what my dad wanted for his life, but not what I wanted for mine."

Sailee listens intently. "So what happened?" she asks.

"I got a girl pregnant the summer before my senior year of high school. I thought we were being careful but... well, accidents happen. She wasn't even my girlfriend. She was just someone I met while lifeguarding at the lake. One stupid decision that changed everything.

"She wasn't from around here – her family was on vacation, camping in the mountains for a week – and she didn't want a long-term relationship with me anymore than I did with her. I thought she was going to give the baby up for adoption, but when my daughter, Jessie, was born, she decided to keep her. I tried to get joint custody, but back then, the courts usually ruled in favor of the mother. And since we didn't live in the same state, joint custody would've been especially challenging. Nora, the girl, told the courts that I only wanted custody so that I wouldn't have to pay child support, which wasn't true. But regardless, I lost. So, strapped with a hefty child support obligation, I gave up my college dreams and took the job at Metal Industries."

"Wow," says Sailee. "That's tough. Where's Jessie now?"

"I had her one weekend a month," Mike continues, ignoring Sailee's question. "But the onus always fell on me to drive to her. Nora was never interested in bringing her to me. I worked long hours at the plant Monday through Friday, and then it was a four-and-a-half-hour drive to where she lived in Georgia. There wasn't much time to bring her back to Marion, so I usually just got a hotel for the weekend. But I wasn't making much money, and with the child support payments, it became a huge financial burden. So I ended up only seeing her a few times a year.

"As Jessie got older, she didn't want to see me anymore because I had rules, and she was expected to follow them. Her mom let her do whatever she wanted. It turns out Nora was always drunk and had no idea what Jessie was up to. But of course, Jessie never told me that. She liked her freedom and was afraid that if I knew, I would have tried to get custody of her.

"And then, when she was sixteen, she got herself knocked-up. One bad decision begets another, it seems. And suddenly, she needed my help. Her mom was unreliable, and she couldn't cope on her own. I found out Jessie had her own issues with substance abuse when she ended up in a car accident, resulting in a DWI, and called me. She had no one else to turn to. That was five years ago. She's been in and out of rehab ever since, and I have temporary custody of Hunter. He's a good kid. He's kind, he's thoughtful, he's smart. I'm just trying to do right by him."

"His dad's not in the picture?" asks Sailee.

"Nope. He found out Jessie was pregnant and ran. She won't even tell us who it is. All she says is that she'd never let that piece of shit near her son." Mike sighs. "She sure knows how to pick 'em. Like father, like daughter, I guess. So anyway, that's how I ended up a forty-two-year-old grandfather who's never getting out of Marion." Mike pauses.

"But honestly, it's okay. I mean, it wouldn't have been my first choice, but I have a good life here. I have a decent job. It's good that I'm near my parents, especially with my dad's illness. And I feel like being here for Hunter makes up for the shit dad I was for Jessie." He meets Sailee's eyes. His are full of guilt and shame, hers full of sympathy. "So what about you?" he asks. "What's your long story?"

Sailee looks over to where Olivia and Hunter are swinging on an old vine. "My story, in some ways, is not all that different," she begins. "I grew up in a strict religious household. Sex before marriage was entirely off-limits. My first college boyfriend wasn't even allowed to stay at my house – he had to sleep next store at my grandparents' house." She laughs at the memory.

"Anyway, halfway through freshman year, I started dating this new guy. We had been together for a few months and were definitely pushing the boundaries of 'purity…'" Sailee makes air quotes with her fingers, "… but, like a good Catholic girl, I was fully intending to wait until marriage to have sex. He knew this and said he was too, but whenever things got hot and heavy, he'd start pressuring me. 'Just once,' he'd say.

"The last week of the semester, I gave in. Just once. And I felt so guilty about it that I was physically ill. I figured once I went home for the summer, I'd feel better; that seeing him every day was bringing back all that guilt, and that's what was making me so nauseas.

"But then I got home and only got sicker. And then I didn't get my period. The day I found out I was pregnant, I was devastated. I didn't want a baby, but an abortion was out of the question. I could hear my mom saying, 'Two wrongs don't make a right.' It also meant that I couldn't go back to that college because it was a Christian school, and premarital sex was against the rules. And one I had obviously broken.

"Olivia's dad, to his credit, tried to do the right thing. He offered to move to Vermont so we could get married, but I said no. He's a good man, but we just didn't work together. I knew it when we were dating, but the pregnancy exacerbated it. So we broke up.

"His story is a sad one too. He was somewhat regular in Olivia's life until he got married and had a child of his own. His wife, who I'm not fond of, is the extremely jealous type and couldn't bear the thought that her husband had slept with anyone else. Since Olivia was living proof of that, she never wanted anything to do with her and always found excuses to keep him away. Then he ended up paralyzed after a skiing accident. So now he can't work, which is tough for his own family, and Olivia's child support disappeared.

"My parents have been a tremendous support, and I couldn't have done this without them. We lived with them for quite a while. I took two years off from school while I was pregnant and the first year after Olivia was born, then completed my final three years at the University of Vermont – the public university near my hometown. I'd been a composition major but switched to music education when I went to UVM because it seemed more practical, and I knew I would need a job. Teaching isn't lucrative but it gives us some stability.

"I taught in Burlington for several years, and we lived with my parents. However, last year I knew it was time for Olivia and me to make a go of it on our own. Unfortunately, the cost of living in Vermont is outrageous, and I couldn't afford it, so I began searching for places where we could manage on a music teacher's salary. And that's when I found this job. I applied, and voilà! Here we are."

Sailee smiles. "As it turns out, my biggest blessing came from my biggest mistake. It hasn't been easy, but Olivia has changed my life. She's a tough cookie. She's kind, intuitive, and so frikkin' smart. I learn something from her every day. Although it has been a hard adjustment for her, we love it here. We love having our own place. It's not much, but it's ours. It's home."

Mike nods. He remembers how he felt when he finally bought his house – his little two-bedroom, one-bathroom ranch. He had saved for years. Like Sailee said, it isn't much, but it's home.

They stare at the horizon, lost in their own memories and absorbing the weight of each other's stories. It's Mike who eventually breaks the silence. "You're a strong woman, Sailee Roberts. I have great respect for you."

Her entire demeanor brightens, and Mike realizes how much this compliment means to her. She meets his gaze. "Thank you, Mike. I have great respect for you as well."

The moment is interrupted when Sailee gets a face full of leaves. Startled, they both look up to discover the culprit, Hunter, standing in front of them with his mouth open.

"I-I'm sorry Ms. Roberts," he stammers. "I was aiming for Papaw."

They burst into laughter, and Mike reaches out, pulling Hunter to him. "Oh really?" he says. "You wanted to give me a face full of leaves? Well, two can play that game!" He playfully drags Hunter to the ground and starts stuffing leaves in his face and down his shirt. Hunter is laughing uncontrollably, and Sailee and Olivia rush to his aid, packing leaves into Mike's jacket and attempting to throw the blanket over his head. And then, when they are all covered in dirt and thoroughly exhausted, they pack up their picnic and descend the mountain.

CHAPTER 23

From that day forward, whenever the kids request a playdate, both Mike and Sailee stay for the duration. Each has been lonely for different reasons – Sailee because she's new to the area, and Mike due to his notorious reputation as the town screw-up – and they find solace in each other's company.

Mike blossoms under the sun of Sailee's friendship. Initially a man of rather few words, now he's a river without a dam, revealing that he used to be outgoing but tucked that part of himself away after Nora got pregnant, tired of the constant whisperings and judgments he faced whenever he went out. "The joys of a small town," he remarks sarcastically.

They continuously learn new things about each other, and Sailee is amazed by Mike's intelligence. He can build anything, fix anything, solve any problem. He's been helping Olivia with her math, a relief to Sailee as she was never proficient in the subject.

Mike, on the other hand, discovers that Sailee is adventurous and creative. She also has quite the temper, which he has witnessed several times when Olivia was misbehaving. Sailee confided in him once, admitting she believed she'd be a terrible teacher due to her impatience. It's challenging, she admits, but having a child of her own has given her better perspective, and perhaps slightly more tolerance.

And then, the night of the spring concert arrives. Mike retrieves a program at the entrance and finds an empty chair amidst the multitude of parents. The children enter the stage, carrying their instruments and taking their designated seats. Olivia sits down in the back row with the brass section, and spotting Mike in the audience, waves excitedly. He smiles, giving her a small wave in return. Meanwhile, Hunter makes his way to the front – the sole boy in a row of girls. He sits very still, staring at the floor. As the house lights dim, Sailee walks onto the stage, pausing at the microphone set up in the corner.

"Good evening!" she says brightly. "I'm Sailee Roberts, the Music Director here at Marion Elementary. Welcome to the 2015 Spring Concert. Your children…" her gaze lands on Mike, "… and grandchildren, nieces, and nephews, have all worked so hard this year, and we're excited to share our music with you. It has been a pleasure getting to know each and every one of them, and we've prepared a wonderful program for this evening. Please remember to silence your cell phones and enjoy the concert." There is polite applause as Sailee proceeds toward the podium.

A small girl with shoulder-length brown hair adorned with a large purple bow approaches the microphone. She momentarily disappears from view, then pushes a large wooden box onto the stage, positioning it behind the microphone, and steps up onto it.

"Our first piece," she recites in a small, high-pitched voice, "is 'Cumberland March' by Ron Cowherd. This composition was designed to introduce first-year instrumentalists to the basics of the traditional march style." The audience applauds, and the girl returns to her seat in the clarinet section.

When she's settled, Sailee raises her arms, taps out four beats in the air, and then… noise. Loud, uncoordinated noise; Mike tries not to grimace. Some of the students seem to be following along with Sailee, while others are fixated on their music, not watching her at all, and some are solely focused on producing any sound they can muster from their instruments, paying no attention to notes or timing. Mike can discern a faint melody, but not a single flute is in tune, and one of the trombones is a measure behind the rest.

Then he notices Hunter's face. He's playing away, occasionally looking up at Sailee but mostly focused on the music, tapping his foot in time to her beat, and his face is positively glowing. Mike can't tell if he's playing the right notes or not – it's impossible to distinguish one instrument in this chaos – but he's clearly having the time of his life, and Mike can't help but wonder if Hunter is seeing the color green. "I'm certainly seeing more of a muddy brown," he thinks, chuckling to himself.

In the third piece, Hunter has a brief solo. Mike has heard him practicing this passage over and over, but it makes more sense in context. While he's no prodigy, he's quite good, at least in comparison to some of the others.

In the final piece, Mike watches Sailee. Even from behind, he can tell she's having fun. It doesn't matter that half the children aren't paying attention to her; Sailee bounces on the balls of her feet, keeping the beat, and cuing the different sections when it's their time to play. "How does she listen to this every day?" Mike wonders, realizing that not only does she endure it, but she genuinely *enjoys* it. Sailee nurtures and encourages each student, not only in their musical abilities but also caring for them as individuals. "She's an angel," he thinks.

And in that moment, he realizes he loves her. He yearns to have this remarkable woman in his life – this creative, silly, not-so-patient yet also incredibly tolerant woman. She has made his life better, has made Hunter's life better. And Mike knows that she'll always make it better. He is so excited to tell her that he doesn't even pause to wonder if she feels the same.

When the final note plays, he claps until his hands hurt. Sailee calls for all the soloists to stand, and Mike enthusiastically yells, "Yeah, Hunter!" when it's his turn. Hunter's face flushes red, his gaze fixed on the floor, his hands a death grip on his flute, but Mike detects the tiniest sliver of a smile. Then Sailee turns towards the audience, beaming with pride for the children. Her eyes meet Mike's, and he smiles at her. She responds with the faintest of nods, then turns back to the children, dismissing them.

Hunter waits for the other children to clear out, and Mike joins him at the foot of the stage. "Well done, kiddo. You nailed the solo."

Hunter gives him a high-five. "I missed two notes," he says stoically.

Then Olivia sprints across the stage and crashes into Hunter, nearly knocking him over. She grabs him in a full-on hug. "You were SO GOOD!" she yells.

"You were too," Hunter replies, grinning at Olivia. "I could hear you the loudest." She grins back, giving him a playful push.

"Do you need help tearing down?" Mike asks Sailee.

"Wow, do you mind? That'd be great!" she responds. "I figured I'd be here all night."

Normally, Mike would enlist Hunter's help, but he wants Sailee to himself. While the kids take their instruments back to the band room, he pulls Sailee to the side of the stage, out of sight from the handful of lingering families. "You're incredible!" he exclaims. "I honestly don't know how you do what you do."

Sailee laughs, "So, what did you think? Hunter did a great job, didn't he? I was so proud of him!"

"Honestly?" Mike replies. "I had a hard time paying attention. I spent most of the time thinking about kissing you."

Sailee's eyes widen. "What?! Are you serious?" She bursts into laughter. Then, drying her eyes with the back of her hand, she says, "Well, that was certainly unexpected. But I love the idea!" Smiling, she tilts her face up to meet Mike's, and he lowers his mouth onto hers in a soft, brief kiss. She tastes both sweaty and sweet.

As they reluctantly pull apart, Mike says, "Maybe it was the nostalgia of being back in my old elementary school, but this is for you."

He hands Sailee his program. Puzzled, she accepts it, and on the back page finds where he has written: *Sailee Roberts, will you be my girl-friend? Circle yes or no.*

Laughing, Sailee walks over to the nearest music stand, where she grabs a pencil and draws a large circle around the "yes."

CHAPTER 24

They decide to tell the kids separately. Hunter takes the news well. He likes Ms. Roberts, he says, and enjoys seeing his papaw smile so much.

When Sailee tells Olivia that she's going to start dating Mr. Black, Olivia says, "I mean, he's nice and all, but ewww, Mom, he's a grandpa."

"He's a young grandpa," Sailee explains. "He's not all that much older than I am."

"How much older?" Olivia demands to know.

"Thirteen years."

Olivia's eyes widen. "That means he was a teenager when you were born," she retorts. "Gross! That's like me dating a..." she does the math, "...a twenty-three-year-old! You would never allow that."

Sailee laughs. "You're certainly right about that," she says. "But age isn't such a big deal once you're an adult. It's life experience that matters. And we share a lot of that."

Olivia ponders that for a moment, then shrugs. "Well, if that's what you want, Mom, then I'm cool with it."

Sailee pulls Olivia into a side hug, planting a kiss on the top of her head. "Thank you, my dear," she replies, her tone laced with a hint of sarcasm, "for being 'cool with it'."

Over the next month, the four of them settle into a routine. Monday and Thursday evenings are spent at Mike's home, while Tuesdays and

Fridays are at Sailee's apartment. Wednesday night is designated as "boys/girls' night only," and if Mike's parents are available to watch the kids, Saturday becomes date night. On Sunday evenings, they typically gather at Mike's parents' place for dinner. Olivia has made herself quite at home there and has taken it upon herself to ensure that Mike's dad completes his physical therapy exercises. While he works on his arms and legs, she alternates between voicing her encouragement and sharing every minute detail of her life since their last meeting.

Tonight is a glorious June evening. The day's heat has dissipated, replaced by a refreshing breeze winding its way through the mountains. It's Saturday, and as Olivia and Hunter walk next door, Mike is opening the truck door for Sailee when a rusty gray Toyota Camry pulls into the driveway. Mike looks up, surprised, as a woman steps out of the driver's seat.

She is bone thin, with toothpick legs that seem barely capable of supporting her frail body. Her hair hangs down her back, scraggly and a dull, mousy brown. Though her eyes, like Mike's, are large and green, they are overshadowed by the prominent red veins streaking through her sclera. Darkly tanned skin stretches tightly over pronounced cheekbones, giving her small face an exaggerated appearance, accentuated by yellow teeth that seem disproportionately large. There's a pleasant symmetry to her features, hinting at a former attractiveness, but it's difficult to determine her age as she appears simultaneously old and young.

"Jessie!" Mike calls out, leaving the truck door open and walking quickly toward her. He gives her an awkward hug, which she reluctantly reciprocates. "To what do we owe this pleasant surprise?" he asks with forced cheerfulness.

Jessie offers a tight smile but keeps her gaze on the ground. "Hi, Dad," she replies in a low, gravelly voice that surprises Sailee. "I just figured it had been a while since…" Her sentence trails off as she looks up and sees Sailee standing by the truck. "Who's that?" she asks sharply, her eyes narrowing into slits.

Mike waves Sailee over. "Sailee," he explains, "this is my daughter, Jessie. Jessie, this is Sailee." Sailee extends her hand, and Jessie looks at it but ignores the gesture, turning back to Mike.

"Yeah, you said that," she replies, and Sailee notices she's chewing on a large wad of gum. "But who is she? Why is she here?"

"She's the music teacher at Hunter's school," Mike responds. Now both Jessie and Sailee are looking at him – Jessie with suspicion and Sailee with curiosity.

"Oh," Jessie says, pointing a finger accusingly at Sailee but still addressing Mike. "So she's the one that talked my *boy*... "she drags out the word, "... into playing the flute."

Sailee is taken aback by the venom in her tone and stammers, "I-I didn't talk him into anything. When he told me that's what he wanted to play, I certainly encouraged him. He has a real talent—"

Jessie cuts her off, snapping her gum. "Yeah, whatever." She looks back at her dad. "So she's Hunter's teacher. What's she doing here? It's not even a school day." She looks around. "And where's Hunter?"

Mike gives a barely perceptible sigh. "Hunter is visiting his great-grandparents. And Sailee is getting into my truck because we're going out to dinner. She's my girlfriend."

Jessie's eyes widen, then immediately shrink back into a hostile glare, which she bestows upon Mike, then Sailee, then Mike again. "Your *girlfriend?*" she repeats disdainfully. "How old is she, anyway? Twenty-one? Twenty-two?" She turns to Sailee. "You look more like a student than a teacher."

Sailee is about thank her for the compliment when Mike jumps in. "She's old enough," he snaps. "What are you here for, Jessie? Is there something I can do for you?"

"I was coming to see Hunter since he is my son and all," Jessie replies sarcastically. "I got out of rehab last week, and I missed the little shit. I was gonna stay for a couple of hours, maybe take him to McDonalds or something, then pop over to Asheville to visit a friend." She pauses, looking back and forth between them again. "But now I'm thinking that I might just take Hunter with me. You must be some kind of creep, Dad, dating a girl who could be your daughter…" Mike winces and tries to interject, but she plows on, "…and I'm… *uncomfortable*…" she says, a disgusting sweetness forming in her elevated pitch, "…with the situation you've put Hunter in. I think he's better off with me, so I'm going to get him."

She turns to get in the car. "Jessie," cries Mike, his voice suddenly desperate. "Let's calm down and talk this through. I have custody of Hunter, so you can't just take him—"

It was clearly the wrong thing to say, and Jessie turns on him. "You shut the fuck up!" she yells. Sailee looks around and can see the neighbors peeking through their windows, curious to know what all the commotion is about. "He's *my* son, and I can do whatever the hell I want with him. Just try and stop me, you…you pervert!"

She begins marching in the direction of Mike's parents' house, with Mike following, pleading with Jessie to think about what she's doing, when Hunter comes running down the road toward them. "Mama!" he cries, throwing his arms around her waist. "I saw your car in the driveway. I didn't know you were coming to visit!" When he pulls away from her, his eyes are bright and happy. But his countenance quickly changes to one of confusion when Jessie grabs his arm and starts pulling him toward her car. "Wait, Mom… what's going on? What are you doing? Where are we going?"

The scene rapidly descends into chaos. Hunter's voice grows higher and higher the closer they get to the car. He is near tears and struggling to keep his feet under him as Jessie drags him across the driveway. Mike is trying to keep his voice steady, attempting to reason with her, but the panic is evident in his tone. "You can't do this, Jessie. You could get in a lot of trouble. There's a process we have to follow. Come inside so we can work it out." Jessie is screaming obscenities back at him. Sailee stands frozen in place, unsure of what to do.

Olivia runs up and throws herself into her mother's arms. She's sobbing. "What's going on, Mom? Who is that woman? Where is she taking Hunter? We have to stop her!" Sailee holds Olivia tightly but doesn't move. Her heart is pounding. Tears stream down her cheeks unchecked, but she can't seem to lift her arms to wipe them away. It feels as if she's paralyzed. She hasn't felt this powerless since the day she found out she was pregnant.

Jessie practically throws Hunter into the passenger seat, screaming at him to "get your seatbelt on and shut the hell up." With surprising strength for someone of her stature, she shoves Mike out of the way and gets into the car, slamming the door. She reverses the vehicle, squealing the tires as she peels out of the driveway. They disappear over the hill in a matter of seconds.

Mike sinks to his knees, burying his head in his hands. His shoulders shake, and Sailee can hear his deep, guttural sobs. The sound of a broken man. Uncertain if he wants to be left alone, she takes a few hesitant steps toward him when Olivia breaks free from her grasp and runs to Mike, wrapping her small arms around his broad shoulders.

"It's okay, Mr. Black! Hunter will be okay. We'll get him back!" She presses her tear-stained cheek against his back, giving it a gentle pat. "Everything is going to be okay," she repeats, softer now, as if she's trying to convince herself as much as anyone.

Sailee kneels down on the other side of Mike, resting her own wet cheek on his shoulder. The three of them stay like this, a still life portrait, until Mike's breathing returns to a steady rhythm. He stands, wiping his eyes, then puts an arm around each of them and gives them a squeeze. "Thank you," he says. "I don't know what I'd do without you girls." He plants a kiss on the top of both their heads, then releases them and begins walking toward the house. "I need to call my lawyer."

CHAPTER 25

A legal battle ensues over the next month. Mike's attorney informs him that if Jessie is clean, as she claims to be, it's likely that he'll lose custody of Hunter. Courts generally aim to reunite children with their parents if they're capable of caring for them. Hunter just turned ten, making it improbable that his preferences will be considered. If he were twelve or older, they might be taken into account. It's difficult to ascertain Hunter's desires because Jessie has forbidden him from contacting anyone in Marion. Mike sent Hunter a birthday card, but doubts he received it. And when Olivia called him, Jessie abruptly hung up on her.

Despite his efforts to keep it together, Mike is grappling with his inner demons. He already failed Jessie as a father. He cannot afford to fail Hunter as well. He wonders if he had fought harder for custody of Jessie from the beginning, that maybe she wouldn't have developed the issues she has. But he tries to push those thoughts from his mind, realizing there's no point dwelling on the past. Besides, that would mean Hunter might not exist, and Mike can't fathom life without his grandson.

Sailee, still burdened by guilt for not doing more to prevent Jessie from taking Hunter in the first place, spends every minute of her free time researching custodial rights and building a case to support why Mike should retain custody. Despite knowing that Mike's lawyer has everything under control, she feels compelled to acquire as much knowledge as possible about the process. While this newfound understanding only weakens her faith in the system, it at least provides Sailee with a better grasp of the situation, making her feel less helpless.

They say that trials and tribulations reveal a person's true character, and Sailee is amazed by Mike's strength. Not only his ability to persevere, but his capacity to maintain a positive outlook, treat Jessie with kindness, and continue looking forward. Although the stress has given him several premature gray hairs, Mike continues to face each day, going to work, taking care of his parents, spending time with Sailee, and helping Olivia with her homework – all while wearing a smile. But Sailee is aware of the weight he carries at not having Hunter with them.

On the other hand, Mike can't imagine how he would cope without Sailee's constant encouragement and warmth. He finds inspiration in her unwavering determination to persevere and fight for Hunter, even in the face of seemingly insurmountable odds.

Then, one day after work, Mike pulls into the driveway and discovers Hunter sitting on his front step. He jumps out of the car and runs to him, wrapping his arms tightly around the boy, only to release him when Hunter lets out a yelp of pain. Stepping back, his hands still on Hunter's shoulders, Mike surveys him. Hunter has another black eye, a cut lip, and bruising on his left cheek and wrist. And though he's always been on the small side, he appears especially gaunt. Mike's eyes widen in horror.

"Hunter," he says, his voice low and quiet, "what happened to you?" Hunter avoids eye contact, looking down at the ground and digging at the dirt with the toe of his worn sneaker. Mike persists, "Who did this to you?" Again, no answer.

He tries a different approach. "Was it a neighbor kid?" Hunter shakes his head no. "Was it your mom?" No. Mike pauses, thinking. "Was it one of your mom's friends?" Hunter keeps his head still, unwilling to lie yet not wanting to admit the truth.

Mike embraces him again, gently this time. His mind is racing. He wants to drive to Georgia and kill the person who did this to his grandson. He's trying to maintain his composure but can feel the rage, the pressure, building in his chest, like a shaken soda can that's ready to explode. He takes a deep breath and asks, "How did you get here?"

Hunter remains silent for a long time. "I took the bus," he eventually replies.

"The bus?" Mike repeats, confused. "What kind of bus?"

"A Greyhound."

Mike runs an impatient hand through his hair. Getting details out of this kid is worse than bathing a cat. "Marion doesn't have a bus station…"

Hunter lets out an exasperated sigh, as if this interrogation is a major nuisance to him. "I took the bus from Savannah to Asheville. I was going to call and ask you to come pick me up, but a nice lady gave me a ride."

Mike's eyes widen. "You hitched a ride with a *stranger*? Do you know dangerous that is?!" His heart thumps loudly in his chest. Hunter has always been so sensible; it's hard for Mike to believe that he would be so reckless. He could have been kidnapped… or worse! "But he's here," he reminds himself. "On my doorstep. In one piece." A wave of relief washes over him. There's no point in getting angry about it now.

"She wasn't exactly a stranger," Hunter explains. "Her daughter, Sarah, sat next to me on the bus. She was really nice to me. Sarah's mom picked her up at the bus station, and when she saw I was alone, she asked where I was going and if I needed to borrow her cell phone to call anyone. When I told her I was going to Marion, she offered to give me a ride since they live in Rutherfordton, and it was right on their way." He gives a small but definitive nod of his head and glances up at Mike, as if to say, "See? Everything's fine."

Mike has so many questions. How did Hunter get to the bus station in Savannah? Where did he get the money for his ticket? Does his mom know he's here? He decides everything can wait except for the last question, which he voices.

Hunter shakes his head no, and Mike puts his arm around the boy's shoulder, leading him into the house. "Well, kid," he says, "we better get some ice on those bruises. Then I need to make a few calls." The screen door slams shut behind them.

When Sailee and Olivia arrive at Mike's that evening, he and Hunter are out back constructing a new fire pit. Olivia squeals with delight and throws herself at Hunter, hitting him with such force that he topples over, landing in the grass. She falls down with him, laughing, until she notices his bruises. "Hunter, what happened to your face?" she asks, her eyebrows furrowed in concern.

"It's nothing," he says, standing up and brushing the grass off his shorts.

Sailee gives Hunter a gentle hug, expressing how good it is to see him again, then raises her eyebrows at Mike in a questioning manner. He nods ever so slightly in the direction of the house, and she takes the hint. They meet in the kitchen, and Sailee wraps her arms around Mike's waist in a long hug while he fills her in on everything he knows.

He's nearly finished, saying how sick it made him having to file an abuse report, when the back door slams, and Olivia calls out, "Ewww, c'mon guys, quit neckin' in the kitchen."

The tension is broken, and Mike laughs, giving Sailee a tight squeeze as she nuzzles her head theatrically under his chin. "First of all, who uses the term 'necking' anymore?" asks Mike. "Second, this is my house, and I can neck in whatever room I want!" He winks at Olivia, who grins back at him, then pulls Hunter into the other room.

Mike looks down at Sailee. "You're the best," he says. "I honestly don't know what I'd do without you. Thanks for always being there for me and not letting all this dysfunction scare you off."

Sailee smiles up at him. "I'll always be here," she replies. "You're my person." Standing on her tiptoes, she plants a soft kiss on his lips. "C'mon, let's start dinner."

Cooking together has become one of their favorite activities. They blast music and have dance parties in the kitchen, singing at the top of their lungs. Today, Mike strums an imaginary guitar while Sailee belts out lyrics into the half-grated carrot she's using as her microphone. Suddenly, Mike seizes Sailee's hand, twirling her across the floor. Although they can't afford dance lessons, they've been practicing a few moves they learned from YouTube. Laughing, Sailee yells for Olivia and Hunter to come join in the fun, and the four of them form a mosh pit in the small kitchen.

When the doorbell rings, Mike leaves the other three dancing in the kitchen and goes to see who it is. Glancing out the window, he finds a policeman standing on his doorstep and feels a weight in his gut, as if he just swallowed one of his dumbbells. The police came out earlier in the day to take pictures and a statement after his phone call, so what could this be about?

"Hey, Pete," Mike says, opening the door. "Is everything alright?" He and Pete played football together in high school and have kept in touch over the years.

Pete shifts uncomfortably. "Hey, Mike," he says, "is your grandson here?"

Mike's heart begins pounding. He knew it. Pete's here to take Hunter back to his mom, but that can't happen. He *has* to make him understand. "Look," Mike explains, "Hunter came back on his own, I swear. I had nothing to do with it. I've been trying to reach his mom, but she won't answer the phone. But you can't take him back there, Pete. Her new boyfriend beat the shit out of him. I won't let you—"

"Mike," Pete cuts him off sharply. "I just got a call from the Savannah police—"

"I know," interrupts Mike, "he ran away from there—"

"It's not *about* that," yells Pete, raising his voice before quickly lowing the volume. His shoulders slump. "C'mon outside and sit down." Mike reluctantly complies.

"Listen," says Pete, "apparently Jessie's new boyfriend was bad news. He got her hooked back on all the shit she'd been into before rehab, and it appears he introduced her to heroin." Mikes eyes widen, but he remains silent. "The cops found her this afternoon, Mike," Pete continues. "She's dead. Drug overdose. I'm really sorry, man."

Mike feels as if he has been slammed in the back of the head with a two-by-four. "Wait, what?" He struggles to process this information. He had expected a lot of things, but not this. His brain can't comprehend it. Jessie... dead? No, it can't be. Maybe she overdosed and is in the hospital, and this is a sick joke. Or perhaps she's pretending because she doesn't want to admit that she can't take care of Hunter. But not dead. So much was left unsaid, undone. He had always hoped that maybe, through Hunter, he could build a real relationship with her, be the father he never was, and help her turn her life around. That maybe, just maybe, they could be a family.

All these deep-seated hopes, perhaps never even consciously acknowledged, now surface in his mind. All the things that could have been but will never be. Mike sits motionless while Pete stands there awkwardly, unsure of what to do.

Then Sailee appears at the door. "Mike?" she asks, her voice sounding concerned. "Is everything okay?"

Pete breathes a small sigh of relief at the sight of her. He nods to Sailee and puts on his hat. "I'll leave you two alone," he says, returning to his car.

Sailee sits down next to Mike. "What is it?" she asks. He tells her, and they sit together on the front step in silence for a very long time. "Will you stay?" Mike finally asks. "I need to tell Hunter, but I can't bear to do it alone. I know this isn't your burden—"

"Of course I'll stay," Sailee replies, placing her hand on his. "Like I said before, you're my person. I'll always be here when you need me." He gives her hand a reassuring squeeze and heads into the house.

Dinner that evening is quiet. It's hard to determine how Hunter is handling the news. Olivia keeps glancing at him from the corner of her eye as she pushes the spaghetti around her plate. Even Sailee has lost her appetite. Once dinner (which mostly ends up in the trash) is finished and the kitchen is cleaned, Sailee signals to Olivia that it's time to leave.

Hunter looks up for the first time all evening. "Will you stay over tonight?" he asks. "Please?" He looks at Mike, his green eyes pleading. "Papaw, can they stay? Olivia can sleep on the floor in my room." He pauses, then quickly adds, "Or she can sleep in my bed and I'll sleep on the floor." Mike and Sailee exchange looks and nod.

Mike feels a wave of relief wash over him. He had dreaded them leaving but didn't feel he had the right to ask them to stay if Hunter needed some time alone. They make a bed for Olivia, who insists on sleeping on the floor. "It's like camping," she says.

Mike feels strange taking Sailee into his room with him. She has never stayed over before, and while he had dreamt of the moment when he wouldn't have to kiss her goodbye, he never imagined it would be under such solemn circumstances. They spend the night in each other's arms, holding onto one another, allowing life to wash over them in a sad yet comfortable stillness. Sailee is exactly what he needs. She is what he has always needed. By the time Mike wakes up in the morning, he knows that he never wants her to leave again.

CHAPTER 26

They get through the funeral, and Mike is granted full custody of Hunter, to everyone's great joy and relief. Over the past several weeks, Sailee and Mike have spent hours discussing the future and what they want it to be. Jessie's death has made them realize that life is precious, and they don't want to waste any more time being apart. However, they have wanted to be sensitive to Hunter, giving him time and space to grieve in his own way.

On Saturday evening, the week before the new school year begins, Mike piles everyone into his truck and takes them to a steakhouse in Asheville. He insists that everyone dresses up, so Hunter puts on kakis and a polo shirt, Olivia wears a flowered skirt with a blue blouse, Sailee looks beautiful in a deep purple dress she found at Goodwill, which accentuates the green in her eyes, and Mike wears his only suit and a tie. There's a touch of salt and pepper at his temples, which Sailee claims to find incredibly debonair.

At dinner, everyone is allowed to order whatever they want. "You mean I can get the biggest steak?!" asks Hunter. And over dessert, Mike and Sailee announce that they've decided to get married. Hunter looks at Olivia. "We'll be siblings!" he exclaims excitedly.

Olivia scrunches her face in thought and then responds with a laugh, "Actually, I'll be your aunt." Hunter makes a face. "That's okay though," she continues. "We'll be family, and that's what really matters. And we'll always be friends." She smiles at Hunter, who grins back at her.

Sailee and Mike exchange glances, and Sailee "winks." Mike laughs. That never gets old.

They live simply, scrimping and saving until, five years after the wedding, they have enough money to build a house on top of the ridge, on the land Mike's parents gave him. It's a small house with three bedrooms and one bathroom but to them, it's a castle. It exceeds their wildest dreams, and their home is always filled with noise, music, dancing, and love.

During dinner on their first night in the new house, they're gathered around the table, expressing gratitude for the blessing of being a family. "We both made some pretty poor choices," says Sailee. "But every decision we made brought us closer together. It was a one-in-infinity chance, and we wouldn't trade it, or you guys, for the world."

"Mom," says Olivia, rolling her eyes, "infinity's not a number."

"So what is then, smarty pants?" asks Sailee.

Hunter has been quiet throughout most of dinner, but now he chimes in. "It would be… one chance in an inconceivably large but finite number," he says. Everyone bursts into laughter, and Mike affectionately ruffles Hunter's hair. Shadow Mike smiles and fades into blackness.

CHAPTER 27

April 7

She's in the car with Mike, driving home. He's saying something about how one in infinity is not a ratio, but she's only half-listening, distracted by a strand of hair curling around his ear. She leans over the armrest to kiss him when there's an enormous crash. Suddenly, they're spinning, and she clings to Mike for dear life. When the whirling finally subsides, something is touching her face, and she pushes against it. The airbag. She punches until she's free of it, then looks over at Mike to make sure he's okay. But where his head should be, there is only a stump. His airbag is red, saturated with blood. His blood. She screams.

Sailee sits up with a start. She's drenched in sweat. It was that dream again; the same one she's been having since the accident. A wave of nausea washes over her. Flinging off the covers, she lies back down but can't shake the image of Mike's headless, blood-soaked body. Unable to bear it any longer, she rises, grabbing her crutches, and heads to the bathroom to splash cold water on her face. Her pajamas are soaked, and she removes them.

She hasn't been sleeping well since the accident, and she's tired. She is *so* tired. Having studied psychology in college, Sailee understands that this dream is a distorted manifestation of her worst fear – that she'll never see Mike again. That he'll never come back to her.

She attempts to push that thought away, to distract herself like she always does, but she doesn't have the energy. The weight of it is too much, and she sinks to the floor, her crutches clattering beside her. The cold tile feels good against her sweaty body. She lies on her side, her broken leg outstretched while the rest of her body curls into a ball, and she cries – deep guttural sobs that tear at her core, as if trying to rip her open. She has fought so hard to hold herself together, to be strong, to be brave. But tonight, she has nothing left.

Hours later, she awakens on the bathroom floor, naked. She must have cried herself to sleep. "At least it was a dreamless sleep," she thinks. Sailee shivers, her body now cold and stiff. She tries to get up but slips. Reaching for her crutches, she hoists herself up on them, using her good leg for support, and makes her way back into the bedroom, where the first rays of daylight are peeking through the blinds. She should try to get more sleep but knows it would be futile, so she showers, dresses, and heads to the hospital.

As she limps into the ICU, the nurses at the station greet her cheerfully. "Good morning, Sailee!" they exclaim. "You're here early today."

They know her well by now and are kind to her. Occasionally, someone brings her food from the cafeteria, or they ask about Mike – how they met, how long they've been married, what drew her to him. She found the questions annoying at first, when all she wanted was to be alone in her grief. But now she appreciates it, grateful for any reason to talk about him, to share memories. To them, he is merely another entry on their medical chart. Name: Michael Robert Black; Date of Birth: February 10, 1972; Status: Coma. But she wants them to know who the man they're caring for *really* is. That he's kind, and funny, and brilliant. That he's a devoted husband, a loving son, and a loyal friend. So now she shares everything with them.

She has also learned about their lives – which ones have children, which ones go out partying after work, and which nurses don't get along with each other. She had friends that used to watch Grey's Anatomy, and Sailee always found the manufactured drama to be ludicrous. Now she realizes it may not have been as fabricated as she had believed. Hospital drama is a real thing!

Sailee hobbles into Mike's room. He's the same as every other day, except his hair is getting long and his customary scruff had morphed into a substantial beard. Swinging herself over to his bed, she perches on the edge, leaning her crutches against the railing. "Hey babe!" she says, mustering a cheerful tone that belies how she feels. "Do you know what today is? April first." She imagines Mike suddenly opening his eyes, sitting up, and shouting, "April fools!" and her jumping in surprise, playfully punching his arm, and yelling back, "Are you kidding me?! Have you been planning this the entire time?" He would laugh and pull her into a hug. "Scared you, didn't I!"

It reminds her of when they first moved into their house. There were numerous corners and closets, and she liked to jump out and scare him. One night, Mike was working late in his office, so Sailee had gone in to give him a kiss goodnight before heading upstairs. She brushed her teeth, removed her contacts, and climbed into bed. They always slept with the bedroom door open to help with airflow. Otherwise, it would get too hot.

As she settled in, she glanced towards the end of the hallway, and there, hidden in the shadows, was a face – not moving, not smiling, just staring at her. Terrified, she leapt out of bed, screaming, "MIKE!" at the top of her lungs. She was frantically searching for something, anything, to defend herself with when Mike emerged from the shadows, laughing so hard he was crying.

"Scared you, didn't I!" he said.

She could've killed him. "I can't believe you did that to me! You nearly gave me a heart attack," she cried.

"You do that to me all the time," he retorted. "This was payback."

She shook her head in relief and returned to bed. After brushing his teeth, Mike slipped in beside her, his breathing soon settling into a slow, steady rhythm. Sailee tried to sleep, but kept imagining that face in the shadows, watching her. Quietly, she got out of bed and tiptoed to the bedroom door, closing it.

"Why are you closing the door?" Mike asked from the dark.

She had thought he was asleep. "I'm cold," she replied.

"You're *afraid*," he accused, a grin evident in his tone.

"I'm so scared!" she confessed, running back to the bed. "That really creeped me out. Now I can't sleep because all I can see is that face at the end of the hallway."

Mike had laughed and snuggled up behind her, wrapping his arms around her waist. "Truce?" he proposed. "No more scaring each other?"

"Truce," she agreed. It still took Sailee awhile to settle down, but she eventually drifted off in his arms.

Oh, how she wishes he would jump up and scare her right now. She wouldn't even be mad. Except, she *is* scared. She's terrified. They're approaching the one-month mark, and she knows it's uncommon for a person to survive a coma beyond a few weeks. "We truced, remember?" she says to him, taking his hand and bringing it to her lips. "You're not supposed to scare me anymore."

CHAPTER 28

Shadow Mike opens his eyes, taking in his new surroundings. He's in Italy – San Gimignano, to be exact. He would recognize this place anywhere. It's where he and Sailee came on their honeymoon. They had planned to tour all of Tuscany but fell in love with this little city on the hill and never left. It's autumn now, his favorite time of year to visit. The harvest is done, and the leaves on the grape vines are changing from their dark green to hues of orange, red, and yellow. The days are cooler, and the throng of summer tourists is gone, leaving the city quiet and walkable. The locals re-emerge.

He's in a small restaurant overlooking the valley. It's midday, and the sun is high overhead. In front of him is a woman in her early to mid-sixties with short hair, blonde streaked with gray. His heart jumps. *Sailee.*

Experience tells him that a version of himself is likely nearby, and he glances around, finding Mike at the table adjacent to hers. "I haven't aged too badly," thinks Shadow Mike. He still sports a full – although thinning – head of gray hair and looks to be in decent shape for a man of his age. Shadow Mike estimates he's in his late seventies. The older Mike is watching Sailee with curiosity. She keeps looking out over the valley, then down at her table. She appears to be drawing.

"It's beautiful, isn't it?" Mike says to her.

Sailee looks up. Her eyes are bright, and Mike notices their almond shape and the rings of green, brown, and gray.

"It's so inspiring," she replies enthusiastically. "But unfortunately, I have no talent."

"I'm sure that's not true," he says.

She holds up her drawing pad, facing him, and he leans forward to see it better. She's right – she has no talent! He's deciding how to respond when she says, "Don't worry. You don't have to flatter me. I know how bad it is!"

Mike lets out a sigh of relief. "I *do* recommend taking a few photos, for memory's sake!" he says with a wink. Sailee laughs.

"Is this your first time in Italy?" he asks her.

"Yes. And you?"

"No, I've been many times. Italy is my favorite country in the world.

"Do you speak Italian?" she asks.

"I'm afraid I don't. I'd like to, but I've never been good with languages." He has tried to learn many times, but it never seems to stick. He was always better with numbers.

Sailee notices the ring on his left hand. "Is your wife with you?"

"No," Mike replies, fingering the ring. "I'm widowed."

"Ah, I'm sorry," she says. "I am as well. How many years?"

"Five. And you?"

"Two." She looks down at her own ring.

There's a moment of silence, and he breaks it with, "Where are you from?"

"Denver, Colorado."

His eyes widen. "You're joking. So am I! What part?"

"Washington Park. On South Gilpin between East Tennessee and East Kentucky. Do you know the area?"

"Of course!" says Mike, shaking his head in amazement. They live in the same neighborhood, less than a mile from one another. "I live on South Josephine."

"What a small world!" Sailee exclaims. "It's a wonder we never met!"

"So, what brings you to Italy, neighbor?" Mike asks.

"I retired last year and this is my gift to myself," replies Sailee. "I always wanted to come to Italy, so my kids finally talked me into joining this tour group."

"How many children do you have?" Mike asks.

"Three," she answers. "And four grandchildren." She's clearly proud of them. "How about yourself?"

"Two," replies Mike. "And three grandchildren, and a great-grandchild on the way."

"That's wonderful!" Sailee remarks. She asks him what he loves most about Italy.

"The wine, of course," he answers theatrically. "And the food, and the people, and the landscapes... Just about everything, really!"

Sailee laughs and invites Mike to join her at her table. From that moment on, they are inseparable. Sailee abandons her tour group and spends the next month traveling with Mike across Europe, much to her children's dismay. "They think I've gone senile in my old age," she says, laughing. Six months later, they fly all their children and grandchildren to Italy for a small wedding ceremony in a vineyard outside San Gimignano. Because, why not? Life is short.

And they have a wonderful life together. They make up for lost years. They make love. They travel the world. They laugh. They spend hours and hours talking. They cherish the time with their blended family and are thankful that everyone gets along so well. They watch their grandchildren grow and welcome three more great-grandchildren. They walk, bike, and play pickleball. People often comment that Sailee must be keeping Mike young, and she retorts that she's the one trying to keep up with him! She learns to play golf for him, even though it makes her angry, and Mike derives great amusement from her temper.

"I wish I had met you in college so I could have spent my entire life with you," he says to her one day while they're sipping tea on their front porch.

"Well," she responds with a chuckle, "I would have been seven, and my parents would not have approved!"

Mike laughs and takes her hand. "Well then, I wish I had had you for my whole life from a respectable age!"

"So do I," says Sailee. She looks at him, and there is so much love in those beautiful eyes. He can't believe this is how he gets to spend his final years.

They're good for each other. It's always easy, and they have fun together; have fun teasing each other. One day, Mike is telling his youngest granddaughter that he doesn't like to think about birthdays as being another year older, he prefers to think of them as another trip around the sun. Sailee comes up behind him, puts her arms around his waist, and says, "Then you must be a regular astronaut!" She grins and winks at him, even though she's as skilled at winking as she is at drawing.

Later that day, Sailee trips over a toy and is limping around the house. Mike turns to the same granddaughter with a mischievous grin and says, "I don't know about her. I might have to find myself a younger, less decrepit woman to hang out with!" Sailee laughs, wagging her finger at him.

She's becoming forgetful in her old age, often misplacing things. "I'm going to put a GPS tracker on the urn that holds my ashes," Mike teases, "so you don't set me down somewhere and lose me."

"You won't have to," she replies. "You'll never be without me."

Fourteen wonderful years. Then, one day, when Mike is ninety-three, he wakes up and can't get out of bed. "I don't think I'm going to be able to get your tea for you this morning, my love" he says weakly.

"That's alright," replies Sailee, getting out of bed slowly. "I can get it for you." At eighty years old, everything feels stiff. "Are you okay?" she asks. "Should I call the doctor?" She makes a cup of Earl Grey tea with milk and sugar and places it on his nightstand, giving him a kiss, just as he has done for her every day since their first morning together in Italy.

"No," he answers, "I'm just tired. Come and lie with me."

Sailee lies back down, resting her head on Mike's chest, and he wraps his arms around her. Her head rises and falls with each breath, then it stops. He is still. Sailee stays there for a moment to be sure, then looks up at him. He's gone.

She knows there are things she must do, but she stays there with him a while longer, holding his hand in hers. She knows this is the last time she'll be with him like this, knows that once she gets up, things will never be the same. Her life will never be the same. *She* will never be the same.

Finally, she gets out of bed, kisses his forehead, and says, "A dopo, amore," then goes downstairs to make the necessary calls. She notifies his children first, then hers, and finally calls 911.

Three days later, on the night before the funeral, Sailee climbs into bed. Their bed. It feels cold. Even as Mike grew older, his body always stayed so warm. She closes her eyes and feels a darkness that is different than usual. Heavier, perhaps? She thinks of the song by Ben Folds that she loved to play when she was younger.

> *Next door there's an old man who lived to his nineties*
> *and one day passed away in his sleep*
> *And his wife, she stayed for a couple of days and passed away*
> *I'm sorry, I know that's a strange way to tell you that I*
> *know we belong*
> *That I know*
> *That I am, I am, I am the luckiest.*

She hears the piano and the strings playing in her mind. The final note. "I am the luckiest," she thinks, and drifts off to sleep.

In the morning, her children find her in bed, her head on Mike's pillow, their wedding photo clutched to her chest. She's cremated, just as Mike was, and six months later, on the eve of their anniversary, their families gather in Tuscany to say their final goodbyes, scattering their ashes together, just as they had wanted.

Shadow Mike sees the vignette forming around the edges of his vision and blinks hard to clear the tears filling his eyes. There is sadness, yet a profound peace in his soul, and he is glad for this Mike who lived such a long and happy life, passing away with his greatest love in his arms. Sailee was the icing on the proverbial cake, the element that sweetened his already wonderful life. She was the half that made him whole, the best part of those many, many years on earth, his soulmate finally found. "Better late than never," he thinks as he slips back into the void.

CHAPTER 29

April 17

It's an uncharacteristically warm day in San Francisco, and Sailee decides to escape the hospital for a while and go for a walk (or the best she can do on crutches) around the city. She heads toward McKinley Square, located about half a mile from the hospital. The day is beautiful, offering sweepings views that stretch for miles. It reminds her of other parks she and Mike have visited together.

While Sailee's family enjoyed hiking, Mike grew up hunting, which he described as hiking with a gun. So, when Sailee proposed hiking together *without* firearms, he was skeptical. But then Covid-19 shut the world down, and they packed up, left the city, and embarked on a four-month road trip, exploring the country, and hiking nine national parks. That experience won Mike over, and now they hike together regularly. When they can't venture far, they seek out local parks, like this one, and she vows to bring Mike here when he wakes up.

Struggling up the steep hill, Sailee reflects on their road trip. It was a remarkable experience, save for one incident. Approximately two-thirds of the way through, while visiting friends in Arizona, Mike tore his hamstring playing tennis. Unfortunately, the next several stops on their itinerary were the four national parks in southern Utah.

They managed to complete a few short hikes in Zion, and although Mike was in significant pain, he pushed through it. The worst part of that day wasn't his leg; it was when the Mexican food he had for lunch decided to wreak havoc midway up a trail, and he was forced to do a one-legged squat in a foot of snow on the side of the mountain, sacrificing his favorite t-shirt since neither of them had any tissues on hand.

The following day, they hiked Bryce Canyon. Mike did fine on the descent, but the switchbacks on the way back up did a number on his leg, and he could barely walk the next day. Though Mike never complained, he winced with each step, alerting Sailee to the amount of pain he was in. She worried that he had further injured his leg and might need surgery.

Their third stop was Arches National Park. Sailee assumed she would have to do the hikes by herself, but Mike was determined not to miss out. Upon arriving in Moab, they stopped at a pharmacy and purchased a cane and a leg brace. For their first stop, Mike suggested that Sailee hike to one rock formation while he hobbled his way to another feature nearby, and she could meet him there.

Sailee agreed, taking off toward the Windows at a brisk pace. When she finally arrived at the Double Arch, she couldn't locate Mike anywhere. Worried that something had gone wrong, she started walking back to the truck when she heard him calling her name. Turning around, she spotted him high up the side of the rock face, directly beneath the arches. It was a steep surface, and she couldn't believe he had managed to climb up there with a bum leg and a cane. She gave him mountain goat status after that. Making her way up this much smaller incline with her own injured leg, Sailee has even more respect for his determination.

Eventually, she arrives at the top. It's a weekday, and kids are in school, leaving the park mostly empty. Sailee meanders over to the playground and sits on a swing, tossing her crutches down onto the ground beside her. She loves to swing, leaning back as far as she can, her toes reaching for the sky, then the exhilarating drop as she hurtles backward towards the earth. "You're never too old to enjoy a playground," she thinks with a smile.

While she swings, Sailee thinks back over the recent weeks. Realizing that she couldn't wallow in her misery forever, she resolved to do something productive with her time in the hospital. Mike always sought to make the most of every situation, and she's determined to do the same. So now, although still spending the majority of her days at Mike's bedside, Sailee has recently begun visiting other ICU patients, particularly those without regular visitors or family nearby. The nurses were thrilled with her idea when she approached them about it, thinking it might boost morale. And when they asked the patients if they would appreciate company, all but two said yes.

Now, Sailee dedicates an hour every day to sitting with different individuals. If they're able to communicate, she engages them with questions about their lives, encouraging them to share their favorite things, their favorite memories. If they need to talk about their pain, or their fear of not knowing how things are going to turn out, she listens attentively, avoiding empty clichés and false reassurances, but instead letting them know that she hears them and genuinely cares. Aware that these individuals are on the precipice between life and death, she wants to make that walk a little better for them.

For those who are unable to communicate, Sailee shares anecdotes from her own life. Usually she recounts lighthearted stories, like the time she replaced her office chair with a large exercise ball, thinking it would provide a good core workout. One day, when her boss was in the office, she had reached for something on her desk and rolled right off of it onto the floor! He had laughed until he cried, and Sailee promptly returned to sitting in a chair.

Sometimes, she reads to them or plays music – anything to alleviate their loneliness. Though it was never intended to be an experiment, both doctors and nurses have noticed the positive impact of Sailee's regular interactions with the patients. They appear more at ease, happier, and in some cases, it seems to be accelerating the healing process.

"Hey, babe," Sailee says to Mike one day. "Remember how I told you I wanted to be a conversational therapist when I grew up? Well, I'm doing it!"

It began as a ploy to mask her own misery. Sailee couldn't bear the pity in people's eyes when they asked how she was doing. The truth was that she was far from okay – her appetite had vanished, she had lost a considerable amount of weight, and she was no longer sleeping. But she didn't want anyone to know how anxious and depressed she really was. This was a way to hide it, to pretend she was fine, and divert attention away from her own well-being.

But over time, the experience has changed her. She now finds she's waking up each morning thinking about the good things that might happen that day, rather than fixating on her fear of losing Mike. And she has genuinely enjoyed getting to know these people. Hospitals had always made her uncomfortable, but now that she's spending so much time in one, she finds joy in making it a better experience for others. And her heart is healing in the process.

CHAPTER 30

Once again, it's sound that pulls Shadow Mike into the next universe. But rather than a barrage of poorly played instruments, this time he's swathed by a loud, raucous roar. He opens his eyes, and the world around him is black. He smells, rather than sees, the mob of bodies surrounding him – warm bodies, sweaty bodies. Eventually, his eyes adjust to the darkness, and he can see the sweat glistening on faces and arms, soaking clothing. He wrinkles his nose. For the first time in a long time, he's thankful he can't feel anything.

Then suddenly, there is light – blinding light that rips through the darkness, illuminating the crowd, and everyone screams louder. It takes Shadow Mike a moment to figure out that he's at a concert. He looks around, hoping to gather clues as to where and when he might be, but all he finds are young, scantily clad bodies. He looks closer, grateful that no one can see him because he'd likely be slapped for ogling some girl's chest. In reality, he's trying to get a good look at her tank top, which reads "Back in Black." He notices the same name and logo on several shirts but doesn't recognize it.

Then a voice booms over the loudspeaker. **"BURLINGTON! ARE YOU READY?!"** More screams. **"LET'S HEAR IT FOR BACK IN BLACK!"** The crowd goes berserk. Everyone is pushing, trying to get closer to the stage. Shadow Mike does his best to move out of the way, but people pass through him at an alarming rate. He feels claustrophobic. Is there another version of himself somewhere in this massive throng? How will he ever find him?

A familiar guitar riff resonates through the crowd, and a voice Shadow Mike knows all too well pulls his attention to the stage. There he is – dressed in jeans and a blue t-shirt, cowboy boots, and a cowboy hat, guitar in hand. He's half singing, half screaming into the mic.

"When I was a little boy
I wanted to grow up and be like Johnny Cash
But daddy, he liked gospel music
And mama said it was trash
But I watched him, and I listened
And I learned to play guitar
I took a stab and writin' songs
But hell, I didn't get too far.
But I ain't gonna give up
And I ain't gonna get mad
Cuz I've always worked towards my dreams
And this is one I've had."

Everyone in the audience joins in now, singing at the top of their voices.

"I wanna sing like Cash
I wanna sing like Cash
Like the man in black, I won't hold back
I wanna sing like Cash

Well I ain't never been to prison
And I never snorted coke
Never shot a man in Reno
And women, they ain't no joke
I ain't never been to Jackson
I've always tried to walk the line

Really, I haven't been anywhere, man,
But I think that's just fine
I'm not all that fond of black
I look better in blue..."

There's a scream of approval from the women in the crowd.

"I'm not too good at talkin' smack
And thank God my name ain't Sue
So I guess I'm not much like him
But I've had a big breakthrough
All that stuff don't matter much
To thine own self be true.

I wanna sing like Cash
I wanna sing like Cash
I'll be the good boy version, post conversion
I wanna sing like Cash"

He ends the song just as he started, with Cash's famous guitar line from "Folsom Prison Blues." The crowd is going wild. The girl next to Shadow Mike jumps up and down, shouting, "Marry me, Magic Mike!" while the electric guitarist yells, **"HOW'S EVERYBODY DOING TONIGHT?!"** into the microphone, eliciting more screams. Mike strums his guitar, and the band launches into another song.

Shadow Mike works his way to the front of the stage to get a better look at himself. He's young here, probably the youngest he's been in the multiverse so far – early thirties, he guesses. This Mike still has broad shoulders, but he's slender, and appears to work out regularly. Shadow Mike can see the definition in his arms as he strums the guitar. He looks massive next to the guy playing lead: a short, skinny man with long hair and a handsome face. Wait – he knows this guy! He's a popular solo artist in his own timeline.

Their music is a blend of country and rock, and they obviously have a large following. Although Magic Mike (Shadow Mike chuckles at this new nickname) does a little singing, he primarily plays rhythm guitar. At one point during the set, he brings out the banjo – a crowd favorite, as evidenced by the decibels of the screams – and they perform a few bluegrass songs with a rock twist.

Shadow Mike looks around for Sailee. Based on Mike's apparent age, she's probably not more than nineteen or twenty in this timeline. Judging by the age of the crowd, mostly college girls it seems, she's going to be difficult to find. He makes his way up and back through the masses, searching for her. He thinks he recognizes her once, wrapped around some boy with spiked blonde hair, and his stomach churns at the sight of her making out with someone else. He knows Sailee has kissed other people, but he doesn't want to see it. When they finally pull apart, he discovers it's not her and breathes a sigh of relief.

And then the concert is over. The band waves to the fans and walks off stage to thunderous applause and screaming. *So* much screaming. Shadow Mike is over it. He has gotten used to the silence in the void and finds this overwhelming. He follows Magic Mike backstage and sees someone hand him a beer, which he opens and chugs. Then he tosses the can and immediately reaches out for another. They hand their instruments to the crew and make their way back to the dressing rooms.

"Quite the crowd," says Mike. "When do we roll outta here?"

A girl with a headset looks at her watch and answers, "In about two hours. You have to make an appearance at the afterparty first."

Mike rolls his eyes. "Ugh," he says, cursing under his breath. "Stupid backstage passes."

The girl smiles and shrugs. "It's part of the gig," she replies, walking away.

Mike goes into the dressing room and takes off his sweat-soaked shirt. Throwing on a clean t-shirt, he runs a hand through his hair, puts his cowboy hat back on, and heads out the door, colliding with a short, dark-haired girl with piercing blue eyes and cleavage hanging out of her loose top. "Er, excuse me," he says.

Her eyes widen in recognition. "Oh my god! You're Magic Mike!" she exclaims. "You were amazing tonight!" She gives him a sultry smile. "I love when you play the banjo. You have such… magic fingers."

Mike smirks, accustomed to the flirting. "What are you doing back here?" he asks. He makes it a point to never be alone backstage with a fan – especially a woman. It's not that he's morally opposed, it's just too risky. People can accuse anyone of anything these days without proof, and he's got too much to lose. He watched it destroy an old bandmate a few years ago and vowed it would never happen to him.

"I'm lost," she explains. "I got separated from my friends on the way to the afterparty and have been trying to find my way back. I suck at directions." She giggles, trying to be cute.

"C'mon," Mike says. "That's where I'm headed. You're liable to get kicked out if one of the managers finds you back here." He indicates for her to follow him and leads the way through the maze of doors and passages under the stage. She never would have found her way if she hadn't run into him. He got lost down here too the first time he played this stage, but that was years ago. Now he knows it well.

When they arrive, the party is in full swing. Kegs and red Solo cups are scattered all over the room. It seems that every scene of Mike's life is dotted with these cups. He should write a song about it. "Better do it before Toby Keith beats me to it," he thinks.

A group of girls rush up to them as they enter the room. "Michelle!" they yell, waving to the dark-haired girl.

"I found her wandering around backstage," Mike explains. Quickly forgetting about Michelle, the girls swarm around Mike, begging for autographs. With a warm smile, he obliges, scribbling his name across the ample chest of a pretty redhead in a low-cut top. He certainly enjoys *this* part of the job.

Then he surveys the room. A skinny blonde rests up against the wall, while Drew, the drummer, leans over her, propping himself up with one hand and holding a beer in his other. He whispers something in her ear, and she giggles. Her chin-length blonde hair is tucked behind her ears, and she has bangs. She looks like she could be in high school, but she's wearing a University of Vermont t-shirt, so Mike assumes she's a student there. He shakes his head. Drew always goes after the younger girls.

Mike works the room, making small talk, signing autographs, flirting, and downing one beer after another. Every time he turns around, someone hands him another cup. Michelle seems to believe they have some special connection and follows him around the room, asking questions and touching his arm every time there's a lull in conversation. He learns that she's a senior at UVM and is here with a bunch of her sorority sisters.

Thankfully, they're interrupted by another girl, this one appearing slightly older. She's wearing short white shorts and a tight black tank top with "Back in Black" emblazoned across the front. Mike can't help but admire her hour-glass figure. She has big boobs, rounded hips, and slender legs. Her thick blonde hair is clearly dyed.

"This is Stephanie," says Michelle, sounding annoyed. "She's my friend's older sister."

"Hi," Stephanie says in a high-pitched voice, extending her hand to Mike. He shakes it, asking if she also attends UVM. "No," she slurs a little. "I graduated from Brown three years ago. I work in New York now."

It's obvious that Stephanie has had too much to drink, but Mike gives her credit for trying to carry on a normal conversation. Noticing something in her hair, a piece of a straw wrapper perhaps, he reaches up to remove it.

"Do you think I'm a natural blonde?" Stephanie asks coyly.

"I always find out," Mike replies, winking at her.

Michelle storms away, visibly upset. Stephanie's eyes widen, but before she can respond, the woman with the headset enters the room and informs the band that it's time to load up. Mike considers offering Stephanie a ride back to New York, thinking they could have some fun on the way, but decides against it. She's too drunk. "Thanks for coming," he says, leaning over and kissing her cheek. Then he walks out of the room.

Drew has his arm slung over the shoulder of the little blonde, and they walk together toward the buses. Drew and Jack, the bassist, almost always leave with a girl. The lead guitarist has a girlfriend back in Nashville, so he (usually) boards the bus alone. While Mike has picked up his fair share, it happened more frequently earlier in his career when the fame and attention were new and exciting. And although he's recently single, he's more selective these days.

He overhears the two girls telling their friends, who all look immensely jealous, that they'll be riding with the band to New York City for their show the next night and will take the train back to Burlington on Monday. Michelle pouts, glancing at Mike as if expecting a last-minute invitation, but he ignores her, getting on the bus.

After saying their goodbyes and making promises to be safe ("as if getting on a bus with a bunch of men you don't know is safe," thinks Mike), the girls are the last to board, and the doors close behind them. The blonde takes a seat next to Drew, while the other, a brunette, settles herself on Jack's lap and immediately begins sucking his face. Turning away, Mike notices the blonde looking at him.

"Hi!" she says cheerfully. Although she does appear young, her smile lights up her face, and Mike can understand why Drew is attracted to her. She extends her hand, about to introduce herself, when Drew cuts in. "This is Sandy," he slurs, tightening his hold around her waist. The girl glances at Drew, then back at Mike. Her hand is still extended, so Mike reaches out and shakes it. She has a firm handshake. He appreciates that in a woman.

"It's Sailee, actually," she replies, looking slightly annoyed.

"Sally?" repeats Mike. "That's a rather old-fashioned name."

"No," she corrects him, "Sailee. Like a sailor on a boat."

"How do you spell it?" he asks, unsure why he even cares. They're all drunk, and she's Drew's girl anyway.

"S-A-I-L-E-E," she spells, seemingly pleased that he's making an effort.

"Pretty." He responds, referring to both her and her name. "I've never heard that one before."

"That's not surprising," she remarks. "There aren't very many of us around."

To Mike's astonishment, Sailee isn't slurring. Most people could barely walk out upright. Is it possible this tiny little thing can out-drink them all? He shakes his head to clear his mind. He drank less than usual, but he's still feeling pretty fuzzy. "You can really hold your booze," he says, impressed.

"Actually, I only drank water," she responds. "I don't like beer, and that's all they had. I just poured it into a Solo cup so people would leave me alone about it."

"Not one to succumb to peer pressure, huh?" Mike can tell he's irritating Drew by talking to his girl, but he doesn't care. Drew can barely sit up and is only managing because he's hanging on to Sailee. Mike knows that he's sobering up just enough to take Sailee back to his room.

Sailee laughs. "Nope. I wasted my first kiss on a dare and vowed I'd never give in to peer pressure again." She pauses. "I do drink," she clarifies, "but only liquor! I don't see the point of being pressured into drinking something that tastes like piss and vinegar."

Mike laughs. She's cute *and* funny! He has been drinking beer since he was thirteen and loves the stuff. But now that she mentions it, it does have hints of piss and vinegar.

"If you're not into peer pressure, why are you on this bus?" he gestures towards Drew, who has his eyes closed.

"Oh," Sailee says, blushing slightly, "I'm always up for an adventure, and I've never been to New York. Or been on a tour bus before. I'm a musician too and wanted to experience what it's like to make it." She glances around. Drew's head is rolled back, and Jack and his girl are noisily making out again.

Mike wonders if she's second-guessing her decision, not necessarily about getting on the bus, but perhaps about being sober. Sailee seems nice and (somewhat) sensible. She's certainly not Drew's usual pick-up – some drunk bimbo who's all over him at the afterparty, practically dragging him to his room the minute they're on the bus, then hogging the bathroom the next morning because she's hungover and puking. No, he thinks, Drew made a better choice with this one.

She asks how he ended up forming Back in Black, and he's about to answer when Drew stands up, taking Sailee by the hand and saying, "C'mon, little miss chatterbox. Let's put that mouth to good use." Sailee stands up and follows him, looking back at Mike over her shoulder with a sheepish grin and a shrug. Jack and his girl are now horizontal, taking up the space that Drew and Sailee just vacated, and Mike smacks Jack on the head. "Get a room," he growls, and they get up to leave as well, knocking into things as they go.

Mike lies down on the couch. He seems to have sobered up, which means he doesn't want to go back to his room and listen to Drew and Sailee next door. It's not as bothersome when he's drunk.

Just as he dozes off, the door to Drew's bedroom bursts opens, and Sailee comes barging out. Her shirt is halfway on, and she's naked from the waist down. "I said *no!*" she yells back into the room.

"Then get off the bus, you little bitch!" Drew's slurred voice calls after her before he slams the bedroom door. Sailee enters the common area, sees Mike, and stops short. She blushes a deep crimson.

"I-I'm sorry," she stammers, turning around quickly and fixing her shirt. "I figured everyone would be in bed." Mike turns away to give her some privacy while she puts her shorts back on.

"Is everything alright?" he asks, although it's obviously not.

"Yes... I mean, no... I guess...I-I just feel so stupid!" she says, sitting down and covering her face with her hands. "Don't get me wrong, I wasn't naïve when I got on the bus. I knew Drew wanted to... you know. And I did too. But... well... he was just so forceful... he wanted me to... I-I couldn't... never mind. I'm such an idiot. If the bus can let me off at the next stop, I'll hitch a ride back to campus."

"You'll do no such thing," Mike says firmly. "It's the middle of the night, and that would be both dangerous and stupid. Just sleep on the couch, and you can take the train back from New York tomorrow. Besides, Drew's so hammered he probably won't remember any of this tomorrow. He'll think you gave him the best night of his life." Sailee gives him a faint smile.

"And I'm sorry," he continues. "Drew can come on a little strong, especially when he's drunk. But I have to say, you're definitely not the type of girl he typically invites on the bus. I'm sure he's really confused about what went wrong if he's not already passed out."

"He just seemed so nice," Sailee says, shaking her head.

"Yeah, well, he can be a real Prince Charming when he wants to be," retorts Mike. He stands up, intending to go to his room, then sits back down. He's tired, but Drew can be a little unpredictable, and Mike wants to make sure he has plenty of time to fall asleep before leaving Sailee out here alone. "So, tell me about yourself," he says.

CHAPTER 31

They stay up the entire night. Sailee shares about growing up in Vermont and living next door to her grandparents and all of her mom's siblings. "It was great if you needed an extra bathroom or a cup of milk, but you couldn't get away with *anything*. I snuck my high school boyfriend over once when my parents were gone, but my grandmother caught us. Needless to say, it was the last time I did that!"

She tells him that she attended Catholic school from kindergarten through her senior year, and how her parents had hoped she would also choose a Christian college. But she decided she'd had enough of the bubble and went to the University of Vermont instead. Adjusting to public school was a shock at first, with everyone drinking and sleeping together – things that were strictly forbidden growing up and considered a sure path to hell. She admits that she went a little wild her first two years, with all that newfound freedom, but she's starting to find some balance. She's currently a junior, pursuing dual degrees in music composition ("because I love to write") and music business ("because I need a job!").

"So, anyway," she says, "enough about me. You don't seem like the typical rock star type. Tell me about you?"

Mike tells her about his small-town upbringing, back when his idea of fun was taking a few fishing poles and a six-pack of beer in his Lil Oscar cooler down to the river with his best friend. He was high school valedictorian, captain of the football team, a triple varsity athlete, and voted most likely to succeed. He had always dreamed of being an engineer, and set his sights on Virginia Tech. His guidance counselor had suggested that he pick a different major, saying that although he was an overachiever in high school, he probably wouldn't make it as an engineer.

"Wow, that's encouraging," Sailee remarks sarcastically. "Did you switch majors?"

"Hell no!" Mike replies proudly. "I proved her wrong!"

"So how did you get into music?" she wants to know.

"It was just luck. I taught myself to play guitar in college, partly to impress girls and also because it's a more versatile instrument than the banjo," he explains. Sailee agrees but expresses her love for his banjo playing.

Mike smiles and continues. "After completing my undergraduate degree, I decided to go back to Tech and get my master's in acoustics. A band was performing on campus one weekend, and they weren't happy with the sound quality in the stadium. I don't know how they got my name, but I got a call to see if I could improve the acoustics. They didn't quite understand that engineering typically deals with design problems rather than on-the-ground fixes, but I thought 'why the hell not? I'll give it a shot.'

"I made some adjustments to the placement of their amps, tweaked a few levels, and they were thrilled with the results. I ended up hitting it off with the guys, and they invited me to hang out backstage before the show. When they discovered I played guitar, they connected me with some of their contacts in the country music scene, and the rest is history. I never did finish my degree. My parents were disappointed that I left engineering for a career in the music industry. It's not that they dislike music, it's all the peripheral parts of stardom that they don't quite approve of."

Sailee shakes her head in disbelief. "I can't *believe* how lucky you are!"

Mike laughs. "I won't deny it, good luck does tend to follow me around. I get it from my Grandpa McCormick. It's the luck of the Irish, as they say."

"Do you still have your Lil Oscar?" Sailee asks.

"No," Mike replies with a twinge of sadness. "I had it for years and years, but when I broke up with my last girlfriend, she stole it. I actually started writing a song about it, but never finished."

"Can I hear it?" she inquires.

"I only have the lyrics." Mike goes into his bedroom and returns with a folder. "All my unfinished ideas," he explains.

He hands Sailee a piece of paper, and she reads it over. "These are great!" she exclaims. "I have an idea for the music if you don't mind. Do you have a guitar?" Mike says he keeps an old one in his room and goes to retrieve it.

"Ok," she says, once he sits back downs. "Play C, F, C, G, C, G, C. Strum on beats one and three, and stop on beats two and four."

He tries it. "Like this?"

"That's it!" she says. She takes the lyrics and starts singing:

"Got my first cooler when I was thirteen
Saved my allowance for a piece of the dream
Bought a Lil Oscar with a bright orange lid
Twenty years later Lil Oscar's no kid
A day at the beach, a ride in the boat
Fishing, chillin', or just gettin' out.
Tie up the anchor that's holdin' you down
Fill up the cooler and turn up the sound…

Ok!" she says, stopping him. "Now for the chorus, play F, C, Em, G, F, C, Em, G!"

Mike complies, and she keeps singing:

"Coolers
The definition of a party
Coolers for ice cold beer, Coke, and Bacardi
When you're feeling low and you wanna go postal
Just fill up your cooler and go coastal."

She stops. "What do you think?"

A smile spreads across Mike's face. "I love it! I've been struggling with the music for this, and you nailed it on the first try. How did you do that?"

Sailee shrugs. "It's what I do!" she replies. "Okay, you sing the second verse."

Mike strums and begins singing:

> *"White, colored, metal and plastic*
> *Filled with ice, it's almost magic*
> *Holds my beer and my water too*
> *Drop in your fish so they stay cool*
> *Igloo, Coleman, Yedi and Engel*
> *It's man's best friend, married or single*
> *Fill em', chill em', seal em' up*
> *'Til you need to fill your Solo cup—"*

He plays the chorus again, then stops.

That's it?" Sailee asks. "You need a verse to complete the story! Something like… my ex stole Lil Oscar much to my dismay…"

Mike chimes in, "With the wheels to my Porsche made a clean getaway!"

"Wait," interjects Sailee, "Did that really happen?!"

"It did indeed!" he confirms.

"That's insane!" she replies, laughing. "And it definitely needs to be in the song." She thinks a minute. "Ok, I've got it." She sings:

> *"My ex stole Lil Oscar much to my dismay*
> *With the wheels to my Porsche made a clean getaway*
> *I had it so long and it made me so sad*
> *But then I realized, life's not so bad*
> *You can always find a friend with a cooler in hand*
> *Ice cold beer and toes in the sand.*
> *Close your eyes and feel the warm sun*
> *Open up the cooler for a drink and some fun!"*

Mike jumps in to sing the chorus again. "*Coolers...*"

Sailee echoes ("*Coolers*")

Mike sings, "*The definition of a party*"

("*Yeah, a party!*")

"*Coolers for ice cold beer, Coke and Bacardi*"

Sailee jumps in with a harmony line. "*When you're feeling low,*"

Mike continues alone, "*And you wanna go postal,*"

She joins him in unison, and they're almost yelling now. "*JUST FILL UP YOUR COOLER AND GO COASTAL!*"

They stop, laughing hysterically. "The only thing this song needs now is a killer kazoo solo," Sailee exclaims, unable to contain her amusement.

"This is incredible!" cries Mike. "We should definitely collaborate on some more music. The band could use someone with your talent."

Sailee beams, honored to be asked. "I'd love to!"

It's now 6:15 a.m., and their arrival in New York is quickly approaching. Mike is exhausted and can see that Sailee is struggling to keep her eyes open as well.

"Listen," he suggests, "we'll be in New York in half an hour. It's usually pretty chaotic when we arrive, so we should try to get a little sleep." He pauses. "I know you had planned to take the train back to Burlington this morning, but I think you should stay. I'd love to hear some of your music, and we could write a few songs together. You can stay through the concert tonight and go home tomorrow morning like you originally planned."

Sailee considers his proposal. "As long as there's no drama with Drew," she says. "I hate drama."

Mike smiles. "I'll handle Drew." He rises from his seat, giving Sailee a friendly kiss on the top of her head, then tosses her a blanket before retreating to his own room. "Sweet dreams, Sailee!"

She chuckles, "Yes, all nineteen minutes of them!" She lies down and is asleep before her head hits the pillow.

CHAPTER 32

They pull into Madison Square Garden at 6:45 a.m., and a crowd has already gathered. The band has some public relations obligations this morning, and they leave Sailee sleeping on the bus. Drew emerges from his room and sees her on the couch. He looks confused, clearly unable to piece together the events of the previous evening.

"She's with me," Mike informs him, nodding to Sailee.

"Oh," Drew replies. "I must have noticed her at the afterparty. She's cute. Awfully young for you though, eh Mike?"

Mike rolls his eyes. Drew is only four years younger than he is, and is notorious for picking up younger women, but he's always giving Mike hell for being the oldest one in the band.

They disembark the bus to a chorus of cheers and a sea of hands reaching out for autographs. With a two-day stay in New York, but only one show scheduled for tonight, they have a slightly less hectic schedule and managed to negotiate the afternoon off in exchange for three hours of PR this morning and a massive afterparty following tonight's concert. Tomorrow they can sleep in, but then are booked solid from noon to 11:00 p.m. Mike is looking forward to the downtime today.

Sailee wakes up and checks her watch. It's 9:30 a.m., and the bus is empty. She goes into the bathroom and runs her fingers through her hair. Then she splashes water on her face and applies a little mascara and Chapstick, which she keeps in her purse. She looks terrible. Perhaps she can stop by a Sephora today and try out a few samples so she doesn't look so tired at the concert tonight, she thinks.

Sailee shakes her head to clear the sleep. Three hours is not enough for her. Yawning, she reflects on the night before. Did Mike Black really ask her to stay and write music with him? She looks down at the floor, and sure enough, there's the evidence of the previous night's collaboration, the words to "Coolers" scrawled across the paper. She reads through it again. "It's pretty good," she says out loud.

She steps off the bus and looks around. A man in jeans and a black t-shirt walks up to her. "Are you Sally?" he asks.

"Yes," she replies with a sigh. It's not worth getting into it right now.

"Mike said to tell you to hang here. They'll be back around ten."

Sailee nods and walks around, stretching her legs. She does a few push-ups to help her wake up. There's some scaffolding on the building, and after glancing around to make sure no one is watching, she jumps up and knocks out a few pull-ups.

"A girl who can do pull-ups, eh? That's impressive." Drew is standing in the doorway. Sailee drops down to the ground, unsure of what to say. He saunters up to her. "I remember you from the afterparty. It's Sandy, right? Mike says you're with him. Just want to say that he's a lucky guy, and if you get bored with the old man, come find me." He winks at her, walking away. Sailee breathes a sigh of relief. She did not want to rehash the events of last night.

A few minutes later, Mike comes through the door, a giant grin on his face. "What did I tell you about Drew? He doesn't have a clue!" He gives Sailee a high-five, and she smiles.

"What do you have going on now?" she asks.

"We have the afternoon off, my friend!" he replies. "We need to be back here at 5:00 p.m. to get ready for the show, but we're free until then. If I remember correctly, this is your first time in New York, and if you're up for it, I'd like to show you around the city."

Sailee agrees. Mike goes into the bus and changes into shorts, sunglasses, sneakers, and a baseball hat. "It's amazing how a small thing like taking off your cowboy hat makes you less recognizable," he explains.

Oh, right – Mike's famous. She hadn't thought about that. Since they're going to be out and about, Sailee hopes she can pop into a store or two and pick up deodorant and a new outfit for tonight. "Lead the way!" she says, excitedly.

First, they visit Madison Square Park and order burgers at Shake Shack. "I need something greasy after all that beer last night," Mike explains. It's fine with Sailee, she loves a good burger. Then they make their way north through midtown, passing the Empire State Building, until they reach Grand Central Station. "I don't come here often anymore," he says, "but I thought it'd be nice for you to see some of the touristy stuff on your first trip!" Sailee is amazed by the architecture, the painted ceiling, and the overall glamour of the place, along with the bustling crowds of people. "And this is a Saturday morning," he adds. "You should see it during rush hour on a weekday!"

From there, they leisurely stroll up to Central Park. They walk along the path surrounding the pond and enjoy people-watching. No one bothers them, though a few runners do a double take as they jog by. "I'm telling you, it's the hat!" says Mike, chuckling.

While walking back down 6th Avenue, Sailee suddenly stops in her tracks! "Hey! That's a Steinway store!" she exclaims, pointing across the street.

"What's that?" Mike inquires.

"They're the best pianos in the world! It's my dream to own one someday, even if I have to sleep underneath it! Do you mind if we go in?"

"Of course not!" With no cars coming, they jaywalk across the street, and Mike holds the door open for her.

They look more like tourists who spent the night on a bus rather than potential buyers of a $75,000 piano, and they receive some disapproving looks when they enter. But Sailee pays them no mind. She marches straight to the concert grand and sits down, delicately placing her hands on the keys. "It's so beautiful!" she says, awestruck.

"Play something!" Mike encourages.

Now that she's here, Sailee is suddenly nervous. She has never enjoyed playing in front of other people. "Ok, let me think," she says. She begins with an excerpt from Beethoven's Sonata Pathetique, then transitions into a slower song with a melancholic melody.

"That's pretty," says Mike. "Who wrote that one?"

"That's one of mine!" Sailee answers proudly. "I wrote it for a class last semester."

"It's amazing that you can do that," Mike remarks. He has only written lyrics and a few simple chord progressions. This was something entirely different. "Will you sing for me?" he asks. "Something you wrote?"

Sailee glances around. It's not exactly the appropriate setting for it. Mike notices her hesitation. "Who cares what people think!" he declares.

She takes a deep breath. "Okay, fine," she answers. After a brief moment of contemplation, she begins singing:

> *"I love it when the sky is blue,*
> *It makes me think of you*
> *I love it when the grass is green,*
> *I think of your eyes and how they*
> *Melt me like ice cream on a sunny day*
> *When I'm stuck in December you are signs of May*
> *Baby, you are my spring*
> *You are my spring."*

Her voice is light and sweet, and Mike notices that everyone in the store has stopped talking, captivated by her singing. The acoustics in the building are amazing, carrying her soft voice throughout the entire hall. Sailee stops after one verse, looking slightly embarrassed by the attention.

"You have a beautiful voice," he remarks.

"Thank you," she replies, pushing back the piano bench and jumping to her feet. She tugs impatiently at his arm. "Alright, let's go."

Mike laughs. "How can you be majoring in music if you don't like performing in front of people?"

Sailee shrugs. "That's why I chose composition as my major. I do the writing, and someone else does the performing. I'm fine in bands and group settings, as long as I'm not on stage alone. Ironically, I have no problem with public speaking, just public playing." She smiles. "I guess I'm weird like that."

Mike nods. Everyone has their quirks.

They have a great time together, and Mike has to keep reminding himself that Sailee is too young for him, still in college, for Christ's sake! However, she seems more mature than many of the women he interacts with on a daily basis. He likes that she's not shy (except when it comes to performing), and when they return to the bus, she quickly makes herself at home with the rest of the band. Despite their exhaustion, they rally through another show and another wild afterparty before finally collapsing on the bus.

The next morning, Sailee has to get back to campus and classes, so Mike dons his "disguise" and walks her to the train station. "This has been a blast," he tells her as they arrive at Penn Station. "I'm glad that Drew hit on you!"

Sailee laughs. "I'm glad, too. Thanks for convincing me to stay and showing me around the city and everything." She gives Mike a hug, and he plants a kiss on her cheek. Sparks are flying between them, and oh, how he longs to taste her lips; but he repeatedly reminds himself that she's too young.

"Let's stay in touch," he suggests. "I still want to write more songs together."

Sailee takes out a piece of gum from her purse, pops it into her mouth, then writes her email, phone number, and Instant Messenger name on the now-empty gum wrapper. "I don't have a cell phone," she explains. "But this is the direct line to my room, and you can always reach me via email or IM. If you call and my roommate answers, say you're Mike Brown. I don't need any drama about a Mike Black calling me!" She winks at him, but apparently can't wink, so it's more of a half-blink. It's awfully cute.

Mike vows to be discreet. After saying goodbye, he makes his way back to the arena, consumed with thoughts of Sailee. In all his years, he has never met anyone quite like her.

CHAPTER 33

They communicate sporadically over the following months. Mike calls Sailee to ensure that she made it safely back to campus, and she follows up with an email containing lyrics and a rudimentary recording of a new song she's been working on called "The Legend of Reenie Black," composed specifically for Mike and the banjo. On the bus, he had told her about his great-grandmother, Reenie, who died in prison at the age of fifty for selling moonshine during the depression. Sailee immediately recognized the potential for a bluegrass song and got to work on it the moment she returned to campus.

After listening to it, Mike is eager to record the song, knowing how much his dad will love it! He calls Sailee immediately, and they discuss different ideas for the music and harmonies before falling into easy conversation about life in general. They talk for over three hours, and when they finally hang up, neither can wipe the smile off their face.

Mike's tour is finally over, and he's been hanging out in Nashville, working on some new music and making occasional trips to visit his parents in North Carolina. With their new album recording scheduled for the following month, and having no pressing engagements, Mike decides it would be fun to drive up to Vermont and surprise Sailee. He calls her room when he's a few hours away, and she tells him that she's in the midst of packing. It's the last day of her junior year, and she's going home. Since she doesn't have her car on campus, she has to wait until her parents can pick her up later that evening, after her dad gets off work. "Perfect," thinks Mike.

He arrives on campus around 3:00 p.m. Mike knows that Sailee lives in a townhouse but isn't sure exactly which one. He drives around until eventually he has no choice but to stop and ask a group of students if they know where Sailee Roberts lives.

"Wait," one of them exclaims, "aren't you Mike Black from Back in Black?"

"Nah," Mike replies, "but I get that a lot." It's obvious that they don't believe him, but they at least point him in the direction of Sailee's townhouse. As he's driving away, Mike looks into his rearview mirror and sees people following his truck. "So much for incognito," he mutters.

Hoping he's in the right place, he walks up to townhouse #3 and knocks. A petite girl with long black hair and brown eyes answers the door. She takes one look at him, and her eyes widen. "You're Mike Black!" she exclaims. "I saw you in Burlington last fall!"

Oh shit. He had forgotten that Sailee attended the concert with a bunch of her college friends. "Hi," he says, putting on a warm smile. "Does Sailee live here?"

"Sailee Roberts?" she asks in disbelief, her eyes now wider than ever, leaving Mike concerned they might pop out of her head. He nods. "Uh… yeah," she continues. "Hang on." Walking away from the door, she calls out, "Sailee! Someone is here to see you."

He hears what sounds like a stampede of elephants coming down the stairs, and then Sailee emerges. Her hair is longer, and she has grown out her bangs. She looks older, more mature.

Upon seeing him, her face breaks into a broad smile and she runs to him, throwing her arms around his neck. "MIKE!" she exclaims, a little too loudly for being so close to his ear, "What are you doing here?!"

He smiles and lifts her up, twirling her around, before setting her back down. He notices the curious faces of her housemates peering around corners. No doubt the brunette went and told everyone that Mike Black was at the door. "I thought I'd surprise you!" he explains. "I didn't have any plans this weekend, so I decided to take a spontaneous road trip and come see you! I didn't realize you were going home today. I'm happy to give you a ride so you don't have to wait for your parents."

"Wow – that's incredibly nice of you!" says Sailee, clearly taken aback by his effort to drive all the way to see her. "That works out perfectly. Besides, I'd love to introduce you to them—" She stops midsentence.

Mike can see that something is wrong. "Is that going to be a problem?" he asks, concerned.

"No..." she replies slowly. "It's just that I never told my parents about my little excursion to New York. They would not be pleased." She pauses, thinking. "I'll just tell them that I met you at the concert, during the afterparty, and we've been writing some music together. I'll say that you happened to be passing through Burlington, thought you'd drop by to say hello, and offered me a ride home so I didn't have to wait for them." She shrugs. "It's partially true."

"I don't want you to lie to your parents. If you prefer, I can just hang out with you here until they arrive—"

"No, no, no." she reassures him. "This is fine. Really. You're my friend. I don't want to keep it a secret forever. I'll give them a call and let them know a friend is bringing me home. They'll be happy about that."

"Well then, can I help you pack?" Mike asks. "Or carry anything to the truck?"

"Sure," Sailee responds, leading him upstairs to her bedroom.

They spend the next hour throwing her belongings into garbage bags and loading them into the back of his F150. A small crowd has formed around the townhouse, and a few people have mustered the courage to request an autograph. Mike considers insisting that he's not *the* Mike Black but decides it's useless.

After loading up, Sailee hugs her housemates, who are all visibly envious of her good fortune, and says she's looking forward to more fun in the fall. As Mike opens the passenger door for her, he hears the click of a camera. Whirling around, he half expects to find someone from the media. Journalists always manage to track him down. Instead, he finds himself face to face with a pimply college student holding a camera, eager to prove to his friends that Mike Black was at UVM. Mike slams Sailee's door and growls, "There's nothing to see here, folks." He gets in the driver side and hits the gas hard. He wants to get the hell outta dodge before he can be followed.

"Is everything okay?" Sailee asks nervously.

"Just idiots and their cameras," he replies.

"Oh," she responds, quiet for a moment. "I'm sorry. Will this cause trouble for you?"

"Not for me," he assures her, "but I don't want it to cause trouble for you. I didn't really think this through. I just wanted to see you. It's all my fault. Sorry."

"It's crazy that nobody recognized you in New York, but here they did right away," she remarks.

"Nah," he retorts. "In New York there are so many people that are famous or those who resemble them that nobody pays much attention. But out here, we stick out like a sore thumb."

Sailee nods, feeling sorry for Mike. She can't imagine being followed around constantly. Soon, however, she has forgotten the incident, preoccupied with wondering how her parents are going to react to her coming home with an older man – and a famous one at that. She imagines they'll assume the worst – that Mike is taking advantage of her, stealing her innocence. It's not true, of course. He has never even made a move on her, to her slight disappointment. At the same time, she's somewhat relieved. She has always gotten along better with guys, but they usually end up falling for her when she just wants to be friends. Then things get awkward because they have been "friend-zoned," and she ends up losing them altogether. She's tired of that cycle. Why can't girls be as easy to get along with as guys? It would certainly make life simpler.

When they arrive at the house, Sailee opens the back door and yells, "Family! I'm home!"

Her mom runs to the door with a big smile, wrapping Sailee in a bear hug. Then she looks up at Mike and drops her arms. "Who's this?" she inquires. Her tone is friendly but tinged with suspicion.

"Mama," says Sailee, trying to keep her voice steady, "This is my friend, Mike Black. He plays banjo in the band Back in Black, and I met him when they performed in Burlington last fall. I've been helping him write some music. He happened to be passing through Burlington today and thought he'd drop by to say hi. When he found out I was going home, he offered to give me a ride."

Mike offers Sailee's mom his warmest smile and extends his hand. "Nice to meet you, Mrs. Roberts."

She shakes his hand. "Nice to meet you too, Mike. Call me Ellie." She turns to Sailee. "Your dad will be home any minute. Mike, would you like to stay for dinner?" Sailee is relieved. It was so nice of Mike to drive all the way here; she didn't want him to have to turn around and leave immediately. Mike gladly accepts the invitation.

"Super!" exclaims Sailee. "Let's go get my stuff out of the truck."

They bring in all the bags and leave them in the family room. Sailee knows her mom would *not* be cool with her taking Mike to her room, even if it's just to drop off her belongings.

Mike doesn't seem to think much of it. Instead, he heads into the kitchen and asks if there's anything he can do to help. Ellie thanks him, saying he can set the table if he wants. "The dishes are in the cupboard to your left."

"How many people?" he asks.

"Four," Ellie replies. "Sailee's brother is at a climbing competition tonight."

"That's too bad," says Mike. "Sailee is always bragging about how cool he is, and I was looking forward to meeting him." While setting the table, Mike makes small talk with Ellie, and Sailee can see that he's putting her at ease... at least a little.

When her dad comes home, he is very surprised to find *the* Mike Black in their kitchen. Although neither of her parents listen to country music, her dad at least knows who Mike is. As he tends to be on the quiet side, Sailee expected her dad to be somewhat standoffish, and is surprised when he's not. To her delight, he takes an instant liking to Mike.

During dinner, Ellie asks Mike about his family, and he tells her that he grew up as an only child in a small mountain town. His mom is a nurse, and his dad is a mechanic. The more Mike talks about his family, the more pronounced his southern drawl becomes, and Sailee finds it charming. She watches her parents gradually relax and realizes that this is likely typical when people meet Mike. He is down-to-earth and exudes a warmth that makes others comfortable.

Eventually, Mark, in a not-so-subtle manner, asks Mike how he and Sailee met and why he's at their home. Sailee, slightly embarrassed by her dad's bluntness, starts to respond, but Mike interjects. "Sailee attended one of my concerts last year, and we met at the afterparty. She mentioned that she's a composer, and I enlisted her to help with a few songs I've been working on. She has a real gift. Since I was in the area, I thought it would be nice to thank her in person." Mark nods, clearly unconvinced that's the entire truth, but decides to let the matter rest.

The remainder of the dinner goes smoothly, and Sailee's parents manage not to embarrass her too badly. At one point, Mike turns to Ellie and says, "Sailee told me you washed her mouth out with soap once!"

Her mom smiles, glances at Sailee, and replies, "Oh, I certainly did. I still wish I could sometimes!" Sailee turns a light shade of pink, and everyone laughs.

After dessert, they're drinking tea in the family room when Mike rises. "I should hit the road," he says. He shakes her parents' hands. "It was nice to meet you both."

Sailee walks Mike to the door. "Thanks again for everything today," she says. "Sorry if my parents were a little weird."

"Not at all," he replies. "They were cool. I'm sure I'd be worse if I had a daughter and she brought me home!" He grins. "Don't be a stranger, ok?"

"Ok," she agrees, hugging him. She watches his truck until it's out of sight, then goes back inside the house where her parents are busy cleaning up the kitchen. Sailee sits down at the table and immediately dives into a conversation about her last week of school, finals, her summer job, and where she's living next year – anything to divert attention from Mike.

Later that night, after getting ready for bed, Sailee steps out of the bathroom to find her mom standing in her bedroom doorway. "What is it?" she asks, even though she already knows.

"Mike seems like a very nice man, Sailee, but you need to be careful…" Ellie begins. Sailee knows her mom is trying to be helpful, but she's annoyed. Mike has never once hit on her. Other than a hug, he has never even touched her! "… because he *is* a man," her mom continues. "Not a boy, not a college guy, a man. I know you're turning twenty-one next month, and you'll be a senior in college, and you feel like you're grown up and mature, but you still have a lot to learn. And you need to think very carefully about being in a relationship with a celebrity, and all that comes with that."

Sailee wants to say, "You have no idea the experience I have," but she restrains herself. Instead, she curtly replies, "It's not like that, Mom. We're just friends." Her mom looks at her with a touch of sadness before leaving the room.

The next time Sailee hears from Mike is on her birthday. He calls the house, and her mom answers. "Hi, Ellie," he says, "This is Mike. I'm calling to wish Sailee a happy birthday. Is she around?" Ellie informs him that Sailee is out with friends but promises to pass along his message.

It's late when Sailee finally arrives home, but she insists on calling Mike back immediately. "Sorry!" she says when he picks up. "Is it too late?"

"No, it's fine," he replies. "I have a birthday present for you."

"You do?"

"Yeah, I got you an internship this summer at a studio in Nashville if you're interested. It's not a glamourous job by any means, but it'll get you in the door to meet some great people. I only learned about it today and had to pull some strings. I even arranged a place for you to live. A friend of mine, Christy, rents out rooms in her house, and she's great. What do you think?"

Sailee is speechless. "I think that's amazing!" she cries when she finally finds her voice. "Thank you! What do I need to do to officially accept it?"

"I'll make an email introduction to Brad, and then you can send him your resume and finalize everything. It's not lucrative, but it's decent pay for an internship."

Sailee is over the moon with excitement. She had planned to work at the jewelry store again this summer, but this opportunity is far better. "Great! I'll take care of everything as soon as I get your email."

She hangs up the phone and wakes up her parents to tell them the good news. Although her mom has some reservations, they both recognize that this is a tremendous opportunity for Sailee. She asks her dad if he would be willing to take a few days off and drive down to Nashville with her, and he agrees. "Mike was very kind to do this for you," Ellie acknowledges.

The internship starts on July 1, giving Sailee just five days to get to Nashville. While her boss at the jewelry store is not thrilled about the short notice, she's understanding. Upon arriving in Nashville, Sailee quickly settles in at Christy's place, then her dad takes her out for dinner downtown. He tells Sailee how proud he is of her, both for her hard work and for the woman she's becoming, "even though your mom and I don't agree with everything you do." When she drops him off at his hotel by the airport, he reminds her to "be smart and stay safe." Sailee hugs him tightly, promising that she will. Her dad doesn't give unsolicited advice very often, so when he does, she tends to listen.

His parting words to her are ones she always loves to hear. "Ya done good, kid."

The next morning, she shows up at the studio early, and Mike is there, waiting for her with a cup of hot tea. "I like a woman who's punctual," he says, jokingly.

Sailee smiles. "I hate being late."

"That will serve you well in this job," he replies. "I just stopped by to grab a few things and see you, but I have to run. The band has a practice session this afternoon. Can I take you out to dinner tonight to celebrate your first day on the job?" Sailee accepts his invitation.

CHAPTER 34

They spend a considerable amount of time together over the summer, and Mike introduces Sailee to everyone he knows in the industry, always bragging about what a talent she is. Thanks to his endorsement, what began as a grunt job quickly turned into opportunities to co-write new songs, sing back-up, and manage public relations for several up-and-coming artists. They frequently hang out in groups, with Mike inviting Sailee to every party he attends under the guise of "helping her network," but they have dinner together alone at least once a week. While she and Mike have grown quite close, Sailee can't shake the feeling that he sees her as a little sister.

The end of summer arrives all too soon, and although Sailee is looking forward to her senior year, she's sad to leave Nashville. She has never worked so hard in her life, yet she loved every minute of it. As their time draws to a close, the interns organize a trip to Wilmington, North Carolina. Sailee convinces Mike and several of his friends to join the excursion, and they spend the weekend playing beach volleyball and body surfing. On the final evening, as the two of them sit on the beach drinking frozen margaritas and gazing out at the water, Mike says, "We should write that song we keep talking about."

"Absolutely!" Sailee responds enthusiastically. They had always meant to, but they were both so consumed by their busy schedules over the past two months that they never got around to it.

Mike starts singing:

> *"Sandy toes and salty lips*
> *Bikini bottoms hugging those perfect hips*
> *Ocean spray blowing through your long, blonde hair*
> *And when we're out here on the water*
> *No, we don't have a care in the world…"*

"I like it!" Sailee replies. Then she adds,

> *"Sun is shimmering on the sea*
> *Baby I love it when it's just you and me*
> *And I can't think of anywhere else I'd rather be."*

They glance at each other, and the tension between them is suddenly palpable. Mike breaks their gaze, looking back towards the water, working out the chorus.

> *"Give us some sun and we'll make the heat,*
> *I want your kisses all over me, both salty and sweet*
> *Girl, don't you know I'm gonna sweep you off your feet."*

Sailee jumps in, finishing his thought.

> *"Let's make some waves and I'll show you some fun…"*

She lifts her glass,

> *"We'll be sippin' margaritas in the hot summer sun*
> *Boy this might sound crazy, but I know that you're the one."*

As soon as the words escape her lips, she knows them to be true; it resonates within her just as certain as the sun's rise in the east tomorrow. Mike is the one. "Don't be silly," she chides herself. "Mike doesn't think of you that way." Besides, she doesn't even subscribe to the notion of "The One." She finds the entire concept of soulmates ridiculous. It's a nice idea, and she would love to believe it's true, but she's too pragmatic. And yet, with Mike, perhaps she could entertain the possibility.

She starts a second verse – singing from her heart now.

> *"Sandy knees and salty kisses*
> *Boy I sure would like to be your missus*
> *Things get hot when our skin is bare*
> *And when we're out there on the boat*
> *No, we don't have a care in the world."*

Mike, seemingly ignoring her first couple of lines, takes up the boat theme.

> *"Throttle down, get lost for days,*
> *My heart is pumping, lets lose our way*
> *When we're together, all I want to do is play…"*

He pauses, and both of them gaze silently out at the ocean, avoiding each other's eyes, not daring to discover how the other feels. Mike clears his throat. "It's really catchy," he says, his voice thick with emotion.

"It is," Sailee agrees. More silence ensues.

"Do you think it needs a bridge?" he asks, more as a way to fill the void than out of genuine curiosity.

"Yeah, probably," she answers. "It should be short and simple. Maybe holding one chord while singing something like,

> *Living carefree…"*

Mike jumps in –

"Baby, you're perfect for me..."

Sailee looks at Mike now, and he is looking back at her. She shouldn't say it, but she can't help herself.

"Lovin' so deeply,
Life with you is serenity...

And then I think we finish with the chorus," she suggests quickly. Mike enthusiastically agrees.

They sit in silence again, sipping their margaritas. It's the first time there has ever been an awkward moment between them. "Look, Sailee..." Mike finally begins, and Sailee's heart sinks. She knows what's coming: 'Look, Sailee... you're great, but I think of you as a little sister.'

"...You've become my best friend over the past few months," Mike continues. "You light up every room you're in. You're smart, you're funny, you're kind, you're hardworking. Damn it, you're even punctual!"

Sailee gives a strained laugh, grateful for a moment of levity even as she prepares herself for heartbreak.

"I love being your friend," Mike goes on. "And if that's how you see me, that's totally cool. But I'd like to be more. I know you still have a year of school left—"

She interrupts him with a kiss, and a year's worth of pent-up tension bursts and dissolves away. His mouth is perfect.

"Damn," Mike utters, when they finally part.

Sailee laughs brightly now, her heart suddenly light. "I'll take that as a compliment?" He responds with another kiss.

The next day, Sailee embarks on her drive back home. She harbors no illusions about the challenges that lie ahead in starting a long-distance relationship. Yet in a way, they aren't really starting it. They built their friendship long-distance, and now they are simply continuing it until the time comes when they can be together again. Sailee's internship went well, and she has already been offered a job at the label when she graduates, ensuring her return to Nashville. She does feel a slight unease about dating a celebrity. As much as Sailee hates to admit it, her mother was right. It certainly introduces an added layer of complexity. Is she prepared to be in the spotlight? She's not sure, but for Mike, she's willing to try.

A month into their relationship, Sailee has only informed her family and closest friends that she's dating Mike. They had mutually agreed, before her departure, to keep it discreet for the time being. One evening, while Sailee is doing homework, her roommate charges into their bedroom. "Sailee, have you seen the front page of Celebrity Rumor Rundown today?!"

"No," she replies. "I'm not particularly interested in celebrity gossip."

"Well, my dear," says Cindy, "you might be today." She retrieves her laptop and opens the CRR homepage. Filling the screen are two photographs. One captures Mike, looking dashing in jeans and a cowboy hat, holding hands with a tall, stunning blonde with large blue eyes at the 2005 County Music Awards. The other photo depicts Mike and the blonde making out on the beach. The headline reads:

IS COYBOY MIKE BACK IN BLACK, OR BACK IN BLONDE?
Mike Black recently spotted making out with his ex-girlfriend.
Have they decided to give it another try?

Sailee promptly closes Cindy's laptop. She has no desire to read the rest. She feels sick to her stomach, and her mind is racing. Is Mike cheating on her? Is that why he insisted on keeping their relationship under wraps? Their communication has waned since he went back on tour, but he's not that kind of person... is he? He always seemed so genuine, so honest. He constantly sends her emails saying that he's thinking about her.

Perhaps he's keeping her on the side – the gullible, doting college girl that makes him feel young. But they were friends… weren't they? Her gut insists that she knows Mike better than that, that he would never betray her in such a manner. But she can't unsee the photograph.

There is only one way to find out. Sailee grabs the phone and dials his number. It goes directly to voicemail. "Shit!" she yells, slamming down the phone. Glancing at her watch, she remembers that they have a concert tonight and likely his phone is turned off. That's the most reasonable explanation for him not answering. Yet, a tiny voice whispers that he purposely declined her call, that he saw the article and is deliberately avoiding her. Sailee shakes the thought away. He'll call her after the concert. He always does. If he doesn't, then she'll know.

She realizes Cindy is still standing there, watching her. "Sorry, girl," her roommate says sympathetically.

Sailee shakes her head. "I'm sure this isn't what it looks like," she replies, attempting to project more confidence than she feels. Cindy nods, but Sailee can tell she doesn't buy it.

She tries to finish her homework but finds it impossible to concentrate. Her brain keeps rehearsing the conversation she's going to have with Mike when he calls. *If* he calls. Maybe she'll never hear from him again. Maybe he'll ghost her – the coward.

The more she ruminates, the more upset she becomes. Abandoning her homework, she goes downstairs and rallies her housemates to go out drinking. She needs something to distract herself. Cindy has apparently showed the article to everyone, because they all regard her with pity – the schmuck who got duped – and no one questions why she wants to go out. Soon, the seven of them are at their favorite dive bar, getting sloshed.

It's after 2:00 a.m. when they stumble back to their townhouse. Sailee checks her messages, but there's nothing from Mike. Her heart sinks. "What is it that Mike always says?" she thinks. "Oh yeah – 'the key to happiness in life is low expectations.'" Clearly, she set hers too high. Without even removing her clothes, she falls into bed, burying her face in her pillow, and cries herself to sleep.

The next morning, Sailee is jolted awake by the ringing phone and pulls the pillow over her face, attempting to muffle the sound. Her head is throbbing. She breathes a sigh of relief when the ringing finally ceases, but it immediately starts again. Groaning, she falls out of bed and snatches the phone. "Hellooo?" she slurs.

"Sailee? It's Mike. I thought maybe I'd missed you!"

"Mike!" she exclaims excitedly. Then, the image of him on the beach floods her mind, and her tone abruptly changes. "I wasn't expecting to hear from you again," she says coldly.

"What?" Mike responds, sounding confused. "I meant to call you last night, but my phone died, and I didn't have a charger with me."

"Hm," Sailee murmurs, trying to sound indifferent. "*I* figured it was because you got back together with your ex-girlfriend." Wait, that's not what she was supposed to say. She had rehearsed this countless times. She had promised herself she wouldn't be accusatory. She was going to give him the benefit of the doubt. But the vodka has washed any rational and practiced response from her mind.

"My ex-girlfriend?" Mike repeats. "What are you talking about, Sailee?"

Taken aback by the sincerity in his tone and the way he says her name, Sailee feels herself melting. She reaches deep into the crevices of her mind, swimming through the alcohol-induced haze, trying to remember what she had planned to say. It slowly comes back to her.

She takes a deep breath. "There was an article in Celebrity Rumor Rundown yesterday that claimed you're back together with your ex. They had pictures—" Her voice cracks, and she stops. She doesn't want to sound like a sniveling child.

"What?!" exclaims Mike. "Hang on." Sailee can hear him rummaging around in the background. Then he picks the phone back up. "I needed to find my laptop," he explains. He falls silent for a moment, and Sailee can hear the clicking of his keyboard. Then he bursts into laughter.

Sailee is furious. Is he laughing at her? Laughing that he got caught? "What the hell is so funny?" she asks angrily.

"I'm sorry," Mike says, trying to stifle his amusement. "I shouldn't laugh, but this is just so… ridiculous."

"What's ridiculous?" snaps Sailee. "That you got caught kissing someone else?"

"Sailee," replies Mike calmly, "the girl I'm kissing on the beach is *you!* Someone must have taken our picture that day, and because of your blonde hair, assumed it was my ex. You can't see your face at all, but look at what you're wearing. That is definitely you!"

Sailee opens her laptop and pulls up the website. She scrutinizes the image closely, then shakes her head, feeling foolish. Yes, that's her alright. Why didn't she see that before? She had immediately believed the headline and gotten upset.

She rests her pounding head on the desk, still holding the phone to her ear. "I'm so sorry, Mike," she says meekly. "I don't know why I didn't see that the first time. I feel like such an idiot."

Mike remains silent for a long while, and Sailee assumes he's angry at her for acting like such a child. She can't blame him. Eventually, he clears his throat. "Sailee," he says kindly, "CRR is a stupid trash column, and in Nashville, it's a big joke to see how many times you can get mentioned. But I know you're not accustomed to this, and I should've warned you that something like this could happen. That's my fault." He pauses before continuing. "Being in a relationship with a celebrity isn't easy, I'm sure, and the long distance makes it even harder. But if we're going to make this work – and I really want this to work – you're going to have to trust me. I have always been honest with you, and I would never, *ever* cheat on you."

Sailee nods her head, even though he can't see her. She feels so small, and Mike's kindness only intensifies her guilt. It would be easier if he were mad.

"Look at the bright side," Mike continues. "If they had identified you, it would be worse. You'd have paparazzi following you around everywhere. You'd never have any privacy, and I'm sure people would be saying all sorts of awful things about me robbing the cradle or whatever. You got off easy this time, Sailee-girl."

She lifts her head off the desk and manages a faint smile. "I acted like such a jerk, Mike, and I'm sorry. Thank you for being so kind. You're a really good man."

Mike laughs. "I don't know about that," he says. "But I try."

The rest of Sailee's senior year flies by. Although Back in Black doesn't come to Burlington on their new tour, Sailee and a group of friends drive up to see them play in Montreal, and the band greets her like an old friend. Drew, having overheard part of their conversation that day, has taken to calling Mike "the cradle robber."

"Yeah," thinks Mike smugly, "I stole her from you, dumbass!"

On the morning of Sailee's graduation, Mike arrives at her townhouse with a dozen roses. She gives him a kiss and tells him she has a surprise for him. Leading him into the kitchen, Sailee points to a box on the table. "Open it!" she says excitedly.

"What is it?" Mike asks, lifting the lid and pulling out a small white cooler with an orange lid. Then he bursts into laughter. "It's Lil Oscar!" he cries. "Where on earth did you get this?!"

"I found it on E-Bay!" Sailee explains, grinning. "It's a vintage one – from 1985! The same year I was born, and the year you bought your first Lil Oscar! Do you like it?"

Mike sets it on the table and wraps her in a hug. "I can't believe you did this for me," he says. "You're the best! I love you!"

Sailee looks up at him, surprised. He has never said that to her before! She squeezes him tightly. "I love you, too."

Mike attends the graduation ceremony with her parents, whom he has now completely won over, and two days later, he and Sailee leave for Nashville. But she's not taking the job at the label. Instead,

Mike tells Back in Black that he's finished after their tour, and he and Sailee form their own acoustic band. A year later, in celebration of their wedding, Mike adds a third verse to his most popular song – The Cash Overture.

But there's one thing Cash did right,
If you ask me what I think
He picked a woman who was willing to fight for him
When he was on the brink.
Well, I've got my own June Carter
And she's my better half
For her I'd jump through a ring of fire
So I guess that makes me like Cash!

I wanna sing like Cash
I wanna sing like Cash
I wanna spend my life singing with my wife
I wanna sing like Cash

They love being together – writing songs, brainstorming, and traveling. Every morning, Mike brings Sailee tea in a yellow mug. "Because you are sunshine," he says. And, in turn, she ensures that he always has the blue mug, remarking, "If I am the sun, then you are the sky. For you make me come alive."

Years later, they find themselves sitting at their dining room table, having completed their final tour. Tired of life on the road, they've decided to give up the band to stay in Nashville and focus on writing music.

As Mike clears the plates, Sailee says, "I have an idea for a new song. It's called 'One in Infinity.' It's about the odds of two people finding each other in this chaotic world."

Mike ponders her idea for a moment. "I love the concept," he responds. "But the engineer in me can't help but point out that infinity

is not a number. So perhaps the song's title could be something like...
'One Chance in an Inconceivably Large but Finite Number.'"

Sailee laughs. "That's quite a mouthful."

Mike grins mischievously. "I'll give you a mouthful, Sailee Black." He pulls her out of her chair, kissing her long and deep, before scooping her up and carrying her, giggling, into the bedroom. The last thing Shadow Mike sees before being pulled from the universe is the bedroom door closing behind them.

CHAPTER 35

May 5

Sailee's alarm blares, and she rolls over to turn it off it. She had debated staying in her makeshift bedroom downstairs instead of sleeping alone in their bed. But that felt defeatist, and she's determined to keep hope alive that Mike will wake up. So, she sleeps in their room, often waking up on his side of the bed, her arms wrapped tightly around his pillow. It used to smell like Mike, but his scent has long since dissipated – a reminder of how much time has passed without him.

She hits the button, silencing that intolerable noise. She has been awake for hours and questions the point of setting the alarm when she no longer sleeps through the night. Four hours is all she manages these days, and it's not nearly enough. The circles under her eyes have become full-fledged bags. Yet, every day she gets out of bed, forces a smile, and tries to focus on the positive things. It's what Mike would do.

This morning, that silver lining is the realization that, for the first time in over two months, she can bend both legs over the side of the bed, rise on her own two feet, and walk to the bathroom without her crutches. Hallelujah! Her hand grazes her thigh, evoking the feeling she experienced when her braces were finally removed, and she couldn't stop running her tongue over her smooth teeth.

Sailee takes a shower and makes her way down to the kitchen, where she prepares a cup of tea. In the aftermath of the accident, she couldn't bring herself to do this simple task. Mike had always brought her a cup of tea in bed – it was their ritual – and drinking tea alone served as a painful reminder of his absence. However, the need to stay awake eventually superseded her grief, and since she hates the taste of coffee, she gave in. It never tastes quite the same, though. It lacks the key ingredient – love. Travel mug in hand, she climbs into the truck, reveling in the ability to bend her leg and effortlessly take her seat. No more contortions required to drive.

Arriving at physical therapy, Sailee is informed that they are behind schedule and is instructed to take a seat in the waiting room. Before the accident, she would have wasted time by mindlessly scrolling through photos on Instagram. However, she hasn't been on social media since that fateful day. It has become too difficult to witness everyone else's lives moving forward while hers remains at a standstill.

She is immensely grateful for the few people who regularly check up on her. Her friend Marie, ever the world traveler, told Sailee she would drop everything and come stay with her if she ever needed. There have been moments when Sailee has held the phone in her hand, overwhelmed by the weight of her situation, but always talks herself out of making the call. Marie is currently in Thailand, and it seems unfair to ask her to make such a long journey when Sailee spends every day in the hospital anyway. Instead, she texts Marie, saying hello and assuring her that she's doing okay, even though she's not.

A few other friends have reached out, and occasionally Sailee agrees to meet for dinner or a drink. But once there, she's never sure what to say. Nothing has changed with Mike, and her days blend into endless monotony. She inquires about their lives, but they answer awkwardly, fearing that they might come across as too happy, yet also not wanting to complain about their problems, which pale in comparison to what Sailee is enduring. She's finding these interactions increasingly exhausting, so mostly she's alone. Making friends was never her strong suit anyway. Acquaintances, yes. She has thousands of them. But true friends? No. And she desperately misses her best one.

The physical therapy proves to be demanding, but it allows Sailee to focus on something within her control. She welcomes the pain. It reminds her that she's alive and healing. And it momentarily distracts her from the unending ache in her heart.

Upon her arrival at the ICU several hours later, the entire nursing station erupts in applause. At first, Sailee is bewildered, but then she realizes the reason behind the ovation – she's *walking*! These individuals have become like a second family to her, and they're all rooting for her and Mike. Sailee laughs, taking a deep bow, then walks into Mike's room, taking a seat on the edge of his bed.

"Hi, love," she says, taking his hand. "Guess what? I can walk again! No more brace, no more crutches. It's a shame you missed all the fun. You would have loved calling me Gimpy and gotten a real kick out of watching me finagle my way in and out of the truck. I still have some strength to get back, and I'm in physical therapy for my leg, but I'm pretty much back to normal." She squeezes his hand gently. "Now it's your turn."

CHAPTER 36

One moment, Shadow Mike is watching Magic Mike carry Sailee to their bedroom, and the next, he's standing on a boardwalk in the middle of the forest. There has been no time in the in-between, the void, for him to process this latest universe, and he is still reeling. Their life together had been loud and chaotic, full of travel, fans, and tabloids.

The worst moment came when they wrote a song titled, "No One Will Ever Know," and a tabloid picked it up before its official release, falsely reporting that Mike was abusive and implying that the song was Sailee's cry for help. They had to issue a joint statement clarifying that the song was purely fictional, emphasizing their wonderful relationship and the fact that Mike has never been physically or verbally abusive towards Sailee.

Following the article, Mike had received all sorts of hate mail, and Sailee was criticized as "weak" for not leaving him. It was all utter garbage, and although Sailee eventually grew accustomed to the attention and gossip, she never stopped feeling the stress it caused. She quickly learned that fame is not as glamorous as it may seem and was relieved to finally step out of the spotlight.

Shadow Mike had been looking forward to watching them settle down together, enjoy a slower-paced life, possibly start a family. But now, he finds himself in an unfamiliar time and place yet again. All he knows is that he's surrounded by a forest, and he's very, very glad that there is a defined trail. He listens attentively, serenaded only by the rustling of trees and the song of birds. It's remarkably serene, a stark contrast from the last timeline which was filled with screaming fans. He wanders down the boardwalk, relishing in the picturesque scenery. The sky overhead is a deep shade of blue. He is alone and enjoying the quiet.

Unaware of how long he has been meandering down the path, he suddenly catches the sound of voices in the distance. Turning, he sees a little boy barreling towards him, and instinctively steps aside.

"Michael!" a man yells. Startled, Shadow Mike directs his attention toward the voice. Is someone calling *him*? "Michael Black, get back here!" The boy halts, turns around and grins, then resumes running.

"Michael, you're gonna get in trouble!" cries a little girl, appearing from around the corner. She has bright red hair and fair skin. Then, a man emerges, hoisting the girl onto his shoulders. At the sight of him, Shadow Mike breathes a sigh of relief. This man is Mike, not the child. The boy must be his son.

This version of himself isn't old, but he looks tired and worn down. "Hold on tight, Maddie!" he says before chasing after the boy.

Maddie squeals with delight. "Get him, Daddy!"

Little Michael is fast, but his dad is faster, and it doesn't take them long to catch up with him. He grabs the boy firmly by the shoulder, bringing him to a halt. "I told you to stop running!" Mike scolds.

"But Dad," says the boy, "didn't you see how fast I am?"

Mike takes a deep breath, composing himself, then says, "Yes, you're very fast, Michael. But it's important that you listen to me and not get too far ahead. Do you understand?" Michael pouts and mumbles that yes, he understands, although it's evident that he's eager to sprint again.

"I wish mama was here," little Michael remarks. "Then she could stay behind with Madison, because she's slow, and you could run with me."

"I'm not slow!" yells Maddie angrily.

"Yes, you are," retorts Michael. "You couldn't even beat a turtle!"

"Daddy," whines Maddie, her voice cracking, "Michael said I couldn't even beat a—"

"Both of you, knock it off—" Michael says sharply.

Shadow Mike stops listening. "Mama?" he repeats to himself. Is he married? He glances at Mike's hand, spotting a wedding band. Is he already with Sailee? Or someone else? He does some calculations, wishing he knew the current year. This version of Mike looks to be about forty, which would put Sailee in her mid to late twenties. He estimates the ages of the children to be about seven and five—

Mike interrupts his thoughts. "I'm sorry I snapped at you, buddy. I miss mama too." He wraps an arm around his son, and they resume walking along the path. The little girl is still on her father's shoulders, amusing herself by playing with his hair.

Turning a corner, they encounter a group of hikers. While passing by, Madison accidentally drops the stuffed animal she's carrying. A woman stops and retrieves it, dusting it off before handing it back up to the girl. Shadow Mike catches a glimpse of her face. It's Sailee. "Here you go, sweetie!" she says cheerfully.

"My name's not Sweetie," the girl retorts. "It's Madison."

Sailee smiles. "Well, Madison, that's a beautiful name, and it's a pleasure to meet you. Hold on tight to your bunny now, okay? Enjoy your walk!" She nods to Mike, gives a warm smile to little Michael, and then jogs after her group.

Shadow Mike gazes after Sailee. Evidently she's not their mother. So who is? He lingers, hoping for another encounter, but Mike proceeds to his car where he straps the kids into their seats and drives away.

He trails this little family throughout the day. Mike makes a quick stop for groceries, treats the kids to ice cream as a reward for their good behavior, and eventually pulls into the driveway of a modest modern colonial. Handing Michael the house key, he asks him to unlock the front door while he gently lifts a sleeping Madison out of the car and carries her inside. Shadow Mike follows them into the house and looks around. The house is cluttered – not with junk, just with toys. It's clear that children live here.

He strolls into the living room and studies the photos adorning the walls and fireplace. They depict a happy family of four – Mike, little Michael, Madison, and an elegant woman, tall and slender, with shoulder-length brown hair. This must be "mama." Shadow Mike does a double take. He knows this woman. That's Caroline! He knew her, was once married to her in his own timeline. They tied the knot shortly after he completed his master's degree, but their careers took them in different directions, and they grew apart. They divorced after thirteen years, their separation mutual and amicable. They never had children. It's surreal to see her now, married to this version of himself. Are they content? How have they managed to make their relationship work?

He continues exploring the house, making his way into what's clearly Mike's office. His degrees hang on the wall behind his desk: B.S. in Engineering, 1994; M.S. in Engineering, 1995; Ph.D. in Engineering, 1998, all from Georgia Tech.

Papers are stacked high on the desk, and he'd like to peruse them, knowing he'd glean a lot of information about when and where he is. But his hand merely passes through the pile, so he settles for scanning the documents on top. It's primarily research. It appears he's involved in some fascinating work in biotechnology.

There's a wedding photo of Mike and Caroline on the bookshelf behind the desk, and Shadow Mike recognizes the picture – it was one of his favorites. She looked beautiful that day. He wonders where she is. Glancing at the clock, he notices it's getting late. Still at work, perhaps? She always put in long hours at the lab. A peculiar sensation stirs in the pit of his stomach, and Shadow Mike realizes he's apprehensive about seeing this Mike and Caroline together. It's simply too bizarre.

He leaves the office, following the children's voices into the kitchen. Daddy-o (his moniker for this new version) is serving dinner on plastic plates – burgers and french fries. He sits down at the head of the table, one child on either side of him, and says, "Ok, which one of you wants to say grace tonight."

Madison raises her hand. "I will, Daddy," she volunteers.

He smiles at her, and they all close their eyes. "Dear Jesus," says Maddie, "Thank you for the birds and the sunshine. Thank you that Michael didn't get in trouble for running away. Thank you for the food, and especially for Daddy." She pauses, taking a deep breath. "And please, please, please take care of mama, so I can see her when I get to heaven someday. Amen."

Mike has tears in his eyes when he opens them. "That was very nice, Maddie. Thank you."

"Do you think mama will still be in heaven when I get there, Daddy? Because I want to see her again, but I don't want to die yet."

Mike reaches over, taking her tiny hand in his large one. "Yes, honey. Your mama will be in heaven forever and ever, and she's waiting for you, but she wants you to live a long, happy life here first. Ok?"

"Ok," Madison says, satisfied, and picks up a french fry.

It all makes sense now – the circles around Mike's eyes, the research papers piled on his desk, the toys scattered all over the floor. In this universe, he's a single dad doing everything he can to stay afloat. Work, maintain the house, and keep up with two busy kids, all on his own. Shadow Mike feels a profound sadness for this man, this family. Even though he and Caroline didn't work out in his own timeline, he knows she's a good woman. A caring woman. She would have been an exceptional mother if they had chosen that path, as evident in this universe. But what happened to her?

Michael has been quiet this whole time, picking at his food. "Dad," he says quietly, "can I get cancer?" Mike looks at him, and there is so much love in his expression that it brings tears to Shadow Mike's eyes. So, that's how she died.

Mike takes a deep breath. "Well," he says, "Anyone can get cancer, and that's a harsh reality of life. But it's very, very rare, especially in children. But, Michael, you can't live your life in fear of getting cancer or any other illness. You just have to wake up every day and be grateful for that day and focus on doing nice things for other people because that's what life is about." Michael nods and takes a bite of his hamburger.

After dinner, Mike takes them upstairs and tucks them into bed. They've wanted to sleep in the same room since their mom died. He reads them each a story, kisses them on the head, and turns off their lights. "Goodnight, you two. I love you both so much."

"Love you too, Daddy," they say. He closes the door and leans against it for just a moment, running his hand through his hair, before descending the stairs to his office, where he prepares for his class the next day.

CHAPTER 37

Shadow Mike observes Daddy-o for months with no sign of Sailee. He watches him juggle work, trying to keep up with his research, classes, and grant proposals, while still spending time with his kids, who need him now more than ever. He could really use a nanny. However, Mike knows there is no substitute for his presence at home with Michael and Madison, so he's making that a priority, even though it means staying up late every night to get his work done. He's exhausted.

Intrigued by the fact that this Mike also married Caroline, Shadow Mike has spent the last several months analyzing every piece of information he can gather about their relationship. In his own universe, he entered the corporate sector upon completing his Ph.D. That choice led to his becoming an entrepreneur, and it was his life on the road that drove them apart. In this universe, Mike chose academia, and he and Caroline moved to Durham instead of Palo Alto. He became an engineering professor, and she secured a faculty position in the medical center. Their lives were much more aligned.

Shadow Mike and his Caroline decided early on not to have children as it would distract from their career focus. But in this universe, they changed their minds after ten years and were immensely grateful they did. He can see that this Mike loved Caroline, just as he once had, but can also sense that it wasn't the same passionate, effortless love that he and Sailee share. It was more of a friendship and a partnership.

"Where's Sailee now?" Shadow Mike wonders. Was that brief encounter all there is? Has he finally landed in a timeline where they don't find each other?

Mike awakens and looks at his phone. It's September 11th, ten years since the attacks on the World Trade Center and the Pentagon. That day will be etched in his memory forever. He was teaching an 8:00 a.m. class on fluid dynamics when the first tower was struck. Turning on the television, he and his students watched in horror as the plane collided with the second tower, and they both crumbled. Class ended, but nobody moved. The room fell into a silence that seemed to stretch on for hours until a student, hailing from New York, burst into tears and ran from the room.

It's astounding to Mike that his children will never know the world before 9/11. They will never know the ease of passing through airport security without removing their shoes or separating liquids. They will only know the New York City skyline with the presence of the Freedom Tower. Though a decade has passed, it still feels like yesterday.

It's important to Mike that his children learn about significant historical events, so he takes them to the memorial service held by Duke University. It's a beautiful day in Durham. The sky is a clear blue, and the summer humidity is beginning to dissipate, a sure sign that autumn is around the corner. The campus quad is packed, so Mike lifts Madison onto his shoulders while holding onto Michael, who stands on a folding chair, trying to see over the crowd.

At precisely 8:30 a.m., the President steps onto the platform. She warmly welcomes everyone, expressing gratitude for their presence in commemorating such a somber day in the nation's history, then asks everyone to rise for the national anthem. Two women take the stage, and the first, a brunette, begins to sing.

> *"O say can you see,*
> *By the dawn's early light*

What so proudly we hailed
At the twilight's last gleaming

Whose broad stripes and bright stars
Through the perilous fight
O'er the ramparts we watched
Were so gallantly streaming..."

The second woman joins in on the chorus with a harmony line.

"And the rocket's red glare
The bombs bursting in air
Gave proof through the night
That our flag was still there..."

Mike glances twice at the blonde, thinking she looks familiar. He wracks his brain but can't place her. At 8:46 a.m. there's a moment of silence, followed by another at 9:03 a.m., during which Madison loudly declares that she's hungry. Mike is mortified, and a few people around him stifle smiles. After thirty minutes, the kids grow restless, and Mike realizes he should have brought something to keep them occupied. Maddie, bored atop his shoulders, covers his eyes with her hands and plugs his ears. Michael is running circles around his chair. Exasperated, Mike takes them to the back of the quad where he can keep an eye on the kids while they play, and an ear on the service.

The blonde woman from the stage is standing a few feet away from them. Madison looks up at her and exclaims, "Hey – I know you!"

The woman looks around, not sure who is being addressed.

"You picked up Bunny for me!" Maddie announces loudly. Mike tries to shush her.

The woman looks down and smiles. "Why, you're absolutely right! You have a good memory. And you are... Madison, correct?" Maddie grins widely, pleased to be remembered.

Michael, eager for the distraction, approaches her. "My name is Michael," he says. "What's yours?"

"My name is Sailee," she answers. "Like a sailor on a boat."

Michael nods. "I like boats," he remarks. "My dad takes me fishing sometimes. It's one of my favorite things."

Mike comes over, taking the kids by the hand and gently pulling them away. "Sorry about that. C'mon kiddos – this nice lady wants to listen to the speaker."

"They're okay," she replies. "I love kids, and they probably find this incredibly boring."

Mike grimaces. "Yeah, I didn't think this through. I thought it would be a good teaching moment, but it's still a bit over their heads." He shrugs. "A friend will be here in half an hour to pick them up so I can get some work done. Hopefully they don't do anything catastrophic before then!"

Sailee smiles. "They are incredibly well-behaved. I would have been running through people's legs and wreaking all sorts of havoc when I was their age."

"Don't give them any ideas!" Mike warns, and Sailee makes an "oops" face, looking around to see if the kids were listening.

"I'm sorry," says Mike, "I didn't catch your name."

"Sailee," she answers. "And you are…"

"Mike," he replies, shaking her hand.

"Pleasure to meet you, Mike. Do you work here?"

"Yes, I'm a member of the engineering faculty. You?"

"I'm a law student," she explains.

"Are you enjoying it?" Mike asks.

"Mostly," replies Sailee. "I always thought the law was supposed to be logical, and it has been a bit disheartening to learn how much of it isn't. But overall, I like it."

Someone turns around and shushes them. They blush slightly, apologizing. Both of them had completely forgotten about the memorial service. "Sorry," whispers Sailee. "My singing voice is like a baby bird, but my speaking voice can be heard from miles away."

Mike smiles. Indeed, her voice does carry.

The service ends, and the crowd begins to disperse. "Well," says Mike, "I need to get these kids to my office. My friend will be there any minute to pick them up."

Sailee turns to Michael and Madison. "I'm glad we bumped into each other again!" she says. They smile at her, then resume their tickling match.

Mike shrugs. "It was nice to meet you," he says. "Best of luck with the rest of your studies."

"Thanks," Sailee replies. "You too." She thinks about what she just said, then clarifies. "On the meeting you part. I'm guessing you're done with school for a while!" Mike laughs, then takes the kids by the hand and walks away.

Sailee returns to the library and immediately gets online, scouring the engineering school website in the hopes of finding more information about this handsome professor. She learns that his name is Dr. Michael Black, and that he joined the Duke faculty in 1998. His expertise lies in acoustics, vibrations, and bionanomanufacturing. He became a full professor at the age of thirty-four and a chaired professor at thirty-eight, just last year. His lab brings in over a million dollars a year in funded research. "He's quite the rockstar," Sailee says aloud, then looks around to see if anyone heard her talking to herself.

During a Google search, Sailee discovers that Mike consults for the Air Force, serves on several boards, and chairs the Advisory Committee for the Swiss Federal Institute of Technology. Then she comes across an obituary for a Dr. Caroline M. Black – born April 12, 1971, died on November 30, 2010 – survived by her husband, Dr. Michael R. Black, and their two children, Michael R. Black, Jr. and Madison M.C. Black. How heartbreaking, she thinks. Those two sweet children are growing up without a mother, and Mike is bravely raising them on his own while managing his demanding career. He really *is* a rockstar. Feeling slightly guilty for uncovering all this information, Sailee closes her laptop and opens her textbook.

Across campus, Mike is in his lab, having trouble focusing, as his mind keeps drifting back to Sailee. He shakes it away. First of all, Caroline has not been gone for very long – less than a year. Secondly, Sailee is a student, albeit a professional one. While it's not off limits, that's not the way he rolls. There are too many risks. He sighs and heads to his class.

CHAPTER 38

It's a chilly winter day on campus, with the temperature hovering just above freezing. Mike is in his office, frantically wrapping up a grant proposal. He is flying to Zurich that evening for a board meeting, and his mom is coming to stay with the kids. He needs to get home and tidy up before she arrives. The house is a mess, and Mike doesn't want his mom to know how badly he's drowning. She would worry, and with his dad's declining health, she has enough on her plate.

As he hits the send button on his final email, there's a knock on his door. "Ugh, not now," he thinks but calls out, "Come on in!" The door opens, and Mike jumps up, surprised. "Sailee! What brings you too my office?"

Sailee steps into the room and begins to unzip her jacket. "Geez – it's not much warmer in here than outside!" she observes.

"I know," replies Mike, grinning. "I intentionally keep it cold to discourage people from lingering. I'm busy and don't time for casual chit-chat. I find this to be quite effective!"

Sailee laughs, zipping her jacket back up. "Well," she responds, "I can take a hint and won't overstay my welcome!"

Mike flinches, mentally kicking himself. "I'm sorry – that wasn't directed at you. I'm certainly not trying to kick you out!" he says, embarrassed.

"I'm just teasing," she remarks. "But seriously, I won't stay long. I'm rarely on this side of campus, so when I happened to pass by your building today, I remembered you and your kids and thought I'd drop in to say hi!"

Mike smiles. "That was thoughtful of you," he replies. "My kids actually mentioned you the other day. We were listening to the radio at lunch when 'The Star-Spangled Banner' started playing. Maddie said, 'Hey, this is the song that pretty girl sang at the party!'" He smacks his forehead. "They clearly missed the entire point of the memorial service."

Sailee grins but doesn't say anything else. Mike looks at her expectantly, wondering if that was really all she came here for. 'I came to say hi, so… hi! And now, bye!'

Suddenly, she blurts out. "I heard about your wife's passing last year, and I wanted to express my condolences. You have such a lovely little family, and I'm sure it hasn't been easy. I don't know much about you, except that you're a brilliant engineer…" Mike blushes at her compliment, "…and that you have two young kids. You probably already have a bunch of friends around to help you, but I was going to ask if you wanted to get a cup of coffee, just for something different to do, and let you know that if you ever needed a night out, I'd be happy to hang out with your kids. I love kids, and they seem great, and I'm sure you could use a break every now and then."

Mike stares at Sailee, not quite comprehending what she said. Did she just ask him out? Or offer to watch his kids? And how does she know about Caroline? His head is swirling.

At his lack of response, Sailee's face turns bright red. "Oh gosh, I'm so sorry," she remarks. "This was completely inappropriate, although I didn't mean it to be… I'm just gonna go." She starts for the door.

"Wait a minute," Mike replies, taking a step toward her. "No, I'm sorry. It just caught me off guard, and it took me a moment to process. And thank you – that was all very kind. I'm sure my kids would be absolutely thrilled to see you again." He pauses, contemplating his next words. "As for that cup of coffee, I would like to take you up on the offer but I'm just heading out the door to pick up the kids from school and go meet my mom, who's staying with them for a few days while I'm away on business." He should leave it at that, just let it go. But it's like a magnetic force is pulling him towards her. "Can I take a raincheck on the coffee? Next week, maybe?"

Sailee smiles, noticeably relieved. "Definitely!" she replies. "I didn't think about the fact that you have to pick up your kids in the afternoon. How about next Tuesday – a week from today? I have class in the morning, but I could meet for lunch at noon."

He says that sounds good. Sailee gives him another warm smile and departs. Mike gathers his belongings, now significantly later than he planned to be, and tells himself that it's fine. Everything's fine. It's not like it's a date or anything. He grabs his briefcase and heads out the door, locking it behind him.

A week later, Mike glances at his calendar and notices that he has the noon hour blocked for lunch with Sailee. Except he can't remember if they finalized where they would meet, and he doesn't have her phone number. But he needn't have worried. At 12:00 p.m. on the dot, there's a knock on his office door.

"Sorry for just showing up," Sailee says, stepping inside. "I realized this morning I don't have your number. I suppose I could have looked up your email, but this way you can't back out on me!" She attempts a wink at Mike. "Does this still work for you?" she asks.

He confirms that it does, grabs his coat, and follows her out of his office. "Where would you like to go?" she asks.

"How about the Washington Duke?" he suggests.

"That's great," she says. "I've never been there. Are you a member?"

"Yes," Mike replies. He opens the door for her at the bottom of the stairs, and she steps out onto the sidewalk.

"Do you play golf?" she inquires.

"Yes. Well, I used to. I suppose I still do. I used to play quite a bit before my wife…" he trails off. Even after all this time, it's still difficult to say. "But I haven't played at all in the past couple of years. I don't have time anymore. Do you play?"

"Oh, hell no!" Sailee responds, laughing. "The last time I played golf was in eighth-grade gym class, and my best friend hit me in the head with a 9-iron." Mike's eyes widen.

"I know what you're thinking," Sailee continues. "I *had* been standing far enough back, but we were talking and she said something I couldn't hear. I stepped forward just as she swung the club, but she swung it like a baseball bat. Suddenly, there was a ringing in my ear. I turned my head sideways, and blood started gushing out. Liz freaked out and started yelling, 'Lay down, lay down, lay down! No – get up, get up, get up!' It turns out what she had said was, 'That flag is a long way away. I'm going to have to hit that ball as hard as I can.'"

She winces at the memory. "They called my dad, who had just finished his night shift, and he took me to the doctor. They examined me and said I needed to go to the hospital. When we arrived at the Emergency Room, a nurse checked me out and sent in the physician's assistant, who sent in the doctor. He looked at it and said, since the cut went straight down into the cartilage, that I needed to see the plastic surgeon.

"Keep in mind, it's now 3:30 p.m. and I got hit at 8:30 in the morning. They hadn't given me anything to stop the bleeding, except for some gauze, and nothing for the pain. My dad, who's usually the quietest, sweetest man you've ever met, had been up for twenty-four hours at this point with no sleep. When we arrived at the plastic surgeon's office, they told us it was going to be another hour of waiting, and my dad lost it. He started yelling at the receptionist, saying that I was a higher priority than someone's new boobs, and he wanted me in there *NOW!*" She laughs. "I was in the room in less than ten minutes!"

"Wow," says Mike, "that's traumatic!"

"Not nearly as traumatic as when they told me I had to wear a head cast for a week!" Sailee replies. "I hadn't cried until that point."

"I bet you never lived that down!" he retorts.

"Nope. And my mom made it worse because while I was sleeping off all the pain medicine they finally gave me, she thought it would be funny to decorate my head cast. When I woke up, she had drawn little flowers all over the front, and over my ear there was a golf club with a big 'X' through it." Sailee rolls her eyes as she mimics drawing a large "X" in the air with her hand.

"Your mom sounds like a real character," says Mike, laughing.

"She's something else," agrees Sailee. "My ear looked like raw hamburger meat for a while, but all I have left now is a small scar." She pulls back her hair and shows him her ear.

"Are you still friends with Liz?" he asks.

"Oh yeah. We've grown apart in recent years, but she was my best friend all the way through college!"

They arrive at the club, and Mike holds the door open for Sailee. Stepping inside, they both come to a halt. Everything is decorated in red and pink. There are roses everywhere, and heart-shaped balloons float from the entryway table.

"Uh…" stammers Sailee. "What day is it?" They look at each other, then back at the room, and Sailee bursts into uncontrollable laughter. "I didn't even think about the date when we scheduled lunch. Happy Valentine's Day, Mike!"

He gives a small laugh, doing his best to conceal his uneasiness. It's not a date, but no one in the club will ever believe that. They proceed into the restaurant and are greeted by the hostess. "Good afternoon, Dr. Black," she says. "Table for two?" Mike nods and motions for Sailee to follow the hostess to the table. It's elegantly decorated with rose petals, and there are little chocolates at each place setting.

"Well," says Sailee, noticing Mike's discomfort and trying to lighten the mood, "this is awfully fancy for our first lunch together. It'll be tough to top this!" She smiles at Mike, then glances around the room and realizes he's probably surrounded by his colleagues, and how this must look to them. She quickly lowers her voice. "I'm sorry if this is awkward for you," she says. "Do you want to go somewhere else?"

"It's fine, really," Mike reassures her. "It *is* pretty funny. I just wonder what kind of rumors will circulate about me bringing a pretty young blonde to lunch on Valentine's Day. Everyone will be trying to figure out who the lucky girl is!" He winks at Sailee, and she laughs.

"Well, I definitely feel lucky!" she replies.

To anyone on the outside, it certainly looks like a date – Sailee and Mike leaning in, fully engrossed in their conversation. They talk about their lives, hometowns, backgrounds, their mutual love of music, Mike's research, and Sailee's post-graduation plans this spring. But mostly, they talk about his children, and Mike finds himself opening up about Caroline. Sailee exudes warmth, and somehow, he feels as though he has known her for ages.

Mike shares that they didn't initially plan on having children, but they eventually changed their minds, and Michael came along shortly after. Madison, he confesses, was a surprise. But she was the best surprise in the world. "She says she wants to grow up to be just like her daddy," Mike remarks. "I wonder how long that will last." He tells Sailee about their standing daddy-daughter dates where he takes her to Panera for chocolate croissants, "because that girl has a sweet tooth like you wouldn't believe!"

Sailee asks if Madison inherited the red hair from her mom. "No," he explains, "that comes from my side. My mom's family is Irish. It must have skipped a generation or two, but Maddie unquestionably has Irish blood and the temper to prove it!" They both laugh at this.

"I can relate," says Sailee. "I'm Irish and have a temper too."

"You?!" Mike asks incredulously. He cannot imagine this cheerful, vibrant woman ever getting angry.

"Absolutely," she replies. "This probably makes me sound crazy, but I don't typically experience a wide range of emotions. I'm either happy or angry. So, imagine this level of intensity, then picture me angry."

Mike contemplates it for a moment and makes a face.

"Exactly," says Sailee, laughing. "The funny thing is, the men in my family are the ones with historically bad tempers. My dad has one, my grandpa had a worse one, and his dad was notorious for it. My mom says that when my brother was born, she prayed and prayed for him, and he has no temper at all. He's the most laid-back person you've ever met. And then there's me. Apparently, mom didn't pray for me!"

Mike is taking a drink and nearly chokes on it. His mom is also the praying type, so this is especially funny to him.

Glancing at his watch, he's shocked to find that it's already 2:00 p.m. He had only blocked an hour on his calendar and he needs to get back to his lab. He signals the waiter for the bill.

"Oh dear!" exclaims Sailee, "I didn't realize it was getting so late. I know you have a lot to do, and I have an exam tomorrow I need to study for."

When the waiter brings the check, Sailee reaches out for it, but Mike grabs it first. "I invited you to lunch!" she argues.

"That's true, but this is my club, and thanks to you, this is the most like myself I've felt in a long time. So please, let me take care of this."

Sailee concedes. "But only if you let me pay next time," she says.

Mike hesitates, unsure if wants to agree to that arrangement. But he does like the sound of a next time. "Deal," he finally replies. He hands her a business card. "Here's all my contact information."

Sailee enters his name, number, and email into her phone, then immediately sends him a text.

Hi Mike, this is Sailee Roberts. Thanks for lunch. Let's do this again soon. "Now you have mine."

CHAPTER 39

Since the Valentine's Day debacle, Mike has had several colleagues stop by and congratulate him on dating again. At first, he insists that he and Sailee are just friends, but eventually he gives up. It's not worth the effort, and no one believes him anyway.

He mentions this to Sailee one day over tea, and she laughs. "This would be a pretty pathetic dating relationship," she says, "considering we only see each other once a month or so." Mike agrees.

Several weeks later, Sailee sends him a text. *Hey Mike! Lunch next week? How about Thursday?*

Mike looks at his calendar. Next week is Parent-Teacher Conferences, and his kids are home all week. He found a babysitter for part of the time, but couldn't get anyone for Wednesday and Thursday, so he has to work from home. With finals week approaching and a grant proposal due soon, he's swamped and staying up far too late every night, trying to keep on top of everything. He's exhausted and doesn't have time or energy to get together, but he also knows that Sailee will be graduating soon and likely moving away, so he doesn't want to miss the opportunity. He sends a reply: *Next week is crazy. My kids are home all week, so I can't really go out. But you're welcome to come over here if you want. Just beware, it's chaos.*

Sailee replies, *Sounds great. I live for chaos. Just tell me when and where.* Mike sets the time for 12:30 p.m. and sends her his address.

On the following Thursday, before leaving her apartment, Sailee texts Mike: *Do you need me to pick up anything on my way?*

He texts back: *To be honest, I have no idea what we have to eat. I'm sure we can pull something together. Maybe hot dogs or mac and cheese.*

Sailee replies: *Leave lunch to me. I'll be there shortly.*

Mike shakes his head, frustrated with himself. He invited Sailee over and then didn't even think to get food for lunch. He used to be the one who always had it together, who made sure everything was done. Now he's just trying to keep his kids alive and not lose his job.

At exactly 12:30 p.m., Sailee shows up, carrying a bag of groceries. Michael opens the door, and his eyes widen. "Hey!" he exclaims, "You're the girl who's named after a boat!" Then he runs off to tell Madison, leaving Sailee alone on the front step.

She lets herself in and is kicking off her shoes when Mike enters the room. "You didn't have to do this," he says, taking the bag from Sailee and giving her an awkward side hug. "We could have scrounged up something."

"I know," she replies. "But this will be fun and easy, and the kids will love it."

Madison comes running into the room. "Sailee, Sailee, Sailee!" she yells, throwing her arms around Sailee's waist. Mike raises an eyebrow in surprise. This is unusual for Madison, who is typically shy around strangers. Madison holds up her stuffed animal. "Remember Bunny?" she asks.

"Of course I do," says Sailee, stooping down so that she's eye-level with Madison. "I'm glad she didn't break anything in that fall." Maddie giggles, and everyone follows Mike into the kitchen.

"So," announces Sailee, "today we're going to make my favorite lunch. Fluffernutters!" Everyone looks at her blankly. "What!?" she asks, incredulously. "You've never had a fluffernutter?"

"What's a 'fruffanutter'?" inquires Michael.

"Oh my goodness," Sailee says in disbelief. "Fluffernutters are the best sandwich in the entire world." She starts taking groceries out of the bag – bread, peanut butter, Fluff.

"What's Fluff" asks Mike, picking up the jar to read the label.

"It's basically liquid marshmallow!" answers Sailee cheerfully.

"Marshmallow!?" echoes Madison. "You're going to put marsh-mallow on a sandwich?"

"I sure am," Sailee replies, "and you're going to love it."

Mike remains skeptical. For the past month, Michael has refused to eat anything but hot dogs. Every meal has been a battle. And Mike can only imagine how little work he'll get done this afternoon if the kids have marshmallow sandwiches. He can feel his stress level rising.

Sailee is oblivious. "Okay, who's ready?" she asks.

Both kids raise their hands in the air. "Meeee!" they shout in unison.

Mike, trying to appear enthusiastic, raises his hand too, although deep down, he's quite unsure about this whole fluffernutter business.

He gets the plates, and Sailee grabs a knife from the drawer and begins making the sandwiches – two slices of bread, a regular amount of peanut butter on one slice, and an enormous glob of Fluff on the other. "Trust me," she says to Mike, who looks dubious.

She makes four sandwiches, cuts them in half diagonally, then hands each person a plate. Mike has set out napkins and cups of milk. They sit down, and Mike explains to Sailee, "We always say a quick blessing before we eat." Sailee nods.

Then he turns to his son. "Michael, will you do the honors?"

They bow their heads and Michael starts praying. "Amen, Holy Ghost, whoever eats the fastest gets the most."

Sailee's eyes pop open in surprise. Maddie giggles, and even Mike can't keep a straight face. He tries to look stern. "Ok, funny guy," he says. "Now try it again – for real this time."

Michael grins, then closes his eyes and says, "Dear Jesus, thank you for Daddy, and Maddie, and our new friend, Sailee. And thank you that we're allowed to eat marshmallows for lunch today!" He pauses. "And please take care of mama. Amen."

Sailee's eyes fill with tears, and she quickly blinks them away. Then everyone takes their first bite. Madison's eyes go wide, and Michael shoves nearly half of the sandwich into his mouth.

"Oh my gosh," exclaims Mike. "This is actually amaz— Hey – buddy!" he quickly turns to Michael. "Slow down a little. Take your time and enjoy it!" He laughs and turns back to Sailee. "This is *really* good!"

Sailee smiles, and her eyes are warm and bright. Mike has never noticed how green they are. "I'm glad you like it! This was my favorite growing up. We usually had to eat healthy, so these were a special treat."

The kids inhale their sandwiches and ask for seconds, but Mike tells them one is enough. "But I'm still hungry," complains Michael. Mike replies that if they want more food, he'll cut up some veggies.

"But I don't *want* veggies," argues Michael, his tone becoming a whine. "I want another fluffernutter. Why can't I have just one more—"

"*That's enough!*" snaps Mike, slamming his fist down on the table. Everyone freezes, and Michael's eyes shine with unshed tears. Mike slumps a little in his chair, then lets out a small sigh and reaches out for Michael, placing a hand on his arm. "I'm sorry, bud" he says. "I shouldn't have yelled like that."

Sailee sits there awkwardly.

"Daddy," Madison says quietly, "I'm full. Can I be excused?"

Mike nods, and both kids leave the table, rushing out of the room. Mike turns to Sailee. "I apologize for that."

"It was my fault," she begins. "I should have brought something—"

"No," he interrupts. "It was a great idea. They were fun and delicious. I shouldn't have lost it over such a small thing. I feel like I'm doing that all the time these days." Mike runs a hand through his hair. "Those poor kids. I'm on edge constantly, like a rubber band that's stretched too tight and ready to snap. And then when I do, it's over something stupid." He puts his head in his hands. "I'm completely failing at this single parent thing."

Sailee reaches over, placing her hand on his shoulder. "You're not failing," she says. "Not at all. No parent is perfect, and you have a lot on your plate." She pauses. "Listen," she says finally, "I don't have any other plans this afternoon. Why don't I take the kids outside to play for a few hours so you can get some work done."

Mike looks up, surprised. "Are you serious?" Sailee nods. "I can't ask that of you—"

"Nonsense," she replies. "I'd love to. I won't take no for an answer." She stands, collecting the plates, and carries them into the kitchen.

"You're an angel," he says.

Maddie pops her head into the room. "Sailee, will you come play with us?"

"I will in a minute," she answers. "Let me help your dad clean up the kitchen first." She rinses the dishes and loads the dishwasher. Mike starts putting the groceries back in the bag. "Oh no," Sailee insists. "Keep them. That way you can surprise the kids with them every now and then, if it won't cause problems."

"That could be dangerous," says Mike. "I might find myself regularly sneaking fluffernutters in the middle of the night. Who knows, maybe it will make me sweeter!" He winks at her.

"You're sweet enough already," Sailee replies, playfully "winking" back at him.

"You *do* know you can't wink, right?" Mike teases.

"Oh yes!" Sailee laughs. "My face is not talented. I can't wink, roll my tongue, flare my nostrils… anything. Talking is pretty much all my face is good for, so it's a good thing I'm planning to be a lawyer!"

Mike is thinking that her face would be pretty good for kissing too, when Madison interrupts his thoughts. He hadn't even seen her come back into the kitchen. "You can't roll your tongue?" Maddie asks.

"Nope," replies Sailee. "Can you?" Maddie sticks out her tongue, shaped into a circle. Sailee tries, but only succeeds in sticking out her tongue and looking quite funny in the process. Madison laughs.

"Okay, guys," Sailee says. "Let's go outside and play so your dad can get some work done. Do either of you know how to play freeze tag?" The kids put on their shoes and race out the back door. Sailee turns to Mike. "Good luck with everything," she says. "Thanks for letting me come over today."

"No," he says, "thank *you*. You're a godsend. Are you sure you won't just marry me?" As soon as the words are out of his mouth, Mike blanches. He can't believe he said that.

Sailee simply laughs. "Mike Black, you better watch what you say because I'd marry you in a heartbeat!" With that, she gives a swish of her hair and walks out the door.

Mike leans against the counter. "Where did that come from?" he wonders. And yet, he knows; he knows in his gut that Sailee is perfect for him. Perfect for him *and* his kids. He lets out a sigh and heads into his office.

Sailee spends the entire day outside with Michael and Madison. They play tag and pretend to be ninjas. They roll down the small hill in the backyard. She pushes them on the swings, and they have competitions to see who can get their head over the bar first. All the while, Sailee tells them stories, like how she and her brother used to pretend they were Godzilla and throw all their toys out the window, or how they played G.I. Joe vs. Barbie, and all her Barbies had shaved heads and amputated limbs, casualties of the many "wars" they fought. Michael gets a kick out of that, but Maddie is appalled at the thought of mutilated Barbies.

Sailee is on the swing, watching Michael go down the slide, when Madison comes up and sits on her lap, facing her. Sailee shows Maddie how she and her friends used to double-swing when they were kids, but soon Maddie's head is resting on her chest, and she's fast asleep, lulled by the motion of the swing. Sailee doesn't stop swinging for a long time because she's certain this is the most magical thing she has ever experienced and doesn't want to break the spell.

When they finally go back inside, Mike meets them in the kitchen. They're tired and filthy, but Mike hasn't seen his kids look so happy in a long time. "Well," he tells them, "tonight is definitely going to be a bath night. But for now, just wash your hands and face and put on clean clothes."

Sailee looks at him sheepishly. "Sorry about that," she says. "We were having so much fun I didn't think about how dirty they were getting. I hope their clothes aren't ruined."

"I couldn't care less about their clothes," Mike replies. "Those smiles are priceless. I grew up in the mountains and was always coming home filthy. That's what it means to be a kid! Thanks for letting them experience that today. They've had to grow up far too quickly over the past year."

Sailee touches his arm. "You're a good dad, and they're lucky to have you." Then, clearing her throat, she asks, "Were you able to get anything done?"

"Tons," he replies. "This was just what I needed."

"Good," she says and begins gathering her things.

"Do you want to stay for dinner?" Mike asks quickly. He's not ready for her to leave.

"I'd love to!" Sailee replies just as hastily, clearly not ready to go.

"I was thinking we could order pizza. I know – banner health day. I promise the kids usually eat better than this. But this has been hell week, and I haven't had time to get to the store."

She smiles kindly at him. "No judgement from me. Plus, I love pizza!"

When the kids come back downstairs, they're thrilled to find Sailee still there, and after dinner and baths, they beg her to read them their bedtime stories. Mike stands in the doorway and observes the three of them, curled up in Madison's bed, engrossed in their book. When Sailee finishes reading, Michael crawls into his own bed, and Mike tucks them both in, kissing them on the head and telling them how much he loves them. As he's turning out Maddie's light, she says, "Daddy, can Sailee stay forever?"

Oh, how he'd like that. "That'd be nice, wouldn't it?" he answers. "Goodnight, Maddie."

"Goodnight, Daddy."

Mike goes downstairs and finds Sailee in the kitchen. "I'm exhausted!" she says, laughing. "I don't know how you do this every day!"

He's searching for an excuse – any excuse – to keep her here. "Would you like a cup of tea before you leave?" he asks.

"That sounds wonderful," she replies.

He carries the cup of tea into the living room, where Sailee has made herself at home on the couch, her legs tucked underneath her. "Here you go," he says, offering her the mug. Gratefully, she accepts it, wrapping both hands around it and gently leaning in, savoring the warmth of the rising steam against her face. "Thanks," she murmurs.

Mike longs to curl up beside her, but instead, he takes a seat the at the opposite end of the couch. They talk for hours, keeping their voices low to not wake the sleeping children. It's after midnight when Sailee rises to leave. Mike walks her to the door and rests his hand on the knob. They are standing mere inches apart.

"Thank you for a wonderful day," he says, his eyes smoldering with desire. "And thank you for being so good to my kids. And to me."

Sailee opens her mouth to reply, but instead leans forward, kissing Mike softly on the lips. A surge of electricity courses through his body. He releases the doorknob, one hand wrapping around her waist, the other moving to her hair. It has been so long since he's been kissed. It's exciting and stimulating, yet soft and sweet – like her mouth. It feels like wrapping yourself in a warm blanket on a cold night or coming home after a long absence.

For years, all he and Caroline shared were quick pecks. Mike can't remember the last time he experienced a deep, passionate kiss. He forgot how wonderful it was.

"I'd ask you to stay over," he says when they finally pull apart. "But the kids—"

"I understand," she replies, touching his arm. She kisses him again, allowing her lips to linger on his, then steps away. Mike opens the door and watches Sailee walk to her car. He should walk her out, he thinks, but he doesn't trust his legs to hold him upright.

From then on, Sailee spends every weekend with Mike and his kids, occasionally joining Mike on his business trips so they can enjoy some alone time and go on proper dates that don't involve peanut butter and jelly or pigs in a blanket. After graduation, she turns down a job offer in Washington, DC and joins a small nonprofit law firm in Durham that provides free legal services to low-income families. It's hard work and abysmal pay but satisfying.

The following February, Mike is driving the children to school when he looks at them through his rearview mirror and asks, "So, kids, what should I do for Sailee for Valentine's Day?"

"Buy her a pony!" Madison yells. "Or chocolate. Sailee loves chocolate!" Michael is quiet.

"Michael? Any ideas?" Mike asks, uncertain how to interpret his silence.

"You could ask her to marry you, Dad," Michael finally says, his voice so soft that Mike can hardly hear him. Mike immediately pulls the car over to the side of the road and turns around to face them.

"Do you mean that?" he asks, his heart thumping. "Do you want me to marry Sailee?"

Michael and Madison both nod. "Well then," Mike says, turning back around, unable to wipe the smile off his face, "maybe I will!"

CHAPTER 40

Mike considers proposing on Valentine's Day but decides that would be too cliché. He does, however, take Sailee back to the Washington Duke for memory's sake. When they pull into the parking lot, she laughs. "I assume it's actually a date this time?"

"It most certainly is," he replies.

Two days later, Sailee parks in Mike's driveway. They are all going to his parents' house for a few days, and she feels slightly apprehensive because the first time she met them was borderline catastrophic. She sits in the car for a moment, recalling that infamous weekend.

The previous fall, after discovering Sailee's love for football, Mike had arranged for a sitter to watch the kids for a long weekend so he could take her to a Georgia Tech game, followed by a visit to Marion, North Carolina to meet his parents.

The drama started as they were leaving town after the game, and Mike got pulled over. "What the hell," he had said, irritated. "I wasn't even speeding."

"They're probably pulling over anyone who might be coming from the game, to make sure you haven't been drinking," Sailee replied.

She was right. After an agonizing twenty minutes of subjecting Mike to all the sobriety tests and making them both blow into the breathalyzer, the cops finally let them go.

But the weekend only went downhill from there. Sailee ended up getting a urinary tract infection and had to make an emergency run to urgent care in the middle of the night. To top it off, she overflowed his parents' toilet with neon orange urine, courtesy of the UTI medicine. She surreptitiously washed and dried all the dirty towels she had used to clean up the mess from the overflow, only to discover, while sitting on the laundry room floor in frustration after spilling spaghetti sauce all over herself at dinner, that the water valve to the washer was closed.

"Seriously?!" she had cried when Mike told her. "You mean I folded and put away all those towels, and they were washed in nothing but dirty toilet water?!" She smacked her head and then raced upstairs, pulling all the towels back out of the bathroom cabinet, and throwing them, along with her shirt, into the washer again.

That weekend will live on in infamy as one of the most embarrassing of Sailee's life. She had called her mom and told her all about it once she got back home, and Ellie had said, "You're a stronger woman than me. I would have jumped out the window after the UTI!"

Sailee shakes her head at the memory and gets out of the car, hoping this weekend goes much more smoothly.

Inside, she throws her overnight bag on the floor and begins to remove her coat. "Don't take that off yet," says Mike. "The kids want to show you something in the backyard." Sailee gives him a questioning look but makes her way through the kitchen and out the back door.

Michael and Madison are on the swings. They're giggling and fidgety, and Sailee wonders if it's the excitement of going to grandma and papaw's house, or a sugar rush from all the Valentine's Day candy they've eaten, that has them so wound up. As she gets closer, she sees they're holding something in their laps. It looks like construction paper. "Hey guys, what's up?" she says. "You wanted to show me something?"

They nod, and then Michael counts to three, and they hold up their signs. The pen is hard to read on the colored paper, so Sailee leans in close to get a better view. She reads out loud, "Sailee... Will... You... Marry... Our... Daddy?"

She steps back in surprise, hands over her mouth.

"Turn around!" yells Madison. She turns, and Mike is behind her, kneeling in the mud, a ring in his hand, and a smile on his perfect, handsome face.

"Sailee," he asks, "will you marry me?"

"Yes!" she cries. "A million times, yes!" She throws her arms around Mike, and the force of the blow knocks him over. They fall into the mud, still holding on to each other. The kids run over and heave themselves on top of the pile. They are all laughing hysterically, and everyone is a muddy mess.

When they finally get to their feet, they go inside, take quick showers, then pile into the car and head for grandma's. Mike tells Sailee they're dropping the kids off, and he's taking her on into downtown Asheville for a weekend alone to celebrate. Smiling, Sailee looks down at the ring on her hand, still unable to take it all in.

Time flies, and before they know it, the wedding is a week away, and they're at the county clerk's office applying for their marriage license. The clerk addresses Sailee first. "State your full name."

"Sailee Ann Roberts."

"Date of birth?"

"June 25, 1985."

"Place of Birth?"

"Jericho, Vermont."

"Parents' names?"

"Mark Daniel Roberts and Ellie Lynn Roberts."

"Mother's maiden name?"

"Collins."

Then he turns to Mike. "Full Name?"

"Michael Robert Black."

"Date of Birth?"

"February 10, 1972—"

"1972?!" interrupts Sailee loudly, her eyes wide. "You never told me that!"

The clerk stops writing and looks up, unsure how to proceed. His eyes flit between them. Mike looks at Sailee, confused, and she bursts out laughing.

"I'm just kidding!" she says, motioning with her hand. "I knew that already. Please carry on." The clerk eyes them dubiously. "Seriously!" she insists. "I just couldn't help myself. Please continue because I need to marry this man!" She takes Mike's hand in hers and gives him a playful "wink." Amused, Mike shakes his head, and the clerk proceeds with his questions.

They get married in the Duke chapel on a perfect spring day, surrounded by friends and family, and after a brief honeymoon, settle into life together. It's not always easy. Sailee struggles to adapt to the challenges of motherhood, particularly learning how to discipline the kids herself instead of relying solely on Mike. And they test her patience, as any child does. But she grows more comfortable with time, and the children love and respect her.

Mike asks Sailee if she would like children of her own. As he's "no spring chicken," he says, it's something they need to start thinking about right away. Sailee considers it but ultimately decides that their family is perfect as it is. They thrive together, the joys and challenges of parenting bringing them closer.

One night, as Sailee is closing Madison's door after tucking her in, she says, "Goodnight Maddie. I love you!"

"I love you too, Mama!" Maddie replies, and Sailee's heart explodes. Neither Madison nor Michael have called her that before. But then she notices the uncertain look on Madison's face, and goes back in, sitting on her bed.

"It's okay, Maddie," she reassures her. "You can still call me Mama, and it doesn't diminish the love you have for your own mama. She will always be with you and in your heart. I can never replace her, nor do I want to. But I'm glad you feel this way about me because I love you as if you were my own daughter." Madison smiles and hugs her tightly. Sailee returns the hug, attempting to hold back tears of joy. Life is good.

Shadow Mike continues to observe them for a few more years as they grow and evolve together until he is eventually pulled back into the blackness.

CHAPTER 41

May 8

It has been a grueling day at the hospital. There is still no change in Mike, and Sailee can sense the restlessness among the nurses. She can almost hear their silent thoughts, wondering how much longer he will occupy that valuable ICU bed, how much longer they should keep him on life support. Sailee's getting restless too and can feel anger bubbling up inside her. She has sat faithfully by his side every day, patiently waiting for a breakthrough, and she's tired of waiting.

Looking down at Mike, she feels a sudden urge to slap him across the face. "WAKE UP!" she yells at him. Consumed with rage, Sailee grabs Mike by his shoulders, intending to shake him out of his stupor, when a nurse enters the room. Embarrassed, she quickly drops her arms, pretending she had been adjusting Mike's pillow. "Pull yourself together," she admonishes herself. Filled with shame, Sailee turns to leave the room when Mike's hand twitches, causing her heart to lurch.

"He's waking up!" she cries excitedly. The nurse approaches the other side of the bed and looks down at Mike, who remains motionless. "His hand just moved," Sailee insists. "I saw it."

Without speaking, the nurse checks all of Mike's vital signs. She shines a small light back and forth in front of his face, as if expecting his eyes to follow the beam. Then she says his name loudly, waiting for some sort of a response, but Mike is as still as stone.

Turning off the flashlight, the nurse looks up at Sailee's hopeful face with a sympathetic expression. "I'm sorry, Sailee," she says sadly. "Sometimes coma patients exhibit involuntary body movements. It appears that's what this was. There are no other indications that he's coming out of it." Devastated, Sailee slumps into her chair. "I am truly sorry," repeats the nurse.

Too upset to remain at the hospital any longer, Sailee drives home, cursing and yelling the entire way. "What the hell is wrong with me today?" she wonders. She is so angry. It likely doesn't help that she's hungry. She never copes well on an empty stomach, and she hasn't eaten all day. Upon arriving home, she rummages through her sparsely stocked kitchen cabinets. Cooking was something she and Mike enjoyed together, but she loathes doing it alone.

As she gathers the ingredients for a fluffernutter, "the dinner of champions," she thinks sarcastically, Sailee replays the events of the day in her mind. No, Mike didn't come out of his coma, but he moved. And that's more than he has done so far. Maybe it's a good sign. She has to think of it that way. She has to stay positive. It's the only way she'll survive.

CHAPTER 42

Shadow Mike has taken to closing his eyes when he's in the void. It's less disconcerting. Lately, though, he has been spending little time here. He's plucked from one timeline and plunged immediately into the next. It's a bit of a mind fuck. "Pardon the expression," he says to no one.

He's relieved to be out of the previous universe. He despised it. Sailee was trapped in a miserable marriage to a possessive and abusive man. To cope, she drank too much and constantly put herself in dangerous situations. Witnessing her pain, anger, and isolation shattered him. Although she ended up with Mike in the end, Shadow Mike had felt her loneliness acutely and tried desperately to escape that universe, to force himself out of the multiverse entirely. But after a dozen unsuccessful attempts to kill himself (how does one kill a ghost?) he concluded that he must already be dead and resigned himself to his multiverse-hopping hell.

Now, he's relaxing in the blackness, amusing himself with a parody he's calling, "Ghost Michael in the Sky." Just as he figures out the chorus, a loud whistle pierces the air. Suddenly, the world around him is bright, and he finds himself standing on a football field, on the brink of being tackled by someone in a red football jersey. Before he can react, the boy runs right through him. Shadow Mike shudders. It's a sensation he has never grown accustomed to, like a cold wind passing through his bones. He turns around and observes a kid in a blue uniform diving at the boy, taking him out at the knees.

The whistle blows again, halting the game, giving Shadow Mike a chance to get to the sidelines. He runs off the field in the direction of the red team when he hears his own voice yelling, "What kind of B.S. call is that?!" Shadow Mike turns, finding a new version of himself pacing on the opposite side of the field. His arms are crossed, and he clearly isn't happy. The referee runs over to Mike, who appears to be the coach of the blue team, and the two of them argue over the play. Then, the referee returns to the field, and Mike throws his hat onto the ground, evidently having lost the dispute.

Making his way around the perimeter of the field, Shadow Mike keeps his eye on the game. He has always loved football, and this is bringing back memories of his old glory days in high school. Glancing up at the scoreboard, he learns that the home team, Lake Travis, is up by three points.

Walking toward the blue team's benches, he can now read "Austin Westlake" on their jerseys. He must be in Texas. The players, though big, are all young, and Shadow Mike ascertains that this is a high school game. Mike won't stand still, so it's difficult to get a good look at his face, but Shadow Mike suspects him to be in his early forties. He's handsome, muscular, and not wearing a wedding ring.

The whistle blows again, and a yellow flag is tossed into the air. The other side of the stadium roars, and Mike, his face as red as the opposing team's jerseys, screams, "You've *got* to be joking!"

From behind him, Shadow Mike hears a woman call out, "C'mon ref, bend over and look out your good eye!" Amused, he turns around and finds himself face to face with Sailee. Her face is contorted with disgust, but even now, Shadow Mike finds her lovely.

She appears to be about twenty-eight, and her dark blonde hair is pulled back into a ponytail under her blue baseball cap. He wonders what she's doing with the football team when Sailee suddenly sprints past him onto the field. Following her with his gaze, Shadow Mike notices a Westlake player lying on the ground, his team surrounding him. Sailee runs into the middle of the group, dropping to one knee beside him, and bends her ear low to his mouth so that she can hear him over the noise in the stadium. "Huh, apparently she's the athletic trainer," thinks Shadow Mike. "That's a new one."

They escort the injured boy off the field, and in the final two minutes, the Westlake Chaparrals score a touchdown and a field goal to win the game by four points. The elated team makes their way to the locker room where Mike congratulates them on the win but chastises them for playing as sloppy as an In-N-Out Burger. "You'll make up for it on Monday," he tells them. "But until then, enjoy your weekend."

As the last player walks out the door, Sailee comes into the locker room. "Good game, Coach," she says, playfully smacking Mike on the butt. Shadow Mike is astonished. In every universe he has visited so far, he has watched Mike and Sailee meet. But in this timeline, they obviously already know each other.

Mike turns to Sailee. "Thanks, but it would've been better if the ref didn't have it in for our guys."

"Well, that's because you pissed him off in the first quarter," replies Sailee, giving him a friendly nudge. "But no matter. You won, and the boys played hard. By the way, I overheard your speech and was slightly offended by your analogy."

Mike laughs. "Yeah, well, there's nothing messier than you eating a burger animal style. Even while I was saying it, all I could see was that sauce running down your arms and smeared all over your face."

Sailee laughs, punching him lightly in the arm. "Oh my gosh," she exclaims. "That was the worst. It was in my hair and everything!" She looks at her watch. "It's not too late," she says. "Do you want to grab a drink?"

"I can't," Mike replies. "I've got a date tonight."

"Ooooh," says Sailee teasingly "is this a new one?"

"Sure is," he responds, grinning.

"Well then, don't let me keep you." Sailee starts toward the door. "I'll see you at practice tomorrow."

"Which one?" Mike asks.

Sailee rolls her eyes. "Band practice."

"Right," says Mike. "See you there." They turn out the locker room lights and walk out to the parking lot together, where they get into their separate vehicles and drive away.

The next evening, Sailee and Mike show up for practice at a man named Titus' house. From what Shadow Mike can surmise, Titus is both the third member of their band and Mike's best friend from college, the two of them having played football together at Texas A&M. He also discovers that, along with being the varsity football coach, Mike is the physics teacher at Westlake High School, and their band, Dusty Boots, is a southern rock cover band. While they aren't good enough to play on Sixth Street, they get plenty of other gigs around Austin. From their interactions, it's evident to Shadow Mike that the three of them are close.

"So," says Sailee, while she's setting up her microphone, "how was your date last night?"

Mike grins. "It was good."

"Where did you find this one?" Sailee asks. "Is this the girl who slipped her number into your front pocket at our last gig?" She rolls her eyes.

"No," says Mike. "I took her out last week. That was definitely a one and done. I met this one online."

"Poor girl," replies Sailee with faux compassion. "She's probably at home with a broken heart right now. Speaking of online, did you ever give that new Tinder app a try?"

Titus bursts out laughing. "Did you not hear that story?" he asks Sailee.

She shakes her head, looking expectantly at Mike, who rolls his eyes. "It was a disaster," he explains. "I swiped right on this chick whose profile said she was thirty-eight and single. I took her out dancing on Rainey Street, which was fun, except she talked nonstop about herself the entire night. I was planning to just drop her back off at her house, but then she invited me in. I figured, what the hell, isn't that what Tinder's for? And she was hot, so how could I refuse. Afterward, I was coming back down the stairs when Brady, one of my freshman players, walked through the door. It got pretty awkward after that."

Sailee doubles over with laughter. "Are you serious? She was Brady's mom?!"

Mike sighs. "In hindsight, I think she knew exactly who I was, which was why she didn't ask me anything about myself all night. It gets around that team moms are off limits in my book. This gave her plausible deniability."

Sailee shakes her head in disbelief and looks over at Titus, who can't stop laughing. "Look at the bright side, stud muffin," she says, turning back to Mike. "You never have trouble getting the moms to volunteer for things. And forget football. No physics teacher in history ever had so much help with their science fairs." Mike rolls his eyes again, but he's grinning, because he knows it's true.

"What about this new girl?" asks Titus. "Being an old married man, I need to live vicariously through you."

"I think I really like this one," says Mike.

Sailee's eyes widen in surprise. "Really?" she asks.

"Yeah. She seems different. She's quiet, but nice. I'm taking her out again tomorrow."

"A second date?" confirms Titus. "That sounds serious."

"Between football practice, band practice, games, gigs, and grading homework, how do you ever find the time?" Sailee inquires, adding a fake drawl to the end of her question.

"Oh, I make time," replies Mike.

Sailee laughs, but when Titus and Mike leave the room to grab a few beers, Shadow Mike notices how she slumps a little in her seat, looking suddenly crestfallen, and he wonders what that's all about.

CHAPTER 43

O ver the next month, Mike and Sailee see each other nearly every day, but their interactions are limited. Then one afternoon, Sailee walks by Mike's classroom between periods and spots him grading papers at his desk.

"Hey, stranger," she says, poking her head into the room. "I haven't seen much of you lately."

Mike laughs. "You've seen me pretty much every day," he replies.

"It's different, though," she answers, coming in and closing the door behind her. "It's been all work, and I miss you. How are you doing?"

She sits on the edge of his desk, and Mike puts down his pen and looks up at her. "I've been good – just busy. You know how much the team has going on, and I'm teaching both regular and AP physics this year. And Titus has been scheduling gigs for basically every night that I don't have a game. On top of that, I've been spending as much time with Jennifer as I can."

Sailee nods. "It sounds like things are going well there."

"They are. I really want you to meet her."

"Just let me know when and where," replies Sailee.

"How about Saturday?" suggests Mike. Then he pauses, watching her face intently. "And what about you?" he asks. "How are you doing? Are you seeing anyone right now? I'm sorry I haven't reached out more."

Sailee shrugs. "I've been out with a few guys. Tinder is a fascinating way to get a date, but it's definitely more about quantity than quality." She gives Mike a friendly push. "You and Titus have ruined me. Knowing men like you sets an awfully high bar, and no one ever seems to measure up!" She hops off the desk. "Anyway, Saturday's good. It'll be fun to hang out, and I'm looking forward to meeting Jennifer. She must be special if you're introducing her to the family already." She gives Mike a small smile. "What time?"

"How's seven-thirty? My place."

"Perfect. See you then."

On Saturday night, Sailee rings Mike's doorbell at 7:30 p.m. sharp. He opens the door and gives her a hug, kissing her on the cheek before welcoming her inside. She sets her keys on Mike's counter and looks around. "Where's Jennifer?" she asks.

"She's running late," answers Mike. "She's always late. I'm trying to get used to it." Sailee is about to make a comment about how much that would have annoyed him in the past, when the doorbell rings again. Mike answers it, and Titus and his wife, Sheila, walk in.

"Sailee!" says Titus, giving her a hug. "I thought you were bringing your new man!"

"Meh," Sailee replies. "He didn't work out. He started sending me dick pics and that was the end of it. I'm not prude, but c'mon, dude – show a little class!"

Titus laughs, putting his arm around Sheila. "Am I ever glad to be out of the dating pool."

Mike pulls out a few beers and some bourbon and the four of them hang out, talking about the team's last game and the setlist for their upcoming gig. At 8:15 p.m., the front door opens, and Mike jumps up. "That's her!" he says excitedly. Titus and Sailee exchange looks. Neither of them have seen Mike like this in quite a while; not since before he got his heart broken a few years ago.

Mike walks back into the room with his arm around Jennifer and makes introductions. When he gets to Sailee, she sticks out her hand, but Jennifer pulls her into a hug. "It's so nice to finally meet you," she says in a thick Texas drawl. "Mike talks about you and Titus all the time."

Sailee smiles politely and gives Jennifer a once-over. She's young, around Sailee's age, and tiny, with long, skinny legs, big boobs, and big blonde hair. "So very Texas," thinks Sailee. She has never quite fit in with the Texas girls and still feels like a transplant, even though she's been here for ten years.

Soon, they're all standing around eating smoked brisket and drinking beer, listening to Titus and Mike regale them with stories of the wild parties they threw in college – how Titus would jump up on the bar and kill a bottle of Jack Daniels, and Mike would drink tequila shot for shot with the first twelve people who dared. Then Jennifer looks at Sailee. "So how did y'all meet?" she asks.

Sailee opens her mouth to answer, but Mike jumps in instead. "We met at Westlake five years ago," he explains. "When Sailee walked into the gym that first day, I thought, 'Oh great, a girl straight out of Texas Christian. Now I'm gonna have to watch my mouth all the time.' But then she dropped her first F-bomb, and I knew we were gonna hit it off. And then one night, I was leaving the school late, and I heard her singing in the women's locker room."

"I thought everyone was gone," interjects Sailee.

"She had a great voice," Mike continues, "and Titus and I had just started talking about forming a band. So, I asked Sailee if she wanted to join us, and that was that. We've been friends ever since." He gives Sailee a warm smile, putting his arm around her shoulder. "She's like a sister to me." Dutifully playing the role of the annoying sibling, Sailee jabs Mike lightly in the ribs with her elbow until he drops his arm.

Jennifer looks back and forth between them, as if trying to decide if she should be jealous of their relationship or not. Then she turns her attention back to Sailee. "Texas Christian, huh? Are you from here originally?"

"No," replies Sailee. "I grew up in Vermont. But I wanted to get out of the Northeast, and TCU had a great athletic training program."

"Were you an athlete?" asks Jennifer, looking at her skeptically. "Why did you become a trainer?"

"I played soccer in high school, but really, I've just always loved sports."

"That's a lie!" cries Mike. "She's just always loved athletes." He winks at Sailee, who gives him the finger.

"Thanks for throwing me under the bus!" she says with a pretend glare before a grin spreads across her face. "But I can't deny it."

Jennifer is about to reply when Titus interrupts them, handing out drinks, and the conversation moves in a different direction.

Throughout the evening, Sailee observes Mike and Jennifer together. He seems quite smitten, but Sailee's not sure what she thinks about this new girl. She's awfully quiet, every now and then leaning over and whispering something in Mike's ear instead of saying it to the group. It's rather awkward. And she has her hand on Mike continuously – on his leg, or rubbing his back, or running her fingers through his hair. And whenever Mike gets up to leave the room, Jennifer follows. "Like a shadow," thinks Sailee. She seems friendly enough, although Sailee notices that she never says anything positive, and has mostly just complained about her retail job and all the idiots she works with. Which is ironic, thinks Sailee, because Mike is one of the most positive, optimistic, outgoing people that she has ever met. She wonders what he sees in Jennifer, short of her figure – which is extraordinary.

At one point in the evening, Mike runs out for more beer, and Sheila and Jennifer are having a conversation in the kitchen, leaving Sailee and Titus alone in the living room. They're whispering about Mike, and how different he is around Jennifer, when Sailee leans forward in her seat. "So, Titus, you were quite the ladies' man in college. What made you settle down?"

Titus laughs. "We were on our first date, and Sheila put her hand on my face, looked at me with those big blue eyes, and said 'You and I are going to make some beautiful brown babies.'"

Sailee snorts her drinks. "She said that on your first date? What did you say?"

"I said, 'Well, honey, what are we waiting for? Let's get started!' and that was that."

Sailee is thoughtful. "So, you just knew right away?" she inquires, her voice tinged with sadness.

Titus puts his hand on her knee. "I did," he states, "but that's not true for everyone." He gives Sailee a questioning look. "Is there a reason you're asking?"

She begins to answer, but then Mike walks in the door, and they both jump up to help him with the booze, and the conversation is forgotten.

Weeks go by, then months, and Titus and Sailee see less and less of Mike, which is unusual. Even when he dated before, he always made time for them. Normally after band practice, the three of them would hang out, but lately Mike has been taking off right away. "Places to go, people to do," he jokes, walking out with a wave.

Then one evening, Titus stops him. "What's up with you, man? You're different."

"What do you mean?" asks Mike.

"You're never around anymore."

Mike rolls his eyes. "You sound like Sailee. You guys see me all the time. I haven't given anything up, I'm just trying to balance it all. Having a serious girlfriend is different than the random banger. And I really like this one." He grins. "But you're right. I miss hanging out with you guys too."

Titus looks at Mike curiously. "You could always bring Jennifer over, and then we can hang out with both of you."

Mike nods nonchalantly. "Yeah, that's an idea. It's just that she's shy. And you know I love you guys, but you can be a little... overwhelming... to someone who doesn't know you."

"Overwhelming?" Sailee jumps in, feigning offense. "Not us. Never!"

Mike laughs, grabbing his keys and giving Titus a one-armed hug, then picking Sailee up and spinning her around a few times before setting her back down on the ground. "I'm just giving her time. Don't worry, she'll come around." Then he walks out the door.

Titus and Sailee look at each other. "Do you think it's me?" she asks him. It wouldn't be the first time one of Mike's girls has been threatened by their friendship.

"I don't think so," says Titus. "Because I never see him anymore either."

Six months later, Sailee is sitting at her kitchen table, cell phone in her hand. She was just offered the job as the athletic trainer for the women's soccer team at Baylor University. She had applied on a whim. She loves working at Westlake, but athletic trainers at the high school level don't make much money, and she thought perhaps getting another job offer would give her some negotiating power. Although she doesn't think she'll accept, Sailee is thrilled to have been offered the position. She's getting ready to dial Mike and tell him her news when she gets a text from him. *Hey – can you meet me at the bar at 9 p.m. tonight?*

Something in his message seems off to Sailee, especially since Mike hasn't asked her to meet him out in months. She types back, *Sure thing. See you there.* Suddenly, she's nervous, harboring the tiniest sliver of hope that perhaps he and Jennifer have broken up.

Looking at her watch, it's already 8:15 p.m. She runs upstairs and puts on makeup, doing her best to fix her hair, which has a giant kink from being in a ponytail all day. Then she hops in the car and heads for their favorite bar, which is about twenty minutes from her apartment. She knows Mike hates it when people show up late.

When she arrives, he's already there and has ordered their drinks. Sailee sits down on the stool next to him and they face each other, their knees casually touching. "That was great timing!" she says cheerfully, trying to sound as normal as possible despite the pounding of her heart. "I was just about to call you when you texted me. I have something to tell you."

Mike's expression is serious. "Really?" he responds. "That's funny, because I have something to tell you too."

Sailee gives him a sympathetic smile, feeling more and more confident that her assumption was correct. "Okay," she replies. "You go first."

Mike takes a deep breath. "So… I proposed to Jennifer last weekend, and she said yes."

Sailee's heart stops. Wait, what? Mike is still talking, but she has stopped listening. She was not prepared for this and can feel her insides crumbling. It's been hard watching Mike date so many women over the years, but she always maintained hope that she would be the next girl. The last girl. But if he's getting married, there will be no next girl. There were so many times she almost said something to him – when he had called her after a breakup, or in a moment where they were sharing some of the most intimate parts of themselves. But she had always wanted him to realize it himself. And now her chance is gone.

Mike is still speaking, and she tries to focus on what he's saying. "The wedding's going to be a little unconventional," Mike continues, oblivious to Sailee's shock. "Jenn and her brother are really close, so she's going to ask him to be a 'bridesman…'" he makes air quotes with his fingers, "… and I want you and Titus to be my groomspeople." He gives her a big grin. "So, what to do you say?"

Sailee's head is spinning, and she thinks she might throw up. Did Mike just ask her to stand up beside him at his wedding? He's looking at her expectantly, and she clears her throat, trying to hide the emotion in it. "I… I'm sorry, Mike… but… I-I can't," she stammers.

Mike looks at her, dumbfounded. "Wait – you can't?" he asks, obviously confused. "Why not?"

She ponders how to answer. "Um… it's too fast," she says, conjuring up all things she has wanted to say to him over the last several months as she watched he and Jennifer get more serious. "You hardly know her. And I don't think she's right for you. I mean, I know she seems great now, but all those little quirks that you find mildly annoying, like how she's always late to everything, are going to drive you crazy someday. And all that negativity, and the way she complains about everyone all the time – someday, when all the butterflies are gone, all that negativity will be directed at you. And you don't really have a lot in common when you think about it—" At the look on Mike's face, she stops talking.

"You mean to tell me," Mike says, an edge forming in his tone, "that you won't be in my wedding because you don't think that Jennifer is right for me? With all we know about each other and have been through together, you don't trust me to make that decision for myself? Even if you don't like Jennifer, I would have thought you'd still support me as a friend." His expression is a mix of incredulity, hurt, and anger.

Sailee looks at Mike, her heart breaking, and knows she has to tell him the truth. "No," she says quietly. "That's not really why." She raises her eyes to meet his. "It's because… I love you, Mike. I've been in love with you for years. And I always believed that eventually, once you went through all the wrong girls, that you'd realize we're perfect for each other. You're my very best friend in the world, and I would do almost anything for you… but I can't be there and watch you marry someone else. I just can't. I'm not strong enough." Her voice cracks on the last sentence, and she desperately blinks back the tears that are forming in the corners of her eyes. She will not cry.

Mike is staring at her, speechless. "You love me?" he says. Sailee nods, and he runs a hand uneasily through his thick, dark hair. "I… I don't even know what to say to that, Sailee," he continues. "You're like family to me. You're my best friend, but—"

Sailee puts her hand over his mouth. "You don't have to say anything else," she replies. And in that moment, she knows what she has to do. "And it's okay, because, well, I'm moving away."

Now Mike's eyes widen in surprise. "What do you mean, you're moving?" he asks.

"That was the thing I wanted to tell you," replies Sailee. "Baylor just offered me a job as the athletic trainer for their women's soccer team. I'll be moving to Waco next month."

Mike shakes his head, trying to take in this information. "Well, congrats," he states, not sounding at all like he means it. "That's great for you. That will be a good job. I'm just surprised, is all. I didn't even know you were looking to do something else. I thought you loved it at Westlake."

"I do," says Sailee, her voiced filled with emotion. "But it's a good opportunity, and I can't pass it up." Silently, she adds, "And you're the reason I can't stay." With that, she rises from her stool and exits the bar.

CHAPTER 44

After that, things are awkward whenever Mike and Sailee run into each other at school, both of them trying to act normal, but neither really knowing how. Typically, Mike would have gone with Sailee to Waco to find a new apartment, but she went alone. She could have asked Titus but was afraid he'd see right through her façade and suspect the real reason for her moving. And she doesn't want that. He's one of her closest friends, but she's not ready for him to know. Not yet. It's still too raw.

On her last weekend in Austin, Mike and Titus come over to help Sailee load the moving truck, and the tension between them is unmistakable. Titus eyes them both curiously, but keeps his mouth shut. When the last box is loaded, he slides the door closed, then turns and hugs Sailee, tears in his large, brown eyes. "I'm gonna miss you, girl. What are we going to do without you?"

Sailee gives him a tight squeeze. "This is Austin," she reminds him. "You'll have no problem finding a singer to replace me."

"I wasn't talking about the band," he says quietly. "I was talking about *us*." He gestures between himself and Mike. "What are *we* going to do without you."

Sailee does her best to give him a bright smile. "You'll just have to visit me in Waco. It's not that far." Titus nods, gives her another hug, then gets into his truck and drives away, leaving Mike and Sailee alone.

Mike walks over to her, clearing his throat. Sailee doesn't know what to do with this awkwardness between them. They have always been so comfortable with each other. But then she went and screwed it all up, and she hates herself for it. If only she had kept her mouth shut, tried to be the best friend he thought she was. Now she has lost him twice.

"I'm going to miss you, Sailee," he begins. "I really am. And I'm sorry…" Not knowing what else to say, he wraps her in a hug, and she dissolves in his arms, hating how familiar his embrace is.

She pulls away and looks up at Mike, her eyes shining with unshed tears. And then, giving in to the impulse that she had repressed so many times before, she puts her hands on his face, stands on her tiptoes, and kisses him gently on the lips.

She can feel the surprise in his body, but he doesn't pull away from her. But neither does he take her into his arms or deepen the kiss, and she lets him go. She has no more words to say. She wants to pull herself together, to put on a happy mask and let their last moment be like old times, but she doesn't have it in her. Instead, she gives him a faint smile, says, "It's been fun, Coach," climbs into the moving truck, and drives away.

Shadow Mike watches in bewilderment. "What just happened?" he wonders aloud. He has observed Mike and Jennifer together, and even though this Mike is quite different than other versions he has witnessed, it's obvious they aren't a good fit. And he can't believe that any version of himself, knowing Sailee, would willingly let her go. Especially after kissing her. Shaking his head in disgust, he follows Mike as he gets into his own truck and heads for home.

Time passes, and nothing has seemed right to Mike since Sailee's departure. Work has been weird, and he's not a fan of the new trainer they hired to replace her. And despite auditioning dozens of new singers, he and Titus haven't found anyone to take Sailee's place in the band. Her absence has left a gaping hole in his life. At first, he was angry with her, for telling him that Jennifer wasn't right for him, then for admitting she loved him and ruining their friendship, for kissing him, and then for leaving. But he could never stay mad at Sailee, and now he's furious with himself for never noticing how she felt about him.

And he's beginning to notice other things that he hadn't before – like how negative Jennifer always is about other people, how everyone around her is seemingly "an idiot." And how, other than sex and going out drinking, they don't have a lot in common. She never comes to his games, has no interest in science, is the opposite of punctual, and hates sharing food – all things that had been on his list of "must haves" on his dating profile. But he has continuously overlooked these with Jenn because she was kind to him, and intriguing, and knock-out gorgeous. He loves Jenn. He really does. And he doesn't want to admit that maybe Sailee was right.

Just the thought of her makes his heart ache. Sailee, his best friend who loved being right, who always made him laugh, who loved sports, and was passionate about working with high school kids even though the money was crap. Sailee, whose level of competitiveness was second only to his own, who was always there for him when he needed someone to talk to, who teased him endlessly but let him be himself, never trying to control or change who he was. He misses her. Wasn't she the girl that he compared all others to, and the reason he let so many go?

Mike tries to distract himself from thinking about her, busying himself with work, wedding plans, and moving in with Jennifer, despite the warnings bells that have begun going off in his head. And then, one night about a month before the wedding, he tells Jennifer that he's going out to meet Titus and a few other guys for some drinks, and she gets angry at him, saying that she isn't getting married just to be left alone all the time. And so he invites her to join, but she refuses that too, insisting that he spends enough time with his friends. She wants to stay home together and watch that new show she's been telling him about.

And in that moment, Mike catches a glimpse of their future – of them sitting in front of the television together, with nothing to talk about, both of them drinking away their misery and regret. And he realizes, finally, how big of a mistake he's making. So he tells Jennifer that he's sorry, but that things aren't going to work out between them, and that he'll move his stuff out of her place that weekend. And when she throws her ring at him, calling him an asshole and a coward, he leaves it on the kitchen table before walking out the door and never looking back.

As soon as he's in the car, Mike picks up the phone and automatically begins dialing Sailee's number, but then he stops, calling Titus instead. "Hey, brother," Titus says when he answers the phone. "You're still coming out tonight, right?"

Mike smacks his forehead. He had completely forgotten that the events of the evening all began with his going to hang out with the guys. "Uh, yeah," he responds. "But I have something to tell you. Do you mind if we have a beer and then ditch the rest of the gang?"

"Of course, man." Titus replies.

So, after a drink and a game of pool, Mike and Titus head down Sixth Street to a speakeasy where they can talk. Titus looks at Mike inquisitively. "What's up with you? You're awfully quiet tonight. Is everything okay?"

Mike looks at him. "I called off the wedding," he states matter-of-factly.

Titus's eyes widen. "You did what? What the hell, man! That's not what I was expecting."

Mike takes another swig of his drink. "She's not right for me," he explains. "I don't know why I didn't see it sooner…" and he goes on to list all the things he has come to realize over the past few months.

Titus nods in agreement. "I knew it," he says, when Mike completes his list. "You weren't the same around her. And then you were never around. I wanted to say something, but I didn't think it was my place—"

"There's something else," Mike interrupts. Titus stops speaking, waiting for Mike to continue. "I...I think I'm in love with Sailee." There's a long pause, and then Titus bursts out laughing. "Dude, what's so funny?" asks Mike, irritated by his response.

"Sheila has been saying forever that you guys should get together," explains Titus. "Every time you dumped a new girl she'd say, 'Good, maybe he'll get a brain in that damn head of his and ask Sailee out this time.' And I was always like, 'Nah, they're just friends.' But the more I watched you, the more I could see it. And then you started dating Jennifer, and it got serious so quick, and it seemed like that was the end of that. Sheila was pissed, man. I mean, she likes Jennifer and all, but she thinks Sailee's way better for you." He gives Mike a grin. "And I have to agree."

Mike shakes his head. "I have been such a dumbass," he says.

Titus's face is suddenly serious. "Have you told her yet?"

"Told her what? That I love her?"

"Yeah, and that you called off your wedding!"

Mike thinks back to that earlier moment in his truck. Even then, he hadn't yet fully realized that he loves Sailee. He just knew that she is the first one he always wants to call, no matter what. Good news or bad. She's his best friend, and yet, she's so much more. And he wants her to be even more still. And that kiss... He hadn't wanted to admit what that did to him, how perfect her lips felt against his own, how comfortable it was, and the bolt of electricity it had sent through him. It had taken everything in his power not to wrap her in his arms. He could have kissed her forever. "No, I haven't," he finally replies, realizing that Titus is still sitting there, waiting for an answer.

"Well then, you should go do that."

An hour and a half later, Mike is sitting in the driveway of Sailee's new townhouse in Waco. It's one in the morning, and all her lights are out. Sitting here now, he's overwhelmed with guilt for all the things he missed the past several months: house hunting with Sailee, helping her move in, popping open a bottle of champagne and celebrating the fact that, with the new job and moving out of Austin where the cost of living is crazy, she can finally afford her own place, no longer having to live with roommates. But he missed all those things because he had been blind. Blind and stupid. He doesn't even know how things are going for her at Baylor. He had started to call Sailee after her first day, but then wasn't sure what to say, so in the end he had hung up before he finished dialing.

Now that he's here, he's still not entirely sure what to do. He doesn't want to knock or ring her doorbell at this hour. Sailee has an overactive imagination, and she'd probably greet him with a baseball bat to the head. So instead, he dials her number. It rings, and rings, and rings. "Please don't let it go to voicemail," he pleads.

On the fifth ring, she answers. "Hello?" Sailee's voice is groggy, and his heart jumps at the sound of it. God, he has missed her.

"Hey, Sailee," he says. "It's Mike."

He can hear her shuffling things around, trying to find a clock. Then he sees a light switch on in an upstairs room. "Mike?" she repeats, a little more alert. "It's late. Is everything okay?"

That's a loaded question, he thinks. Everything is not okay, and at the same time, everything is great. It has been a rollercoaster of a day, and yet, for the first time in as long as he can remember, he knows he is exactly where he is supposed to be. "Yeah, he answers. Everything's good. I'm actually sitting in your driveway. Can we talk?"

He sees her peer out the blinds, then look again, as if not believing her eyes. "Yeah," she says. "Give me a second and I'll come unlock the door."

A minute later, she's standing in front of him wearing gray shorts and a Baylor tank top. She has bed head, and no makeup on, and she is absolutely beautiful. Gesturing for him to follow her inside, she leads him into the living room, which is sparsely furnished with a futon and a giant beanbag. "Sorry," she says, "I'm still saving for furniture."

Mike sits down, and Sailee begins to sit on the floor when he taps the spot next to him, and she joins him on the futon. "I missed you, Sailee. I'm sorry I didn't call you sooner."

She gives him a confused look, and he can see that she's still not entirely awake. "You came all this way in the middle of the night to tell me that?" she asks.

"Well, no," he explains. "I really came to say that…" And what he intends to tell her is that she had been right about Jennifer, about everything, and that he had broken off the engagement, and, most importantly, that he realized he's in love with her. But he's nervous and excited, and what comes out of his mouth instead is, "…you were right, and I love you."

For a moment Sailee just sits there, stunned. And then that mischievous grin that he knows so well spreads across her face. "Wow," she replies. "I'm not sure which of those two things I like hearing more!"

And before she can say anything else, he puts his hand tenderly on her cheek. "I mean it," he says. "I love you, Sailee Roberts. I'm sorry it took me so long to figure it out. But I am all yours if you'll have me." And this time, when she leans forward to kiss him, he takes her into his arms, and can feel her melting into him. And at the same moment, Shadow Mike, smiling, melts away.

CHAPTER 45

May 11

In her downtime, Sailee has been trying to find the best medium for processing her emotions. She doesn't want to burden Mike with her anger and fear if he's listening and trying to get back to her. She considered writing a song, but everything she composed seemed rote. Then she tried writing a letter expressing what he means to her, but it felt lackluster.

She's at his bedside once again, making another attempt to articulate her feelings when it comes to her: a poem! She grabs a pen and paper and scribbles furiously. Twenty minutes later, she stands up and leans against his bed, still favoring her uninjured leg. Holding the paper with her right hand, she places her left hand on Mike's thigh. It's always better when they're touching. Then she reads aloud.

"When There Are No Words

I tried to find a word that describes life with you,
But letters and syllables just don't come close to
Capturing what I feel inside –
Every word leaves me dissatisfied.

I've tried "full," "overflowing," "gorged," and "bursting,"
But they aren't the performance, just merely rehearsing.
It seems no word will ever make do,
When it comes to depicting my love for you.

So I thought I'd find a phrase to express how I feel,
But nouns and verbs still don't reveal
The depth of emotion I want to convey –
It's like longing for sex, but there's only foreplay.

You're "the warmth of the sun on a cool spring day,"
Or "the soft gooey center of a chocolate soufflé" –
These are things I could say as a last resort,
But all of the phrases forever fall short.

If words won't suffice, then maybe a smell –
Like freshly folded laundry or chocolate caramel,
A brand-new book or rolls that are baking,
The cinnamon tea we sip as we're waking,

Newly cut grass, or air thick with rain –
Maybe one of these scents could begin to explain
Why my knees are so weak and my face is aglow.
But even with these I don't think you would know.

I thought maybe I could define it by sound,
A particular vibration that would be so profound.
The crack of a baseball or waves on the beach –
But even deep-throated laughter comes out like a screech.

If words, smells, or sounds can't spell it out,
How then, my love, will you ever find out?

I realize now, the only thing I can do —
Spend every last second just showing you."

Her voice cracks with emotion on the last line.

"That was lovely," says a voice from behind her. "Did you write it?"

Sailee turns and sees a nurse entering the room. She blushes slightly. She didn't expect anyone to hear it but Mike. "Yes," she admits.

The nurse comes around the other side of the bed and checks Mike's chart. "I didn't mean to eavesdrop, but I didn't want to interrupt you either. He's fortunate to have you. This is the best thing you can do for him, even if it doesn't feel like much."

Sailee is surprised by how these words affect her — it feels like a weight has been lifted. She doesn't feel like she's doing anything. Nothing is making a difference. But somehow, this small encouragement is just what she needed to hear.

"Thanks," she replies. "I'd do anything for him."

"I know," says the nurse. "Keep doing it." With that, she slips out of the room, leaving Sailee and Mike alone again.

CHAPTER 46

In and out. In and out. He's in a universe, he's out of it. Shadow Mike has lost count of the number of timelines he has dropped into. Some weren't so different from his own life, while others he can hardly believe – like the one where he and Sailee met at NASA and spent six months together on a space station. That was one wild ride.

Sometimes he lingers in a universe for what seems like an eternity, while other times he's in and out swiftly. The duration often depends on how the Mike and Sailee of that universe cross paths and how quickly they fall in love. Sometimes Shadow Mike observes the entirety of their relationship, while other times it's more of a synopsis. Time has lost its constancy, slowing down and speeding up unpredictably.

It's certainly entertaining, this endless stream of movies where he is the star, but it's also unbearably lonely. He never used to talk to himself, but now finds he's doing it regularly. A byproduct, he supposes, of not being seen, heard, or felt. He has only himself to confide in, and he's growing weary of his own company.

Then, suddenly, light breaks through the darkness, and he finds himself standing in an atrium, sunlight pouring in through a wall of windows. Enormous banners hang from the ceiling, displaying the words "Aviation Global." The sight of them triggers a sense of déjà vu, and Shadow Mike wracks his memory. Ah, yes, he's been here before. This was one of his earliest "stops" when he first entered the multiverse. People move about, and a small stage is set-up in the corner, just as he anticipated. Curious. Throughout all this time, he has never been pulled back into the same universe twice.

"C'mon," he mutters aloud. "I don't need to watch this again." Memories of this timeline come flooding back. He was here for what seemed like forever. Mike and Sailee were so adamant about just being friends, it took years before they finally acknowledged their chemistry and embraced the possibility of something more. And then they went through all that bullshit with the lawsuit. It was excruciating to witness, although he admired their resilience and unwavering commitment to each other.

So why is he here again? He closes his eyes, hoping that when he reopens them, he'll either be back in the void or somewhere else entirely. Whoever or whatever is running this train will have to realize their mistake. If there's some lesson he's meant to grasp from this experience – and he's unsure what it is, apart from admitting that he was absolutely wrong about there being a "one in infinity" chance that he and Sailee end up together – he certainly won't learn it by watching this repetition.

He ventures another glimpse. Alas, he's still here. Having no other choice, Shadow Mike observes the speeches, watches Sailee introduce herself to Mike, and witnesses them at the bar in Chicago. "Did I miss something the first time?" he wonders. Some small spark? Is that why he's here again? But everything seems unchanged.

He watches them at the game, observing the tension between Sailee and David, and noting Sailee's visible relief when David leaves early. As soon as he is out of sight, Sailee transforms into a different person – lighter, bubblier, and more flirtatious. Was she like this before? If so, he must've been so engrossed in watching Mike that he missed it. He watches Mike carry a drunk Tiffany to the car. No change there.

Sailee joins the softball team, and Shadow Mike keeps a vigilant eye on their developing friendship. Everything appears the same, yet occasionally he catches glimpses of things he doesn't recall seeing before:

Mike's lingering gaze as Sailee walks away, the grin she gives him when something inappropriate is said, the way he winks at her. It's driving Shadow Mike crazy. How could he have missed this the first time?

Then Sailee confides in Mike about her new job offer, seeking his advice. Shadow Mike senses an unfamiliar emotion emanating from Mike – perhaps sadness at her departure, and... excitement? But the conversation unfolds just as he remembers. Mike assists her in negotiating her contract terms, and she is appreciative of his guidance. End of story.

Now it's Sailee's final week at AG, and they gather at Matt's after practice. They drink three bottles of wine, get into a push-up competition, and have a dance party in the kitchen. When they eventually glance at the clock, it's late. Very late. Mike and Sailee exchange knowing looks and grimace, aware that they'll both face trouble when they get home. As Mike recounts one last story from his college days, Sailee remarks, "I wish I had known you in college. I would have liked you!"

Mike replies, "If I had known you in college, I would have gotten you into a lot of trouble!" He winks at Sailee, and she giggles flirtatiously. "Someday, you and I are going to get hammered together, and I'll tell you some crazy stories," he promises. Sailee says she looks forward to it.

Shadow Mike looks on, baffled. He definitely doesn't remember this. The push-up competition? Yes. The dance party? Yes. The overt flirting? No.

Sailee gathers her belongings and hugs Matt, giving him a kiss on the lips. Then she hugs Mike, and he wraps his arms tightly around her waist, lifting her off the ground. "Be careful," he says, "and text me when you get home so I know you made it okay." She agrees.

A week after Sailee starts her new job, Mike sends her a text. *I've been traveling this week, but would like to take you to dinner when I get back. You've been a great asset to the company, and I want to say thank you. Are you free?*

She replies: *Sure. Sounds like fun!*

Mike types back: *I want you to be able to enjoy yourself and relax, so I'll pick you up at your house at 5:30 p.m. when I leave the office.*

Sailee replies: *Sounds good. See you then.*

When Mike pulls into Sailee's driveway, she is ready and waiting. "You look great," he compliments her as she hops into the passenger seat. She's wearing skinny jeans, ankle boots, and a leather jacket.

"Thanks," she responds. "You don't look so bad yourself!" Mike is dressed in jeans and cowboy boots, and sporting a blue button-down with the sleeves casually rolled up to his elbows. He looks relaxed in his sunglasses, with one hand resting on the top of the steering wheel.

Shadow Mike enjoys seeing them together, knowing how this friendship blossoms into a beautiful love. However, something is off, and he feels uneasy as he watches them drive away. He just can't put his finger on the reason why.

CHAPTER 47

Apart from the one time when they had drinks in Chicago, Mike and Sailee have never been alone together. They've always been with colleagues or the team. Although they find it slightly awkward at first, they eventually settle into comfortable conversation.

Their first stop is a bar, and Sailee asks if this is where they get hammered and Mike starts telling crazy stories. He laughs, surprised she remembers that. "Well, it was," he replies. "But I have to be the responsible driver. Don't worry, though. I'll still tell you a story or two." He grins at her. "However, I do think we should begin the evening with a shot of tequila." He requests two shots of Patron and a couple of lime wedges. The bartender brings them over, and Mike places the saltshaker between them.

"What am I supposed to do with the lime?" Sailee asks. "Do I squeeze it into the tequila?" Mike looks at her quizzically. Is she messing with him?

"Uh," he says, "you suck on it."

"Oh," she replies, looking confused but picking up the lime. "Now?"

He gives her another funny look. "Have you never done a shot of tequila?!" he asks her, dumbfounded.

"Nope," she replies. "I've done other kinds, but never tequila."

Mike can't believe they're having this conversation. Sailee is an un-apologetic flirt, drinks like a pirate, and swears like a sailor, but in some ways, she seems so innocent. She's a conundrum. A smart, sexy conun-drum, he thinks, then shakes his head to clear his mind from that line of thinking. "Um," he says, trying to focus on the conversation at hand, "you have to remember the three steps: lick it, slam it, suck it."

"Are we still talking about the tequila?" Sailee asks coyly.

Shadow Mike is watching in utter bewilderment. Yes, they had dinner following her departure from Aviation Global, but it did *not* go like this. They shared a bottle of wine and discussed Sailee's experience at AG, how she balanced music and sports growing up, and how Mike learned to play the banjo. He surely would have remembered the te-quila shots, the sexual innuendo.

Then it dawns on him. This is *not* the same timeline. It's a parallel universe where they're making similar choices to the other, but not exactly, which explains the side comments and subtle flirting he didn't remember seeing before. And it appears the paths are beginning to diverge. Leaning forward, he observes intently as Mike instructs Sailee on the art of shooting tequila.

"First," Mike says, "you sprinkle salt on your wet hand so that it sticks." He demonstrates. "Then, you lick the salt, slam the shot, and suck the lime. Got it?"

Sailee nods. "Lick it, slam it, suck it," she repeats. "I could write a great drinking song about that!" She licks her hand and shakes some salt onto it.

"Are you ready?" Mike asks.

"Yes, sir."

"Okay – cheers to you, Sailee," he says, raising his tequila. "Best of luck in your new career." They clink glasses, then lick the salt, down the tequila, and suck the lime.

Sailee makes a face. "That is… sour," she says, smacking her lips. "But really good. Let's do another one!" Mike agrees and orders another round.

After two more shots each, Mike settles the bill, and they drive down the street to have dinner at a nearby Thai restaurant. He entertains Sailee with wild stories from his college days, and she shakes her head in amazement. "My life has been so tame in comparison," she says. "Not that I haven't made mistakes…"

"We all have," replies Mike, intrigued by her comment. Sailee talks a lot – chatters constantly – but he realizes now that it's been mostly small talk. And though they've been slowly building a friendship, he really doesn't know much about her life. He'd like to change that.

"You've always said how much you loved your job," he begins. "Why are you leaving?"

Sailee thinks for moment about how to answer. "People have always told me that I'd both excel in sales and enjoy it. Since this opportunity practically fell into my lap, it seemed silly to turn it down."

She pauses. "But honestly, it came down to money. Recruitment doesn't pay very well. I'm the sole income-earner in my house, and this new position is a substantial pay increase for me. David doesn't work, which is a story in itself, and despite budgeting and doing everything I can to save, it always feels like we're pinching pennies, and I'm tired of it. Hopefully, this will alleviate some of the stress, and maybe we won't argue as much. I constantly feel like the bad guy, always saying no to everything, but we simply can't afford it all, and I refuse to get into credit card debt. I've always lived within my means, and I always plan to. It'll just be nice to have a bit more means."

Mike is both surprised and pleased that Sailee has opened up to him. He reaches across the table and places his hand on hers. "I didn't know that about your life," he says, "and I'm so impressed that you manage all of that. It's a heavy burden to bear." He withdraws his hand but can see that Sailee appreciated the gesture and the sincerity behind it.

"It is," she replies with a sigh. "So, I'm really hoping I enjoy this new job. Anyway," she says, suddenly brightening, "that's enough about me. I want to know about you! There's something I've been meaning to ask you for a while."

"Sure. What is it?"

"David never wants to come with me to anything. You've probably noticed that he rarely shows up to our games and never joins us afterward. I can tell that Tiffany is also introverted, and even though she's quiet, she still attends stuff with you. How have you guys managed to make it work? Any insights that could help me out?"

Mike frowns. It's clear Sailee thinks it's a lighthearted question. He contemplates how to respond and decides to be honest. "Actually," he says slowly, "I don't have any tips for you because I haven't figured it out. Tiffany comes to things, but I get hell for it at home afterward."

He pauses, wondering how much more he should reveal. That's probably sufficient, but it has been a burden for so long. He knows it's the tequila talking but decides to speak his mind anyway. "We put on a good show in public, but we're not happy. We're miserable, actually. We've been miserable for a long time. I should never have married Tiffany. I was young and stupid, and ignored the advice of my parents and closest friends. I knew it was a mistake within the first year, but then my daughter was born, and the twins came shortly after, so I stayed for the kids. I kept hoping I could improve things, but I've finally come to the conclusion that I can't. I have to stop taking responsibility for Tiffany's happiness. That's on her, and she has made it abundantly clear that I'll never make her happy."

He stops. That was definitely oversharing, but he has never voiced those thoughts before. Ever. And it is liberating to be honest for a change. He's tired of putting on a façade for the world. Mike looks down at his plate. "When I was a lifeguard, one of the things we learned was that if the person you're trying to save is going to drown you, you have to let them go and save yourself." He looks up at Sailee, his green eyes full of pain. "And I'm drowning."

Sailee places her hand on his arm. "I understand," she says quietly. "I really do. And I'm sorry."

Suddenly, the pieces fall into place – why Sailee enjoys being on the road so much, her reluctance to go home after practice, the excuses she makes for David's absence, and why she seems less buoyant when he's around. She's not happy either.

"Why don't you leave?" Sailee asks bluntly.

"I've been working on it," says Mike. "But it's easier said than done. It's daunting to think about dealing with the properties, assets, lawyers... We've discussed getting divorced so many times, but actually saying, 'I'm pulling the trigger' is a whole different story."

Sailee agrees. "I know. I've been trying to figure it out as well. It's a shame that getting out of a marriage isn't as simple as getting into one. If the process of getting married were as difficult and expensive as getting divorced, people would think twice before tying the knot." Mike nods, acknowledging the truth in her words. "So, are you just going to continue like this until you get the courage to do it?" she asks him.

"I don't know. Are you?" Mike redirects the question back to Sailee.

"If I'm being honest... probably." She shrugs, looking down at the table. "Unless..." she pauses, clearly contemplating whether or not to voice her thought. "...unless we do something to speed things up."

Mike sits up straighter. "Like what?"

Sailee remains silent, but when she looks at him, there is fire in her eyes. Mike could melt under the intensity of her gaze. He should let it go, he thinks. Change the subject. Excuse himself to the restroom or accidentally spill his wine. Any distraction that would allow them to stay what they are – just friends. But the words spill out before he can stop them. "Like... maybe you and I make things a little less miserable for each other?"

Sailee blushes. "That's what I was thinking."

She can't meet his eyes now. Mike's stomach tightens, sensing that Sailee shares the same mix of nerves, excitement, lust, and guilt. He knows it's wrong, but he has been unhappy for so long that he no longer cares. "So, how do we do that?" Mike asks.

"I don't know," Sailee replies. "Let's play it by ear." And just like that, the moment dissipates, and they resume talking about their favorite sports teams, their favorite foods – anything and everything.

Another two hours pass before they exit the restaurant. Mike opens Sailee's door, then settles into the driver's seat and starts the car. It's a cold night, and he lets the vehicle warm up for a moment while they sit facing each other, engaged in conversation.

Shadow Mike flashes back to a similar scene in another timeline, to the universe that started out so much like this one. Back to their first date, more than a year from now, when they're in the car together after dinner. He watches this Mike and Sailee come together, just like before, and knows the kiss will be perfect. But his feelings about it this time are not the same.

"No, no, no, no, no..." he utters loud. "It will all come together in due time. Just be patient! *Stop!*" But his plea falls on deaf ears. He's thinking of all the things they were accused of in that other timeline – the lies told, the damage to their careers, the hurt it caused them both. They were accused of *this,* despite their innocence. What lies ahead for them now? Shadow Mike buries his face in his hands. If only he could get through to them.

Looking back, he recalls how he felt in that other universe – how he'd wanted Mike to disregard his marriage and sweep Sailee off her feet; how restlessly eager he was as he watched them inch ever so slowly toward one another. But now they are barreling towards each other like a high-speed train, and he realizes he was wrong. This isn't the way.

There were numerous instances with his own Sailee when he was tempted to push the boundaries. But she was engaged, and he respected that, even though he didn't want to respect it. He has often wondered what might have unfolded if he had made a move. Would she have responded like this Sailee? Now, observing the present circumstance, he's glad he waited.

He knows, statistically, that they won't make a good choice, the right choice, every time. They've made mistakes in other universes. He has made his fair share of mistakes in his own. Yet, it's still difficult to witness, especially knowing that it could be different. Perspective is paramount, and Shadow Mike reminds himself that this version of Mike doesn't know what he knows. He is acting on desperation following years of anger, hurt, and disappointment. The same can be said for Sailee. Life has posed challenges for them both... he's just afraid they are going to make it a whole lot harder for themselves.

Shadow Mike follows them, reluctantly at times, over the next several months, as Mike and Sailee seize every opportunity to steal moments together. And while they are driven by their passion and their need for affection, their yearning to be wanted, and their desire to be loved, their connection goes beyond physical intimacy. They spend countless hours engaged in conversation, baring their souls to each other, and Shadow Mike can feel their hearts opening. He sees them learning to trust again as they share their most painful and humiliating stories with one another – things they've never been able to share before. And with each revelation, a burden is lifted. Admittedly, that burden is sometimes replaced by guilt, knowing that what they're doing is wrong. Yet, this wrong thing is somehow changing them for the better. Shadow Mike recognizes the complexity of it and is as torn by it as they are.

CHAPTER 48

Six months pass, and Mike and Sailee are in South Carolina. It's been nearly a month since their last secret rendezvous, and Mike has arranged for a beachside cabana where they meet after wrapping up their respective conferences. The wind is blowing, and while it may be warm by Vermont standards, there's a bite in the air. Exchanging their swim gear for jeans and sweatshirts, they snuggle together on the day bed beneath the canopy, seeking refuge from the breeze.

Their lust has not dissipated, but with it has grown a deep-seated love and friendship. They dream of a future together. Mike has received the same promotion in this universe and is in the process of re-vamping his office, creating that new role that Sailee would be perfect for. Not only is she exceptionally suited for the position, but the prospect of seeing her every day is tantalizing. Meanwhile, Sailee is miserable at her new job; her only consolation being her ability to occasionally meet up with Mike in a different city. But he can't hire her now. He knows better than that.

Sailee interrupts his train of thought. "What are we going to do about them?" she asks, leaning against his chest. Mike's body radiates heat, and she is like a barnacle, clinging to him for warmth.

"About who?"

"David and Tiffany."

Mike lets out a sigh. "I don't know. Our relationship was over before I ever kissed you, but I've been trying to figure out how to extricate myself without causing too much drama. We've been together for so long that I think Tiffany assumes we'll just continue living like this indefinitely. She says she hates me, yet she'll never actually leave. She's too dependent on me."

Sailee nods, understanding the struggle. David is dependent on her as well. It's difficult to leave someone in such a vulnerable position. She doesn't love him, but she does care deeply about his well-being. David isn't particularly kind, supportive, or affectionate, but he isn't a bad person. And he doesn't deserve this. That's why she has to do something about it, even though she hasn't figured out how.

"David and Tiffany would be a perfect match," she says, laughing. "Neither of them likes to work, or enjoys socializing, and they'd both be content staying home, watching television, and ordering take-out. We should arrange a spouse swap! How do we set them up with each other?"

Mike chuckles. "They would indeed," he replies. "Unfortunately, I don't think either of them would take the suggestion well!"

As if on cue, Sailee's phone rings. It's David. Whenever he calls, a sick feeling settles in the pit of her stomach. She's unsure if it's due to guilt or because he usually only calls to yell at her about something. She doesn't answer. Then her phone buzzes, and she reads the text: *You need to call me back NOW.* The queasy feeling intensifies, and her heart pounds. Every fiber of her being is telling her that this is it – the gig is up.

She calls him back. "Hey Dave," she says, trying to sound normal. "What's up?"

"Where are you?" he asks, his voice seething with anger.

"I'm at the conference in Hilton Head," she replies innocently.

"Who are you with?"

"What do you mean? A bunch of salespeople from my team are here—"

"Don't fuck with me, Sailee," David interrupts. "You know what I mean. Are you there with Mike?"

Sailee's breath catches in her throat. How could he know that? She attempts to play dumb. "Mike who?"

"I'm not stupid, Sailee!" David yells. "I know you're there with Mike Black. Tiffany just called me. She said Mike left his iPad at home, and she saw a message from you saying you were at the beach and would meet him there. What the hell is going on? Is he there with you? You better not lie to me, you slut."

Sailee can't breathe. She feels like she's going to vomit, and her mind is racing. What should she tell him? She has lied to him so many times it has become second nature. But now, she can't think of anything to say.

Mike watches her, concerned. Though he can't make out the words, he can hear the anger in David's voice, and he's fairly certain his name was mentioned. He feels like he's been punched in the gut. They both knew this day would come but had convinced themselves they could keep up the charade until they found a way to end their marriages gracefully, without drama, fighting, or hurting their spouses. What fools we were, he thinks.

Sailee is floundering. Mike shrugs and silently mouths, "Just tell him." It's the only way forward now. They'll face the consequences together.

Sailee takes a deep breath. "Yes," she replies. "I'm with Mike."

David is silent. Sailee waits...and waits... until the silence becomes unbearable. "I'm so sorry, David," she says softly.

"Don't you *dare* tell me you're sorry, you lying whore," hisses David. "You're not sorry. You're just sorry you got caught."

"I never wanted to hurt you..." her voice trails off. It's true, but it sounds so pathetic now.

David falls quiet again, and Sailee can tell that the truth, the betrayal, is setting in. She's certain his anger will resurface, but this – this is worse. Her heart aches. Part of her wants to rush home this instant, kneel before him, and beg his forgiveness, try to make it work… again. But she knows, in the end, it won't make a difference.

"How long?" he asks.

"Does it matter?" she counters. She doesn't want to admit – *can't* admit – how long she's been cheating on him, lying to him. More silence. This time, Sailee doesn't break it.

"Why?" David finally asks, his voice cracking. The pain in his tone shatters her. "What did I do…? I tried so hard… we were so young…" He can't get it out. She can tell that he's struggling to hold himself together, but he's falling apart. Sailee feels her insides crumbling. She longs to reach through the phone and hold him, to tell him it was all a mistake, a terrible dream, to take away his pain. She never wanted to hurt him like this. She has been so selfish.

She's deciding how to respond, but he doesn't give her a chance. "So, now what?" he asks, his voice hardening. "What are you going to do?" He's regaining his composure, holding onto the anger to shield himself from the bone-shattering pain.

"I don't know," she replies. "I need some time—"

"You don't get time," David says firmly. "You don't get to live two lives anymore. You have to grow up and make a choice. No more lies. Are you coming home on the next flight to work this out and face the consequences of your actions? Because there *will* be consequences. Or are you staying?"

This is the moment. Whatever she chooses, it will define the path she's on now. There's no turning back. It's the moment she has been dreading, when she has to speak the words aloud that she has rehearsed so many times over the past sixteen years. Words she never imagined she would utter when she walked down the aisle all those years ago. She was just twenty-one then. So young. Too young.

"I'm sorry, David," she says, and it's true. Her heart is breaking. She thought she had experienced pain before, but she has never known this kind of anguish. "I'm not coming home. I want a divorce."

He doesn't say anything for so long that Sailee thinks he hung up on her, but then she hears the muffled sob. This has been a long time coming, but she knows he still wasn't expecting it. Finally, his voice hoarse, he says, "You're really leaving me? For Mike?"

Tears stream down Sailee's face. "I'm not leaving you for Mike. I'm leaving you because we should have divorced years ago. We've tried so hard to make this work, and we both know that we failed every single time. The wounds are too deep. There's too much scar tissue. Our marriage isn't failing because of Mike. He's a byproduct of an already broken relationship. But I *am* sorry. I never should have betrayed you. I should have had the courage to do this earlier, but I wasn't brave enough. I'm sorry…" She has said the words so many times that they're starting to lose their meaning.

David's voice is hard again. If Sailee weren't completely numb, she would get whiplash from the emotional rollercoaster. "Fine. When you come home on Wednesday, I'll be gone, and you can pack your shit and get out. I want you out of the house by midnight. I don't care what you do or where you go. You can go to hell for all I care. But I don't want to see you."

"We need to work through some things—" she starts.

"I don't give a shit," he interrupts. "You figure it out." Click.

Sailee drops the phone in her lap. She has been trying to hold herself together, but now the dam breaks, and her body is wracked with violent sobs, her shoulders heaving. She thinks she might vomit. She's torn between an enormous sense of relief – it's finally over – and more pain than she ever imagined possible. What God has joined together, let no man put asunder. She thinks about the definition of "asunder": apart, divided, into pieces. Her heart is like her marriage – asunder, shattered. She has broken so many of her vows – to love, honor, obey (she always hated that one), cherish, be faithful – and now the final one. 'Til death do us part.

Mike gazes at her sympathetically, tears welling up in his own eyes. He reaches out to touch her leg. "Don't…" she chokes out, and he pulls it away. Assuming she wants to be alone, he starts to rise. "Please… no…" she manages, prompting him to sit back down beside her.

Finally, after what feels like hours, when she has no tears left, Sailee takes a deep breath, hiccups, wipes her eyes and nose on her sleeve, and looks up at Mike. Her face is full of agony. "I guess that's that," she says, sniffling. "I knew it would be hard, but I never imagined it would hurt like this." He reaches out again, and this time she leans into him, burying her head in his shoulder. "I'm sorry if I snot all over your shirt," she mumbles.

"I don't care about that," he responds softly. "Just you. And I'm sorry. I'm so sorry for everything."

She shakes her head. "We made our choices together."

Mike knows his turn is coming. Sure enough, twenty minutes later the call comes from Tiffany, who has obviously talked to David. She has lost her mind – screaming, swearing, and crying – and he can hardly make sense of what she's saying. "I HATE YOU!" she screams. "Fuck you! Fuck your soul to hell. You don't get to do this to me, you asshole. You're coming home right now, and you're never going to see that bitch again. You will never talk to her again, you are never traveling without me again, and you are most definitely quitting the softball team."

Mike sits there quietly. In some ways, this is easiest. This is a normal night for him. The only difference is that this time he knows he deserves it. He had hoped to bring things to a quiet end, with respect and civility. But he had been weak, unsure of how to broach the subject and not wanting to deal with the repercussions. And now, here he is. He can already sense that this is going to be a long and acrimonious process.

When Tiffany's tirade finally subsides, Mike says quietly, "I'm sorry, Tiffany, but I'm done. I'm tired. I gave you everything I had for almost thirty years and received nothing in return. No love, no affection, not even a kind word. I can't do it anymore."

"I'm going to ruin your life," Tiffany spits into the phone. "I'm going to destroy your career. Everyone is going to know what a cheater you are. You always thought you were such a hotshot, but you are *nothing*, and I'm going to make sure you stay that way for the rest of your life."

The situation is deteriorating rapidly, and Mike quietly hangs up the phone. He's having difficulty processing. This was so long in coming, but then it all happened so fast. He looks at Sailee, managing a weak smile. "Well," he says, "now what?"

"I don't know," she replies. "But I'm here for you, always." She reaches out her hand and takes his. What a mix of emotions – relief, love, pain, sadness, guilt – it's almost more than a body can take.

The divorces are difficult, as they always are, but these are particularly brutal. Word spreads, of course, and Tiffany makes good on her promise, doing her best to tarnish Mike's reputation and sabotage his career. Luckily for him, while having an affair is frowned upon, as Sailee is no longer employed at AG, there are no professional consequences.

Their families struggle with the news. Not the divorces, which they suspected were coming. But they do not approve of the affair. Over time, however, they come to accept the relationship, observing how happy Mike and Sailee are together, witnessing their love and the way they consistently treat each other with kindness. It becomes difficult to ignore the positive influence they have on one another, despite the less-than-honorable circumstances of their start. Once the divorces are finalized, Mike and Sailee wait a year for the gossip to settle down, then have a small wedding ceremony with a few friends and family in attendance.

In an unexpected and delightful twist, David and Tiffany do end up together. Tiffany emails David one day, saying she has no one to talk to and asks if he wants to get coffee. He almost says no, but then thinks, "Why not?" They can commiserate over their betrayals. And they hit it off immediately, their bitterness being the initial connection, but they soon discover how much more they have in common. When Mike and Sailee hear about it, they share a good laugh.

"I always knew they would be a perfect fit!" Sailee chuckles, sincerely glad for them both. "I hope they're as happy together as we are!"

Shadow Mike shakes his head, feeling mixed emotions. Looking forward, he sees Mike achieving his career ambitions and becoming the CEO of Northrop Grumman, while Sailee quits her job in order to maximize their time together. In the grand scheme of things, this Mike and Sailee endure far less suffering than their counterparts who tried so hard to do the right thing. It seems unfair. "But life isn't always fair," he reminds himself. Nevertheless, he takes solace in the fact that they ultimately find each other. And they live a long and happy life, although their happiness will forever carry a tinge of guilt. With this final reflection, Shadow Mike dissipates into the enveloping blackness.

CHAPTER 49

May 13

Today marks their four-year wedding anniversary. A mere four years that somehow feels like forever, in the best sort of way. Life prior to Mike seems like a distant world, almost like a dream, and Sailee finds it hard to believe that she almost settled for someone else.

They had planned to be in Italy today, and Sailee put off cancelling the flights and hotel until just two days ago, holding onto hope that Mike would wake up and she could whisk him away.

But alas, it's not to be. At least not this year. Instead, she brings him a dozen red roses, placing them in a vase on the small table in the corner. "Happy Anniversary, my love," she whispers, planting a tender kiss on his forehead. "You have changed my life." She perches on the edge of his bed, her favorite spot now that she has the use of both her legs again. Pulling out her iPad, she begins scrolling through photos from their wedding and honeymoon.

In truth, they had two honeymoons. Initially, they planned to get married on October 5, 2019, in a small ceremony at their country club in Redwood City, then fly to Santorini for a week. The honeymoon was already booked – a stunning villa in Oia overlooking the Aegean Sea. But in mid-April, they decided not to have a wedding after all. Mike's dad's health issues prevented his parents from being able to attend, and it didn't seem right having a wedding without them. Moreover, the guest list kept expanding, filling up with obligatory invitations. In the end, they decided to elope.

As a result, they concluded there was no reason to wait until October. Why not the following month? Mike had a speaking engagement in Barcelona, and they could venture to another European destination afterward – Venice, Tuscany, or perhaps even both!

And that's precisely what they did. Sailee had already purchased a dress, although its completion was scheduled for October. She promptly called the shop, asking if she could expedite the order. "How soon do you need it?" the woman asked.

"Three weeks?" replied Sailee sheepishly.

"Well, honey," the woman had said, "for a price you can have anything."

Sailee bit the bullet, paying the exorbitant fee to have the dress finished in record time. She has never regretted her decision. The dress, a light cream in a sleek silhouette, exuded elegance. Its neckline featured a pearl collar, and a graceful fabric cascade descended from her shoulders, highlighting the low back. A black ribbon tied at the nape of her neck, adding a whimsical touch. "Business in the front, party in the back," she had joked. It was elegant, modern, and unique, and she felt absolutely stunning in it.

They decided to get married in a vineyard, finding an Italian-style villa in Santa Rosa. The pergola, nestled between the meticulously manicured lawn and the vineyard, offered a charming setting. While weekends in wine country are typically reserved for weddings years in advance, their Wednesday afternoon elopement allowed them to secure exactly what they wanted, even with less than a month's notice. It was an idyllic occasion, with only an officiant and a photographer present. They exchanged vows under the pergola and spent the ensuing hours strolling through the vineyard, capturing cherished moments with the photographer. Without the obligation of entertaining guests, they were able to focus solely on one another, etching every detail of the day into their memories.

Afterward, they retired to a nearby Bed and Breakfast. They consummated their union, then donned pajamas and stretched out on the bed, eating a block of cheese and drinking a bottle of Brunello di Montalcino while calling their parents and recounting the events of the day.

Upon concluding their calls, dinner was served in their suite. They ate their fill and retreated back to bed, where they snuggled up and watched Top Gun until they could no longer keep their eyes open.

The following morning, they drove to San Francisco, catching a flight to Barcelona. While Mike delivered his presentation, Sailee napped in a hotel near the airport. From Barcelona, they took another flight to Venice, where they spent a week exploring the island city, followed by a week at an agriturismo just outside San Gimignano in Tuscany.

However, their Greece trip was still booked. So when October arrived, they decided to take a second honeymoon. They ended every evening on their balcony, sitting in the hot tub with a glass of wine, listening to an accordion player serenade the setting sun. And as the last of the sun dipped below the horizon, the gathered onlookers would erupt in cheers and applause. The memory still evokes goosebumps for Sailee.

Concluding her photo journey, Sailee sets down the iPad and gazes at Mike. Time has not diminished his handsome features, nor her love for him. A small sigh escapes her lips. They had promised to read their vows to each other on every anniversary. Although circumstances prevent Mike from reading his, a promise is a promise. Sailee pulls up the document and begins reading aloud:

> *"My dearest Mike,*
> *The road to this moment has not been smooth or straight.*
> *It was your kindness, friendship, and unconditional love*
> *that brings us here today, and I am so incredibly grate-*
> *ful for you. I once read that intimacy is being able to*

share your innermost thoughts and secrets without fear of judgement or retaliation. This was something I both lacked and craved in my life, and it's a gift you've given me above all else.

So, Mike, from now until death parts us:

I promise to make decisions that continue to foster that intimacy.

I promise to be your best friend and your confidant.

I promise to be your biggest champion and cheerleader, in good times and in bad.

I promise to treat you with kindness and respect, whether we're with others or alone.

I promise to adventure with you and rest with you.

I promise to treat our life together as a journey, not a destination.

I promise to love and embrace your family as my own, and welcome you wholeheartedly into mine.

I promise to build a life with you together as one unit, always working to better the lives of those around us.

I promise communication, commitment, and an equal partnership in all things big and small.

I promise to be open and honest with you.

I promise to trust you, and be trustworthy.

I promise that I will get angry, but that I will also get over it, and I will not harbor disappointment, grudges, or resentment.

I believe that love is an action, and I promise that I will make the choice to love you every day, even if the feeling is not there.

I promise to laugh with you often, and cry with you when necessary.

I promise to care for you emotionally and physically, in whatever ways you may need."

She stops, choking on those last words. She clears her throat, trying to keep the tears at bay.

> *"I promise that I will work harder at our relationship than anything else.*
> *I promise I will read these vows to you every year on our anniversary, and sometimes when we simply need a reminder."*

The tears are flowing steadily down her cheeks now, but she's determined to finish.

> *"I don't know what the future holds, or how easy or hard it will be to keep these promises over the years, and I will probably fail every now and then. But I promise that when I do, I will admit my wrong and try again. You have brought more joy to my life than I dreamed possible, and I can't believe I get to be your wife from this day forward. I love you."*

Her last words are but a whisper. Sailee lays the iPad down and slides off the bed. She remembered the gist of her vows but reading them now to the lifeless man lying before her is more than she can bear. Overwhelmed with emotions, she collapses into the chair beside his bed and buries her face in his mattress, sobbing.

Outside the curtain, hushed voices can be heard. "This isn't a good time," one voice says. "We should come back later." There is the sound of retreating footsteps, and all is quiet again.

Once her tears have subsided, Sailee raises herself upright. It feels incomplete, she thinks. While Mike may not have the ability to read his vows to her, he would if he could. How she longs to hear those heartfelt words spoken in his beloved Southern drawl. But reading them, and knowing that he meant them because he lived them every day, will be enough. It has to be enough. She retrieves the iPad and reads:

Sailee, you're the love of my life, and my life is better because of you.

First and foremost, you're my very best friend. You were my friend before we were anything else, and you will always be my best friend above all else. You bring sunshine and joy to those around you, and you brought that to my life when I needed it most. You are a treasure, and I promise to treat you as such for as long as I have mind and body to do so.

We both know that life is full of unexpected turns...

"You have no idea how true that is," she says out loud to him.

... but there's no one that I'd rather face those turns with than you, my love. You checked every box on a wish list of qualities I'd dreamed of in a partner, and added to that list in ways that I never knew was possible. Throughout our friendship and ever evolving relationship, I've been careful to only promise things that I can deliver. So it is in that spirit that I write these vows.

I promise:
- *To treat you as my best friend first, and to share all of myself and what I have to offer with you.*
- *To give you all the freedom to take care of yourself, yet provide you with the comfort and security of knowing that you have someone else in your life that will always go the extra mile to take care of you.*
- *To be the person you can share everything that you think and feel with, and to listen with an open heart and absent judgement, to the best that I can as another human being.*
- *To engage you in conversation when our opinions differ or my feelings are hurt, and be open and*

> *honest about how I feel, no matter how difficult the topic, until we determine how to move forward together.*
> - *To accept you for who you are and celebrate our similarities and differences.*
> - *To openly debate you on topics small and large, and whenever you're right, to say, "you're right and I love you." Because as long as one of us is right, we both win.*
> - *To tell you I love you before I close my eyes at night, and the minute my eyes open in the morning, unless, of course, it is physically not possible to do so.*
> - *To hug and kiss you every day that I can.*

Sailee pauses. Mike has read these vows to her four times now, but she never paid much attention to the caveats. Today, they stand out to her more than anything. Even in his coma, Mike hasn't broken any of his promises. He always made it clear that he would do these things *as long as he is able.* "Oh, my love," she says. "You thought of everything." She continues reading.

> - *To blow off steam when I need to, knowing that I'm in a place that's safe to vent and share my frustrations.*
> - *To remember that small acts of kindness are ways of showing your love for someone, and finding new ways to show you my love every day.*
> - *To remember that you love me even when you're mad at me, or I'm mad at you.*
> - *To not take you for granted, and I expect you to tell me if you're feeling that way, and I will do the same.*
> - *To do my best to make you feel like you're the most beautiful and cherished woman in the world.*

- *To work harder at our relationship than any-thing else.*
- *To be human and make mistakes along the way, and rely on you to help me work them out with you.*
- *To read these vows to you every year on our anni-versary, or whenever we need a reminder.*
- *To entrust you with my heart, and make sure you know every day that you can entrust me with yours.*

I love you, Sailee. Thank you for being my wife.

Having finished, she places the iPad on the table and gently clasps his hand in both of hers. "Thank you, Mike," she whispers to him. "Thank you for loving me the way you do." She wipes her eyes, takes a sip from her water bottle, then settles back up on the bed and opens the book she's been reading aloud to him. "*A Man Called Ove*, Chapter 5..."

She's still reading to Mike an hour later when a nurse peeks through the curtains. After a few moments of whispered conversation on the other side, they whip open, and four nurses enter the room, carrying a small cake. "Happy Anniversary!" they call in unison.

One of the nurses, Jessica, adds, "We knew this would be a diffi-cult day for you, and we wanted to do something special. Mike is so lucky to have you, and your presence in the ICU brightens our days. You truly are a ray of sunshine."

Sailee is deeply moved by the gesture. "That's incredibly kind," she says. "Will you stay and enjoy a slice of cake? I can't possibly finish it all by myself!"

Josh, another nurse, produces paper plates, napkins, and some plastic forks from behind his back. "No need to worry," he assures her, "we came prepared!"

Though their time is limited, the nurses provide wonderful com-pany, offering a much-needed respite. They ask Sailee about her wedding, and she shares a few pictures, recounting the last-minute elopement and the bouquet that Mike surprised her with – roses and calla lilies. Her favorites.

She tells them the story of how, after they were declared husband and wife, Mike swept her off her feet for a kiss, followed by a high-five, eliciting laughter from the photographer and officiant. Sailee grins. "I suppose most couples don't do that," she admits. She tells them about the breathtaking sunset over the vineyard, the sky ablaze with hues of orange and red, the same as her bouquet. She recounts the cheese and the wine, the pajamas, and Top Gun.

"Now *that* sounds perfect," remarks Josh, clearly unaffected by the other wedding details.

Sailee, now lighthearted, regales them with some of her other favorite Mike stories. She recounts a Florida vacation they took with her parents. They had been discussing how Mike was dragging Sailee out of bed early to go fishing, even though the seas were predicted to be slightly rougher than she preferred. Mike had said, "When we get home, I'm going to give Sailee a 24-hour boning. That should help." The table fell into stunned silence.

"Excuse me?" Sailee responded, mortified. "First of all, my parents didn't need to hear that. Second of all, I believe that's something we should discuss first!"

Her parents burst into laughter, while Mike looked at Sailee, perplexed.

"What are you talking about?" he asked. "I always give you one before we go fishing!"

"No wonder she doesn't want to go fishing every day!" her dad managed to interject through tears of laugher.

Mike appeared even more bewildered. "What on earth is so funny?" he asked. "I'm giving you a Bonine – like a Dramamine – so you don't get seasick!"

"Oooooh," they all chimed in unison.

"That makes way more sense," quipped Sailee.

"What did you think I said?" Mike inquired.

"I thought you were announcing to my parents that you were going to give me a 24-hour bon*ing!*"

Sailee can barely tell the story because she's laughing so hard, and everyone is in stitches. But soon their time is up, and as the nurses depart to attend to their other patients, Sailee hugs each of them. "Thank you. Truly. You have no idea what this meant to me."

Once they're gone, Sailee squeezes Mike's hand and playfully declares, "Well sir, when you wake up, I'm going to take you up on that 24-hour boning. Just you wait!"

CHAPTER 50

Shadow Mike is engulfed in darkness once more, his mind spinning from the whirlwind of timelines he has just visited. Without a moment to collect himself, he spots the first rays of light breaking on the horizon, signaling his next adventure. It has become a puzzle for him, seeing how fast he can figure out where he is, when he is, and who he is. Initially overwhelmed by the multiverse hopping, he now approaches each new timeline as a game. He seemingly can't escape it, so he's trying to make the most of it, which is how he always approached life. He supposes he can maintain the same attitude even in death.

Scanning his surroundings, he realizes he's in an airport. He likes airports as they offer quick clues about his location. Glancing at the screen behind the ticket counter, he reads the date: June 25, 2015. Today is Sailee's birthday! She's turning thirty, which means he must be forty-three in this universe. Finding a clean-shaven version of himself sitting near the gate, engrossed in work on his laptop, Shadow Mike murmurs, "I guess I'm not the captain in this universe."

He looks back at the flight board. The time is 8:00 a.m., and he's apparently flying from Sydney to Los Angeles. Having followed himself on many flights, he knows the long ones can be particularly arduous, and judging by the number of people already gathered at the gate, he predicts there won't be an empty seat available.

He keeps a watchful eye out for Sailee, wondering if she'll be a flight attendant again. Perhaps this Mike will impress her with his refined wine order, and when everyone's asleep, Sailee will give him a "come hither" expression, and he'll ravish her in the bathroom. That would be quite the universe. Or maybe it won't even take that long. Maybe she'll see him sitting at the gate, be instantly smitten, and drag him into the family bathroom. It wouldn't be their first time engaging in such airport escapades, nor the wildest thing he's witnessed from them.

Shadow Mike shakes his head. "Stop it!" he chastises himself. But damn, he misses sex. Lately, it's the only thing occupying his mind. No, not sex, he realizes. He's missing the closeness and intimacy of lovemaking. Being an observer for so long, he yearns for human touch, human connection.

The crew approaches the gate, pulling Shadow Mike from his reverie, and he scans their faces but doesn't find Sailee among them. Then the gate agent gets on the loudspeaker, announcing that they'll begin the boarding process in a few minutes. Mike puts his laptop away and takes out his phone, pulling up his boarding pass. Shadow Mike peers over his shoulder, noting his assigned seat: 4D. Mike (whom he jokingly dubs Baby Face Black) rises, grabs his carry-on, and joins the line. Shadow Mike looks around again for Sailee, but there is no sign of her.

He follows Baby Face onto the plane, watching him stow his suitcase in the overhead bin before taking his seat. Mike turns on his screen and is browsing the movie options when a flight attendant approaches. "Would you care for champagne or orange juice?" she asks, offering him a glass from the silver tray she's carrying. Mike selects the champagne. Shadow Mike can tell by the flight attendant's flirtatious smile that she finds Mike attractive, but Baby Face is oblivious.

An attractive young black woman passes by. "Excuse me," she says, tapping Mike's arm, "are you famous by any chance?" He smiles and assures her that he's not. Shadow Mike exhales in relief. Being famous is nothing but a hassle. "Well, you look like you could be!" the woman remarks before continuing to her seat, leaving Mike grinning in her wake.

The plane is nearly boarded, and there's still no sign of Sailee. Shadow Mike navigates through the economy cabin, scanning each row in search of her. "Maybe she's the pilot!" he muses, turning back towards the cockpit. And that's when he spots her. She's the last one to board, and he can tell she has been running. Even red-faced and disheveled, she's beautiful.

Shadow Mike smiles. He always loves seeing Sailee for the first time. Sometimes she's old, sometimes young, most often she's somewhere in the middle. Her hair has been short, long, all shades of blonde, brunette, highlighted, and in one timeline, even red. She has been skinny as a pole, super muscular, average build, or sporting some curves. She's always lovely – her eyes big, bright orbs taking in the world with curiosity and a touch of skepticism. And while today marks her thirtieth birthday, she looks more like a twenty-five-year-old.

Brushing her shoulder-length blonde hair away from her face, Sailee scans left and right, then drags her suitcase down the far aisle and places it in the overhead bin above 4F. Then, flopping down into the seat beside Mike, she wipes the sweat from her forehead. Glancing up, Mike smiles politely, then goes back to what he's doing.

The flight attendant approaches, offering Sailee champagne or orange juice. "Um... orange juice, please," Sailee says loudly, taking the flute off the tray. She turns to Mike, who's now looking at her, and raises her glass to him. "Cheers," she says. "To not missing the flight." She has a big smile, and Mike notices how it lights up her entire face.

"Cheers," he responds, raising his now half-empty glass back to her. "Close call?"

"Too close," Sailee retorts. "I really suck at jet lag and have been screwed up all week. And then I stayed up far too late last night. I was so out of it this morning that I didn't hear my alarm go off." She wipes her brow again and laughs. "At least I got my exercise in!"

"Sounds like you needed champagne," says Mike.

Sailee laughs. "I don't do bubbles. They give me the hiccups, and that's the last thing I need on a fourteen-hour flight!"

"No bubbles?" Mike repeats. "How about soda?"

She shakes her head no.

"Seltzer?"

No.

"Beer?"

No.

"So what do you drink?"

"Wine, mostly," she replies with a laugh. "And water, when I re-member. And tea. *So* much tea."

He laughs. "Well, that I understand. I'm a tea drinker myself."

Sailee smiles at Mike, then focuses on getting herself situated, pushing her pillow and blanket down toward her feet before perusing the menu.

"Just an FYI, they're out of the chicken," Mike says, leaning over toward her.

"Ugh," replies Sailee, annoyed. "That's what I was going to or-der. Though I'll probably be asleep before they serve dinner anyway. There's something about the engine noise – I sleep like a rock on air-planes." She pauses to take another sip of her orange juice. "I wrote a haiku about it on the flight over," she continues. "Care to hear it?"

"Uh, sure," Mike answers, amused.

Sailee closes her eyes and recites dramatically,

> *"Engine lullaby –*
> *a constant whirring white noise*
> *singing me to sleep."*

She opens her eyes and looks at Mike expectantly.

"Very nice," he remarks, thinking that while her poem was lovely, he never did understand the point of haiku. "Are you a poet?"

"No," replies Sailee. "I just dabble." Mike nods, unsure of what to say. He's getting ready to put on his headphones and start a movie when she asks, "What were you doing in Sydney?"

"I'm working on a project for the concert Hall in Melbourne," he explains. "When they renovated it several years ago, they messed up the acoustics, so I'm getting it back to where it needs to be. Since I'd never been to Australia before, I decided to make a trip of it. I flew into Adelaide, drove the Great Ocean Road to Melbourne where I met with the rest of the engineering team, then flew up and spent a few days in Sydney, and now I'm flying home."

Sailee's eyes widen with excitement. "You're working on Sater Hall?" she exclaims excitedly. "That's great news! It really needs it. What exactly do you do?"

"I'm an engineer," Mike replies. "More specifically, an acoustician." Before Sailee can respond, he asks, "And how about you? What brought you to Sydney, and why do you know so much about Sater Hall?"

"I'm a pianist," explains Sailee. "I was performing with the Sydney Philharmonic this week."

Mike's jaw drops. "Seriously? That's incredible!"

"It's a good gig," she admits. "Although, to be honest, I don't particularly enjoy performing."

"You're a concert pianist and you don't like to perform?" he asks incredulously. He finds that hard to believe.

"Yeah," she says sheepishly. "Don't get me wrong – I love playing the piano. It's my passion. I've been performing since I was a kid. I played my first recital when I was four years old. But unlike most of my peers who thrive on the adrenaline rush, I get incredibly nervous, to the point of becoming physically ill sometimes. I always manage to pull it together once I'm on stage, but the day of a performance, I'm a wreck!" She laughs.

"Was there ever a time when you didn't get nervous?" he asks curiously.

"Not that I can recall," she responds. "When I was little, like four or five, they asked me to play the offertory during the evening service at our church. Now, you have to understand that no more than twenty people ever came to the evening service. But this was my first 'public performance' so to speak…" she makes air quotes with her fingers, "…and I practiced and practiced. I had this short little piece mastered. I asked my mom if she would come sit with me at the piano, but she said no, that I was a big girl and didn't need her.

"When the time came, I confidently marched up to the piano, hopped up onto the bench, and began playing. I played through the song once, and when I didn't see the ushers return to the front, I played through it again. And then again. And then *again*. When I started the fourth time, my mom came up to see what was going on. Still playing, I had tears streaming down my face, and I asked, 'Mama, are they done? I can't see over the piano.' She says she felt like the worst mother in the world. She came and sat next to me, told me they were finished and reassured me that I'd done a great job, gave me a big hug, and walked me back to my seat. Everyone applauded, but I was so embarrassed. Ever since that incident, I've always felt nervous playing in front of people."

Sailee shrugs. "But I kept doing it. I competed throughout high school. I'd throw up, then go on stage and perform, come off the stage, and puke again. It was a truly delightful experience." She laughs at her own sarcasm. "And then, just to torture myself further, I decided to major in music in college. I pursued a bachelor's degree in music composition, hoping to steer away from performing, but that didn't happen. I was accepted into Julliard for a master's in performance, and here we are. I've made a career out of something that makes me sick. How's that for nuts?!" Sailee takes a deep breath. "Sorry. That was a really long-winded answer to your question."

Mike chuckles. "Where did you perform?" he asks.

"In Australia? At the Sydney Opera House. In the concert hall. I played Grieg's Piano Concerto in A Minor. It was a dream come true for me, and I didn't even puke!" she says proudly.

Mike laughs. "Congratulations! Was this your first time in Australia?"

"No," she replies. "I actually lived in a small town called Toormina, about five hours north of Sydney, for a year after college."

"Doing music?"

"No," she answers. "My ex-husband (I got married right out of college. It was stupid.) got a job over here. It was a terrible year. His job was dreadful and I couldn't work on our visa, so I was home alone all the time. When we decided to move back to the States, I applied to Julliard and was accepted. He got into a graduate program in Tennessee. He didn't want to put his life on hold for a year to follow me to New York, and I didn't want to follow him to Tennessee and spend another several years in limbo while he pursued his career. So we split.

"We were only married for a little over a year and we were both broke, which made the divorce fairly straightforward. Fifty percent of nothing is nothing. My parents didn't approve – they thought we should have tried harder to make it work, but I have no regrets. All we did was fight. It was horrible." She pauses. "Sorry, that was probably oversharing. I ramble when I'm tired."

"I don't mind at all," Mike says truthfully. "Hopefully this isn't impolite, but do you mind if I ask how old you are? It seems you've experienced a lot in a short period of time."

Sailee grins. "Not at all. I'm twenty-nine. No wait – I'm thirty! Today's my birthday!"

"Well, happy birthday!" he says, raising his now empty glass to her. "You certainly don't look it!"

She taps her empty glass against his. "I get that a lot," she replies. "On one of my first tours, when I was twenty-five, I was in the hotel pool and got hit on by a fifteen-year-old who thought I was his age." She shakes her head. "It was depressing." Mikes laughs.

Sailee asks, "Since you basically know my entire life story, how about you tell me yours?"

"I'm a lot older than you," replies Mike. "It'd take a while."

"We do have fourteen hours!" she retorts.

"There really isn't much to tell…"

But she looks at him eagerly, so he goes on to share about his family and growing up in the mountains, the sports he played, and how he was being recruited to play Division I football at Yale until he got injured his senior year.

"You went to Yale?" asks Sailee, impressed.

"Well, no." Mike replies. "They were recruiting me but I didn't go. I went to Virginia Tech instead." He shakes his head. "I didn't think I could afford it, so I never completed my application. I didn't realize that being valedictorian and a first-generation college student from a low-income family meant that I wouldn't have to pay anything. I wish I knew then what I know now."

Mike and Sailee talk all throughout the dinner service, discovering they have much in common. They both hold motorcycle licenses, share a love for music, enjoy traveling, and appreciate good food. Several times, they find themselves saying the same thing simultaneously. Noticing that Mike isn't wearing a ring, Sailee inquires if he's married.

"I'm not," he answers. "I was engaged once to my high school sweetheart. I proposed the summer after we graduated from high school. But she dumped me my sophomore year of college, which, in hindsight, was definitely for the best. We were too young and not a good match." Sailee nods, understanding. "Since then, I haven't found anyone I wanted to spend a significant amount of time with. I've been focused on my career and have great friends. I've dated casually, but no one has ever really captured my attention."

"Do you want kids?" Sailee asks. She realizes she's being nosy, but Mike doesn't seem to mind.

"I don't know," he replies. "I didn't think I did, but as I've gotten older, I find myself considering it more. I suppose it would depend on meeting the right person. You?"

"I don't know either," Sailee answers. "I always thought I'd have a large family, but the year I was married made me realize the importance of being with a like-minded person to raise children. Then my career took off, and I can't imagine being on tour pregnant or with a baby. So, I'm unsure. I have a niece who's the joy of my life. She's three years old and amazing. She's already rock-climbing and kicking my butt at anything athletic. She calls me her 'best girl' and has me wrapped around her little finger. I think I'd be content just spoiling her for the rest of my life."

"She sounds awesome. What's her name?"

"Charlie." Sailee takes out her phone and shows Mike a video of her niece, wearing a red velvet dress, climbing a wall and traversing the ceiling. "Can you believe she's three? That's their living room. My brother has turned their entire house into a jungle gym."

"Lucky kid!" Mike exclaims.

The lights in the cabin are dimmed, making it difficult to carry on a conversation without leaning in close to one another. "I'm going to get some sleep," says Sailee, lowering her seat down into a bed. Though she had hardly been able to keep her eyes open when she first sat down, talking to Mike gave her a boost of energy. Now that the cabin is dark, she feels her exhaustion again.

Sailee sleeps for the remainder of the flight and is awoken by the flight attendant nudging her, saying they're preparing to land and that she needs to return her seat to its upright position. She rubs the sleep from her eyes and looks over at Mike, who's watching a movie.

"Did you sleep at all?" she asks.

"A little," he replies. "I don't sleep well on planes."

"That's a shame," she remarks. "How many movies did you watch?"

Mike does a mental count. "Six," he responds.

"Wow," says Sailee. "That's a lot of movies!" Then she checks the time. "It's always strange when flying from Australia to the United States. You get to relive the same day. On the bright side, it's my birthday again!"

Mike chuckles. "Happy Birthday... again! How do you feel?"

"Not a day older than yesterday!" Sailee exclaims, laughing at her own joke. "Is Los Angeles your final destination?"

"No," Mike replies. "I have a four-hour layover until my flight to Raleigh-Durham."

"Is that where you live?" Sailee asks, realizing she hadn't asked before.

"Yes. Well, technically I live in Chapel Hill, but I work in the research triangle park. How about you?"

"I live in Manhattan," she replies. "But this is my final stop for now. I'm playing in LA this week, and San Diego next week. I'll be more than ready to get home."

"I'd love to hear you play sometime," says Mike.

Sailee ponders this. "I don't get to North Carolina very often, unfortunately, but I'll be performing in New York a fair bit this fall. Do you ever come to the city?" she asks.

"I'm there a few times a year for work," he replies.

"I'll give you my number," Sailee remarks, pulling out her phone. "Let me know the next time you're in the city. I'd enjoy getting together."

"I'd like that too," Mike responds. He hands Sailee a business card, and she adds his number to her phone, sending him a text: *Hi, this is Sailee Roberts from the plane. It was great to meet you.*

He replies: *This is Mike Black. It was great to meet you too. I look forward to connecting again sometime.*

He hits send, and she smiles. "Got it!"

As soon as they're parked at the gate, they both jump up and grab their bags. Mike follows Sailee up the jet bridge. At the gate, they stop and shake hands. "That's a nice firm handshake you have," Mike observes.

"Thanks," Sailee replies. "My granda told me once that you won't go anywhere in life with a weak handshake. I took it to heart!"

"Well, you're definitely going places!" responds Mike with a laugh. He wishes her luck in her upcoming performances, and she wishes him safe travels home. They part ways with a friendly goodbye.

CHAPTER 51

Mike makes two trips to New York City over the following months, but he and Sailee never manage to connect. The first time, she's in Vienna, then Tokyo. The third time proves to be a charm, and they meet for dinner at Ilili – a Mediterranean restaurant on the corner of 27th and 5th. At Sailee's suggestion, they order an array of dishes and share everything. Despite not having spoken since their farewell in Los Angeles, they fall effortlessly into conversation.

Intrigued by Sailee's life on the road, Mike inquires about her experiences. Sailee nonchalantly replies, "I arrive in a city and am escorted to my hotel. I have a few rehearsals with the orchestra, then put on a gown, and it's showtime. After the concert, I'm usually whisked away to some sort of fundraiser or event, sometimes not getting to bed until well after midnight, only to wake up and repeat the cycle all over again. I'm sure it seems glamorous from the outside, and I suppose it is to some extent. But since I'm typically a guest artist, I don't have a consistent set of musicians that I travel or perform with, and it can get quite lonely. I always wished I played an orchestral instrument, but my small school didn't offer a strings program, and my parents couldn't afford private lessons in addition to my piano instruction."

"If you could play an orchestral instrument, which one would you choose?" he asks her.

"Cello," Sailee responds without hesitation. "I've always been drawn to the deep tones of low instruments. In high school I played the euphonium."

"What's that?" Mike asks, feeling slightly ignorant for not knowing.

"It's like a small tuba," she explains. "Ironically, it's the only wind instrument not in an orchestra." She smacks her forehead lightly. "Do you play any instruments?" she asks Mike.

"Yes," he replies hesitantly. "I play the banjo. But not well. I'm mostly self-taught."

"The banjo?!" Sailee repeats, her eyes widening. "That's fantastic! I've heard it's a challenging instrument to master. I love bluegrass." She takes a bite of shawarma. "And what do you do for fun?" she asks.

"I have a lot of hobbies," he replies. "I play music, fish, waterski, golf, lift weights, hunt… I have no problem keeping myself occupied." He pauses, contemplating whether he should share the rest. "I'm also writing a book," he finally confesses.

"A book?" Sailee repeats, looking surprised. "About what?"

"It's a guide to dating for engineers and scientists. I've titled it, 'The Thermodynamics of Love.' I relate relationship principles to the first, second, and third laws of thermodynamics."

"Unfortunately," says Sailee, "I'm unfamiliar with the laws of thermodynamics. Care to expound?"

Mike takes a deep breath and plunges into his explanation. "The first law of thermodynamics is about the conservation of energy. Energy cannot be created or destroyed; it can only be transferred or transformed. Another way to put it is that the best you can do is break even. As humans, we consume food to store energy, and then we expend that energy on useful activities like running or playing the piano. Even thinking expends useful energy. In relationships, you invest useful energy into another person by investing time in them.

"The second law deals with entropy, which basically says that you can only break even at absolute zero. Entropy reflects the tendency of the world and all things within it to move towards a higher state of disorder. When you run for exercise, part of your stored energy is used to propel your body over a distance. However, some of that energy is lost as heat, or sweating – a form of non-useful work. Similarly, if you invest energy into a relationship once, that's fine, but it will naturally dissipate over time, just like any other system. If you wish to keep your relationships progressing, you need to continue putting energy into them. Simple, right?" Sailee nods in understanding.

"The third law of thermodynamics, in lay terms, states that you can never reach absolute zero. This ties back to the second law and conveys why you have to put in constant effort and invest energy into a relationship every day. Think about balancing on one leg, like the tree pose in yoga. When you're in balance, it's relatively easy to maintain the pose. However, if you start losing your balance, consider how much energy it takes to regain that stability. Relationships work in a similar way. If you consistently invest positive energy, it's much easier to sustain a healthy relationship compared to waiting until the relationship has lost its balance. The energy required to restore stability at that point is significant, and sometimes even impossible, just like the effort needed to regain balance after falling."

"Oh baby, talk nerdy to me!" says Sailee, playfully "winking" at Mike.

He flushes slightly. "My only concern is that I don't feel entitled to write a book on relationships."

"Nonsense," Sailee replies. "I think you'd make a great partner." She pauses awkwardly, then quickly continues, "It sounds like an interesting book, and I'm sure engineers will love it!"

"So, how about you?" Mike asks, changing the subject. "What are your hobbies?"

"I love to read," Sailee replies. "And work out. I take pride in being a girl who can do pull-ups. I also enjoy running, and I absolutely love to eat, as you can see." She points to her empty plate. "I enjoy writing as well – mostly parodies, poetry on occasion. And music, of course. It's great to have friends that are musicians because I can usually convince someone to play one of my compositions."

"Is there anything you don't like?" he asks.

"Games," she responds matter-of-factly. "I hate games. I'm too competitive, and they make me angry. And I'm not a nice person when I'm angry." Mike finds that difficult to imagine. "Also, olives." she continues. "And drama." She pauses to think. "But that's about it!"

Mike laughs. "That's a respectable list," he says.

When the topic of relationships arises, Sailee reveals her cynicism about marriage. "I feel like I was duped the first time," she says. "My ex turned out to be a very different person once we got married compared to who he was when we were dating. Although our marriage was short-lived, he did some things that hurt me deeply. Regrettably, I reciprocated. The final straw was when we prioritized our individual careers over each other, but there was a lot of anger and resentment behind that decision."

She pauses to take a bite. "After our divorce, I dated a bit, mostly for something to do, but I never found anyone who made me confident in marriage as an institution, or even humanity, for that matter. Besides, I'm too busy to invest much time or energy, as you would say, into someone right now. So, mostly I just have superficial relationships with men that I meet in my travels. How's that for honesty?"

"I actually appreciate how open you are about it," Mike replies. He can't help but wonder if that's the category he falls into – superficial relationship with a guy she met on a plane – and how many more of them there are.

They finish their meal, and Sailee offers to pay, but Mike says there's no way he's letting her buy his dinner, so they split the bill down the middle. After all, it wasn't a date; just two almost-strangers getting to know each other. As they step out onto the street, a skateboarder zooms past, nearly running into Sailee, and Mike pulls her out of the way just in time.

"Geez – that was a close call," says Sailee. "Thanks for saving me! Now you're my favorite engineer *and* my hero." She grins at Mike flirtatiously, then glances around to ensure no other unexpected dangers are approaching before asking, "Where are you staying?"

"In midtown, near Grand Central," Mike replies. "It's an easy walk from here."

"Ok," says Sailee, her disappointment evident as she realizes they're heading in different directions. "I live uptown, near Lincoln Center. My station is just around the corner." They share a hug and bid each other goodnight, promising to make an effort to meet again soon.

On his walk back to the hotel, Mike thinks about Sailee. He has always considered himself a happy person, but Sailee's infectious energy and joie de vivre are truly inspiring. She reminds him of Odie from Garfield, always bouncing around with excitement. She's definitely someone he'd like to have in his life. However, based on their conversation this evening, he's not sure she feels the same.

CHAPTER 52

Time flies by, and despite their best efforts, Mike and Sailee haven't been able to synchronize their schedules since their initial dinner in New York. Sailee's constant touring and Mike's demanding work have made it challenging to connect. Besides, Mike has met someone else. After their dinner, he often thought about Sailee but ultimately concluded that their busy lives and age difference would likely prevent anything from blossoming between them. Months passed without any contact from Sailee, and although Mike contemplated reaching out to check on her, he never hit the send button. He didn't want to be a bother. So when his friend arranged a blind date with a friend of his wife, he reluctantly agreed, but ended up enjoying himself.

Patty, at forty-five, is divorced with no children. She's pretty, although she wears a bit too much makeup for Mike's taste. Nevertheless, she's a kind person and an engineer. She attended Virginia Tech as well – graduating a year ahead of Mike in chemical engineering – but given the size of their classes, it's not surprising their paths never crossed. Aside from her love of smutty romance novels, Patty doesn't appear to have many hobbies. However, Mike decides to overlook this, as she seems eager to try new things.

Over the next several months, they spend a considerable amount of time together. Mike takes Patty fishing, but she can't stand the idea of putting a hook into a living creature. He introduces her to golf, but she struggles to hit the ball. When he suggests getting her some lessons, Patty takes offense and storms off. So that's out. Hunting is also off the table, since he suspects Patty's aversion to baiting a hook would extend to shooting animals. Moreover, she avoids sun exposure to prevent wrinkles, ruling out all other outdoor activities. Mike takes her to a country music concert, but she complains that the music is too loud. He tries to talk about engineering – at least they have that in common – but she dislikes discussing work outside of the workplace, finding it too draining.

Mike discovers that the one thing Patty does enjoy is shopping, and their outings typically involve dining out (with Patty barely eating, as she's always conscious of maintaining her figure) and leisurely strolling through shopping malls, where she indulges in an Auntie Anne's pretzel (because they're "walking off the calories") while trying on expensive shoes. Mike makes a sincere effort to focus on Patty and put continuous positive energy into the relationship, as he advises in his book. However, his mind frequently wanders to Sailee—her myriad of interests, her natural beauty even with minimal makeup, and her overall ease and self-assurance.

Eventually, he decides to end things with Patty. She gets teary-eyed and blows her nose loudly into her napkin, saying she had been sure he was "The One" and lamenting that no one will ever love her. Mike feels a pang of guilt but also an overwhelming sense of relief as he walks away.

Then, April arrives, and Mike is astonished at how swiftly the year has passed. It's late one evening when he finally pulls into his driveway after playing golf in the morning, enduring a long day at the office, and stopping at the gym on his way home. He has noticed his metabolism slowing down, and he's determined not to let age defeat him. Tossing his gym bag onto the kitchen counter, he begins sifting through the mail. "Junk, junk, fishing magazine, junk, utility bill… what's this?" he wonders, noticing a white envelope bearing his name and lacking a return address.

When he opens it, something falls out onto the counter. Picking it up, Mike finds a ticket to the Performing Arts Center in Raleigh, granting him access to see the North Carolina Symphony, featuring guest artist Sailee Roberts, at 8:00 p.m. on Saturday, April 23. His heart quickens its pace, and he reaches back into the envelope, withdrawing a piece of paper. Unfolding it, he reads a note scrawled in messy handwriting.

> *My dearest Mike,*
> *I'm sorry I've been so negligent at keeping in touch. As I haven't heard from you, I assume you've been busy as well. In a wonderful turn of events, I'll be performing in Raleigh at the end of April. I'm playing Rachmaninoff's 3rd piano concerto, which is my all-time favorite, and nothing would make me happier than having you in the audience. I've enclosed a ticket for you. Pardon my rudeness for not including a companion ticket, but I had my manager clear my schedule of all obligations after the performance, and I would like very much to take you to dinner. Please send me a text and let me know that you've received this and confirm if you are able to attend. If not, you're welcome to give the ticket to someone else who enjoys classical music, but the dinner invitation is for you alone. ☺*
> *Warmest regards,*
> *Sailee*

Astonished, Mike reads the letter again, and then again. He assumed Sailee had forgotten all about him. He grabs his phone and types out a text. *I just received your letter and the ticket. Thank you for thinking of me. I wouldn't miss it for the world and look forward to seeing you in a few weeks.*

"Is that too formal?" he wonders aloud. Does he sound too excited? Not excited enough? Annoyed with himself, he mutters, "Oh brother, I'm acting like a middle school girl." He hits send. After what feels like a very long minute, he receives a response: *Fabulous! See you soon! Xoxo* His heart skips a beat.

The rest of the month crawls by. Mike tries on every suit in his closet and deems them all too engineer-ish for such an occasion. Eventually, he finds himself at a high-end shop where he purchases an Italian-made suit. Although he balks at the exorbitant price, he decides to have it tailored as well, something he has never splurged on before. With the concert merely four days away, he stands in the shop, trying on his new suit and feeling pleased. The medium gray hue brings out his green eyes, and he realizes the difference that tailored clothing can make. The cut accentuates his broad shoulders and slim hips while hiding the slight paunch he has been fighting. He has long legs, and the pants reach perfectly to the tops of his shoes. He has a real James Bond look going on, he thinks.

"Very sharp!" exclaims Valentino, sweeping into the dressing room. After taking a few measurements, he hangs the measuring tape back around his neck. "I think that fits just right. Would you like me to hang it for you?" Mike nods, removes the suit, and puts on his jeans and button-up. He hopes he won't appear too overdressed.

Finally, the evening arrives, and Mike dons his suit, pairing it with a white shirt and a dark gray tie. He didn't appreciate the way Patty constantly touched his face, so he grew a beard, which he ended up liking. It's more like manicured scruff, but he thinks it suits him. He wonders what Sailee will say. Patty hated it, complaining that it scratched her face when they kissed, but as he doesn't anticipate kissing Sailee, he isn't worried.

He's unsure what the protocol is for a performance like this but feels it would be inappropriate to arrive empty-handed. He leaves early, making a stop at a florist where he chooses a bouquet of roses in red, orange, and yellow. Bright, like Sailee, and hopefully not excessively romantic. The florist bundles them up, wrapping the stems in a small pouch of water to keep them fresh. Then he sets off on his way.

His ticket includes premier parking, so he valet-parks his car, takes the flowers from the passenger seat, and ascends the front steps of the concert hall. He is familiar with this building, as he was on the team that designed it. The acoustics are impeccable, and he eagerly anticipates hearing Sailee play in this venue. He presents his ticket to the usher, who nods and guides him into the hall, indicating his seat. Mike chuckles to himself. He's positioned in the very center, about two-thirds of the way back, and he knows exactly why Sailee chose this seat for him – this is where the acoustics are best.

The orchestra is already on stage, some individuals doing last-min-ute run-throughs of difficult passages while others are chatting with one another. Mike examines the program. Three pieces will be performed, with Sailee slated for the final one. He recognizes the Beethoven but is unfamiliar with the second composer, Ravel.

He reads through the program notes, descriptions of each piece being performed, but doesn't really understand any of it. This must be how Sailee feels when he talks about engineering. Then he peruses the schedule for the rest of the spring concert season. "I really should come to more of these," he muses. Flipping through the pages, he pauses at a full-page photograph of Sailee. She's leaning on a grand piano, stunning in a floor-length, off-the-shoulder hunter green gown. Her blonde hair is pulled back in an elegant up-do, and long diamond-studded earrings show off her long neck. It takes his breath away. He has only ever seen her in jeans before, and she was pretty then!

He reads through her biography, much of which he already knows – a bachelor's degree in composition from a small liberal arts college, a master's from Julliard, and her accomplishments as a globally re-nowned performer. He discovers bits of her personality embedded within the list of her impressive achievements. She gives a special mention to Charlie, her niece, as her "best girl," and expresses gratitude to her family for their unwavering support.

Mike stares at Sailee's photo until the lights dim, then shifts his attention as the principal violinist strides onto the stage. The audience applauds politely. The concertmaster bows and turns to the orchestra, gesturing to the principal oboist who plays a note, and all the wind instruments tune accordingly. Then the strings tune, and Mike experiences a surge of anticipation coursing through his spine. There is something incredibly warm and inviting about the sound of stringed instruments.

The concertmaster takes her seat, and there's more applause as the conductor proceeds to the center stage. He shakes the concertmaster's hand, bows to the audience, and assumes his position on the podium. The room falls silent. Mike double-checks his phone to ensure that everything is turned off. He doesn't want to be *that* person. And then, the first notes of Beethoven's second symphony resonate throughout the hall. Mike closes his eyes. The sound is perfect.

He smiles to himself when they play the Ravel. He didn't recognize the piece, Bolero, by name, but he's certainly familiar with it. Then comes intermission. Although thirsty, Mike refrains from getting a drink, not wanting anything to distract him from Sailee's upcoming performance. As he watches the grand piano being rolled to the center of the stage, someone interrupts his thoughts, saying, "Excuse me, sir. Are you Michael Black?"

He looks around and notices an usher leaning toward him over the seats. "I am," he replies.

"Miss Roberts has invited you backstage after her performance. If you don't mind waiting in your seat for a moment when the concert concludes, I'll meet you here and escort you to her dressing room."

Nodding in acknowledgment, Mike tries to appear calmer than he feels. "That will be fine," he responds.

The lights flash, signaling the end of intermission. Mike settles into his seat but finds it difficult to sit still, his leg bouncing nervously.

As the lights dim, a roar of applause erupts as Sailee makes her way across the stage.

Mike gasps. She is absolutely lovely! She's wearing a vibrant pink satin gown, with the front hemline falling just above her knees and a gentle train cascading at the back. The dress billows as she walks, creating the illusion that she's floating across the stage. Her hair, longer than when he last saw her, cascades in curls down her back. Sailee walks to the center stage, taking a low bow before seating herself at the piano. The room falls into silence as she adjusts the bench, her dress, and then, finally, gives a small nod to the conductor, prompting him to raise his arms to the orchestra.

Mike will never find the right words to describe what happens next. The closest he can come is to say that Sailee transforms. For the next forty-five minutes, she ceases to be Sailee Roberts. Gone is the bright, cheerful, smiling, and chatty woman he met on the airplane. Instead, she is passion and intensity personified. He can see the focus on her face, the muscles in her back, as those small hands hammer out octaves so fast that her fingers become a blur. He recalls her telling him during dinner that this was the piece that made her want to become a concert pianist, that she cried the first time she heard it. And as the final notes of the third movement fill the concert hall, he understands.

The piano and the orchestra converge in a sweeping crescendo, and Mike's vision blurs, goosebumps covering his body. And when they hit that final climactic chord, he feels as though his heart might burst. He's on the edge of his seat, and on the last note he is out of it, joined by everyone in the concert hall in a standing ovation for Sailee's masterful performance. The applause is deafening.

Sailee rises and smiles, taking a bow. "Ah, there she is again," Mike thinks. Then she motions toward the conductor, who reciprocates a bow before gesturing back to her. She takes another low bow. When she lifts her head, her gaze sweeps across the audience, and their eyes meet. Mike knows she was searching for him, as her smile widens even further. "Bravo!" he yells, raising his hands in the air, clapping harder than he has ever clapped.

And then the conductor signals the orchestra to rise. The applause goes on and on until Sailee and the conductor finally take their leave of the stage. The clapping gradually subsides, and people begin to collect their belongings and make their way toward the exits. Mike sits back down, still attempting to grasp the magnitude of what he just witnessed.

"Sir?"

It's the usher. Mike grabs the bouquet and follows him out a side door near the front of the stage. At Sailee's dressing room, the usher knocks before nodding to Mike and departing in the same direction they came from. He stands there alone, outside the door, feeling a bit self-conscious.

And then it opens, and Sailee throws her arms around his neck in a bear hug. "Mike! Thank you so much for coming!" She momentarily steps back, studying him, before breaking into a smile. "I love the beard! It suits you," she exclaims. "And that suit looks fantastic on you too!"

Mike presents her with the flowers, and she accepts them, inhaling their scent. "These are beautiful – thank you." Then she leads him into the room, which is filled with flowers, and places his bouquet on the dressing table. He should have brought chocolates, he thinks.

"Thank *you*," Mike says, "for inviting me. That was…" he falters, unable to find a word that does her performance justice. "I had no idea…" he tries again, but to no avail.

Sailee laughs. "Oh, it's nothing," she replies modestly. "But I'm so very glad you got to hear my favorite piece. Isn't it extraordinary? Rachmaninoff's melodies have a way of penetrating one's soul."

Mike agrees, not verbalizing what he's thinking – that she has a way of penetrating *his* soul. "I almost didn't recognize you up there," he remarks. "You're a completely different person on stage."

"It's true," she confesses. "I have to be. It's requires intense focus. I forget anyone else is in the room. It's just me and the music." She pauses. "Which is a good thing, because if I were aware of the audience, it would make me too nervous to play!" She smiles. "Anyway,

I hope you're hungry, because I'm famished." Mike says that he is. "I hope it's not presumptuous, but I gave my driver the night off, assuming I could ride with you."

"But of course," Mike replies.

Sailee takes the flowers from the dressing table, carrying them along. "My manager will handle the rest of these," she mentions casually, "but I'd like to bring these to my hotel room." Mike wonders if she's trying to flatter him but decides it doesn't matter. When he offers Sailee his arm, she accepts it.

It feels strange being in the empty concert hall. Most of the lights have been switched off, and only the janitor remains, picking up the litter that has fallen between the seats. Mike notices that the piano remains in the center of the stage and pauses. "Would you play something for me?" he asks. "Not Rachmaninoff or anything. I'd like to hear something you composed."

Sailee hesitates for a moment, then agrees. She ascends the stairs on the side of the stage, and Mike moves to sit in the front row. "No, no," she interjects. "Come up here with me." He complies, surprised at how much more expansive the hall appears from the stage.

Sailee pats the bench beside her. "Sit here." After a brief reflection, she begins to play. The piece commences with an intense, somber melody, both hands playing in unison. Then, the accompaniment evolves, while the melody stays constant. It progresses in this manner, gaining complexity. It's played in a round, haunting in the way the two melodies weave in and around one other. Then it ceases to follow typical chord progressions altogether, becoming atonal and chaotic. In the final variation, Sailee's hands are flying over the keys, yet that same simple melody resounds beneath the movement. Mike is astounded that this composition came from her brain. She finishes with a flourish and looks at him.

"That was incredible!" he says. "I can't believe you wrote that!"

"I actually composed that my freshman year of college," she replies. "It sounds complicated, but it's really quite simple. It's called a Passacaglia – a musical form which is essentially a series of continuous variations over an ostinato pattern. It's not Rachmaninoff, by any means, but I've always loved it because it allowed me to explore multiple musical genres, or styles, within a single piece."

Mike laughs. "I wish I understood what you just said. What was the phrase you used at dinner? Talk nerdy to me?" He winks at her. "All I know is that I thought it was amazing!"

Sailee grins and hops up off the bench. "Alright," she says, "I'm hungry. Let's go."

When they reach the front steps, Mike can see that the valet is annoyed at their delay. Everyone else has left, and he had to wait for them. The car is already pulled up to the curb. "Sorry about that," Mike apologizes to the valet.

"This is your car?!" Sailee exclaims, gawking at it.

"Yes," Mike replies proudly. He adores this car. It was a splurge, and he purchased it used and in pretty rough shape, but he had always wanted one. When he received a big promotion several years ago, this was his present to himself. It took him a year to restore it.

"This is my favorite car ever!" she remarks. "It's a 911, right?" He confirms that it is. "I've wanted this car ever since I watched *Gone in 60 Seconds* in high school. Do you remember that movie?"

Mike laughs. "The one with Nicholas Cage?"

"That's the one!"

"Oh yes, I remember." He also loved that movie. Mike opens the car door, and Sailee slides in, pulling her train in behind her. Her pink dress stands out against the car's black interior. She could easily be a Porsche advertisement.

"Best night ever!" she cheerfully declares.

Mike agrees. He settles into the driver's seat and turns to her. "So, where are we going?"

Sailee blushes slightly. "Sooooo, please don't think me too forward, but going out after a concert is a nightmare because someone always recognizes me. They come over and say hello, wanting to talk and take selfies, when all I want to do is eat. So I thought we could go back to my hotel and order room service. I've already had them set up the table." She pauses, then clarifies, "I have a suite with a separate living room and dining area, so it's like not I'm inviting you to my bedroom or anything!"

Mike laughs, although he can't deny feeling a bit disappointed that she felt the need to explain. "I'll take you wherever you want to go, my dear," he says, shifting the car into gear.

Sailee grins and relaxes. "So, what did you think about the concert? Not just the Rachmaninoff, but the entire performance."

"It was wonderful!" Mike responds enthusiastically. "I sat there the entire time wondering why I don't have season tickets. I've always been a fan of Beethoven. And the Ravel—" he stops, contemplating whether or not to continue.

"What about it?" she prods.

"I didn't recognize the composer by name, but as soon as they started playing, I knew the piece. I think it's one of the sexiest pieces of music ever written. It was featured in an old movie from 1979 called *10*, with Bo Derek. I saw it when I was in high school and had a massive crush on her. She played this song while seducing Dudley Moore, and I used to think he was the luckiest bastard on the planet."

Sailee laughs. "I've never seen that movie."

"But the Rachmaninoff..." he continues, attempting to steer the conversation, "...blew my socks off. How do your fingers move so fast? I thought I had nimble fingers from playing the banjo but I'm no match for you!"

"Just years of practice," she responds. "Ok, turn in here."

He pulls into the Heights House Hotel. "Nice digs!" he comments.

"It's definitely a perk," Sailee replies. "My manager knows I need peace and quiet on the day of a performance, so he's good at finding these little gems for me. This is a lovely one."

Mike jumps out of the car and hurries around to open Sailee's door, but she has already stepped out.

"Good evening, Miss Roberts," greets the man at the front desk as they enter. "We've been expecting you. You'll find your menus on the table. Please call down when you're ready to order."

Sailee thanks him and leads Mike up the stairs. It's a charming room – and enormous! There is a spacious living area with a fireplace, and a table for two is set up by the expansive windows. "I'm going to slip into something a little more comfortable," says Sailee, giving Mike a smile and a half-wink that he doesn't know how to interpret. "Please make yourself at home." She goes into the bedroom and closes the door.

Mike walks around a minute, then takes off his suit coat and tie, draping them over the arm of the couch. He unbuttons his top button and rolls up his sleeves. "Much better," he thinks.

He wasn't sure what to expect from her comment, but Sailee emerges from the room in lounge pants and a sweatshirt, her hair in a loose ponytail. She looks like a college student. "That's more like it," she says, gesturing for Mike to grab a menu. He's hungry, and everything looks good.

"Do you want to order a number of items and share again?" she suggests.

"That sounds great. Order whatever you want," he replies. So she does. She selects eight different dishes, and they talk, and laugh, and drink a bottle of mediocre wine ("Compliments of the hotel," she explains) before their food arrives.

"I hope you liked your seat," remarks Sailee. "I was going to seat you in the opera box for a better view, but considering you're an acoustician, I thought you'd prefer the sound from that section."

Mike tells her he immediately understood why she chose that seat, and that the acoustics were amazing. Every instrument blended perfectly.

It's past midnight when their food finally arrives. "I'm sure this wreaks havoc on my digestive system," Sailee explains, "but I can't eat before I perform, so I'm always starving afterward and end up eating too much too late at night. I hope it's okay and I'm not keeping you up." Mike wants to say that he would stay up all night for her, but he refrains.

They savor every last bite, and when they finally put their forks down, it's two o'clock in the morning. Exhaustion creeps over Mike, and he can barely keep his eyes open, which Sailee notices. "I'm sorry I kept you so late," she apologizes. "I've been enjoying your company and lost track of the time. How long is your drive home?"

"About thirty minutes," he tells her.

"Well," she says, "I'm not flying home until Monday morning. I was supposed to perform at a private function tomorrow afternoon, but the host got sick and cancelled. I was planning to ask my manager to find me a flight out tomorrow, but maybe I'll stay. Would you like to spend the day with me? I've never had a chance to explore this area, and I'd love for you to show me around."

Mike's heart quickens its pace, and he tries not to read too much into her request. He can see that Sailee is a friendly and extroverted person, and being on the road all the time must be lonely. "I'd love to do that," he replies.

"Ok, then." Sailee pauses a moment, thinking. "Well, if that's the case, does it make sense for you to go home? You could stay here…" She's looking at Mike with an expression he can't read.

"I *am* really tired," he admits. "I'll sleep on the couch, and in the morning, you can get ready, and then we'll swing by my house so I can shower and change, and we'll go from there. Does that work? I promise I'll be a gentleman," he adds, winking at her.

"Are you *sure* you want to be a gentleman?" Sailee asks coyly, giving Mike a mischievous grin that makes his heart pound.

"Uh…" he stammers, not entirely sure if she's joking or not.

"It's up to you," she replies, her tone now serious. "But the way I see it, we're both adults, and I think you're pretty amazing. I can assure you my bed is more comfortable than the couch…" she takes a step toward Mike, "…although I can't promise you'll get much sleep there." Sailee grins and takes another deliberate step. "You already know how I feel about relationships, but I'm certainly up for spending more time together if you are."

Mike leans in, now wide awake. Yes, he is definitely up for that. "I think…" he says slowly, moving his hand to Sailee's waist and pulling her towards him, "that I'd like to not be a gentleman."

"Well then, Mr. Black," she replies, wrapping her arms around his neck, "either take me to bed or say goodbye to me forever."

"I suppose I'll be taking you to bed then," he says, scooping her up and carrying her into the bedroom.

CHAPTER 53

It is very late when they finally retire to bed. Mike sleeps like a log and wakes up at 8:00 a.m., which is sleeping in for him. Usually, he manages around four hours of sleep, five on a good night, awakening around 4:30 in the morning. His doctor tells him it's unhealthy, but he doesn't know what he can do to fix it. He doesn't like the way sleep aids make him feel.

He glances over at Sailee, sprawled on the other side of the bed, still fast asleep – proof that the previous night was not, in fact, a dream. Mike is uncomfortably warm under the covers, so he tosses them aside, allowing his body to breathe for a minute, then rises, dressing in his suit pants and shirt. He steps into the bathroom, splashing cold water on this face and through his hair. He would jump in the shower, but he doesn't want to disturb Sailee.

Heading to the kitchenette area, he searches for tea bags. Thankfully, he locates some. It's not Earl Grey, but it's better than nothing. He also finds an electric kettle in one of the cupboards. "Excellent," he murmurs. He's switching it on when he hears Sailee's alarm go off.

A few minutes later, she emerges groggily from the bedroom. She's wrapped in the bed sheet, and her hair's a mess. Mike thinks this is the prettiest she has ever looked. "Good morning, beautiful!" he exclaims. "Would you like a cup of tea?"

Sailee rubs her eyes and quips, "Who are you – Prince Charming? I'd love one."

"I hope black tea is acceptable. It's all I could find." She nods, sitting down at the table. The water boils, and Mike pours her a cup, placing it in front of her. "Based on what you said last night, I didn't expect to see you for another couple of hours," he jokes.

Sailee gives a small laugh, still in the process of waking up. "Normally, you wouldn't see me until at least 10:00 a.m., but I remember you mentioning being a morning person, and I didn't want to keep you waiting around, so I set an alarm." She gazes out the window. "Besides, it looks like a beautiful day, and I don't want to waste any of it." She takes a sip of her tea. "I'll be back in a few minutes," she says, carrying her cup into the bedroom. Mike hears the shower running and resists the temptation to join her, recognizing that Sailee might need some solitude in the morning. Ten minutes later, she appears in the living room, dressed in jeans, wedge heels, and a light sweater, her tousled curls from last night falling loosely around her shoulders.

"That was quick!" Mike remarks, impressed.

She smiles. "Do you want to shower here, or would you rather wait until we get to your house?"

"I'll wait," he replies. "That way I don't have to put my dirty clothes back on."

"You could always go commando," she suggests, giving him a flirtatious smile.

"I could," he responds, his heart suddenly knocking excitedly against his chest. "But then we'd probably never leave the room." He grins at her, grabbing his suit jacket and tie from the couch. "Ready to go?"

She is, and he follows her out the door.

They have the best day together. Sailee gushes over Mike's house, exclaiming, "You have so much space compared to my apartment!" Then they explore downtown Chapel Hill, stopping for lunch at an Indian restaurant. Sailee shares that Indian and Ethiopian cuisines are her favorite ethnic foods, while he confesses that Italian is his preference."

"I remember you mentioning on the plane that your dad has Lou Gehrig's disease," she says, suddenly serious. "How's he doing?"

Mike is touched that she remembers. "He's doing alright. Every day, he deteriorates a little more. It's tough on my mom since she's his fulltime caregiver. I wish there was more I could do to help."

"Do they live far from here?"

"About three hours."

"We should go see them!" Sailee says excitedly. "It would be the best surprise!"

Although not entirely practical, Mike can't resist her excitement and spontaneity. Besides, he hasn't seen his parents in a while. "It's after 1:00 p.m. already," he states. "We wouldn't get there until nearly 4:30, and then we still have another three-hour drive back."

"That's ok!" she insists. "It will be a fun road trip, and you know it will make their day!"

That is definitely true. Mike agrees, and they request the check.

They talk non-stop during the drive, discussing their favorite books (hers: "A Tale of Two Cities"; his: "Treasure Island"), favorite foods (hers: cheese; his: pepperoni pizza), favorite movies, funniest memory, most embarrassing moment (his: the time he got a straw stuck up his nose while trying to pick up a girl in college; hers: when she curtsied to a university president after a concert, as if she were being announced in a royal court. There were over two hundred people in the room, and everyone looked at her like she was an idiot.), past relationships, favorite tacky pick-up line, favorite subject in school (his: math; hers: English), things they wanted to be when they grew up (her: astronaut, dancer, composer; him: astronaut, country singer, fighter pilot), stupidest thing they've ever done, biggest regret... Nothing is off-limits, and the three hours fly by.

When Mike pulls into his parents' driveway, Sailee exclaims, "Wow, we're here already?"

They walk up the sidewalk, and Mike knocks on the door. When his mom sees him through the window, she cries, "Good Lord, it's Mike!" and flings open the door, throwing her arms around her son. "This is the best surprise!" she says. "What are you doing here?"

"It was Sailee's idea," Mike replies, smiling.

"Who's Sailee?" his mom asks, confused.

"I am," Sailee says, stepping around Mike and extending her hand. "I'm a friend of Mike's! He talks a lot about you, and I wanted to meet you!"

His mom shakes her hand. "Well, that's lovely. I'm Carol. Come on inside. I was just starting to think about dinner."

"Don't worry about dinner, Mom," says Mike. "We'll run to the store and pick up some steaks, and I'll grill. Do you have any potatoes?"

"That sounds wonderful," Carol says. She turns to Sailee. "Have you ever had one of Mike's steaks?" Sailee confesses that she hasn't. "Well, they're the best," Carol tells her. Then she turns back to Mike. "I have potatoes and onions down in the basement, and some frozen broccoli. Do you like broccoli, Sailee?"

Sailee assures her that she eats everything, and Mike confirms it. "You've never seen a girl eat the way Sailee does, Mom!" he says, laughing.

The rest of the evening is filled with conversation and laughter. They all gather around Mike's dad's bed in the living room and share stories. Sailee finds it difficult to understand Bill as the Lou Gehrig's has affected his throat and tongue muscles, making speech difficult. But Mike and Carol act as translators, conveying his anecdotes to Sailee, who laughs wholeheartedly, realizing where Mike inherited his sense of humor from.

Then the conversation shifts to music, and Bill tells Sailee that he once saw Lester Flatt and Earl Scruggs perform in his small town back when he was in high school. "Do you like music?" he asks her.

Mike chuckles. "Sailee is one of the best pianists in the world," he explains.

Sailee blushes and modestly states that while it's not entirely true, she does love music and earns a living playing the piano. Mike pulls up a YouTube video of her performing at the Kennedy Center in Washington, DC. She's playing Liszt's "La Campanella" – a very technically challenging piece.

"This is Sailee," he says proudly, showing the video to his parents.

"Wow," Carol exclaims, her eyes widening. "You're very good!"

Mike's dad appears unimpressed. "Can you play honky-tonk?" he asks. "Like Floyd Cramer or Jerry Lee Lewis?"

Mike laughs. "My dad has very singular taste when it comes to music," he explains to Sailee.

She grins, confessing that she hasn't played honky-tonk before and that it's a very different style from what she was trained in.

"You should give it a try some time," Bill suggests. "I bet you could pick it up." Mike rolls his eyes, knowing his dad's unwavering preferences.

When it's time to leave, Sailee hugs Mike's parents, and his dad remarks, "I'm not letting you go. You can tell your manager you've been kidnapped!"

Sailee laughs. "I wouldn't mind being kidnapped by you," she replies playfully, kissing his cheek.

They're quieter on the ride home, happy and content just to be together. After a while, Sailee reaches over and takes Mike's hand in hers, intertwining their fingers. His heart quickens.

They are on a dark, desolate stretch of road when she turns to Mike. "I think you should pull over," she says, her voice low and sultry. Without questioning, he promptly complies with her request. As soon as the car is in park, Sailee leans in and softly kisses his cheek. Then she turns his face toward hers, planting a delicate kiss on the tip of his nose, then one on his lips.

Then the tenderness gives way to passion. Without breaking the kiss, Sailee unbuckles her seatbelt and crawls over the center console into Mike's lap, straddling him with her knees. The confines of the small car make it difficult to maneuver, and the back of Sailee's head hits the ceiling. When she leans over, her rear end presses into the steering wheel, blaring the horn and shattering the night's silence. Giggling, she reaches down and reclines Mike's seat, holding onto him as they fall backward with a thud.

When they finally pull apart, both of them are breathless. As much as they'd like to take this further, there just isn't room in the tiny vehicle. "I think I need to work more North Carolina venues into my schedule," says Sailee. "I like you."

Mike wholeheartedly agrees. Yet he notices, with a twinge of disappointment, that she doesn't say anything about dating him. He can envision a future with her, but her comment from months ago at the restaurant nags at him. They haven't discussed it, and perhaps it's unfair to assume, but he can't help but wonder how many other men she might be seeing at the moment. Is he willing to be another fish on her hook? He gazes at Sailee, her eyes shining mischievously in the darkness, and thinks, "Probably so."

CHAPTER 54

Although scheduling continues to prove challenging, they find ways to be together. Sailee has almost no say in her tour schedule, but Mike does his best to align his trips to New York when she's there. Sailee has never invited him to her apartment, opting instead to visit his hotel when he's in town, and Mike assumes it's because she considers their relationship a fling – and perhaps one of many. It's about the only thing they haven't discussed. Mike knows Sailee would be honest if he asked outright, but he's not entirely sure he wants to know. From the beginning, she was clear that she's skeptical of marriage. But does that mean she's opposed to any kind of committed relationship? He's uncertain. Regardless, he adores spending time with her, and they often stay up late into the night talking and laughing. He has never been so happy – or so tired!

Although his parents keep asking about Sailee, Mike honestly doesn't know what to tell them. It feels like they're dating, but every time he brings up the topic, Sailee becomes skittish and changes the subject. He's reaching a point where he can't ignore it anymore. He's serious about Sailee, but if she doesn't feel the same, he needs to know.

They're walking arm-in-arm back to his hotel after dinner one evening when he finally broaches the subject. "Sailee," he begins, his tone serious, "there's something I need to say."

She frowns, concern evident in her expression. "Is everything alright?" she asks.

"I don't know," replies Mike, contemplating how to begin. He decides it's best to be direct. "We've been... seeing each other... or whatever this is, for almost a year now, and I've loved every moment of our time together."

She furrows her brow. "Go on," she urges.

"The truth is," Mike continues, "I've grown to really care for you. I know this began as a casual thing ..." he pauses briefly, gathering his nerve, "...but I want more."

Sailee doesn't move away from him, but he can feel her body tensing up. Without hesitation, Mike takes a deep breath and plows on, knowing he must follow through with what he started. "You're an important part of my life, Sailee. I love you. I'm no longer satisfied with casual trysts in the city. I know your reservations about relationships, and I'm not trying to pressure you. I'm certainly not asking you to marry me or anything. But I've reached a point where I want to officially date you. Openly. Exclusively. I want you to be my girlfriend. I understand that you've been hurt before. I also realize that part of hesitancy is your fear of hurting me. And if you don't want to date me exclusively, or can't, that's fine. We can keep on being friends. But we can't continue on this current trajectory because my feelings for you are too strong." Having said it all, Mike looks at Sailee expectantly. For once, her face is impossible to read.

Sailee struggles to maintain a neutral expression, her mind racing. She knew this was coming. It had to happen eventually. The complicated thing is that she *does* love Mike. Unbeknownst to him, she ended all her other "relationships" a while back because it felt unfair to him, even though he never asked it of her. In truth, all those other men paled in comparison to Mike. But formalizing their relationship? She's not sure she's prepared for that level of commitment.

When she replies, her voice is strained. "I need to think about it." Mike's face falls, his disappointment evident. "That doesn't mean 'no'!" she adds quickly. "I care about you a lot, Mike. But this is a big step for me, and I don't want to say I'm all in if I'm not."

He assures her that he understands, though she can tell her response has hurt him, and it creates an awkward atmosphere between them. Sailee continues to hold his arm, but as they arrive at the hotel, she says, "I think I'll to go back to my place tonight, Mike. I'm not upset, but you've giving me a lot to think about, and staying with you just doesn't feel right after our conversation. I'm aware you leave in the morning, but I don't want to spend the night together distracted. Okay?"

Mike reluctantly agrees, although he is clearly disappointed, leaving Sailee wondering if she underestimated their ability to set aside their discussion and have a normal night together. Nonetheless, he hugs her tightly, planting a light kiss on her cheek. "I won't push you," he assures her. "Just reach out whenever you're ready to talk."

Sailee acknowledges Mike with a nod, then walks away, turning to blow him a kiss before she disappears around the corner. She walks the two miles back to her apartment, ignoring her aching feet, which scream at her from within the four-inch heels that imprison them. Her head is reeling, and the cool night air feels good on her face. "What the hell is my *problem*?!" she exclaims aloud. A passing couple raises their eyebrows, and Sailee realizes how crazy she must appear walking down Broadway talking to herself.

She knows Mike; she knows that he's not going to suddenly change once they become "official." In addition, he understands her better than anyone, and loves her for who she is, flaws and all. He hit the nail on the head – her hesitation doesn't stem from him or his love. She's afraid of herself. Mike is truly the best person she has ever met, and she's afraid that someday she might do something to crush him. She can't bear the thought of that.

She reminds herself that she was just a kid when she got married the first time. Since then, she has gained years of experience, growth, and self-reflection. She doesn't have to repeat those same mistakes. She doesn't have to run when things get hard. And she doesn't have to run from commitment indefinitely, either. While she has relished the freedom of flitting from one man to another, popping into a fling when it suited her, and swiftly moving on when she grew bored with it, she realizes that's not the life she wants forever. And it's not the kind of relationship she wants to have with Mike. At least, not anymore. He's too good for that. He's too good for her, really. Yet, he loves her. Deep in her heart, Sailee knows that Mike is worth every sacrifice, but being with him entails making significant changes. Is she ready to do that?

Mike tosses and turns all night. He misses Sailee's body curled around his, misses the smell of her hair on his pillow. He's grappling with the uncertainly of their future. Does her reluctance to commit have anything to do with him? Maybe he's not successful enough for her. He's not intimidated by her achievements, but maybe she's looking for someone more accomplished. Someone who shines as brightly as she does. Perhaps a boring old engineer is fine to sleep with, but not openly date. Or maybe his age makes him an unsuitable partner. It could be any number of things. "Or," he tells himself, "it could have nothing to do with me at all."

And what about him? If she *is* unwilling to date him exclusively, will he stay on her hook – meeting her in hotel rooms whenever he's in New York? Or will he be cast back into the dating pool? The thought of losing Sailee leaves a gaping hole deep inside him. Could they just be friends? He'd like that but doesn't know if he's capable of it.

The next morning, Mike wakes early and checks his phone. No messages. Disappointed, he gets out of bed, showers, and catches a cab to the airport. He wonders when he'll hear from Sailee. She won't ghost him – he's sure of that.

As much as he hates to admit it, his hopes are dashed when she's not at the airport. When he lands in Durham and turns on his phone, there are still no messages. There are no emails. A day goes by, then a week. Then another week. "Maybe she *would* ghost me," he thinks. He had thought her better than that.

A month later, he's pulling into his driveway, returning home late from a work trip to Atlanta, and is shocked to find Sailee sitting on his front steps. She's wearing jeans and a hoodie. Her hair is tied up in a messy ponytail, and she has no makeup on. When Mike sees her face, red and splotchy from crying, his heart sinks. At least she didn't drag him along forever before cutting him loose. And he respects that she came to deliver the news in person rather than over the phone or by text.

He grabs his suitcase and gets out of the car, making his way toward her. Before he can utter a word, Sailee blurts out, "I'm sorry it took me so long, but I couldn't talk to you until I was absolutely certain. I've been doing a ton of soul-searching and have barely slept in weeks. And then, once I knew, I couldn't wait one more second to see you, to tell you, so I booked the first flight out of New York this morning, and I've been here on your doorstep all day. When you didn't come home, I started to panic, thinking that maybe you'll never forgive me for the way I treated you, or that maybe you've already moved on. But I love you, Mike! I love you so much. I'll be honest and say that I'm scared – not because of you, but because of me. But you're worth it. And I *do* want to be with you. Only you. Please say you'll still be mine."

Overwhelmed with surprise and joy, Mike drops his suitcase and picks Sailee up, twirling her around so vigorously that she kicks over one of his potted plants. When he finally sets her down, they're both laughing, and Mike can feel tears moistening his cheeks – a blend of Sailee's and his own. Tenderly cupping her face in his hands, he whispers, "Sailee, I promise I will take care of your heart."

"I know," she replies. "And I will take care of yours."

Sailee will discover that she never has to sacrifice a thing. She didn't need to change herself or relinquish anything to be with Mike. On the contrary, she gained everything – intimacy, unconditional love, a best friend. Their relationship doesn't confine her; it sets her free.

Several months later, they embark on a drive from New York City to North Carolina. With two whole weeks together before Sailee's month-long tour in Russia, they decide to spend it at Mike's home. It's the longest stretch of uninterrupted time they've had together, and it's long overdue. In the car, Sailee reads a book aloud to Mike. They categorize every chain restaurant they can think of. They sing along to the radio. They write a song titled, "You're Wrong and You Love Me," a bluesy tune that playfully twists the phrase that has become a staple in their relationship: "You're right and I love you!"

As they approach Chapel Hill, the conversation turns serious. "I know we've only been officially dating for a few months," Mike begins, "but I've been contemplating something, and now feels like the right time to discuss it." Sailee turns down the music and swivels in her seat to face him, her expression curious.

"I love you, and I would marry you tomorrow," Mike continues, "but I never want you to feel pressured into anything. So I will never propose to you unless you propose to me first. That way, I'll know you're ready, if you ever are. How does that sound?"

Sailee's face lights up with a smile, and she takes Mike's hand in hers, kissing it. This man truly understands her. "That sounds perfect," she replies.

They navigate the challenges of a long-distance relationship, arranging their schedules to maximize their time together whenever they can, wherever they can. When the weariness of living apart takes its toll, Mike finds a new job, selling his house in Chapel Hill and moving to New York City. And Sailee begins to truly believe that things could be different this time.

On their first Christmas Eve together in Sailee's apartment, now their apartment, they're dancing in the dark, their silhouettes backlit by the light of the Christmas tree. Sailee wraps her arms tightly around Mike's waist. Giving him a squeeze, she kisses his cheek, and sings,

> *"What's a kiss without a squeeze?*
> *It's the mac without the cheese,*
> *A tickle with no sneeze,*
> *It's the A's and B's without the C's,*
> *It's a big old bra without the double D's*
> *No, a kiss without a squeeze is not for me.*
>
> *It's a car without a key,*
> *It's a fish without the sea,*
> *It's liberty without the free,*
> *A windward ship without the lee…"*

Grinning, Sailee takes Mike's hand in hers and gets down on one knee.

> *"…It's a proposal when you are not on one knee,*
> *So, Michael Black, will you please marry me?"*

On their wedding night, Mike comes out of the bathroom to find Sailee grinning mischievously at him, Bolero playing on the Sonos, and thinks to himself, "Dudley Moore has nothing on me. *I* am the luckiest bastard in the world!" And in the early mornings, when he's restless, Sailee rolls over and lays her head on his chest, lulling him back to sleep.

They navigate a pregnancy and learn how to juggle touring and a baby. After a time, Sailee grows tired of the constant travel and gives up performing to stay home with her little family. She exchanges the grand stage for a small studio where she gives piano lessons. Occasionally, she's enticed back as a guest artist, but mostly she's content teaching and composing. She sings lullabies to her daughter and love songs to her husband, and their home is always full of music and laughter.

When Aila enters elementary school, they leave the city and move to Vermont to be closer to Sailee's family. Aila and Charlie become the best of friends despite their age difference, and although they couldn't be more dissimilar, they're inseparable. "Sister-Cousins," they call themselves. Charlie, with fine blonde hair (like her aunt), possesses incredible athletic abilities and can do anything she puts her mind to. She obtains a degree in engineering, like her Uncle Mike, but becomes a professional climber. Aila, with thick dark hair (like her dad), learns to play the violin but abandons her classical training and becomes a world-class fiddler, much to her grandfather's delight.

Mike and Sailee love their life in Vermont, the friends they make and their proximity to family. Then, one day, after feeling unwell for a while, Mike comes home from the doctor and tells Sailee he has cancer. They cry together, and Sailee reassures him that they'll get through it. And even though things get hard, she doesn't run. She stays with him throughout the chemo, telling Mike how handsome he is even as his hair falls out. She holds him while he's sick from the radiation treatments. She helps him to the bathroom when he's too weak to manage on his own. She never leaves his side, remaining steadfast in her belief that he will overcome it.

When Mike goes into remission, he leaves his firm in pursuit of a lifelong dream – to open a restaurant – because he realizes that life's too short to wait. He names it "North Carolina Smokin'," and his vinegar-based barbeque sauce becomes legendary in Burlington.

"I didn't marry him for his meat," Sailee remarks playfully during a dinner party, "but it's certainly a perk!"

After a few glasses of wine, Mike begins recounting the story of their first meeting, concluding with, "We were so lucky. If either of us had made any other choice, we never would have met. The odds were one in... well, an inconceivably large number."

Shadow Mike smiles, shaking his head. "If Mike only knew," he thinks. After all he has witnessed in the multiverse, he now knows beyond a shadow of a doubt that he and Sailee are destined to be together, will be together, in every life. They are two halves of a whole, and regardless of the choices they make, their paths will invariably intersect, and they will fall in love. With this thought, the world around him goes black.

CHAPTER 55

May 25

Sailee finishes her lunch in the cafeteria, a small salad and a few french fries, and makes her way back to Mike's room. Her appetite has significantly diminished as of late, and she has to force herself to eat. Exiting the elevator, she unexpectedly collides with someone turning the corner. Apologizing, she looks up and recognizes the attending doctor.

"Ah, Sailee," he addresses her warmly. "I've been looking for you. Would you mind coming to my office for a moment?"

She nods and follows him, her heart suddenly pounding. Dr. Wilson, whom Sailee assumes to be in his late fifties or early sixties, is tall and broad-shouldered with graying hair. He has bright blue eyes and a kind smile. He is usually cheerful, and Sailee can sometimes hear him whistling in the halls. But today she can't read his tone.

He guides her into his office and motions for her to take a seat. Then he settles down behind his desk, sitting opposite her. "Sailee," he begins softly, learning in towards her. "It's approaching three months since your accident." Sailee senses what's coming and instinctively tightens her grip on the wooden chair arms, bracing herself. "Although Mike's vitals remain stable, there hasn't been any change in his condition. No sign of improvement whatsoever. It's remarkable that he has endured so long, but we need to start considering what lies ahead."

"What do you mean?" Sailee asks.

Dr. Wilson sighs and folds his hands on the desk. "I mean," he continues, "that we need to begin discussing, at the very least, the possibility of removing Mike's life support if there is no improvement in the coming weeks."

Sailee's heart seizes at the suggestion, and she finds herself gasping for breath. She leans back against the chair, her knuckles turning white from the intensity of her grip. Her body grows ice cold, yet perspiration forms on her brow. She can't think. She can't speak. It feels as though she is trapped in a vacuum. Images of Mike flash before her eyes – his expression when he spilled the wine on her dress, his smile when he picked her up from her apartment on their way to meet his parents for the first time, the tears glistening in his eyes when she read him her vows, the playful wink he gave her in the car before... before...

She shakes her head violently. No. NO! The thought is so abhorrent to her, she can't even fathom considering it. He will recover. He *will*. He *must*. He just needs more time. Mike was never one to be pushed into anything. He did things his own way, and it always worked out. This is just one more thing. No. No way. "No fucking way," she says aloud.

"Sailee," Dr. Wilson says calmly, "I understand how difficult this is for you, but please just think—"

"No," Sailee interrupts sharply. "You *don't* understand. You're asking me to kill a part of myself. You're asking *me* to make the choice to live without him. No. I can't. I'm not that strong. He *will* come out of this. I *know* he will. Please, Dr. Wilson, he just needs more time. Please..." She's pleading now, leaning forward, her hands clasped together.

Dr. Wilson exhales a long, slow breath and sits back in his chair. "Okay, Sailee," he says placatingly. "We don't need to discuss this further today. We can give it a little more time. But it's something you need to start preparing yourself for. I'm sorry, truly. Hopefully, Mike will recover. But if not..."

Sailee sets her jaw stubbornly. She stands, nods brusquely to the doctor, then swiftly turns on her heels and exits the office.

As soon as she rounds the corner into the hallway, she breaks into a run. It's awkward, given the muscles in her injured leg are still rebuilding, and she feels a twinge of pain with each step, but she doesn't care. She needs to get out of there.

She pushes the door to the stairwell open with such force that she nearly falls face-first into it. Regaining her balance, Sailee rushes down the three flights of stairs, through the lobby, and out the front doors. Breathless and in pain, she inhales the fresh air. Her leg is throbbing, but she can't feel it for the agony in her heart. She collapses against the wall, slumping down to the ground like a deflated balloon.

Her mind continues playing its montage of memories. Mike with his cane, standing high on the wall beneath the double arch, a triumphant expression on his face. Mike bringing her a cup of tea in bed. Mike's face, scrunched and red, tears of laugher streaming from his eyes. But then, it interjects other images. Mike lying comatose in his bed. Mike wasting away from starvation. Mike convulsing with his final breath as she stands by his side, clutching his hand. Mike's body being wheeled out of the room. Mike's ashes resting in a box on her mantle.

She's sobbing now, pummeling the pavement with both fists. She's aware of the people around her staring, but she doesn't care. Sorrow and grief engulf her, drowning her. It would be better for *her* to die than to make the choice to let Mike die. She cannot fathom life without him.

"But he's not gone yet," a tiny voice reminds her, cutting through her anguish. She grasps hold of that thought, hanging on to it for dear life. Gathering herself, she inhales the air in deep, desperate gulps. That's right, she thinks. He's not gone yet. It is hope that has sustained her, and she cannot, must not, lose hope. There is still time.

CHAPTER 56

Shadow Mike never knows exactly how much time he spends in the void. Sometimes he's there and out again, pulled into another universe before the darkness fully sets in. Other times, he lingers, alone with his thoughts. This time, it seems, he's been here for a while. With nothing better to do, and having already dissected every moment of his life, he's using the time to analyze the various universes.

He has discovered that, despite the countless choices made by each version of himself across the different timelines, he often exhibits a remarkable predictability. In every universe, Mike is intelligent, kind, hard-working, and loyal – sometimes to a fault. Consequently, many of his decisions lead him in the same direction, although never to quite the same result. At some point, there will be a divergence, no matter how minor, setting him on a different yet similar path.

Take his college choices, for instance. In most universes, Mike ends up being the high school valedictorian, and as such, could likely have gone to any college of his choosing. But being born to two working-class parents in the mountains of North Carolina, he wasn't aware of that. Instead, he focused mainly on public schools because he thought that was all he could afford. Therefore, in most timelines, he ends up attending Georgia Tech or Virginia Tech.

In nearly every universe, Mike pursues engineering in college, as it was what he wanted to be from the time he was young. His subsequent decisions guide him along a few primary paths: academia, corporate life, or entrepreneurship. Naturally, there are a few exceptions, with each timeline offering a unique variation, but the overall patterns remain consistent.

And then there are his relationship patterns. Shadow Mike has observed him with dozens, perhaps even hundreds of women in different universes before he encounters Sailee, with varying degrees of success. In many universes where he attends Georgia Tech as a traditional student, he meets Caroline. But it never lasts, for one reason or another. Shadow Mike has to give himself credit, though. He's nothing if not consistent.

When he goes to Georgia Tech as a co-op student, he never meets Caroline, and several times ends up with Tiffany in his fifth year. That relationship is always a trainwreck. In fact, Shadow Mike just came from a timeline where Sailee was their marriage counselor. That was awkward! Despite the valiant efforts of both Sailee and Mike, he and Tiffany couldn't make it work. Not surprisingly, Tiffany didn't take the news well when, a year after their divorce, she learned that Mike had recently begun dating their therapist.

Fortunately, in some timelines, Mike heeds the advice of his friends and parents and breaks off their engagement. His life is easier in those universes. And, of course, different colleges and alternative choices lead to other women. Shadow Mike always wishes he could reach out to these different versions of himself and encourage them to be patient, assuring them that the best is yet to come. Unfortunately, he can't, and they have no way of knowing.

Sailee also makes different choices, but her paths don't follow the same overarching patterns. Perhaps it's because she never truly knows what she wants and tends to go wherever the wind blows her. Her core qualities include being creative, passionate, quick-tempered, logical, and extroverted. She has attended a myriad of colleges and studied subjects ranging from music to literature, psychology, law, medicine, finance, and computer science. She has been an author, a fundraiser, a salesperson, an administrative assistant, a paralegal, a lawyer, a composer, a conductor, a teacher, a pianist, an airman in the US Air Force, an astronaut, a dancer, a journalist, a social worker, a politician, an accountant... the list is endless. Ultimately, it's the unique combination of their core qualities and their choices that determine who Mike and Sailee become in each universe, their compatibility, and when, how, and where they meet and fall in love. And their choices *do* change them. Even though their core characteristics remain consistent, Sailee in one universe may not be compatible with Mike from another.

Shadow Mike once told his own Sailee he believed that if someone ever found a way to travel the multiverse, they would never want to return to their own, being constantly driven to seek the "best" timeline. But he was wrong there too. Although he has grown to love witnessing the different versions of himself finding their own versions of her, more than anything, he wants to go home to *his* Sailee. He misses her. Needs her. He needs the one who first caught his attention, the one he married in Sonoma, the one with the wine-ruined dress. He has never found *her.*

And then, there it is – dawn on the horizon. "Please," Shadow Mike wills with all his might, "please let me go home. Let me wake up in my bed with my own Sailee beside me. Let this all have been one enormous dream. Please... please... please..."

CHAPTER 57

May 29

Days pass, each one blending into the next. Sailee's days all look the same: attempt to sleep, get up, go to the hospital, return home, attempt to sleep, repeat. But with every passing day, her heart beats a little faster, her blood pressure rises a bit higher. Her stomach tightens in knots whenever the doctor reviews Mike's chart and finds no signs of improvement.

To make matters worse, Sailee's boss has started inquiring about her return to work. Could she work remotely? Maybe start by reconnecting with some of her old clients? Concerned inquiries pour in from everyone. They all care about her well-being. Perhaps easing back into work would be beneficial, they suggest. A few hours a week, perhaps? Initially, Sailee wondered if it might serve as a helpful distraction, but she quickly realized she would have no ability to concentrate. She is far too anxious.

Now, she finds herself in the hospital cafeteria. She has been humming a tune all day without paying much attention to it. While adding tomatoes to her salad, she suddenly realizes what song she has been singing. The lyrics originated from a poem crafted by her friend, Marie, and upon hearing it, Sailee had asked if she could set it to music. Years have passed since she last thought of this song, but today she can't get it out of her head. Now cognizant of the tune, she contemplates the words.

> *To say goodbye, I cannot simply walk away*
> *Say no, and purge myself of you, my love*
> *In love, I am tied to you*
> *Bound, and fight the boundaries I make to lose you to myself.*
>
> *To say goodbye, I must not stab you*
> *Slice the memory of you from my mind*
> *Can I annihilate you, love?*
> *Can I live as less of myself*
> *With this piece of you that is me, now gone?*
>
> *I close my mind*
> *Travel deep into the hiddenness of my heart*
> *My soul, where you reside*
> *Where we are together,*
> *And I touch the walls which move*
> *At the very sense of my will*
>
> *To say goodbye, I change the place where we live entwined*
> *Change the context of our love*
> *So we are together*
> *Have always been, will always be*
> *Can still be, just differently,*
> *Two flowers on a hill*
>
> *To say goodbye*
> *I catch the string of feelings that bind you to me,*
> *One by one I pluck my fingers off.*
> *And I sit in that hidden place*
> *And smile for the wonder of where you will go —*

To say goodbye, my love,
Goodbye, and be whole.

Sailee loves the song, but today she would rather have any other earworm – even the ones that typically drive her crazy, like the Christmas carols or "I'm a Little Teapot" – because she doesn't want to think about saying goodbye. Despite grappling with the possibility, she is simply not ready.

CHAPTER 58

It's light now, and Shadow Mike finds himself in a large, windowless room. Positioned across from the double doors on the back wall is a stage, featuring two large chairs facing the audience, and a central microphone. People are slowly filing in, taking their seats, always attempting to leave an empty chair between themselves and others. A PowerPoint presentation is displayed on the screen:

The Value of Board Members in a Start-Up
Michael Black
Founder & CEO, Fast Forward

Shadow Mike takes a step back, startled. He looks again. He recognizes this presentation – it's one he has delivered numerous times. That's *his* company. The clock ticks: 2:00 p.m. A woman wearing a navy pantsuit walks toward the stage. "She's going to drop her papers," he thinks. As if on cue, the woman stumbles while ascending the stairs. She catches herself but drops the papers she's carrying. She quickly gathers them up and proceeds to the microphone, straightening her jacket.

"Good afternoon," she begins, "and welcome to TechSphere Summit 2015. I'm Veronica Nielsen, Director of the Startup track. I'm pleased to see both new and familiar faces this year. This is our largest turnout yet, and we have an exciting line-up of speakers for you! Kicking us off today is someone likely familiar to many of you. He was recognized as one of Time's 40 under 40 in 2010, and was named Entrepreneur of the Year by Ernst & Young in 2013. His latest venture, Fast Forward, is revolutionizing the way we think about multi-media streaming. So without further ado, please give a warm welcome to Michael Black!"

Shadow Mike observes himself saunter confidently across the stage. He's wearing a tailored navy suit and a silver tie. He takes the microphone out of the stand and...

Shadow Mike shuts his eyes. He can't bear to watch this. He knows this stage, this speech. This is *his* life. He has been here already. Lived it himself. This Mike isn't some different version of himself, it is himself exactly. He wanted so badly to have his life back. Why is he here, watching it unfold instead of living it? He's confused. Angry. He's... scared, even. What can this possibly mean?

A slight hitch in Mike's speech pulls Shadow Mike's attention back into the room. He follows his gaze. Of course, it's Sailee – her blonde hair cascading around her face as she leans forward, scribbling furiously in her notebook. He had thought she was captivated by his presentation, but now it's evident she isn't paying the slightest attention to him.

The sight of her, *his* Sailee, pierces him like a knife in the gut. He has endured all the other universes by reminding himself that they aren't her – not quite. But this one is. He can't resist; he moves across the room and sits down in the vacant chair beside her. He reaches out to touch her hair, remembering how it felt slipping through his fingers. But his hand passes right through, and her hair remains undisturbed. He feels nothing. A profound ache settles in the pit of his stomach. Glancing at Sailee's left hand, he notices the engagement ring. It's a small solitaire set in rose gold. It strikes him as funny, seeing this now, as he knows she prefers white gold or platinum.

Suddenly, Sailee jumps up, snatches her notebook and laptop bag, and hurries out the door. Shadow Mike looks around. It appears the session is over already. He was so taken by her, by being so close to her, that he lost track of time. He turns his gaze toward the stage and spots himself scanning the crowd, searching for her, wanting to find her and strike up a conversation, wanting to get her name, her number.

And then he's at the cocktail reception, witnessing himself spill wine all over her dress. He loves that dress. She still wears it occasionally, and it always reminds him of their first encounter. *This* encounter. He sees her expression, which he failed to notice before because he was too pre-occupied, mortified by her dress mishap. He observes the mix of shock, annoyance, and amusement on her face, the way her eyes flash angrily before she regains her composure. It all happens in an instant.

He observes them together at dinner, leaning in towards each other, partly to be heard but mostly because they are so enthralled with one another. He watches Sailee throw her head back in laughter, drawing the attention of those around the table, everyone momentar-ily pausing their conversations and smiling because her laughter is so infectious.

He sees everything now – everything he missed before. But he doesn't want to see it. He wants to *live* it. He would even be content to go back and relive it all over again, "but *please* don't make me stay here and watch this," he begs. But his pleas go unheard.

Their life together passes by in a blur – the drinks at the bar, the hours spent pouring over emails, the long phone call after her break-up, introducing her to his parents, asking her to marry him. Then their wedding, that perfect elopement in Sonoma. He wouldn't change a thing.

He sees their joy and the knowing glances they exchange, rolling their eyes when people comment on their marital bliss and follow it up with, "Yeah, but you're still newlyweds. Just wait." They brush off such ignorance and continue on with their contented lives. And that happiness endures long after they cease to be newlyweds. He observes them waking up every morning, saying, "Merry Christmas!" because they both understand that each day together is a gift.

Then they meet Steve and Katie in a bar and make plans for dinner. They sit around the dining room table, recounting the story of how they first met. Shadow Mike sees himself taking Sailee's hand in his, and he's jealous. He's so very jealous.

And then they're in the car driving home, talking about the multiverse, and he hears himself saying that there was only one chance in the universe, in any universe, one chance in an inconceivably large but finite number that they would meet and fall in love. "Oh, Mike," he says aloud, "You are so very, very wrong about that."

Sailee leans forward to retrieve something from her purse, and that's when Shadow Mike notices the SUV barreling towards them. Its headlights are off, and he only catches a glimpse of it when the moonlight momentarily glints on its roof.

Mike and Sailee are still moving toward the intersection. Their traffic light turns green. "Stop!" Shadow Mike screams at them. "STOP! Look to your right! Slow down! Do something! Do *ANYTHING*!"

Driven by desperation, he rushes into the road, placing himself directly in front of their car, but the vehicle passes right through him. Powerless to stop it, Shadow Mike watches in slow motion as the SUV plows headlong into the passenger door of the Porsche with a thunderous crash.

And then, everything is still. Silent. Shadow Mike falls to his knees, burying his face in his hands. His eyes are tightly shut. He cannot bring himself to open them, cannot bear to see the wreckage, cannot bear to face the truth.

He finally understands why he can't remember anything else from that evening. Why he doesn't remember getting home or getting into bed. They never made it home. His hypothesis was correct – he must be dead.

CHAPTER 59

Shadow Mike remains motionless, unaware of how much time has passed in his frozen state. And then he hears a noise. He doesn't want to see what happens next – he wants only to melt away into nothingness. Yet, he's still here. Slowly, he opens his eyes.

The wreckage lays before him like a war scene. Shadow Mike is numb, his brain unable to process what he's witnessing. The passenger side of the Porsche has been completely crushed, reducing the car's width by half. The obliterated passenger door is where the center arm rest should be, while the smoking engine of the SUV occupies the area where the door should be. There's no way a passenger can have survived this crash. "There's no way Sailee can have survi—" he can't finish the thought.

A Nissan pulls up to the intersection. A man jumps out of the driver's seat and rushes to the scene, yelling at the woman with him to dial 911. First, he opens the door of the SUV, which is closest to him. Smoke pours out of the vehicle as he tries to pull the driver, a man, out of the car. He's bleeding profusely from a head wound. He's alive, but barely.

Next, the man rushes over to the Porsche. The mangled passenger side offers no entry – it no longer exists. He pauses, blanching, before racing to the driver's side. The door is jammed, but he forces it open and leans over Mike, struggling to unbuckle his seat belt. He clears the deployed airbag out of the way and removes Mike's limp body from the vehicle. Laying him carefully on the pavement, he places an ear to Mike's chest. Then he returns to the car, and after glancing inside, doubles over and vomits. The woman approaches him, placing a comforting hand on his back, saying something that Shadow Mike can't hear. The man gestures toward the Porsche, shaking his head.

Suddenly, wailing sirens pierce the air, and emergency vehicles swarm the scene. A police officer dashes to the center of the road, prepared to divert any oncoming traffic. Firefighters spill out of the truck, and one of them rushes over to the man on the roadside, who points to the two bodies lying on the ground and then motions toward the car. The fireman shouts something, and they all converge on the SUV, working together to push it out of the way. The tow truck has yet to arrive, and time is of the essence.

They manage to push the SUV far enough to access the passenger's side. The window is shattered, and it takes three men to pry what remains of the door from its hinges. Shadow Mike turns away, unable to watch. His Sailee, his beloved Sailee. He does not want to see her like this. He wants to remember her like he last saw her – smiling at him.

Then, one of the men reaches inside and ever so gently lifts Sailee out of the wreckage. An EMT wheels over a gurney, and the fireman places her on it. Shadow Mike can't see her – they're standing in front of him, blocking his view. The EMT is checking her vitals, looking for any small sign of life. They retrieve a sheet, wrapping it around Sailee, and Shadow Mike's heart lurches with hope that maybe, just maybe…

But then they pull the sheet up over her head, and he dies inside. There's an emptiness now, a void, where his heart used to be. And of course there is. Because his heart is lying there on that gurney.

CHAPTER 60

June 7

Sailee sits beside Mike's bed, reading aloud. She's nearing the end of the book, knowing that he would love it if he heard any of it. Her throat is dry from the exertion, and she needs a drink. Setting the book down on her chair, she leans over the railing and plants a tender kiss on his forehead. "I'll be right back," she assures him. "Don't go anywhere!" Smiling at her joke, Sailee exits the room.

She's only gone ten minutes, but as she's walking back down the hall toward the ICU, Sailee can tell that something is wrong. Doctors and nurses rush towards a patient's room – Mike's room. Instinctively, she breaks into a run. Drawing nearer, she can hear the beeping. It seems every monitor in the room is going off.

Pulling back the curtain, she finds Mike surrounded by his medical team, rendering her unable to reach him. Sailee scans the room, searching for the source of the commotion – the heart rate monitor. For the past three months, his heart has maintained a steady rhythm of 50 beats per minute.

Her gaze focuses on the monitor, a component she has largely disregarded due to the absence of concern. Now, panic seizes her as she attempts to decipher each displayed metric. The blood pressure is too high. The heart rate reads... 172?! That can't be right. But the incessant beeping confirms its validity. And it continues to climb: 185bpm... 194... 200... 207... 215... 245...

Sailee is terrified. She doesn't know what this means. Could his heart give out? Might he suffer a stroke? No one has ever talked to her about this possibility. She has been gradually accepting the likelihood of losing him, but not like this. She had envisioned a quiet farewell, where loved ones could gather and bid their goodbyes. It wasn't meant to be this chaotic, this deafening, preventing her from even reaching his side. "Not like this!" her inner voice screams in desperation.

Her own heart is racing. She feels so helpless. What can she do? Then, she starts praying. She grew up praying but hasn't done it in a long time. And she has never prayed like this. She has no words, she simply pours everything she has toward God, hoping desperately that he's there, and that he's listening.

And then, suddenly, everything stops. The heart rate is slowing, the blood pressure is dropping. "Thank God!" Sailee cries aloud. She watches the monitor. 217...205...196...174...138...127...120......105 ......98......93......91......86............85......

Gradually, the heart rate returns to normal.

71............64............62............60....................57.................

53.........50......... 48.........47............46............43.....................

Wait, it's still dropping. No, no, no. That's not right either. It's too slow. The blood pressure is now too low. The heartbeat too feeble. Mike's breathing is becoming shallow.

The doctors exchange glances, and Dr. Wilson approaches Sailee, placing his hand gently on her shoulder. "I'm sorry, Sailee," he says softly. "The erratic heart rate, accompanied by a sudden decline in blood pressure, often indicates that a person's body is giving up. You need to prepare for the worst. I'm so very sorry."

"That's it?!" she cries out. "Isn't there something else you can do? Give him a shot of adrenaline? Anything?!"

He gives her shoulder a sympathetic squeeze, and she looks up into his kind blue eyes. "Is this really the life you want for him?" he asks. "Is this what Mike would want for himself? To waste away in a hospital bed?"

He drops his arm, and Sailee slumps against the wall. She knows he's right. Mike would despise seeing himself like this. Keeping him alive is not what he would want. But what about what she wants? Does that matter at all anymore?

Dr. Wilson exits the room. There's one nurse left, adjusting Mike's wires and the feeding tube that was disturbed in the chaos. Then he leaves, and it's just the two of them. Sailee knows she should probably call his parents, call her parents. But right now she can't do anything. She's numb.

Slowly, she moves toward the edge of the bed and gently clasps Mike's hand in hers. She refuses to relinquish hope. She can't. "Come on, my love," she whispers. "Stay with me. Stay strong. Fight for me."

CHAPTER 61

Time is no longer linear. Shadow Mike moves from the present – the scene of the accident – into the past, to memories and moments with Sailee, both mundane and extraordinary. Then forward, into the future, envisioning what could have been – growing old together, him first. Then back into the past – the way he held her while they brushed their teeth – then returning to the present.

Sailee's body has been moved into an ambulance, while the other driver is placed on a gurney. Mike still lies by the car. They had always said they wanted to go out together with a bang, and it appears they did, except it's unfair. He should just be lying there now, oblivious to the pain, oblivious to the emptiness inside, oblivious to her death.

The other two ambulances have departed, the one carrying Sailee moving slowly, the other speeding away with sirens blaring. They approach Mike's body, transfer him onto a gurney, and check his vitals. Shadow Mike anticipates them shaking their heads and pulling the sheet over him, as they did with Sailee. He is taken aback when they instead tuck the sheet around his body and load him into the ambulance. "Head injury…" he hears one say. "…coma…" They close the doors behind him and speed off toward the city.

Shadow Mike has no choice but to follow. He arrives at the hospital and witnesses the doctors swiftly whisking him into the ICU, connecting him to various machines. Everyone is shouting instructions, taking notes, and then suddenly, he's alone. He observes them calling his parents, delivering the news first about Sailee and then about himself. Although he cannot see her, he can hear his mother's cry, her pain, resonating through the phone. It hits him like a gut-punch. Why did he wish to return to this life? He would have been better off exploring the multiverse indefinitely. It would have been better not to know that this is how it ended for them. He's not present for the call to Sailee's parents, and he's grateful for that. The mere thought of being on the other end of that conversation is unbearable. He feels nauseated.

Standing next to the bed, he looks down at Mike – at himself. Not another version of himself, but his actual self – the body, the face, a mirror of his own. They made the same choices. Have the same memories. Loved the same Sailee.

Shadow Mike doesn't wonder what's going on in this Mike's head because he already knows. He knows that he is just now commencing his journey through the multiverse, that he's somewhere watching a version of himself fall in love with a version of Sailee. And he feels a twinge of envy for this Mike, who doesn't yet know that his own Sailee is gone.

He will learn the devastating truth when he comes out of the coma, *if* he comes out of the coma. But that is many, many lifetimes from now. Or perhaps he'll die. Maybe *he*, Shadow Mike, can finally let go and end this horrific cycle, knowing he won't be going back to Sailee.

Shadow Mike can feel the darkness closing in, and he welcomes its arrival. Gazing down at himself lying in the bed, he utters, "Godspeed." And then he's gone.

CHAPTER 62

June 1

4 1......38...........35..............33............
Sailee tightly clasps Mike's hand, willing him to hold on.
31........................... 29.........................26..............

Then, she shifts her gaze downward, toward Mike's body, which was once so strong but has weakened with each passing day, and something inside her breaks. It's not painful, like a shattering or a fracture. It feels more like a sigh. A release. And she recognizes a sensation that has been evading her for a long time: peace. She knows it's time to let go.

25................22.....................19........................15.......................

With one hand still holding his, she takes her other and traces the contours of Mike's face. Her finger glides along his hairline, down the side of his jaw, around his chin, and up the opposite side. Then, she traces the center of his face – between his eyebrows, down his nose, over his lips – trying to memorize every line, every detail of this face that she loves more than any other face in the entire world.

15......................15.............................15...........................

The moment seems to hang in the air, and she cradles Mike's face in her hands. There's so much she wants to say, needs to say, but there is no more time. Leaning over, she delicately presses her lips against his, a tear falling onto his cheek. Then, she pulls back slightly, her face hovering just above his, and whispers, "I love you."

15...............14.........................13............................12...................
He's falling.

CHAPTER 63

"What is that awful beeping?" he wonders. It's akin to a smoke detector with dying batteries – slow and sporadic, and incredibly annoying. He knows he's in a new universe because of the light in his face, but he cannot muster the will to open his eyes. He doesn't want to be here. He doesn't want to exist *anywhere*. He cannot bear to be in a timeline where she is alive, when his own Sailee is dead.

Then, he notices a peculiar sensation in his hand – like being touched. The surprise jolts him, forcing his eyes to open, and simultaneously, the beeping ceases. Surveying his surroundings, he finds himself lying in a bed, with Sailee standing beside him, fixated on something above his head. His heart aches at the sight of her, and he instinctively tightens his fist.

Suddenly, he feels a pressure, accompanied by an all-too-familiar voice. "Mike? Oh my God! Mike, are you awake? Can you hear me?"

He looks upward, and she's looking… at him. *Directly* at him! He meets her gaze. Her eyes, that exquisite blend of green and brown, reveal excitement tinged with nervousness. He clasps her fingers, and she reciprocates the gesture. The connection is tangible, and it fills him with profound joy. But how…?

He tries to speak, and his voice cracks as words escape his lips. "You can see me?"

Sailee emits a sound that combines laughter and a sob. "Of course I can see you! Oh my God, Mike! Thank God!" She's trying to hug him and kiss him, and she's laughing and crying all at once, leaving him bewildered yet so happy – happy to feel her touch, to be seen. But then he remembers.

"Hold on," he says, extending his hand. He has to know where he is. "What year is it? How did we meet? Where did we get married? When did we get married?" The questions tumble out.

Sailee appears concerned but replies, "It's June 1, 2023. We met at a conference when you spilled wine on my dress. We eloped in Sonoma on a perfect day in May of 2019. You've been in a coma for three months, Mike. I thought I'd lost you." She leans over to kiss him again. "I've missed you *so* much."

"But how…?" He can barely get the words out. "You're… you're dead."

Sailee laughs. "I assure you, my love, I am not. A little busted up maybe, but definitely alive. You, on the other hand, just gave me quite the scare."

But Mike doesn't hear her. He's replaying the scene in his mind, watching the sheet being drawn over her lifeless body. The ache in his soul resurfaces. "You were leaning forward to get something out of your purse when the guy hit us. You were crushed." His eyes fill with tears. "I saw it."

Confusion flickers across Sailee's face. "No…" she responds slowly, "I was leaning over the armrest, kissing your neck when the car hit us. The doctor said that's what saved my life."

And now he remembers, seeing her leaning forward and sensing that something was amiss. But in the chaos of the collision, and the aftermath of her death, he hadn't stopped to give it a second thought. So… that *wasn't* him. Or her. They were others versions of themselves in a timeline that was parallel until that critical moment when Sailee chose to reach into her bag instead of kissing him, altering the course of their futures. And that means… he's home!

"My Sailee!" he cries, "It's really you!" His heart swells with emotion, threatening to burst. "I've been trying so hard to get back to you."

Sailee strokes his hair. "Where have you been, my love?" she asks softly.

Mike doesn't know where to begin. "I know this sounds crazy," he replies, "but I was trapped in the multiverse. Universe after universe, I observed our lives and all the different choices we made, seeing what roads they led us down and how those choices changed us." He pauses. "But you were right, Sailee. There is such a thing as soulmates – a force powerful enough to transcend time and space. I have been in hundreds of timelines, and in all of them, I love you."

Tears are running down Sailee's face, and she leans over, giving Mike a long, lingering kiss. A kiss as perfect as their first one was, and their last one will be. "I believe you," she says. And then a grin spreads across her face. "But there's something you said that I think I missed. You were saying that I was right and…?"

Mike laughs, taking her hands in his and pulling her into the bed beside him. Sailee nestles herself between his body and the bedrail, and he tenderly kisses the top of her head. "You're right," he says, "and I love you."

"And I love you," she replies. She rests her head on his chest and they lie like this for a long while, too overwhelmed with joy to even speak.

There will be hours, days, months, years to talk about it all. Sailee will recount the details of the accident, her arduous recovery, and the void of his absence. In turn, he'll tell her about all the universes he visited – regale her with stories of how they meet and fall in love. They will laugh and cry, occasionally cringing at their stupidity, at the choices they make. But for now, they're content to be in each other's arms.

He ponders whether the Mike he left behind in the hospital will embark on his own odyssey. He hopes so. He wants his counterpart to realize that their meeting was no arbitrary chance, that he and Sailee are intrinsically bound together in every universe. It's a longing born of compassion, hoping it brings him solace when he wakes up and finds her gone in his.

A little while later, a nurse enters the room and sees them lying together on the bed. She discerns from the clasp of their hands, the lingering touch of his lips on her head, and the peace in Sailee's face that Mike has reawakened. She won't disturb them now; everything can wait until morning. She smiles as she pulls the curtains closed around them and lets them sleep.

EPILOGUE

May 13

Sailee awakens and lies still for a moment, her eyes closed. She can feel the sun pouring in through the window of their agriturismo, warming her face. While they've returned to San Gimignano several times since their honeymoon, this time is special – their thirtieth wedding anniversary.

It's hard to believe she and Mike have been married thirty years. The time has flown by. Sailee sifts through her memories, beginning with the most recent and working her way backward. Their post-retirement adventures – wine tasting in South Africa, a safari in Tanzania, climbing Machu Pichu in Peru, eating their way through Argentina, India, and Singapore, Iceland ... the list goes on and on; buying a boat – a long-time dream for Mike – and spending a month in the Bahamas; her niece's wedding (how did she grow up so quickly?); the passing of Mike's parents. Then back further – Mike being elected to the National Academy of Engineering; Sailee getting her first book published – a memoir of their life together and Mike's experiences in the multiverse. Then back further still – moving to the East Coast to be near their aging parents; Sailee quitting her job to focus on writing; their struggles with infertility as a result of her injuries; Fast Forward selling to a major media conglomerate; the accident. Here, she pauses.

At the time, those three months that Mike was in the coma felt like an eternity, and she wondered if life would ever be the same. Now, twenty-six years later, they're but a blip. And while the accident and subsequent coma are distant echoes of the past, their impact remains. Not a single day goes by that Mike or Sailee takes life, or their life together, for granted, and Sailee is thankful every day that the difficult period was truly just a comma, a pause in their wonderfully fulfilling life.

And then, going back even further – their wedding; their friendship formed over years of emails and phone calls; and finally, their first encounter. Sailee chuckles to herself, reminiscing about that fateful day when she was so preoccupied with her career and strained relationship, utterly unaware of what awaited her.

She rolls over and gazes at Mike, this man who unexpectedly blew her world apart in the very best way. He has changed some over the years – there are a few more lines etched into his face, his hair now more gray than brown. Yet his heart, his character, remains the same. Sailee smiles and leans over, planting a gentle kiss on his cheek, waking him. "Good morning, my love," she says softly. "Happy Anniversary!"

"Happy Anniversary," Mike replies, smiling. Then, throwing off the covers, he asks, "Would you like a cup of tea?"

"Of course," she replies.

And just like that, another day begins. Unaware of the looming shadow, they have no idea that another Mike, just beginning his journey, is drifting out of their room and into another universe.

AUTHOR'S NOTE AND ACKNOWLEDGEMENTS

My husband and I were out with friends one evening when he made the comment that if either of us had made any other decisions in our lives, we would never have met. Although the conversation quickly moved on, his statement stuck with me and became the catalyst for this story.

Music has always been an integral part of my life, and it seemed impossible to write a book incorporating elements of my own music, and music that I have loved over the years, and not share them with you. Therefore, if you are interested in listening to any of the music referenced in the novel, you can access links to all of the pieces here: onechance.substack.com.

I could not have published this novel on my own, and I have many people to thank for joining me on my journey. To Libby Jordan, for guiding me through the publication process and ensuring that my novel was the best it could possibly be, to Danna Steele, for the cover and interior design, and to Hal Leonard, for granting me permission to use the Ben Folds lyrics.

To my beta readers: Heather, Kate, Suzanne, Maureen, Rick, Betsy, Lois, Kim, and Alaiya – thank you for investing time in this, and in me, and providing your invaluable feedback. And a very special shout out to Heather, who wrote the poem, *To Say Goodbye,* and for letting me both set it to music, and use it in this book.

To my parents, whose love and unconditional support is vital to who I am as a person, and especially to my mama, who was my first and last reader and editor. To my stepchildren and in-laws, thank you for loving me and accepting me so readily into your family.

And last, but definitely not least, to Rob – my partner, my best friend, my soulmate, my inspiration. Words cannot express how thankful I am for you – for being the man that you are, and for the endless hours that you have listened to me prattle on about this book. Thank you for all your ideas and feedback, for laughing with me at the memories, and crying with me at the imagined futures. Mike and Sailee may be fictional, but the love they share is real, and I'm thankful I get to share this love with you. If there is a multiverse, I sincerely hope that every version of me ends up with you. And if this is the only universe there is, then I'm even more thankful we get to spend it together. I love you.

Milton Keynes UK
Ingram Content Group UK Ltd.
UKHW011808010124
435297UK00005B/474